Alisia,
love yourself first!

Jasmine Aziz

SEX
& SAMOSAS

A Novel By
JASMINE AZIZ

Shubblie Publications © Jasmine Aziz 2009. All rights reserved.

Published by Shubblie Publications, Ottawa, Canada
www.shubbliepublications.com

Jasmine Aziz asserts the moral right to be identified as the author of this work.

All rights reserved. No part of this publication may be reproduced, stored in a retrieval system, or transmitted, in any form or by any means, electronic, mechanical, photocopying, recording or otherwise, without the prior and express written permission of the publisher.

This book is sold subject to the condition that it shall not, by way of trade or otherwise, be lent, re-sold, hired out or otherwise circulated without the publisher's prior consent in any form of binding or cover other than that in which it is published and without a similar condition including this condition being imposed on the subsequent purchaser.

The opinions in this work are not to be taken as factual but are for pure entertainment. Any and all statistical information is used for the purposes of fiction and should not be considered absolute or accountable and accurate.

This novel is a work of fiction. The names, characters and incidents portrayed in it are the work of the author's imagination. Any resemblance to actual persons, living or dead, events or localities is entirely coincidental. No reference to any person is intended or should be inferred.

Library and Archives Canada Cataloguing in Publication

Aziz, Jasmine

Sex & samosas / Jasmine Aziz.

Issued also in an electronic format.
ISBN 978-0-9877357-0-6

I. Title. II. Title: Sex and samosas
PS8601.Z59S49 2011   C813'.6   C2011-905487-6

Shubblie Publications
Sex and Samosas/ Jasmine Aziz

Printed and bound in the United States of America
Cover design by Partner Publishing (www.partnerpublishing.com)

For my Mother
*This book, as is my life,
is dedicated to you*

You never forget your first orgasm...

Chapter 1

It was a Saturday night *sex party*.

How could I turn it down?

Truth be told, in my infinite desire to get out of going, I could have come up with at least a dozen different reasons why I couldn't, shouldn't, didn't *want* to go.

What exactly is a sex party? Does it involve naked people? Naked people on top of other naked people? Whips? Latex? What *is* latex? Okay, so maybe there was a small part of me that was actually more than a bit curious but how could it be better than the Saturday night I had planned at home with my husband in front of the television eating a bag of *ghatia* and wearing my fat pants?

I changed my outfit four times before I settled on a mocha turtleneck with beige pants. I clipped my mess of curly hair into a banana clip at the back of my head. When my best friend Mahjong arrived at my house she blurted out: "What are you wearing? You look like an overcooked spring roll. *Change!*"

"No way!" I insisted. "It took me forever to pick this out! And besides I like it, what's wrong with it?"

"Nothing if it was still 1981. Come on, let's go. Sorry I'm a bit late. I had last minute customers in my store."

On the car ride over, I refrained from commenting on what Mahjong had done to her hair. She had dyed the top of her head bright red and left the bottom black. Her almond-shaped eyes were outlined in heavy black liner. She had found red mascara, God only knows where, and had applied it so thickly that I wondered how she could see through her lashes. On the side of her right eye she had glued a small diamond trio. "Like my *bindis*?" she asked.

"Those are *bindis*?"

"Yup. Funny eh, you're the Indian and I've never seen you wear them. I wear them more than you ever have!"

"Screw you, Mahjong. I do wear them. I wear them when I go to functions."

"Oh, *functions*," she mocked. "Tonight's a function. Why aren't you wearing one now?"

Tonight was not a function. Born to two South Asian parents who were landed immigrants meant the only functions I ever went to were the ones where three quarters of the guests were either related to me or married to someone that was related to me. They were almost all events designed to celebrate the engagement of a couple, the marriage of a couple or the birth of the couple's first child. Though this was a celebration of my friend Jenny's wedding, I had a suspicion it wasn't going to be like a typical Indian function.

The truth is I had never been to an *Outside the Box* party. I had only heard stories about them from Mahjong who is notorious for exaggerating.

"Is this what happens to you when you get out of your comfort zone?"

Mahjong cursed out loud as she cut off a van to get on the highway waving her middle finger over her head.

"Out of my comfort zone?" I shrieked, "I'm so far out of my comfort zone that I'm in another time zone!"

Standing on the porch of Isabelle's house waiting for her to open the door, I had the sudden strong premonition that everything was about to change.

I looked at Mahjong and just as I was about to fake an epileptic seizure, despite having no history of the disease whatsoever, the door I had willed to stay shut forever suddenly flung open.

"Hi!" Isabelle's smile was almost as wide as her cleavage. As joyfully as our hostess shouted her greeting, it was still hard to hear her over the loud rise and fall of women's voices coming from just beyond where she stood. Mahjong instinctively pulled me into the foyer of Isabelle's house, immediately handed her coat to her and with only a casual greeting to our hostess, headed towards the cackling crowd abandoning me. I slowly crept backwards towards the door. I contemplated becoming a permanent fixture in Isabelle's entrance. I'm already brown, so what's the big deal if I get mistaken for a bloated wooden coat rack, I thought. People could just hang their coats on my head; weather permitting I could hold umbrellas. No one would notice me.

"Hi Isabelle." I reluctantly took off my jacket. I tried not to stare too openly at her heaving cleavage barely contained in her red and black leopard print bustier. I handed her a tin foil pan of fresh mini samosas I had picked up at a local Indian grocery store. My original plan to bring brownies backfired when I ended up eating more than half the batch in a hormonal fit the night before.

"Thanks, Leena! Oh samosas!" she said peering under the foil. "They look so good! Did you make them?"

"I made the chutney from scratch." It was an old recipe of my paternal grandmother. My sweet *Dadi* would probably never guess I would introduce her secret coriander chutney to a bunch of drunken Westerners at a party to buy vibrators.

"Well I'm so glad you came." Isabelle flashed her usual party-till-we-puke grin. She paused and studied me for a second as she felt my grip tighten on my jacket. In my reluctance to leave the foyer, I had inadvertently gotten into a tug of war with her over my coat, her massive breasts jiggling in her top from even the slightest yank on my jacket.

I feigned a fake laugh, finally surrendering my coat.

"You look nice." I suspected she was just being polite.

"Would you like me to take off my shoes?" I asked stalling for more time.

"Don't be ridiculous Leena. Keep your shoes on. Go on in and enjoy yourself."

There was no getting around it. It was time to face down my fears. My mother had filled my head with stories of bohemian Western culture since I could first remember. She was convinced that behind closed doors, Westerners engaged in satanic type rituals that were not part of my culture. I was Indian, according to her despite what my North American passport said and I'd never been allowed to mix with the *besharam* before school, after school or during the day in school. I did however manage to break free of her judgmental eyes while away at university and never once saw someone drink chicken blood or partake in group orgies with goats as she often warned me I would if I hung out with heathen *ghoras.*

I heard a loud scream of joy as soon as I entered the living room behind Isabelle. From the pitch alone I could tell we had arrived late and the alcohol had already begun to flow. I needed a drink too.

"Yippee! It's Leena!" screamed Jenny, the bride-to-be and guest of honour. She was sitting in the middle of a group of at least a dozen women. Someone had covered her long blonde hair in a silver plastic crown with blown up condoms hanging from its side. She was wearing a pink penis necklace and was drinking from an oversized black plastic penis. I suspected from the glazed look in her eyes it had something other than water in it.

I'd met Jenny in high school. She hung out with the pretty popular types while I spent my lunches under the stairwells. That is until the head bangers found my spot and the smell of their drug soaked clothes drove me to find another hiding place. I hadn't seen her in years until I met her again at Isabelle's birthday party. She always seemed warm and sincere. I wanted to believe she liked me.

I stepped over and around two girls on the floor to hug and kiss the bride and smiled nervously at a few unfamiliar faces. I instantly found myself longing for Mahjong like a safety blanket. Suddenly I was so grateful for her quirky style; her dyed red head should jut out like a matchstick above the sea of smiling faces.

As I looked around the main floor my eyes landed on the dining table in the adjoining room. At first glance I could see black canisters with Japanese figurines on them, several bright pink containers, a few game boxes, a large white feather on a stand and small silken black bags neatly stacked off to the side.

My eyes spotted a set of pink fuzzy handcuffs and a plastic whip next to what looked like a child's paint set with the word *edible* blazed on the front of it. I tried not to seem overly interested or like I was staring, but at the same time I couldn't figure out exactly what the two Japanese characters were doing on the long canister in the centre of the table. *Was that his leg?*

I could see the outline of Isabelle's large black marble island in her kitchen with what appeared to be an enormous spread of food. Only food in the kitchen; check. No naked people; check. So what was I so worried about? I doubled checked that there was no one there that might know my mother and tell her that I was at a sex party before moving forward. I ventured in looking for my safety blanket.

"Grab something to eat. You *must* have a drink!" Isabelle's large breasts bounced like they were nodding in agreement with her.

I surveyed the long island. I saw plates loaded with homemade cookies and peanut butter and cream bars. Next to them were apple dome tarts with cherries provocatively place on top. There was a loaf of sourdough, the centre carved out and filled with spinach dip. The pieces from the centre of the loaf had been arranged in two round circles at the base of the bread creating a phallic image. And just in case anyone wondered what shape Isabelle was trying to simulate with the loaf, one of the girls had drawn a long white trail out the top of the bread with sour cream.

"That looks like my boyfriend Zach!" one of the young ladies said dribbling cream out the side of her mouth.

"I dated Zach in high school and he ain't that big!" the pretty brunette next to her said.

I waited for the two of them to break into a fight, but instead they turned and high-fived each other snapping pictures of themselves with their mouths open near the front end of the loaf.

I spotted a big bowl of tortilla chips with salsa, guacamole and homemade cream dip next to it; each bowl had a phallic shaped spoon in it. I saw a plate of mushroom caps that looked less embarrassing than the rest of the food. After I had picked up three and put them on my paper plate, a girl next to me whispered, "Those nipples are really good! She stuffs them with cheese." I looked down at the serving tray and realized that I had plucked the brown mushrooms from small beds of rice that had been shaped into breasts, the caps forming the nipples. *How was I supposed to eat them now?* With no one else around me I grabbed three kinds of chips, salsa, guacamole, a nonsexual piece of bruschetta, the only two brownies that did not have dyed coconut simulating pubic hair on them, one peanut square, one chocolate chip cookie and one of the bars with the apple on top. The cherry one made me blush too much. I paused and added a carrot for good measure careful not to place it anywhere near the mushrooms on my plate.

"Leena!" Mahjong screamed as I entered the living room. "We're sitting over here." She pointed to a spot on the floor by the end of the sofa. I hurried over toward her. A young girl sitting near us passed over two cushions to make us more comfortable. "Thank you," I mouthed to her. Was she as new to this as me? I had never seen her before but from her French manicured hands, expensive shoes and purse I could tell she was one of Jenny's friends. She smiled back then directed her attention to the paper in her hand. Before I could figure out what she was reading, I felt a tap on my shoulder. I looked up to see who it was.

Towering above me was a large woman with auburn hair, her smile kind and inviting. She had green eyes the same shade as my guacamole. I became so distracted trying to remember the last time I ate Mexican food that I hadn't noticed she was trying to hand me the same piece of paper that the young lady who passed us the cushions had been studying. Mahjong nudged me roughly, snapping my eyes away and forcing me to focus on the paper and pencil the woman had put in my hands. Suddenly all I could hear was a sharp-pitched wail coming from Mahjong's throat.

"For fuck's sake! I love it!"

I scrambled mentally to make sense of what had happened trying not to drop my plate of food while juggling the paper and pencil at the same time. The tiny pencil had a small plastic purple penis nestled on the top. Mahjong began to perform fake fellatio on hers.

"I know this guy!" she said extending her long tongue around the top of the pencil until the penis disappeared from sight. I heard the women all around us respond in uproarious laughter; someone from behind me poked me in the head with their penis pencil. I hid mine under my plate of food. "I'm taking this to work!" one woman screamed. "I can't wait to see their faces when they ask me for a pencil to take their order!"

"Last call for alcohol before the presentation starts!" Isabelle called out. "Anybody? Drinks?" Several glasses went into the air including Jenny's plastic penis which caused another eruption of laughter.

"Have a drink, Lee," Mahjong whispered to me. "I'm driving so I'm not drinking and I figured you'd need to more." I glared at her for a moment. She smirked and within seconds I acquiesced. Mahjong went into the kitchen with a few other girls and came back, handing me a large stein with liquid too dark to be beer. "It's a rum and Coke. Heavy on the rum." I coughed initially at the sharp taste of booze and then downed a quarter of it without tasting it as soon as I regained my composure. Mahjong smiled as she popped the top off her bottle of juice.

"Okay ladies," the auburn haired woman in front of the table said, sharply clapping her hands to emphasize her point. "Can I have your attention please?" It took a few minutes for everyone to settle down. "My name is Clarissa," she said, smiling at everyone. "Those are your order forms, or as I like to call them, your menus, so that you can choose what you like. And for those of you who have never been to an *Outside the Box* party before please remember that you will get what you want tonight as I have tons of stock in the sales room ready to go home with all you horny women!" There were several loud screams, a general explosion of whistling from all around me and someone poked me with their pencil again.

Sales room? What the hell does that mean? I had no intention of buying anything. I wasn't some liberated Westerner; the kind my mother said was responsible for sexually transmitted diseases, global warming and overpriced rice in North America. No, no. I was a respectable, thirty-two year old second generation Indian girl married to a good Indian boy. I did what my mother said and cleverly hid from her and her large network of spies the things I didn't want her to know. I had nothing to feel guilty about aside from a few light beers or the occasional store-bought curry I tried to pawn off as homemade.

Okay I *was* guilty of lying to my mother about the nature of the party at Isabelle's house. I told her that Mahjong and I were helping make centrepieces for the wedding. I remember when my mother first met Isabelle. It was at my engagement ceremony at Uncle Varki's house. My mother must have envisioned the person responsible for bringing her beloved son-in-law Manny to her to be a dignified woman with a refinement accredited to those astute enough to understand the subtleties of a proper match. She was visibly disturbed when she saw Isabelle wearing a pink leather jacket with sequins over a black lace camisole that barely covered her breasts. It was so see-through Uncle Varki dropped his plate of food twice. Despite the fact that Isabelle's appearance put her off, my mother, in true hypocritical fashion, was full of praise and compliments to the greatest matchmaker of all time.

"Ladies! Ladies!" Clarissa said clapping her hands loudly. "Back here! Remember me?" The noise level in the room slowly subsided. I became increasingly more uncomfortable with the seats that Mahjong had picked. We were too close to the front which meant every pair of drunk and sober eyes would see my reactions first.

"Okay, let me explain some things for those of you who have never been to a party like this before. There will be some information passed along to you that might shock and surprise you."

Information? What could she possibly say that was so shocking? I knew there were probably more than three sex positions but what was the point in trying different ones? Missionary worked for when I was tired, sideways meant I was the only one who could see my rolls of fat and I only used doggy style when I wanted to plan out my grocery list but didn't want Manny to see my face in case he figured out what I was doing.

"Who here has been to an *Outside the Box* party before?" she asked. Several hands went into the air including Jenny's, Isabelle's and Mahjong's. "And who has not?" I put my hand up barely past my shoulder. "Well that would make all of you *virgins*," she said with a mocking tone and a monstrously huge smile.

"Ha! Virgins!" Jenny said as she tapped the heads of each of the ladies, including me who had their hands in the air.

"You're a virgin!" a dark haired, long-nosed woman behind me slurred as she pointed at me and laughed.

Clarissa cleared her throat to speak. "I always like to start my presentation with a few true and false questions that I want you ladies to feel free to answer out loud. Are we ready to start?" There was an array of excited shrieks. "Okay, let's start with an easy one," she said studying a battered piece of paper in her hand. "True or false, most couples stop masturbating after they are married?"

The women were silent for a brief moment and then Jenny yelled: "False! That's when they start doing it more!" Everyone with the exception of me began laughing. I heard a few of the girls at the back high-five each other. How could they be so cavalier about touching themselves? My mother always told me masturbation would make me blind, deaf and shorter; none of which made for a good bride.

Clarissa redirected her gaze to the paper in her hand. "Correct that's true. Now here's another one, true or false, masturbation is a healthy and natural way to learn about one's own sexual responses and capabilities." I pulled on the fabric of my turtleneck and avoided anyone's eyes. This just wasn't a subject I felt comfortable talking about. For God's sake, I blush when I set my cell phone to vibrate.

"Masturbate! Don't hesitate!" the petite young girl next to Jenny said.

What in the hell was I doing at this party? I felt the first bead of sweat start to trickle down my back.

"Correct. That's true," Clarissa said with a smile. "Okay, next question on that similar subject, true or false, women who masturbate with a vibrator become indifferent towards intercourse with men." The women had only slightly hushed when one of Jenny's friends shouted: "Screw that! I love my BOB!!"

I looked at Mahjong who could read the question in my eyes. She leaned in and whispered in my ear "Battery operated boyfriend" as she wrote it out on the back of my menu.

"Ah, I see," I mumbled. I had no idea what she meant. From the moment I walked in I felt like I had checked my brain with my coat and nothing anyone said made any sense to me.

"Not so fast ladies..." Clarissa said. "Actually if you'll turn to your order form, you will see the last item is our $120 toy. Now this toy won't make you indifferent towards men, it will however make you care less if you don't have one, or if the one you have doesn't pick up his socks!" There was another rousing roar of laughter. This time I joined in more as a result of the rum hitting my bloodstream than actual comprehension. "That toy is the best one I have ever seen in fifteen years of working with this company and he shall henceforth be known as *The King*." I followed the lead of the girls around me and searched out the item she was referring to. I wrote the word "*Raja*" next to it, drew a smiley face and put the pencil back under my plate. I was never one to not pay attention in class; when all the other girls were out on dates or having sleepovers, I was studying or writing papers to maintain an A average. Heaven forbid I fail a class and have my mother remind me that no one wants a stupid bride.

"Okay, true or false, most couples rarely discuss their sexual relationship openly with each other." Several women started whispering but no one answered. Clarissa repeated the question.

I could still see the huge smile on Manny's face when I told him a few weeks ago about the party. I expected him to react with horror, shock or disgust but he didn't. He'd even heard of the parties and knew more about them than I did. What I hadn't anticipated was how he would light up like a firecracker when I told him I was going. Why was *he* more excited than I was? What did that say about our sex life?

We had been married for just over five years. Our sex life was fine. After all, we *had* sex .... occasionally ... when time allowed and fatigue wasn't an issue ... or a great television season ... or I didn't feel extremely fat. The truth is we fit in sex when it was convenient to our busy schedules. Between Manny's hockey practice and my general lack of desire, sex easily slipped off the radar after the first year or so we were married. It just never seemed as important or pressing as tending to the garden, cleaning out the attic or taking up scrapbooking.

No one offered an answer to Clarissa's question so she answered it herself. "The answer is true. Most couples rarely discuss their sexual relationship with each other. It seems the longer you're with the same person, the *less* you talk. Moving on, true or false, approximately 50% of all women have never had an orgasm."

"No, no, no!" Jenny said covering her ears and causing the plastic penises and condoms to rattle around her hair. "That has to be false!"

"Is it?" Clarissa asked cocking one perfectly plucked eyebrow and waiting for a reaction. I hastily stuffed a piece of bruschetta into my mouth, chunks of salsa jumping from the bread like passengers on a sinking ship trying to escape death. I then scooped up the escapee tomato pieces with the tortilla chips, the sound of crunching doing a lousy job of drowning out my own thoughts. I looked over at Mahjong with my mouth stuffed and feebly smiled accidentally spewing small bits of tortilla dust and tomato in her direction. As close as we were, my sex life was something I managed to avoid talking to her about. *How could I tell her that I had never had an orgasm?* What difference did it make anyway? Sex with Manny was nice; it was pleasant. There is nothing wrong with pleasant. It's not like I hadn't thought it was odd before that I had never had an orgasm, it just didn't seem to be that pressing of an issue.

At my marriage ceremony, my Aunt Jumma took me aside to give me a sex talk providing me with the same advice she had been given on her wedding night. "Listen to me Leena. I tell you vat to do na? Sex is wery simple dimple. You just let him do vat he need do and you count to forty in your head." She looked me square in the eye with a seriousness that chilled me. "*Heyna*? When it be ower, den you make *dahl*." There was no talk about love, no talk about emotional connections or technique, just the basic understanding that sex is the man's domain, and mine was the *dahl*.

"It's true that approximately 50% of the female population has never had an orgasm," Clarissa said. She sounded stern, the playful glint in her eyes momentarily gone. I thought she was staring directly at me. I felt the heat in my body rise. Even a mocha-skinned person like me could turn pink with the right provocation. Before she could catch me blushing, I looked away, stuffed two mushroom caps in my mouth and chased them with a large swig of rum.

I was sure every woman in that room owned a vibrator, had multiple orgasms and open communication with their partner. I had never masturbated in my life, never had an orgasm and the only thing Manny and I really communicated about before I left the house was whose turn it was to empty the dishwasher. It was mine.

"That means statistically, there is probably someone here who has never had an orgasm. And if you *think* you've had one, I can definitely guarantee you haven't. The good news is that if you have never had an orgasm, don't worry, you will. Today's your birthday!" Peals of laughter exploded all around me. I was only half-aware of Mahjong muttering: "Now *that's* what I call a happy birthday" under her breath as she doodled pictures of penises on her order form.

If it was true, who else fell into that category besides me? I longed to look around, to catch someone's eye, to feel a certain kinship with another woman but I was too afraid.

"Here's another question," Clarissa said. "True or false, the clitoris retracts under the hood just before the point of orgasm?" Suddenly it was silent save the sound of ice clinking in someone's glass. I fidgeted with the pillow under me. The vinyl cover made a rude farting sound against Isabelle's hard wood floor.

No one would have noticed if I hadn't snorted out a laugh through my nose trying to cover it up which only echoed the sound and made it worse.

Clarissa repeated the question before she finally revealed the answer. "That is true." She pointed to a large fake diamond ring on her right hand. "See this ring? Okay, for the rest of the night we are going to *pretend* that this ring is my clitoris. We're just *pretending*." There was a bit of nervous laughter but for the most part all the women stared at the large bauble. She dropped the ring down to the front of her pubic area. "Now let's pretend I'm getting some loving."

She wiggled the big diamond up and down. "This is the hood that protects the clitoris." She cupped the fingers of her left hand over the top of the diamond. "So here I am getting my loving, and just at the point of orgasm, the clitoris retracts." She pulled the diamond ring toward her hiding it under the cup of her left hand. "At this point, the clitoris is so over-stimulated that it hides. It then needs to be gently coaxed back out." She curled the diamond ring slowly out from where it was hidden by her other hand, blowing gently down on the large stone. "Then Blam! There's your orgasm!"

So all I had to do to have an orgasm was get a big diamond ring like hers? Nothing made sense. I felt more lost and unsure with every word.

Clarissa looked confident without a hint of smugness to her. She had at least eighteen women fixated on her pubic area and yet she didn't seem at all fazed. She was a heavy set woman, close to the size of my mother and most of my Aunties with large round hips, a wide belly and robust breasts squeezed into a white lace top. I marvelled at how comfortable she looked.

Clarissa surveyed the women in the room. I must not have been the only one with a daft expression on my face. "You see ladies, you all know what I'm talking about without actually *knowing* it. This point, where the clitoris is hiding under the hood," she emphasized by hiding the diamond under her hand, "this is the moment that you have all experienced at one point or another. It's the moment during sex that you are lying there thinking…hmmm…it's not going to happen tonight…so….what should we eat for dinner tomorrow? Maybe chicken? Or you're thinking I should probably get to the laundry. And my point is?" She waited but no one said a word. I started to get anxious sure that she was about to impart the most important piece of wisdom of the night on us. "My point is, your orgasm is where ladies?"

No one spoke. Surely someone knew the answer? I sure as hell didn't.

Finally one woman in the corner said, "Under the hood?"

I wanted to laugh as I felt the second wave of rum hit my bloodstream but felt too self-conscious.

Clarissa shook her head. She waited and when no one produced an answer, she slowly drew her finger to her head and pointed. "Your orgasm is up here," she said tapping her temple for emphasis. "It doesn't really matter what you have going on down here," she pointed to her pubic area again. "You have to be up here." She moved her hand up toward her head. "Or there's no orgasm. Your orgasm is in your brain."

Some women started to whisper among themselves. I yearned for Mahjong to make eye contact because as the rum started to tear down my barriers one by one, I was eager for my secret to finally be revealed. When I looked over at her she was drawing pictures of gaping mouths with long curling tongues hovering over the penises she had doodled on her order form.

"Again, I reiterate," Clarissa said, "if you've never had an orgasm, today is your birthday!" Several of the women in the room laughed. I took a deep breath and polished off the stein trying to make eye contact with Mahjong again.

"Mahjong," I whispered. "Are you paying attention?"

She looked up at me through her red eyelashes. "I have two of everything she has on that table."

Mahjong could talk about sex anytime, anywhere. She was frank and honest when it came to everything in life, often to my embarrassment or social discomfort. She was born Mae Wong but at some point during our time in high school she said her name to someone who didn't quite catch the correct pronunciation and responded, "Mahjong? Like the game?" The name has stuck ever since.

I still remember the day we met. It was on the fifth anniversary of my father's death, which was also my 17th birthday. A boy from school named Glen asked me to go to the movies with him. My mother said that dating was something only the *besharam* did. It was a conspiracy brought on by condom companies to sell their products and make Westerners more promiscuous than they already were.

When I told Glen I wasn't allowed to be alone with him, he cleverly disguised our date by including me within a larger group of kids already going to the movies. My mother, unaware that there would be boys present, acquiesced. The movie started and not two minutes into the playlist Glen slipped his hand onto my knee. The feel of his hot fingers on my leg startled me. I pushed his hand away. Ten minutes later he put his arm on the rest between us and brushed his hand against my right breast. This time I was so alarmed that I screamed out loud.

"Relax Leena," he whispered in my ear. "I actually like your exotic looks. I'm the only one in school who does." I couldn't process what he was saying because I saw the silhouette of his hands approaching me in the flickering lights of the movie theatre. Glen attempted to lift my sweater up and slide his hand under the fabric despite the fact that I was clawing my fingers into his palms. My nails were so deep into his flesh I was sure I was going to draw blood and have to find a way to explain the stains to my mother.

"*Stop it*!" I whispered and then with more panic and insistence, "Stop it! Glen, no! Stop that!"

"Don't make me call the usher on you!" I heard a voice from the row above us shout. "Cause they will hose you horny bastards down!"

"Doug was right." Glen growled at me, finally giving up. "Indian girls are all stupid virgins!" Then he threw his middle finger up in the air to the person behind us, and without one look back at me turned to Debbie Anderson sitting on his right and began to grope her instead. They left after the movie in the same car stranding me at the theatre.

I stood in the parking lot uttering every Hindi curse word I knew my mother would hurl at me when I tried to explain what happened. As I contemplated which would be worse, showing up three hours later than my curfew because I walked home or showing up in a police car because I got arrested for hitchhiking, I heard the voice from the row behind us shouting at me to get my attention.

"Where you heading?" she asked.

"I live on Elm drive," I said, wiping tears from eyes.

"I live right near there. Want a ride? If you're worried about stranger danger, I assure you I'm strange but you're in no danger."

"What's stranger danger?"

"You've never heard the term stranger danger? Didn't your mother ever tell you not to talk to strangers?"

"She told me not to talk to *anyone*."

"Well that's good advice too. My car is over here. Come on. My name is Mae."

"I'm Leena."

"Well Lee," she said extending her fingerless gloved hand, "I'm happy to meet you."

"Did you come here alone?" I said suddenly aware that she was all by herself at the movies.

"Yup. I don't hang with the high school bunch much. I've seen you in school before."

I didn't want to tell her that I'd seen her too, mostly hanging out alone, wearing weird clothes and always smelling like some strange kind of herb. It didn't really matter though. That night she was my salvation and for the next fifteen years my truest and dearest friend.

Clarissa clapped her hands to bring the ladies back to focusing on what she was saying. I fidgeted with the pillow underneath me causing it to quack and burp against the wooden floor. I felt even more uncomfortable and self-conscious. I looked at Mahjong. She had started to doodle vaginas on the opposite side of her order form. When she caught me staring at her, she smiled and lifted the purple penis to her lips flapping her tongue around the top of it.

"Okay, where was I ladies?" Clarissa said when the noise level had subsided. "Oh yes. Your orgasm! It's all up here," she said pointing to her head again. "I can't stress that enough. You have to play the movie up here or it won't happen. I don't care what it is, just make it work up here and your orgasm will come…no pun intended!" Clarissa didn't wait for anyone to laugh, she redirected her attention and everyone else's in the room to her tattered piece of paper. "True or false, it can take between ten and fifteen minutes for a woman to reach orgasm."

Almost every woman in the room shouted true in response and Mahjong lifted her head long enough to say "Fuck that, I need an hour!"

"True or false, approximately 80% of all males reach orgasm within two minutes of entering the vagina." Clarissa had barely finished asking the question when Mahjong shouted, "It's true! But he never gets a second date from me!"

Clarissa smiled. "You're right, it's true. And what a difference! Ten minutes for us and two minutes for them. That's a whole hockey period! Or at least it can feel like one!"

Maybe that was the reason I never understood hockey, no matter how many times Manny tried to explain it to me. I would hear the word "icing" and all I could think about from that moment on was *cake*.

"Moving on, true or false, approximately 50% of couples experience sexual difficulties." Suddenly everyone was quiet again. As the rum floated through my veins toward my brain I reasoned that with Manny our sex life might not have been a wild adventure ride but at least it was worth the price of admission more than half the time.

I felt heat rise in my chest as an unstoppable flood of memories from my past threatened to overtake me. My delectable suppressor was gone; not a drop of rum left in my stein. As I looked down at the last piece of ice floating at the bottom of my glass I heard Clarissa direct the question again to someone in the room. I was surprised to see her staring at me for the answer.

"I'm sorry?" I said choking back my own saliva. "What was the question again?"

"True or false, approximately 50 % of all couples experience sexual difficulties?"

Mahjong instantly rose to my defence.

"Why don't we ask the bride-to-be that question?" Eventually all the women focused on Jenny. I heaved a deep sigh of relief as Mahjong put her hand on mine and squeezed it.

"Yes, Jenny!" one of the drunker girls said. "Tell us about your sexual difficulties with Johnny!"

"Your fiancé's name is Johnny?" Clarissa asked. "So it's Jenny and Johnny?"

Jenny smiled. She seemed to revel in the dreamy satisfaction of how people reacted to hearing their names together. Though Jenny had completed her degree in business at university and had interned with a top-ranking company, she chose not to take a permanent position in marketing but opted to work as a receptionist for a downtown law firm when she graduated. She wore very provocative clothes to work and enjoyed watching the young clerks fawn over her vying for her affections. She never let any of them get farther than a kiss on the cheek. The moment Johnny was hired to the firm with rumours of being fast-tracked for partnership she made her move like a well trained panther securing his undying love, a two carat ring and the promise she would never have to work again - all within eight months of his arrival.

"We don't have any sexual difficulties," Jenny said slurring her words. "We fuck like rabbits all the time! He's an animal!"

"Woohoo!" several of the girls to the left and right of Jenny said at the same time.

"Well I'm happy for you. But the answer is true. Most couples experience sexual difficulties at some point. Communication is the key."

I had heard it so many times before: *Communication is the key*. Communicate your needs to another and then they will know what makes you happy; communicate your goals at work and you will rise to the position you have longed for; communicate your feelings and others will listen with open hearts. When I communicated my needs to my mother, she told me to shut up and stop being so sensitive. When I communicated my need for more money at the accounting firm where I worked, my boss told me they were experiencing cut backs and instead gave me more work to do for the same pay. When I communicated feeling insecure about my body and the extra weight I had put on after we got married, Manny simply said, "All couples get fat after they get married." The extra weight he gained on his long frame only made him look healthier while my extra poundage made me look shorter, dumpier and frighteningly close to a brown troll.

"Okay, last question." Clarissa said. "True or false, when the G-spot is properly stimulated, a woman can ejaculate one to three quarts of liquid." I looked over at Mahjong who had a devilish smile on her face. She winked at me, sat back against her pillow and quietly watched the women around her gasp in both horror and amazement. I was one of the women gasping in horror.

"*Has that happened to you?*" I whispered to Mahjong.

"It was a freaking tsunami the first time. I thought I peed all over the guy and the dumb jerk got all cocky and wouldn't stop smiling. But let me tell you Lee, it put the ah in ah-mazing!"

How had I known Mahjong all these years and somehow I never knew this? She shared details about each of her lovers from girth, width and duration but this piece of information was news to me. In fifteen years of knowing her I could recite the nicknames she gave to all her lovers from Andrew Apple Balls to Thick Dick Victor. I could tell you her shoe size, how she cheated on her exams in university and which one of the Spice Girls she would have sex with but somehow *this* was a subject we had never discussed.

"The answer is true," Clarissa said. "The first time it feels like you have peed all over your partner." Mahjong had a smile on her face and an *I told you so* look in her eyes. "But let me take the time to explain this because it's important." Clarissa positioned herself squarely in the middle of everyone's gaze and looked down at her pubic area drawing everyone else's eyes down at the same time.

"The G-spot is on the outside wall right here," she said poking her belly just below her navel. "If you put your finger inside you and crook it like you are motioning *come here, come here* you will be pressing against it." She looked back down to her pubic area and made a circle with her other hand over the hub of her bottom belly. Then she bent her finger as though it was stimulating the circle from the inside. "Now as I continue to stimulate this area, it goes from about a dime-size to a quarter-size and with clitoral stimulation… well let me put it this way, you'll have to change the sheets!" She smiled broadly.

"I've heard about them but I've never had one," a woman with bright red lipstick said. "Is it pee?"

"No," Clarissa said. "Everyone thinks that it is but it isn't urine. It's natural and it will feel *unlike* anything else you've ever felt. It's really quite incredible." She resumed her position by the side of the table, directly in front of me.

In under an hour's time my mind had become flooded with too much information, some of it getting lost in the cloud of rum that had firmly settled into my blood stream.

"There is one thing I can't stress enough ladies," Clarissa said resting one leg over the other and leaning against the table. "You need to know your bodies better than anyone else. If you don't enjoy sex with yourself, how can you expect someone else to?"

Suddenly there it was in a language I could fully understand despite the fog of rum: *If you don't enjoy sex with yourself, how can you expect someone else to?*

When I had arrived at the party, I had no idea what to expect but after hearing Clarissa state it so plainly, the words formed an inescapable truth I could no longer hide from. I knew from that moment on, there was no turning back.

Chapter 2

"I'm going to present a lot of product in a short period of time," Clarissa said. "Before I do, let's look at some lingerie." She reached behind her and brought out a straw basket covered in a gold cloth that in my slightly inebriated state looked like a giant samosa. She even folded the fabric back like my grandmother taught me when she first showed me how to make them. "Remember ladies, your lingerie says a lot about you."

She pulled out a brown teddy with ruffles. It would make me look like a misshapen *chappati*. If your lingerie *says* something about you, what was mine saying about me? My bra was over eight years old and had three holes in the lace at the back which only marginally exceeded the number in my thick cotton underpants. I cancelled out the section marked lingerie on my menu. A blazing red pen would have made me feel better, but I only had the little penis pencil to work with.

Clarissa smiled politely at everyone's reactions to the pretty lace outfits and then widened her grin when she brought out a few costumes. Police Officer, French Maid and the School Girl all got rousing applause. The runaway hit was the Nurse's costume.

"I'm a nurse!" a pig-tailed buxom blonde said twirling her hair in her hands. "I love that costume!"

"And the last thing I want to show you ladies is my best seller. Crotchless panties!" She held up a pair of underwear with white lace at the sides and two strings hanging down from either end of the front joining into one small bow at the back. It looked like a parachute cut in half at the top with its strings suspending down towards an invisible jumper.

"These are a wonderful addition to every woman's wardrobe. Let me show you why." To the roar of a delighted crowd Clarissa reached down, slid the white panties up over her black pants and snapped the strings into place creating the striking visual of a large black triangle in the centre of two white stripes. Thank God she put them on because there was no way I would ever have figured it out by myself.

"There are four reasons these panties will go home with you tonight. One, women always complain they can spend $80 on an outfit and it ends up on the floor in two minutes, so what's the point? Well, with these you spend under twenty dollars and they *stay on*." Someone clapped. It might have been Mahjong.

"Let me give you reason two. If you're having sex with a man, he's *visual*. Never underestimate that. It's not the same as wearing nothing at all. Just the *thought* of you wearing them will make him crazy. And when he sees them on you it will make him even crazier."

She held up three fingers. "And if you are having sex with a man, let's face it, he might not get it. With these panties you make it really simple for him and tell him to *stay inside the lines*," she said as she pointed to the black space between the two white strings over her pubic area. Every woman in the room, myself included, howled with laughter in response.

"And lastly ladies, what I most recommend these panties for are those bad days when you just feel really low. You know what I'm talking about? We all have them. Put on these crotchless panties, wear a skirt, and go grocery shopping." I saw looks of intrigue, shock and delight. "Trust me ladies, you wear these panties and if you were depressed before you left the house, you won't be by the time you come home. It has nothing to do with sex, and everything about making you *feel* good."

I tried to think of the last time I felt good, really good. In the confusion of rum and mushroom nipples exploding in my stomach, it saddened me that no single event stood out in recent memory.

Then, with a sudden impulse of pure drunken determination, I boldly wrote *Parachute Chuddy* on my paper menu in the top right corner.

Clarissa refolded the golden fabric and slid the basket under the table. While she began to explain the bubble bath line, Mahjong slipped into the kitchen, got herself another juice bottle and a cold cooler for me. Years of friendship and a deep desire to get drunk eliminated the need for me to properly thank her. I popped the top off and swallowed half the frosty drink.

The consultant extolled the virtues of bubble baths with our partners and how sexy it was to play with edible products. I almost choked on my cooler at the image of Manny and I both trying to fit into our small bathtub at home. I could see him sloshing around, his long six foot frame struggling to stay inside the tub. I envisioned his feet on either side of my head with mine in his groin just trying to get both of us in at the same time. Comical yes, sexy no.

"This product is also edible so you can use it as a mouthwash, toothpaste, deodorant, shampoo or for washing your pets, your car and your dishes.

"And it has vitamin E in it so it is exceptionally good for shaving." She ran the bottle along her legs. "And shaving." She waved the bottle under her armpit. "And *shaving*." She held the bottle over her pubic area.

Thankfully I had no cooler in my mouth or it would have ended up spewed across the room. "The afro went out in the seventies ladies," Clarissa said. "Clean it up. It's your best chance it will get found!" I pulled my legs closer to my chest.

"This next product is a body lotion that you can put anywhere on your body. *Anywhere* you put it you'll be perfectly edible from head to foot." She winked. "This lotion is peppermint flavored and really good for giving foot rubs so I suggest since your feet are clean and edible, well, why don't you get your toes sucked?"

Toe sucking? Did she actually just say *toe sucking*? What a hideous thought! My big toes had three very stubborn hairs on each of them that made them look like beetles lying on their sides doing Pilates leg stretches. Though I plucked them on a regular basis, they still seemed to grow faster than any other follicles on my body. I could just picture my toe in Manny's mouth, the hair protruding from the edges of his lips as though they were trying to make their escape from his teeth.

"That's so gross!" Jenny slurred.

"I love it!" screamed one of Jenny's bridesmaids, someone so conservative she made me look like a pole dancer.

My eyes instantly turned to Mahjong.

"Oh yes my little brown friend," she said pointing to her feet. "Toe sucking is good." She leaned back against the end of the sofa tucking her arms behind her head and closing her eyes.

"Toe sucking," Clarissa said, "is actually pretty cool. Try it. I'm just trying to get you to think *outside the box*." She smiled at her own joke and waved the round black container in the air.

"Now this stuff is not only good for toe play, it has many other uses. Are you ready?" She waited until everyone stopped talking. "This body lotion is also exceptionally good for analingus." Clarissa paused. I felt tension rise all around me. "What's analingus? Well we all know what cunnilingus is right?" She looked around the room. No one moved or spoke.

I stopped breathing in case the slightest shift in position caused the pillow beneath me to roar another loud farting sound in the dead silence.

"Okay, so imagine you're freshly showered and covered in this lotion and someone is performing cunnilingus on you and then whoops their tongue slips and hello there it is! Analingus!"

She looked every woman in the eye as though she wanted to make sure her advice registered with each one. My brain had completely abandoned ship, setting sail in a sea of malted liquid.

My first introduction to the word *anus* was quite memorable. I heard the word for the first time in science class. I rushed home to tell my mother about the other planets in the universe and when I got to Uranus she slapped me across the face and shouted, "Dat place only for *besharam*!"

A few months later at a dinner party my mother was hosting for someone's arranged marriage, one of the Aunties commented about how badly Westerners behaved. "Ve know how to act na? *Ghoras* are tooo liberal. Vhere oh vhere do all dese *besharam* come from?" To which I loudly and proudly replied, "They come from Uranus!" I was slapped and sent to my room. Needless to say after our sex education class when the word came up for real, I knew better than to bring it up to my mother. If a planet got me a hard slap to the head, I didn't want to think what a rectal discussion would get.

"The next product is something that heats up!" Clarissa held up a tube shaped bottle. "Now I'm supposed to tell you it's good for muscular aches, pains and cold feet but what it's really good for is… oral sex!" Mahjong's eyes shot open. She sat upright and grabbed her penis pencil in hand. "When you blow on this product it makes your skin hot! And speaking of hot ladies, what is the key to performing oral sex on a man?"

No one answered for a brief moment. The long-nosed lady behind me snidely said: "Get someone else to do it."

Clarissa ignored her.

The pretty brunette next to Jenny said: "Lots of lubrication."

"No teeth?" the buxom blonde offered, twirling one of her pigtails.

"Good one," Clarissa said and smiled. "But let me get straight to my point. The key to performing good oral sex on a man is *enthusiasm*."

I can't lie. Oral sex had never interested me. Manny made no secret of his desire for fellatio but I was never that comfortable doing it. It felt awkward and embarrassing. Eventually he stopped asking for it. For the last few years, we both seemed content to treat his penis like a melting ice cream scoop. I gave it just enough licks to form it into a peak and then straight to penetration.

"The more energetic and enthusiastic you are," Clarissa said, "the happier the penis. With this product, it does some of the work for you warming your mouth and heating him up at the same time. I blow on it and it gets hot and the penis says… wow!" A few women giggled. She had everyone's attention.

"So now let's say I want to change it up the next time, you know, practice my enthusiasm. This time I might have a piece of ice tucked into my mouth and now it's hot and cold. Try it!" Mahjong was smiling at me. I looked down at my order form. I hadn't taken any decent notes and I was suddenly angry with myself for not paying more attention.

"If you want to liven it up even more, you can buy popping candy from the corner store and put them in your mouth and then lick the penis for special effects!"

When I was eight years old at my cousin's wedding, my other cousin Vargoo slipped me a handful of popping candy. We laughed riotously as it exploded in our mouths. That is until we got caught by one of his uncles who exclaimed wildly that we were eating crack in the back alley. I wasn't allowed to hang out with Vargoo again. My mother made a point of telling me that candy would only rot out my teeth and no one wanted a toothless bride.

Mahjong smiled widely. "I love popping candy. It's a poppy good time!"

"When do you sleep?" I asked Mahjong sarcastically. She smiled and flicked me in the knee with her penis pencil.

"Yes or no, things can get lost inside the vagina?" Clarissa said. She waited for an answer and when no one put one forth she offered it on her own. "No. Nothing gets lost in the vagina. What that means is that it's closed. So if you put anything in there, it will come out. Just relax. It's not *lost*. It's in there."

The long-nosed lady behind me put her hand up to tell the story of a friend who lost a ring in her vagina. Her boyfriend at the time, thinking it was a clever way to propose shoved the diamond inside her but when it came time to ask her the question he couldn't find it.

They went to the hospital and once it was retrieved, he got down on bended knee and proposed.

"But it wasn't *lost* was it? On to the next question then, true of false, things can get lost inside the anus." She waited a bit longer for an answer.

Like a voice in the fog, I heard, *true* from someone near me.

"You are correct." Clarissa smiled at Mahjong. "Now ladies, this is important, the anus is not like the vagina. The first few inches of the rectum are empty and then after that there is a natural vacuum which means whatever I put in there had better have a loop on the end of it, something I can hold on to or it should flare out at the bottom. Like the lamp, but *not* the lamp." I felt my sphincter involuntary spasm against the cushion.

"So always remember this about the rectum, ladies, because if you don't, and you lose something in there, well that's a trip to the hospital and you better hope the doctor is cute!" She winked. Two women laughed. I felt my dinner coming up.

She put down the canister of liquid that got hot and while she reached over to get another product, I took my first real notes: Hot stuff = oral. Anus = no lamps.

"Now the next product is lubricant. This one is especially good because it is water-based." Clarissa held three oval bottles in her hand. "It comes in three flavors. Strawberry is the best seller. Lubricant is important because at different times of the month, you may feel dryer than normal. After giving birth, your body's lubrication changes too. As you get older, vaginal dryness becomes an issue. Lubricant tricks the brain into thinking you are more aroused than you actually are so it helps you feel more excited."

Clarissa went on to present a numbing cream, two kinds of body chocolate and several products for enhancing internal tightness and one for promoting multiple orgasms.

Like a student cheating on an exam, I tried to spy the menu of the woman lying on the floor next to me to see which items she was checking off. She caught me looking at it and moved her paper away. I looked over at Mahjong's paper but couldn't see any check marks in the mess of erotic doodles on her sheet. I faked a sneeze to take a quick glance at the paper in the lap of the lady who had handed me the cushion and noticed she had ticked more than five items. I took my penis pencil and made five random checks of my own as Clarissa brought out a game box.

"Now this is a great way to increase communication and have fun while playing," she said, holding the box up to her chest. "The aim is to win favour coupons which are good for thirty days after the game is played. Remember the most important part of the word foreplay is *play*!"

The game seemed like a good deal all around. It had a blindfold I could use to sleep in with on the weekends, the timer would replace the one my mother broke in Yahtzee when she caught me cheating on my score card and the pretty pink note pad was perfect for grocery lists.

Clarissa then presented a few other stimulating liquid products, some edible body paint and five kinds of massage oil. When she was done, she asked if anyone wanted to take a break before the toys. Almost everyone shot up from their seats without hesitation and lunged at the island of food in Isabelle's kitchen.

I headed straight for the coolers in a bucket near the fridge.

"I'm so glad you came out tonight!" Jenny said to me. Her eyes were completely glazed making them appear like two shiny blue marbles. "I didn't think you would come. Cum! Ha! Leena did you hear what I said?"

Everyone, including Isabelle's neighbours, probably heard her.

"I'm so happy for you," I mumbled looking instinctively for Mahjong. "I guess I'll see you at the wedding next week."

"Are you going to wear a len-goo?"

"Sorry?" Despite the fact that she was still shouting, I had no idea what she meant.

"A len-goo. You know, a len-goo. Your traditional clothes. The clothes of your people." *My people?* My people were the same people as her people. I saw Jenny picking out a blouse in the mall two weekends ago in the exact same shop as me.

"You mean a *lengha*?" I asked.

"Yes! A len-goo! Oh please wear it! Johnny will just love it! Oh my God Lee, did you make these samosas?" She stuffed the entire triangle into her mouth. "So good!"

"I bought them. But I did make the chutney."

She dipped another triangular pastry in the green liquid and then stuffed it in with the half-masticated heap already in her mouth. "That chutney is so good! I'll have to barf tonight or I'll never fit into my dress!" She darted off to talk to the other girls in the kitchen.

Isabelle topped up everyone's drinks, served some warm brie from the oven with a crusty French bread and then loudly insisted that people resume their seats.

"Jenny wants me to wear a *lengha*," I said to Mahjong as we sat back down on the floor.

"Are you going to?"

"You must be high! All my *lenghas* are heavily embroidered. She showed me a picture of her dress last month. Even my cheapest one makes her dress look like she bought it at the dollar store."

"So what are you going to wear?"

"Whatever fits my fat ass."

Clarissa clapped her hands. "It's toy time!"

She began the second half of her presentation by showing us a laminated picture of two vaginas. One showed the clitoris directly over the vaginal cavity, a phenomenon she said approximately 15% of the female population enjoyed. The other picture showed the clitoris higher up, with a greater space between it and the opening. This she said was the case for about 85% of the female population.

"Men are born with their genitals on the outside of their bodies," Clarissa said. "Lucky them! Women, on the other hand, need to go and get a mirror and physically look at themselves and we don't often do that. And if no one has told you before, then I'm telling you, you're beautiful. You're unique." I felt like everyone was staring at me. I shifted on my pillow. I was just drunk enough to start to enjoy the sounds it made.

Clarissa's first toy was a cyber-skin penis that had a suction cup on the end. She called it Hank. Mahjong dated a guy named Hank once. She called him Stanky Hanky after he dropped his drawers on their second date and the smell from his penis almost made her faint. They never went out again.

"Now this little bullet vibrates." Clarissa held up an egg shaped toy with a cord attached to a control. "I'm going to put it in your hand so you can feel what vibration feels like." She walked around the room, placing the toy in each lady's hand. The buxom blonde squealed with joy and proclaimed to everyone in the room that she already owned one just like it. Jenny in her drunken state needed her friend's help to steady her hand. The long-nosed lady refused to hold the toy. Mahjong curled both her hands around it and smiled.

I was next.

I held out my hand like I was waiting for my teacher to hand me back an assignment I knew I had failed. The first wave of vibration coursed straight through my veins on a highway of alcohol fast-tracked to my brain. It felt at once invigorating and frightening. I closed my hand over it as Mahjong did, feeling the pulsations dance like little sparks inside my fingertips. Before I could fully begin to enjoy the sensation, Clarissa pulled the toy away and continued her presentation. I was surprised that I instinctively wanted to hold the bullet longer to see what other reactions it would elicit.

"That's just a sample of what it's like." She pulled a small silver bullet similar to the one she had in her hand from one of the black satin bags on the table. "Here's a great toy that I recommend. It has six speeds and it fits into this piece." She pulled a small pink gel-like rabbit out of the bag.

Clarissa demonstrated how to slide the bullet into the back of the bunny causing its nose to vigorously vibrate. She slipped two fingers into the round strap under the base of the bunny so it appeared as though it were perched on a ledge. She recommended it as one of the best beginner toys. *Beginner*, now that sounded like me. I put a star next to the number for the bunny.

She demonstrated two waterproof toys, a crooked one for the G-spot and a ring for use around the testicles to increase sensitivity and prolong an erection.

"Now while we're on the subject of him." With a smile she pulled a rubbery pink sleeve from a golden box behind her. "This is for *him* ladies. You pour warm water through it and slide some of our water-based lubricant down the centre and when the penis goes in here, it *feels* like a vagina. He can use this for self-stimulation, or you can use it with him. If you give it to him, you can have the whole night off to read a book! Imagine that! And if you want to play together, here's how." She grabbed Hank from the table and inserted him inside the sleeve. "Hold it at the base. Then I pull on the sleeve… gently! And as I tug on it up and down, I am caressing the penis with my hands on the outside but it feels like a vagina on the inside."

Jenny clapped and laughed awkwardly.

I thought about buying the sleeve for Manny. My mother had been telling me to buy him a leather briefcase for work with his initials on it for his upcoming birthday. Somehow in my drunken state, I reasoned they were pretty much the same idea: a thing he held in his hand at his job or a hand job for his thing. Either way his birthday present was taken care of.

"Okay ladies," Clarissa said after everyone was quiet again, "are you ready for the King?" She turned to the table and picked up the last black bag behind her, slowly revealing its contents. From the black satin emerged a white see-through toy with a dolphin attached at the base. The dolphin looked like its mouth was open, split into two angular pieces. The shaft of the toy was topped with the face of a knight which formed the crown of the penis.

"This is the King!" Clarissa's dark eyes flashed like green electricity. "Now ladies, let me show you something about this toy. Not only will he light *you* up, but he lights up himself!" She flicked a switch at the base and the white shaft came to life flashing bright green, then pink then blue. She went on to extol the virtues of how the toy was made but more specifically how it was designed to please the female form. "Ladies as women we can often justify getting something for someone else before we treat ourselves to anything special. Too often we don't assume responsibility for our own sexuality. We rely on someone else to figure us out. Bring home a toy and you bring home personal satisfaction. Because it's like I said earlier. If you can't enjoy sex with yourself, how can you expect anyone else to enjoy it with you?"

There it was again.

So simple and true and for some reason resounding even more clearly to me than it had when I first heard it.

"Hallelujah!" Mahjong said saluting Clarissa.

"Johnny who?" Jenny slurred to the delight of the women around her.

I looked up at Clarissa and was surprised to see her looking back at me. Was it the alcohol that made me think she could see right through my soul? Like somewhere deep in those dark green eyes she could see past my facades and fears. Everything she had said resonated like crystal chimes above the growing murky fog of liquor sloshing around my brain. Could she know what a deeply profound impact her presentation was having on me?

"And with that dazzling light show ladies, I end my presentation for the night. I'll be in the bedroom down the hall to take your orders." Clarissa bowed gently then turned her back to the clapping mass of drunken women. Within minutes she had loaded up her display bag and slipped off to Isabelle's bedroom.

Isabelle handed out pieces of paper with a number on it to everyone. I held on to my piece of paper flipping it from 6 to 9 and giggling at my own idiocy until the buxom blonde friend of Jenny's came up to me and tapped me on the shoulder.

"Are you an Indian? Jenny said there was an Indian coming to her wedding."

I didn't know whether to correct her and tell her the term was South Asian or to tell her I was as North American as she was.

"I guess that's me," I said, hiding my numbered piece of paper in my palm.

"She said you were going to wear some kind of traditional Indian clothes at the wedding. I think that's so cool!"

Where the hell was Mahjong?

"I'm not planning on it. I have a nice blue dress I can wear."

It was the only one that fit.

She leaned her massive chest toward me and twirled her pig tails. "So I guess that you know all about the Kama Sutra right?"

"Oh no," I said tipping against her in my own drunken numbness, "my people may have *written* the Kama Sutra but we forgot to *read* it." I saw the momentary pause for comprehension in her eyes and then marveled at how large her mouth was when she threw it open to laugh out loud.

"So you must know about tantra too. Do you do tantra sex?" Her eyes were wide, her anticipation as big as her heaving breasts.

"Tantra? It's my mantra!" I lied. "But I can't-ra tell you or I'll have to kill you." She laughed so hard I thought I saw her teeth rattling in her head.

"There you are!" Mahjong said pulling me away from the blonde. "Do you want to go home?"

"But I'm number 9. Which is also number 6. Look! Which could also be 69." I laughed so hard I snorted through my nose.

"So you're ready to go home then." Mahjong smirked at me.

"No!" I said with more urgent insistence than I intended. "My people wrote the Kama Sutra dammit! I should go in there and reclaim my place in the sexual history of my ancestors."

"What the fuck are you talking about Lee? Your people are suburbanites that drive SUV's. You can't twist like those people in the Kama Sutra. You're not some bendy brownie. You don't have to prove anything."

Then why did I feel like I did have something to prove?

There was a hint of a challenge in Mahjong's eyes that made me instinctively want to rise up to it. It wasn't just the liquor talking. It was years of suppression and personal angst bursting out. In under two hours, I felt the seams of my entire existence begin to unravel.

Your people wrote the Kama Sutra.

You're not some bendy brownie.

If I wasn't those things then what was I?

I heard number 9 called out.

I removed Mahjong's hand from my arm and grabbed my purse. As I crossed the threshold into Isabelle's bedroom, the sight of the consultant's bag spilling open with product was almost enough to send me screaming back to my safety blanket. It looked like the carnage of a sex store being beaten to death; vibrators and bottles of lubricant strewn everywhere where blood and guts would be.

"I'm sorry," I apologized as I closed the door behind me. "I'm very nervous. It's my first time."

"I won't bite," Clarissa said with a smile flipping a fresh bill of sale open.

"I think the last brave thing I did before tonight was pick the bold coffee in the cafeteria instead of the light blend."

"You have a good sense of humor," Clarissa said and smiled.

"You haven't met my mother. You need one to survive living with her."

"What's your name?"

I hesitated. I could just imagine that somehow word of my presence at this party would get back to my mother. Quick! Think of another name! Polly – no I don't look perky enough to be a Polly. Maria – I don't look Italian enough. Sushmita – I wasn't even sure how to spell it.

"My name is Leena," I said.

"That's a very pretty name. Do you know what you want to buy Leena?"

"Everything!" I blurted out. I dropped my gaze. "I'm embarrassed to say I think I have never had an orgasm before." The sentence tumbled from my mouth with surprising ease. When the words were finally out of me, I felt an overwhelming feeling of release.

"Then today's your birthday!" Clarissa wrote down my name in the bill book in front of her.

"It's in December actually." The edge of my drunken buzz had worn off and I realized what she meant. "Oh, I get it. I'm sorry."

"It's okay, Leena. Take your time. When you're ready, you can buy a toy and have another kind of birthday. For now, take baby steps."

I looked down at the check marks and tiny notes I had scribbled on my paper menu. I had made them small enough so that no one else could read them but in the dim light of the room the joke was on me. I couldn't make out any of the markings either. Just as I tried to decipher my own handwriting I noticed the words *battery operated boyfriend* that Mahjong had written on the back page, the first letters of each word suddenly making it clear to me why vibrators were referred to as B.O.B. I laughed out loud in a delayed reaction to the joke that had taken place nearly two hours ago. I squirmed when I saw Clarissa patiently smiling at me.

"The bunny seemed good," I said, with a bit of hesitation. "I don't think I'm ready for the King."

"Absolutely. That's a great choice." Clarissa's warm green eyes looked even more endearing in the soft lights of Isabelle's bedroom.

"I want to live!" I suddenly yelped like some second rate actress in a B horror movie. Clarissa smiled and although she was receptive and warm, I felt embarrassed at how I must look to a complete stranger. Something was bubbling up inside me and it wasn't just the rum.

"What I meant to say was I want to buy all of these things." I tried to sound calm. I handed her my list hoping she could make more sense of the scribbles than I could. To Clarissa's credit, she took out each item I had put a mark next to and explained again how to use it while I decided whether or not I really wanted them.

"And the parachute *chuddy* too!" I said as she put the last item I ordered in a bag.

"Sorry, what is that?"

"The underwear with the hole for those bad days when you want to grocery shop and forget your troubles."

"Oh, you mean crotchless panties!"

"No more bad days for me."

In the end, I handed Clarissa my MasterCard and my trust hoping in the sober light of day I wouldn't regret what I had purchased and would remember the sweet excitement burgeoning in my chest as I said yes to every item she held up to me. I walked out with two large black bags packed with products that filled me with equal amounts of extreme anxiety and extreme anticipation.

Mahjong waited for me at the front door with the most peculiar smile curling her lips.

"Good thing you brought your credit card eh, Lee?" Her eyes twinkled as she handed me my coat.

"I didn't have any idea, Mahjong. It's like I've been sleeping for thirty-two years." Mahjong smiled at me and wrapped my coat around my shoulders as Isabelle came over to say goodbye.

"Did you have a good time, Lee?" she asked.

"I sure did. I was just blown away."

Isabelle looked down at the two big bags in my hands and then to Mahjong. "From the size of those bags, it looks like Manny is going to be the one getting *blown away* tonight. Now if you'll excuse me I have to round up some cabs for these horny drunk bitches!"

Once Mahjong and I were in the car, she immediately threw her bag in my lap. "Open it if you want." A part of me was more than curious to see what she had bought for herself since I didn't see her go into the sales room. I peered in and found a satin bag with the King inside. She had also bought some lubricant in the grape flavor and then much to my surprise I suddenly found my hands on Hank.

"Holy crap! That does feel like skin!"

"You better believe it!" Mahjong said reaching her hand over to pet the top of the penis. "He reminds me so much of Huge. I mean Hugh. Ah, I miss that loser sometimes."

I studied the cyber-penis in my hand with unabashed excitement. Mahjong smiled at me but said nothing.

"Do you want to know what I bought?"

"Only if you want to show me Lee."

"I *want* to show you what I bought." I marveled at how much more excited I felt about showing Mahjong what I had bought than I had been making the purchases. "I bought the blue bubble bath for making your muscles relax." She seemed uninterested. "I bought this hot stuff in a few flavors to begin with."

"I have that."

"And I bought some lubricant."

"Me too."

"I bought… I bought… the rabbit toy too." I paused to create dramatic effect. It was after all the first vibrator I had ever purchased.

"What else?" Mahjong asked matter-of-factly.

Her reaction disappointed me. I could feel my buzz completely fizzle.

"The game," I said flatly refusing to act like it bothered me that she didn't congratulate me on my monumental purchase.

"That game looks lame. But let me know if it's any good. I think you'll get laid the second he sees you come in the house with the big bags alone!" Mahjong howled out loud laughing at her own joke.

"Mahjong?"

"Yup?"

"I have to tell you something."

I took a deep breath.

"Sure." Mahjong's eyes were focused on the highway ahead of us.

"I've never…"

"Had an orgasm," she finished. "I know."

It took all my courage and bravery to make my confession for the second time that night and instead of a reaction of shock or surprise, she made it seem like it wasn't a big deal.

"How did you know?" I wailed.

"What the fuck? It's obvious! I've known you like fifteen or sixteen years now, right? You think I never pay attention? Anyway I blame that fucker Nick for messing with your head all those years. He screwed up your self-esteem and he made you feel bad about yourself. Anyway, forget that jackass. I'm not going to waste any more time being careful how I put things to you. What I don't know is why you felt like you needed to lie to me all these years."

I was reminded of a few conversations we had in the past. Once when we were in university Mahjong flat out asked me if I had ever had an orgasm and I lied. A second time, a year into my marriage to Manny, she asked again. I lied again. She never pressed the issue after I gave her my answer both times.

"I don't know why I lied," I said, fidgeting with my seatbelt. "I can't believe you knew all along and never said anything."

"Don't put this on me, Lee. I wanted to help you but every time I asked, you said, "Yeah sure Mahjong." What the hell was I supposed to say? Prove it? I knew you were too embarrassed and I wasn't going to put you on the spot."

"Thanks," I muttered under my breath.

"What I don't get is why you're telling me now. I've asked so many times over the last few years and suddenly we go to this party and you say it just like that." I could tell instantly that she was hurt that it took a total stranger to bring it out of me.

"I would never have said it if you hadn't forced me to come to the party tonight."

Suddenly there was too much tension in the air between us.

"Well, anyway, whatever. I'm glad you got a toy," Mahjong said, her pride obviously still a bit wounded. "Do you know how to use it?"

"I – uh. I – well…"

"It's really very instinctual. Don't be embarrassed to ask me questions. Cause you can ask me anything Lee."

She sounded so sincere but I found it hard to get past how awkward I suddenly felt. "For sure," I said as easily as I could. "I will ask you, but I hope to be able to figure it out on my own. I'm not a total sexual loser. The toy goes in my ear right?"

It took her a few seconds before she let a smile curl her lips and then Mahjong quickly reached over and squeezed my knee with her hand.

"Leena," she said, taking a deep breath, "I'm really proud of you."

I felt tears sting my eyes.

"Well I don't know how Manny will react," I said "I never talked to him about it really. All this time we've been married and I've never talked about it."

I was getting more and more anxious as we approached the house. How do you come home from a sex party with a big bag of toys and bring up subjects with your husband that you haven't ever broached the entire time you have been married? Where do I start?

By the time Mahjong drove me home, it was just past 11:30 p.m. I scurried upstairs and, like a drug dealer trying to hide a stash from the police, I frantically scouted out a suitable hiding place for all my newly acquired loot.

I decided to hide the bags in the spare room behind the plastic totes I had been asking Manny to go through since we first moved in. I reached into one bag, found the golden box with the sleeve toy for him and removed it from its casing. I figured it would be easier for him to accept how much money I had spent if he saw that there was something in it for him.

I lay down on our bed, my mind still racing, as I flicked the pink sleeve back and forth in my hands hearing it flop and crackle with each whack of my palm.

How did a night of a few drinks, some racy underwear and a bunch of vibrating toys suddenly force my eyes wide open?

Why was it that suddenly something didn't feel right anymore?

I'd only had sex with two other men before Manny. My first boyfriend Jonathan was a cook in the university cafeteria. He was a soft-hearted romantic that doted on me, constantly professing his love. I was so convinced that my mother would die from a heart attack if I brought home the kitchen staff that I ended our brief love affair before it really got a chance to start. I met Nick in my second year of university. I was enamoured with him from the moment I saw his large muscular frame and heard his deep booming voice. Despite all my efforts, I never felt secure enough in his love to justify the wrath I would get from my mother because I had fallen in love with a *ghora*. When we broke up, I lost all hope I would ever meet anyone, until Manny came along.

I looked over at the alarm clock on the side dresser: 12:09 a.m. Just as I started to panic about whether my husband was dead or alive, I heard a key in the door downstairs.

Chapter 3

The fussing downstairs was all too familiar. I heard the click of the door locking and the sound of Manny opening the foyer closet to put his shoes neatly in their place on the shoe tree inside. He had a *thing* about shoes in the doorway and never liked to come home to see anyone's slippers or boots in the entrance. The closet door closed followed by the sound of his bare feet shuffling across the wooden floors until they were muffled by the beige carpet in the living room. He went into the kitchen, opened the fridge door and then closed it. I heard him pour a glass of water and then wash it out in the sink. I grew more and more anxious and even became a little agitated that he wasn't rushing upstairs to see how my night went or if I had purchased anything.

I heard Manny shuffle some of the mail on the island in the kitchen until he finally thumped his way up the stairs to our bedroom. I had left the French doors open but was still a bit surprised to suddenly see him standing in the doorway. There was my husband of five years with the face I had lain beside for all that time and with the body I had come to know every inch of and suddenly I was more nervous at that moment than I had been our first time together.

"Hey baby," he said with his usual warm grin. "Did you have fun tonight?"

I tried not to read too much into his question. Was he making polite conversation because he thought I probably wouldn't buy anything? Was he trying not to embarrass me in case I did buy something? Did he forget that I went to a *sex party*?

"Yeah, I had fun tonight." My gaze directed him to the sex sleeve lying on the top of the bedcover.

"I hate driving George around!" He stripped off his clothes ignoring my gaze and what I thought was a fairly provocative tilt of the head. "What part of being the designated driver means I have to drive him to the grocery store to get eggs for tomorrow? Just going to jump in the shower and rinse off the stink, okay baby?"

Within seconds Manny was in the shower, his sweaty clothes in the hamper, his pyjamas out of their drawer and waiting for his freshly washed body. I started to feel my blood boil. Maybe his normal behaviour would have been fine if it had been one of my regular Saturday nights staying at home stuffing myself while I read or rented movies. But this was no regular Saturday night!

I heard the faucet turn off and watched him shake the water from his ears and inspect his nose for errant hair before he finally flopped down in his wet towel on the duvet next to me.

"What's this?" He picked up the tube in his hand.

Waiting for him to finish his shower, I went from nervous anxiousness to irritable anger to suddenly being caught off guard.

"It's uh..." What do I say? How do you put something like that?

It's a sleeve for your cock, dear. Or a warm blanket for your dick? What had Mahjong called it during the party? Pocket something. Pocket rocket? Pocket Pita? What was it called again?

"We won the game, eh?" Manny said excitedly. "You should have seen it! There was hardly any time left and suddenly out of nowhere Rodriguez totally scores on their team and after that, it was bam, bam, bam we had three goals!"

It was all too much to absorb at once. My night had some sort of surreal quality to it which was only enhanced by the image of my husband excitedly recanting details of a hockey game while unconsciously squeezing and smacking a pink sex toy in his hand.

Deep down, under the anxiousness and anger, I was starting to feel hurt that Manny seemed more excited to talk about his game than my night in a room full of drunken screaming women and vibrators.

"You won? That's great Manny," I said with as much enthusiasm as I could muster. "Won? No baby, we didn't just win, we pulverized them! I think Marcus even tore his leg up again."

"That's horrible!"

"He's a dick," Manny said. "Don't worry about him. No one likes him on the team. Hey, what is this thing anyway?" He looked down at the pink sleeve still in its plastic wrap and gave it a tentative squeeze.

"Well… speaking of dicks…" I said, trying to make a clever segue.

"What?" he said with alarm. "This is a fake dick? You bought a fake dick?"

"No, no! It's more of a sleeve actually." I was mortified. This wasn't how I had pictured things going at all. He hadn't even kissed me hello yet.

Manny studied the outside plastic casing, inspected the ridges on the side and squeezed open the hole at the top. "Oh! I get it!" he said. "It goes *on* my dick." He sat on the edge of the bed with the pink sleeve flopping back and forth between his hands.

I would have paid a million dollars to know what was going on in his mind at that moment.

"What did you get yourself?"

He smiled warmly at me and started a step by step routine I had grown accustomed to over the years. One: Towel gets hung up damp on the side of the tub. Two: Pyjama top goes on before boxers and pyjama bottoms. Three: Teeth get brushed. Four: Slippers are left neatly at the edge of the bed. Five: Pillow is removed from under his head and placed at the foot of the bed. In ten minutes, he would be snoring.

He was half-way through brushing his teeth when he popped his head out of the bathroom and shouted, "What did you buy, Lee?"

"Just some stuff. And I bought some other stuff too." I paused to see if he was going to say anything or press for more details. When he didn't, I made my dramatic declaration in a voice barely above a whisper. "And I bought a toy too. For me."

"What?" he asked turning off the faucet. "I couldn't hear you. I had the water running." He shut the bathroom light and sat down on the bed. He lined up his slippers by the edge of the bed. "What did you say baby?" he said, stifling a yawn.

From the fatigued and exhausted look on his face, I could tell that sex wasn't going to happen. And sadly, for the first time, I was really ready for it. I was in fact so anxiously anticipating it that I found myself deeply disappointed when I realized it wasn't going to happen.

"I just bought a few things," I said in a low voice. "Do you want to see them now? You look kinda tired." "I am, Lee. If I didn't have to drive George to the grocery store on top of everything else, I wouldn't be so late." He took the pillow out from under his head and placed it past his feet. I stared at the five-year-old symbol at the edge of the bed that signalled it was time for sleep.

"I understand Manny. Goodnight."

"Goodnight baby."

I turned over to the side lamp by our bed and switched it off. I sat in bed while Manny nestled into the mattress and tucked the sheets up to his neck. Visions of lubricants, a large pink diamond ring and a bunny with a vibrating nose swirled through my mind until sleep finally overtook me.

Sunday morning started out like any other. Manny and I rose around the same time we usually did on the weekends: 9:30 a.m. We would both brush our teeth and head downstairs to our usual routine of coffee, breakfast and the morning paper.

"Hey, tell me how the party was last night," Manny said putting his section of the paper down on the table.

His attention was completely on me. I didn't know where to start. Everything felt like a dream in the bold light of morning.

"I had a good night actually," I said. "It was fun. I learned a lot too."

"Really?"

What did he mean by *"Really?"*

Did he know more than he was letting on?

Was he being sarcastic?

Did he know that I had never had an orgasm?

If he did know, was now the time to tell him?

I decided that wouldn't be nice. It's simply not something one says over scrambled eggs and toast.

"Yeah I did learn a whole lot." I smiled. "Nothing Mahjong doesn't already know of course."

Manny burst out laughing. "She could write a book I bet."

"Well she wasn't as surprised as me by some of it. The consultant was a really nice woman. She's been doing the parties for fifteen years. She was really nice. I liked her a lot."

"I guess I wasn't picturing your night being an information session."

"What were you picturing?" I wondered if his vision was anywhere close to what I had in my mind before I got there.

Manny flashed his big smile. "A bunch of girls in their pyjamas hitting each other with pillows."

He smiled more broadly.

I crossed my arms and furrowed my brow until his smile vanished and I knew the image of young, chesty women in lingerie flailing linens at each other was out of his mind.

"Sorry to disappoint Manny but it wasn't anything like that at all."

"Hey, what's the deal with that thing you showed me last night?" he said. "How much was that?"

I suddenly felt a pang of both guilt and fear. Would he be mad when he found out how much money I had spent? Should I really have bought *that* much stuff? In the sober light of day I wasn't even sure I could remember what some of it was for.

"I got that for you," I said, praying he wouldn't ask me to show him the receipt.

"I don't think I got a good look at it last night."

Was he trying to be coy or was he using the toy as an excuse to have sex? I couldn't read his expression.

"I can show you," I said, sounding more like a teacher than I wanted to. He shrugged and followed me upstairs.

Our sex routine had become as regimented as the pillow-at-the-foot-of-the-bed habit. It was always the same. One of us undressed, then the next undressed, we would slip under the covers, kiss and touch, usually in the same places with unvaried pressure and for approximately forty seconds a body zone, until the act itself was complete.

With all the new information floating around in my head and my burgeoning desire to make things different, I felt compelled to strike while the loins were hot and not settle for tried and true.

"Wait here," I said.

I left our bedroom and headed towards the storage room. I rummaged through the black bag and removed the bottle of lubricant and toy cleaner I vaguely recalled was supposed to be used with the pink sleeve. While foraging through the rest of the bag I reached into the tiny sac that had my vibrator neatly enclosed inside and decided to leave it where it was for the time being.

I wasn't ready yet.

I closed the bag, took the two bottles in my hands and headed back to the bedroom.

When I re-entered our room, Manny was lying on the bed absently tapping his toes against the bed railing. It wasn't exactly the kind of sex scene I had imagined as I told him I should probably clean the toy first before we used it. He nodded in agreement and then promptly began to tell me about his plans to play squash with his buddy later that afternoon.

I grabbed the pink sleeve from where it was sitting on the nightstand and took it into the bathroom removing the plastic wrapping while Manny carried on a conversation he could have easily had without me. He was mentioning something about one of his squash buddies cheating in a game and I half-heartedly responded with the odd "Oh you don't say," here and the occasional, "You must be kidding!" there.

Was this what all couples do when they play with sex toys – make idle conversation and pretend not to feel awkward and a bit foolish?

Was this how they do it in porn?

I sprayed the cleaner on the outside of the toy and on the inside of it. When I put my fingers inside the pink sleeve it suddenly became very clear what it was for. I felt a strange tingle of excitement.

What had Mahjong called it at the party? A pink pocket? A pizza pocket? No! A pocket pussy! That was it! It was all coming back to me.

I started to get excited.

I poured warm water down the centre of the toy to make sure all the cleaner was washed out. I opened the bottle of lubricant and placed a small bubble of it on my fingers shoving it inside the toy. I giggled feeling the rubber react to my slippery touch.

Manny was still talking about how he got jilted out of ice time when I walked out of the bathroom with my hands behind my back. He must have noticed my expression because he eventually stopped talking and waited for me to say something.

"Look what I have," I said slowly bringing the soft pink toy to his view. His mouth twisted and I couldn't read his expression. "Do you know what it's for?"

The truth is I was hoping he would tell me so I wouldn't have to figure it all out myself.

"I think so," he said, slowly getting up from the bed and walking towards me. "Is that what you showed me last night? It's pink." Before he could ask me how much it cost, which might threaten the light-heartedness of the mood, and before I lost my nerve completely, I pushed him back against the bed away from me and the toy. He willingly lay down and propped his arms behind his head, making himself comfortable.

I opened the buttons of his pyjama top. He unfolded his arms long enough to free himself and then promptly returned them back behind his head. I was determined to stay in control even though I had no idea what I was doing. Unfortunately, my cell phone was too far away to text Mahjong to ask her what I should do. I figured stopping every ten minutes to get instruction by text would probably spoil the mood.

Once Manny's pyjama bottoms were off, it was obvious to me that there was much work to do. I looked down at his semi-erect penis, looking like a beleaguered snake in a charmer's basket too tired to get up and wave to the tourists. It reminded me of a Discovery program I saw on India when I was younger, with one major difference: I didn't have a *cinnai* flute, I had lubricant.

I took Manny's penis in my hands and gently stroked it with the same rhythm as I had so many times before. I placed one knee between Manny's legs and the other against his outer thigh. I reached for the lubricant. When I squirted it onto my hands I was shocked to feel how cool it was.

I knew instinctually the snake would retreat back into its basket if I doused it with the coldness of the liquid so I made a spectacle of warming the gel in my hands until I was covered in its silken warmth. Somewhere along the way Manny's expression changed from relaxed to excited.

With the liquid dripping between my fingers, I slowly placed my warm, wet hands down the shaft of his penis. He smiled. I watched as his eyes closed and his head sank deeper into his pillow. He brought his arms down to his sides. It almost looked like he was melting into the sheets.

He moaned. I took it as a sign that I was doing something right.

I spread the lubricant all over his genitals until he was one beautifully glistening masterpiece of manhood. I was heady with my accomplishment as his fully erect penis indicated my work was well done. It was time to find out exactly what the pink sleeve did.

SEX & SAMOSAS

I reached over and grabbed it putting some of the lubricant still left on my hands into the opening. It felt squishy and warm against my fingers. I couldn't help but wonder what it would feel like for Manny.

I stretched the opening of the toy over the head of his penis and slowly slipped him into the sleeve. His eyes were still closed. As the sleeve descended down, he let out a guttural moan from his throat.

I felt a rush of confidence.

Once the sleeve was completely on his penis, I sat and stared at it, unsure what I should do next.

I was glad Manny's eyes were closed so he couldn't see me looking around for inspiration, almost expecting someone to be there to give me some tips or guidance. I struggled to remember what Clarissa had said we were supposed to do with the toy once it was on. In a sudden flash, I had an image of her stroking the pink sleeve on the cyber-skin penis she called Hank. Somewhere in my drunken state I remembered thinking how sensual it looked to see her pulling and twisting the pink sleeve up and down on the fake penis.

I started to yank at the toy but it was so slippery that as soon as I pulled it up, it began to ooze lubricant and threaten to fly skyward. I securely anchored the sleeve down at its base with one hand and then began to squeeze the sides in and out with the other.

Manny's back started to arch.

I nestled into my position like I was glued to the sheets and then continued to gently tug, twist and pull on the pink sleeve. With each movement his face contorted into a new expression. He started to breathe heavily and erratically.

The toy felt like warm dough in my hands, just like my mother made for samosas. I started to knead the sleeve like it was *atta*.

With every twist Manny arched higher, moaned a bit louder. Somewhere in the midst of preparing the dough for samosas, I lost sight of the most important aspect of the toy - anchoring it to the base.

I began to tug, twist and pull with more vigour when I suddenly lost control of the pink sleeve. Just as I felt Manny rise to his climax my hands slipped and lost their place. In the split second that Manny bucked upwards and ejaculated, the pink sleeve shot at bullet-like speed into my left eye bounced off my face and ricocheted toward the lamp at the side of our bed. The base cracked and split in two colliding with the sound of Manny's groaning and the crash of my ass hitting the ground as I slipped from the bed to the floor.

When I opened my right eye, I looked down at my hands which were covered in a combination of volcanic eruption from Manny's penis and a sea of lubricant. Without thinking, I raised my left hand to my left eye to alleviate the throbbing sensation, which resulted in an even more shocking sting from the combination of lubricant and sperm I had just introduced to the delicate tissues of my eye.

I screamed out loud and darted from the floor to the bathroom. I instinctually cleaned my hands and began to douse my eye with cold water in an attempt to ease the burning sensation.

When all was said and done, I emerged from the bathroom with my left eye red and starting to swell, the black mascara I had forgotten to remove from the previous night dripping down my cheeks making me look like a swamp zombie. Manny came to his senses when I returned to the bedroom. He struggled to sit up, a confused expression on his face. He looked from the side lamp to my pathetic figure by the bed.

He smiled sheepishly. "Good luck explaining to your mother how you got that black eye."

I instantly burst into tears.

Though the swelling around my eye healed fairly quickly, it took a full week before my ego did.

After a long week at work, Manny and I planned to do little more on Friday night than catch up on some television shows we had missed or possibly rent movies.

Sitting on the sofa, fat and full from a dinner of dosas in an Indian restaurant, I watched Manny flip through a series of sitcoms on television. I felt restless and bored. My mind drifted to the sex party. I found myself mentally going through what was in the bags in the spare room. For some reason, I continually returned to the same image of a large black box marked with the words *Sex Games for Couples*. It showed a picture of a man's hands massaging a woman's bare backside.

"Want to play a game?" I asked. Manny began to randomly flip through the sports channels.

"You want to play Rumi for cash? I'll let you win if you're nice to me." He smiled without taking his eyes off the TV.

"I wasn't thinking about beating *you* at Rumi, I had another kind of board game in mind."

"Monopoly? Sure. We haven't played that in a while." He raised the volume on a sports channel he had locked onto.

"No, not Monopoly. I was thinking we could play *Sex Games for Couples*. I bought it at the party. Jenny's party," I added at the last moment.

"Seriously?" Manny focused on my face and muted the station.

"Yeah." And then more emphatically, "Yes! It looks like fun!"

Manny turned the television off.

"Okay," he said. "Sure."

I studied his expression for sincerity. Finding nothing but slight intrigue and what I thought was a small dose of fear, I decided to seize the moment and got up from the chaise. In no time I returned from my secret stash. Manny sat on his chaise, hands neatly folded in his lap. He looked like a nervous young school boy. I handed the game to him and sat down at the end of his chaise.

"I thought you might bring down Monopoly as a joke." He tore open the cellophane wrapping on the box.

I chewed on my lower lip as Manny rifled through the contents of the game. He unfolded the board onto the coffee table in front of us. It had the same image from the cover in the centre, the woman's backside slick with massage oil. In the middle of her tailbone was a dial that spun around to different coloured squares. Manny put out a small sand-filled hourglass, a white vibrator shaped like a torpedo and a black silk blindfold.

Of all the things on the table only one scared the hell out of me: five inches of satin in the shape of a figure eight. The vibrator didn't scare me half as much as the blindfold.

When I was fifteen years old, my friend Julia invited me to her house for a birthday party. I was shocked when I saw a few boys from school were also there. I sat awkwardly in the corner of her basement unsure of how to engage with anyone. When Julia's mother said she was going to leave to go pick up more chips, someone suggested we play the racier version of pin the tail on the donkey. The idea was to blindfold someone, place them in the centre of everyone else, spin them around and wherever they stopped, they had to kiss the person who was standing in front of them.

Julia went first. Her long red hair spun like a blanket in the wind as she twirled and giggled with delight. She stopped right in front of Dack Grover, a lanky but handsome senior. He reached down to kiss her while the others quietly smirked. When she took off her blindfold she was glowing. Carrie, Julia's best friend spun next. Her kiss was with Trevor Hamm. They locked lips so tightly I thought they were going to melt into one person.

Then it was my turn.

I put on the blindfold and spun around, excitement building in my chest. I would have been happy to smooch any one of the boys there. It was to be my first kiss after all. After a few moments of twirling around I started to get a bit queasy and stumbled forward. When I finally stopped I felt something in front of me so I leaned forward and planted my mouth on it. I heard the kids behind me suppressing their laughter. I wondered why the person I was kissing seemed to resist my mouth so I pressed harder until the others were screaming and clapping. I removed the blindfold and stared blankly at Julia's father's punching bag wet with my saliva. To make matters worse, my stomach revolted from all the twirling and I suddenly threw up all over her basement floor. I was never invited over to another one of Julia's parties again.

"The game seems pretty straight forward," Manny said. "We spin the wheel and pick up one of these cards to win favour coupons. You want to go first?"

I was nervous and breathing heavily. I could hear my heart thumping loudly in my ear.

Maybe the game wasn't a good idea.

Manny seemed calm as he laid out the cards on the board.

I stared at the blindfold and then the vibrator.

Then from the vibrator to the blindfold again.

I grew more anxious.

"Ready?" Manny asked.

The board was fully set up. I nodded, my eyes fixated on the wheel in the girl's back. I tried to think of a clever decoy so that I could distract Manny long enough to either set the blindfold on fire or *accidentally* drop it into our personal shredder upstairs.

"I'll spin first," Manny said. The white disk in the centre of the board game whirled until it landed on a section labelled *Challenge*. Manny picked it up and read it aloud. "Blindfold your partner and before the time is up, guess what part of their body they have put in your mouth."

That damn blindfold!

"What! What does that mean?" I hated how hysterical I sounded.

Then in a split second, my memory raced back to the night of the sex party and I remembered Clarissa's description of the game.

"This is so much fun for couples. You play the challenge cards in order to win favour coupons that are good for thirty days outside of the game. If your partner is a man then I can assure you every time you're blindfolded he will try to put his penis in your mouth. So now that you know the answer, you'll win the challenge for sure!"

Her description had the room of drunks roaring with laughter. I vaguely recalled hoping to cheat in the game by writing "answer = penis" on my order form.

Manny reached for the black silk blindfold and motioned for me to come closer.

I had no choice. The shredder was upstairs and there were no matches in sight. What's worse, I could only imagine what Manny would say when I backed out of playing after it was *my* idea.

I leaned in half expecting the blindfold to be one that you can see through or one that you can successfully peak out the bottom of. Instead I saw nothing but blackness as soon as he put it on. Almost instantly, I felt my heart beat faster and my hearing become more acute.

"You ready?" I could make out the sound of him shifting on the chaise and the rustle of what I thought was his shirt coming off. There was the unmistakable sound of his zipper going down and the thud of his pants hitting the floor.

"Open your mouth." A faint touch of laughter accompanied his instruction.

I suddenly didn't trust him, feeling the sweat on my lower back begin to mirror the dewy slickness of my palms, I cautiously opened my mouth. Cold air rushed against my tongue. Before I had a chance to think, something was gently placed in my mouth.

Well, I reasoned, it definitely wasn't his penis. Clarissa was wrong. It was a different kind of hard. I would have tried to explore it with more zest if it were not for the smell I couldn't quite place. I immediately recoiled making what must have been a horrified face.

"Trust me," Manny said guiding my head back. I could hear him starting to breathe heavier, the hard knob back in my mouth again. "Try and guess."

I started to press my tongue against it and assessed that it must be a bone of some sort since it seemed hard under the surface of the skin. I started to suckle it to try and figure out its shape hearing Manny's breathing getting harder and deeper with each stroke of my tongue.

He seemed to have trouble keeping whatever it was in one place as it kept jerking in and out of my mouth. My mind was racing but I couldn't think of anything that it might be. Since it obviously wasn't his penis, there was no harm in me possibly biting it off so I scraped my teeth against it which caused Manny to let out what sounded like a squeal, a deep moan and a gasp all at once. It was a noise I had never heard him make before but it was a decidedly satisfied sound.

I leaned back and tried to think.

Hard and bony = shoulder? No. Nose? No. Toe?

"It's your - your elbow," I guessed.

Manny began to giggle between short, shallow breaths. "Open your eyes!"

I removed the blindfold to see him contorted on the chaise, clutching his calf in the air, the sight of his ankle in front of my face still bearing faint lipstick marks from my mouth around it.

"Your ankle?" I threw my hands in the air. "I'd never guess!"

"It's really erotic," Manny said in a low rumble. He grabbed me closer to him and gave me a long deep kiss.

Was he turned on by having his ankles sucked? I looked down at his boxers and could see his penis trying to periscope out as if to watch us play the game.

"You like that?" I asked with hesitation. "Having your ankles licked?"

All the times we had been together, and I never licked his ankles. I never even *knew* that he liked it.

"Okay Lee," he said. "It's your turn next before we re-spin."

"What do you mean?" I asked pulling myself up on my haunches on the chaise.

"Give me the blindfold. Now you put a part of your body in my mouth and I'll guess."

"Okay so it's my turn," I said out loud hoping to motivate my brain to think of something to do.

Manny smiled and opened his mouth wide in anticipation, the blindfold firmly in place over his eyes. I laughed out loud at the sight of him sitting on the chaise, his tongue flopping forward like a dog in summer heat.

My mind raced. What do I do? Put my elbow in his mouth? Put my ankle in his mouth?

I removed my blouse and pants and prayed for inspiration. I left my lingerie on. My black bra was starting to fray badly at the edges and was held at the base with a safety pin. My faded black control top panties with the elastic escaping slightly from both edges was stretched to its capacity attempting to hold in my heavy dinner.

What if I put my finger in his mouth or my wrist? They both seemed too easy. I felt competitive and wanted to win, to surprise Manny the way he had surprised me. I asked him to ease his head forward to stall for more time.

Impulsively, I placed the inside of my elbow near his mouth, being careful not to get too close to him but close enough to watch his expression. His tongue probed around the gentle curve of my arm causing me to giggle from the ticklish sensation and instantly jump back.

"Sorry, sorry!" I leaned his head forward again putting my arm back up to his mouth. He licked slowly at first and then more rapidly. The sensation started to drive me wild. I wanted to scream, cry and laugh all at once.

"I think it's your shoulder," he said tentatively.

"I win!" I said triumphantly. "Open your eyes!"

Manny removed the blindfold and smiled at me. "Your elbow?"

"*Inside* of my elbow," I corrected. "I win."

"You do not!" he said. "We both got it wrong. You didn't guess mine either."

I enjoyed the playful banter between us so much that I wanted it to continue more than I wanted sex. It had been so long since I felt so energized and playful with anyone. Any thoughts of nervousness or tension were completely gone. I wanted to play and what's worse, I wanted to win.

"Is it my turn to spin?" I asked.

"Yes." Manny slid back against the chaise.

I spun the wheel. It landed on a section labelled *Action*. I picked up the first card on that deck. "Do a sexy striptease for your partner." I sat back on the chaise away from Manny. "Can I pick another one?"

"Why? Seems pretty simple, you just do a sexy striptease." Manny folded his arms, a faint smile curling his lips.

"Most of my clothes are off already!"

"Okay, so you forfeit?" he said and smiled reaching for a favour coupon.

"No!" I grabbed his hand to stop him.

I put my blouse back on and began to wish we had started drinking before opening the game.

It's not like I hadn't ever seen a strip tease before. During my first year of university, my entire dorm floor had decided (with Mahjong's guidance) to visit an after hours club and take in a strip show. By the time we got to the club most of the girls were already at their drunken saturation point. I wasn't close enough to mine to plunge as easily into the noisy room like the others. I was convinced I would run into someone I knew, or worse, someone my *mother* knew. I surveyed the club to see if there were any brown faces I might recognize until Mahjong screamed at me to let go of the front door frame forcing me to give in.

Our group took up an entire table at the back. The centre stage was empty and the club was alive with screams from women who were being goaded by the D.J. The lights dimmed, music began to crescendo from two loudspeakers hidden in the dark when suddenly a tall, very well built blonde came charging out of the back curtains wearing red and orange fire fighter cover ups and no shirt underneath. He began to gyrate and swing his plastic helmet about much to the delight of the frenzied women in the club. With deliberate skill he removed his uniform piece by piece until he was standing in only a pair of loose boxers with red and yellow flames on them.

"I respect the attention to detail," I shouted to Mahjong commenting on his shorts.

"I want to see his hose!" Mahjong screamed.

Several rum and cokes later, I began to feel the energy of the crowd infuse me. I whooped and hollered with the rest of them even when I wasn't sure what we were yelling at. Mahjong was happy to see me so animated. She encouraged me to call "Officer Pete Pecker" over to our table. I raised my arms over my head and started to flap them around to get his attention which caused me to accidently elbow a nearby dancer in the groin. He doubled over in pain, lunging towards a server with a tray of drinks that ended up flying through the air. We were asked to leave immediately. I have never been to another strip club since.

"I'll put music on," I said as I did up my buttons slowly to stall for more time. My top was long enough to drape down to almost mid-thigh though it was badly wrinkled from being shoved in my slacks at work all day.

I walked over to our stereo system at the side of the big screen and pushed the power button on. As it fired up, my mind started to race again. What can I play that's *sexy*?

I glanced over the compact discs but nothing seemed even remotely appropriate. I picked up Anne Murray's Greatest Hits, got temporarily distracted by some of the tracks on the back, but decided in the end she wasn't the right choice. I loved Anne, but her music only conjured up images of snow birds and spring time, not sex poles and strippers.

My well worn Air Supply disc wouldn't motivate me to do anything more than sit on the sofa with a box of chocolates and cry like I did for months after my break up with Nick. I put it back.

In a flash, I remembered a George Michael disc I had just purchased and put it in. I moved the selector over to track eight. I vaguely recalled thinking the song "Freek" sounded like something my mother would hate, which meant it must be provocative and sexy.

I pressed play, took a deep breath and stared at the wall in front of me away from Manny.

The song started out slow for a brief and awkward ten seconds until the tempo jumped slightly with a heavy pounding beat. I turned to Manny who was sitting back in his chair, one leg propped up and the other lying flat. He had one hand behind his head, the blindfold resting on his temple and the other hand on his thigh.

I tried hard not to look him directly in the eye at first because I knew I would lose my nerve. Instead I focused on the music, attempting to move my hips back and forth in time with the rhythm. I smacked the fabric of my top in patches at first. When I realized it looked like I was swatting flies off my blouse I stopped.

Manny looked bored. When I slowed down the strokes, his expression softened.

What else do strippers do? I walked in small circles until I ended up with my back against the door frame. I leaned back against it and saw Manny's eyes widen slightly. I slid down against the wood slowly, then more vigorously so I could scratch the itch in my back. On the way up, I got a mass of my curly hair caught in the dimmer switch. I turned sharply trying to yank it free which in turn eased the lights down but cost me a wad of curls.

With the basement not as bright, I felt more empowered by the music, more in the mood. I walked over to just in front of the chaise and began to touch my arms, shoulders, breasts and the top portion of my thighs. What I intended to look provocative ended up looking like I was giving him baseball signals in slow motion. Manny was unimpressed and I was nervous. It was time, like it or not, for some clothes to come off.

I took a deep breath, closed my eyes and turned my back away from Manny slowly unbuttoning my blouse out of his sight. I looked over my shoulder to see what he was doing causing the blouse to slide half way down my back. His eyes widened. I bent over and flung my head down between my legs to peak at him while giving him a long view of my sizeable underpants. I saw him smile slowly and lean back farther into the chaise, his hand moving up his thigh to his lap. When I flipped my head back up, I felt a rush of blood course through me, the *dosa* in my stomach churning in revolt to the disruption of its digestive process.

I winced and rubbed my belly. His gaze became more intense. As the *dosa* settled, I slowly undid the buttons of the bottom half of the shirt. I was still clutching the fabric close to my chest allowing him to only see the top of my underwear. I let the shirt slide back over my shoulders again slowly revealing my bra one breast at a time, the dimmer pot lights gently gleaming off the safety pin on the side.

I swayed closer and just barely missed nicking myself in the knee on the coffee table. I straddled it deciding it was easier to do that than to stop to move the table over to the corner and continue. There were probably a whole field of dust bunnies under it anyway. What would Manny do if I stopped my version of an erotic dance to grab the vacuum and do a quick clean up? The thought was so ridiculous it made me smile. When I looked back at him his eyes looked more intense, the dome of an erection peeking through his boxers again.

I felt more confident so I dropped my blouse to the floor. I crawled over the long part of the chaise toward Manny like a cat, feeling my tummy drop loosely in the cold air. In an effort to minimize the droop, I twisted my hips backwards rocking my body like it was in a boat on choppy water. All the writhing made my hair clip suddenly pop loose. In frustration I started to wildly toss my head back to get the hair out of my face and just as I was mentally cursing such a long song choice the music finally drew to its climax and ended. The room was silent for a brief second as the c.d. moved to track nine.

I lay on top of Manny who slowly raised his hands to my bare back.

"Good job," he said in my ear.

"I felt like a fool."

"No it was good. I was impressed. Where did you learn that?"

"Learn what?"

"To move your hips like that."

I didn't realize I had moved my hips at all.

"Bollywood I guess. All Indian girls can sway their hips, na?"

He laughed out loud and then laid me back on the chaise so that I was sitting in the same position as he had been. He walked over to the stereo to change the c.d.

I looked down at the folds of fat curling down my stomach and quickly grabbed my shirt off the floor to put it on while Manny's back was to me. I couldn't find my hair clip so I let my curls hang loose around my head.

Manny turned and looked over his shoulder at me. "It's my turn now," he said with a twinkle in his eyes.

I nestled back on the chaise and drew my legs up to my chest eagerly clapping my encouragement.

With extreme drama, Manny tapped the play button on the stereo and in moments the heavy tabla beat of an Indian song began to thump through the air. I instantly burst out laughing from the expression on Manny's face. He mimicked the actions of a Bollywood actor in sync with the lyrics. His expression changed from sorrow to fleeting happiness as he thrust his hips rigidly from side to side.

His mocking impression of an Indian movie star dancing in the rain and looking around imaginary trees had me holding my sides with laughter.

He chose to pick up his clothes and begin to dress instead of undress. He put his pants on and as soon as he raised the zipper he began to thrust his hips back and forth while holding his hands up in a "U" shape over his head. At one point I think he was swatting an imaginary tabla drum but it looked like he was playing basketball.

"For the love of Bollywood please stop!"

"Here comes the strip tease part," he said between jagged breaths. He reached behind him and turned the music up. As the bangra beat rose to its crescendo, Manny started to undo his pants slowly. He had them half way down over his boxer shorts when he stopped to smack his butt to the rhythm of the beat. With his pants half way down his legs he began to hop up and down again flailing his hands about as though he couldn't decide if he should pull up his pants or push up the roof.

"You're killing me!" Tears of laughter streamed down my face.

Manny pounded the power button off in one fell swoop and then leapt onto the end of the chaise by my feet. I could see beads of sweat starting to form on his forehead.

"That was awesome!" I said clapping my hands. "You were amazing!"

Manny flashed me a big smile and dramatically patted himself on the back.

After we caught our breath, we both looked back at the coffee table and the game. I think we were both wondering at the same time if we should continue playing or just start having sex.

"You tired?" he asked.

"No," I said quickly. "Maybe a little," I added a second later.

"That wore me out," he said with another big smile. "It was fun though."

"It was really great! Do *you* want to keep playing?"

Manny paused before answering. "Let's have one more go of it if you want. Do you want to?"

"Sure," I said straightening out in the chaise. "It's your turn to spin."

Manny spun the wheel and it landed on the section marked *Challenge* again. He picked it up and read it aloud: "Tell your partner exactly what you would like to do to them. Be explicit."

I instantly felt myself get tense.

What was I supposed to say? Talking dirty was something that had never come naturally to me with any of my partners. It wasn't like I was a complete prude. I could call my lady bits by their common *cat* reference even though it felt weird but stringing out a full sentence with the word was much more awkward.

"Mahjong, how does one talk dirty exactly?" I asked in a study break for calculus once.

"You just say wicked things to your lover while you're having sex."

"I don't know how to do that."

"Okay, then try phone sex. You don't have to be face-to-face for that."

"Phone sex? What's that? Do you just pick up the phone and say 'Hello, it's me Mahjong. I am going to give you a blowjob'?"

She rolled her eyes at me.

"You need some build up woman. It's more like he asks me what I'm wearing and I tell him. Then he asks me what I'm doing to myself. I tell him. I ask him what he's doing and give him *graphic* details about what I am going to do to him and the next you thing you know, badda boom, cum everywhere."

It seemed simple enough.

So one day, with Jonathan, I mustered my courage and decided to surprise him with some dirty talk to get the wheels in motion for when we would see each other later that day.

"Hello?" Jonathan answered his phone.

"Hello Jonathan," I purred into the receiver. "It is me Leena."

"Hi Lee!" he said in his naturally exuberant tone.

"Are you wearing your brown pants?" I'd lowered my voice like I had strep throat.

"What? No. I'm wearing my jeans." Jonathan said.

"I have black socks on," I continued, purring like a cat with pneumonia.

"Okay…"

I could hear the hesitation in Jonathan's voice.

"Hello?"

"Yeah I'm here. I heard you say you have black socks on. Why are you telling me this?"

"I thought we might have phone sex," I said flatly.

"Oh!" Jonathan said with a hint of laughter in his voice. "Okay we can do that. Well you know what I'm gonna do? I'm gonna take those black socks of yours off and lick between your toes."

"Gross!"

That ended my experiment with phone sex.

With Nick I decided to be a bit more bold and obvious. On an outing to a friend's cottage, he and I were sitting on lawn chairs with some of the other students from my class when I decided to repeat what I had overhead Mahjong say to a lover on the phone. I leaned in and whispered in his ear: "I want to suck your dick".

He looked perplexed at me.

I said it again.

He still looked confused.

I said it a bit louder over the chatter of the other drunks but he still couldn't hear me.

"You want to soak the deck?" he finally asked.

"No!" I said raising my voice in frustration. "I WANT TO SUCK YOUR DICK!"

The entire group fell silent.

What felt like a lifetime later one of the guys in my accounting class shouted, "You go Lee! You go girl!"

Everyone laughed.

I wanted to die.

Before we were married Manny and I were always sneaking around to have sex, so being quiet came naturally to us. We lived with my mother for the first six months of our marriage and refined the art of noiseless lovemaking.

There was no way this challenge was going to go well. I wanted to ask Manny to spin again but he placed the card down and began to clear his throat before I could suggest it.

"I'll go first," he said. He held my head in his hands, paused and looked me straight in the eye. "I want to lick you all over."

He said it so deliberately and so precisely that it took a moment for my brain to register what he was saying.

Where did that come from?

Ever since I'd known him, I couldn't remember him ever being that direct or erotic.

Manny must have sensed my hesitation. He leaned in closer to me and nestled his mouth by my ear.

"I'll repeat," he said. "I want to lick you all over." His deep and seductive voice in my ear made me instantly aroused. To hammer it home, he started to nibble on my ear lobe and the sensation coupled with the mental image he had just placed in my mind made me eager with anticipation. Just as I started to lean in to him, Manny pulled back.

"Your turn!" he said.

My turn? My mind raced. I knew I was either going to make a fool of myself or end up starting a discussion about the backyard deck.

"Okay."

I drew in a deep breath.

I cleared my throat to buy more time.

Then I shifted in the chaise to lean in closer to him to buy myself even more time. Nothing was coming to me. Manny helped me by leaning his head in closer and giving me his ear to whisper in and still nothing would come.

What the hell should I say? One simply can't pull words out of nowhere!

Nothing sexy or remotely erotic would come to me. The only words that came to mind were the ones I had meant to say to him all day like "Did you empty the dishwasher?" or "Don't forget to buy wine for Saturday's dinner".

I cleared my throat again until I started to sound like an outboard motor on the fritz.

I took a deep breath and plunged forward.

"I want you!" I didn't mean to be so loud. Manny instantly jumped back. "Sorry Manny! I didn't mean to shout that!" My voice continued to rise with every word.

"Uh, it's okay." He said tugging his ear and wincing.

I asked for another chance. He sat farther back in his chair and nodded for me to go ahead. I cleared my throat two more times.

"I, uh, I want you," I said in a voice above a whisper.

He didn't move.

"I want you all night long."

"Like the Lionel Ritchie song?"

I hit him on his shoulder.

"I can't do this!" I slouched back against the chaise and crossed my arms.

"Why not?"

"It doesn't feel… natural."

Manny pulled back and studied me with his eyes. I willed myself not to cry under his gaze. I tried desperately to regain a feeling of playfulness but it was too late. It was gone.

"Are you tired?"

I knew if I lied and said that I was it would put an end to the game. It was my out. I didn't feel like risking more humiliation. I didn't feel like having sex and I especially didn't feel sexy.

I feigned fatigue and we headed up to bed.

For what seemed like the first time in a long time Manny crawled into bed and instead of dozing off on his back, turned to his side and spooned me, pulling me tightly to his chest. I fell asleep, gentle tears dropping softly on my pillow.

Chapter 4

Manny was part of a special team designed to expand his company's public image and therefore required to take a series of courses offered in New York City on marketing and management. When the first course in the series came up, he asked me to come along with him to ensure that he wouldn't have to share his room with his teammate Borgis, an overweight Russian man that Manny described as "smelly and simple."

I happily joined him expecting it to be a romantic getaway or at the very least a better honeymoon than the one we had moving his stuff into my mother's basement while we house hunted.

"'Dere are muggers and bums in New York," my mother yelled at me when I told her about the trip. "'Dey vill beat you and kill you and cut out your kidney for da drug money."

I didn't believe her, but while waiting for Manny I made the mistake of watching the local news in the hotel which made me too scared to go out on my own. By evening when he would come back to the hotel room after a full day at the seminar, he was too tired to go out on the town with me so we would grab a quick bite at a nearby restaurant and then head back to sleep. *Sleep, that's it.* There was no sex that weekend.

Subsequent conferences would find Manny returning home with loads of papers to study, grumbling that he had too much responsibility for someone at his level and that the company might be taking on more than it could handle. As a result, he always came back in a bad mood, tired and cranky. I had no interest in going with him again. Manny stopped asking me after the third seminar.

Much to my surprise, he asked me if I wanted to tag along for the upcoming weekend.

"I can take our air miles and put them towards another ticket if you want to join me." His excitement was infectious but my desire was still faint. With my big black bag of goodies from the sex party still patiently awaiting me and the mystery of the as of yet unachieved orgasm looming ahead I was loathe to give up a chance to spend some time by myself. Maybe I would have better luck with the toy like Clarissa had said.

"I'd love to Manny," I said with as much genuineness as I could fake, "but I might have to work this weekend."

It wasn't a complete lie. It was the busiest time of the year for the accounting firm.

"Okay, well I gave the number of the hotel to you right? I guess you'll go over to your mother's this weekend."

I was expected to go over to my mother's house whenever possible to do little things for her like change a light bulb, clean the fridge or help her stuff hundreds of homemade samosas. I wasn't in the mood for a weekend of fat comments, pregnancy pushes and general negativity.

I drove Manny to the airport, went home to a quiet and reasonably clean house and calculated all the little things I could putter time away doing. I lacked the desire to initiate doing anything. I called

Mahjong and told her I had finally decided to try a spin class with her. Somehow in the aftermath of Isabelle's party, it seemed a lot less scary.

"Are you fucking serious?" Mahjong screamed into the phone. "I'm so excited! If I had known all it would take was one sex party I would have thrown one for you in my own house!"

"That's not the reason I want to try the spin class. I just thought I might as well give it a chance since you've been bugging me about it for so long. I just want to come once to see if I like it."

"Speaking of cumming, have you used your toy yet?"

"Uh – uh," I said getting caught off guard, "Um, there wasn't any time. I meant to. I mean, no."

"If you do plan to use it, you have to clean it first. Did you buy cleaner?" She spoke in a very clinical tone of voice.

"I bought cleaner." I sounded like an indignant child. "I bought it that night."

"Actually that's good stuff cause it's a spray. So you spray the toy and just hold it at the base and then after a minute just rinse off the toy and leave it on a face cloth or something. Let it air dry and then you put the batteries in it and away you go! Woohoo! Damn I'm so excited for you Lee! This is what a mother must feel like when her daughter takes her first steps."

"You need so much therapy, Mahjong."

"Yippee! You don't know what this means! Lee you're gonna come unglued when you have your first orgasm! I wish I could be there!"

"Okay, you're creeping me out now."

I was starting to get a bit nervous. What if it didn't live up to my expectations? What if it didn't live up to *her* expectations? What if I fried my *wonton* as Mahjong referred to her genitals and electrified myself? Images of my mother coming to pick me up at the hospital with a bandage wrapped between my legs like a *dhoti* flooded my mind.

I hung up, all at once anxious and nervous, and went straight to the black bag in the spare room before I completely lost my nerve. I rifled through its contents until I found the little satin bag that held the vibrator. It reminded me of a stuffed rabbit I had as a child that I named Bunti. It had the same big bulgy eyes, long floppy ears tucked tightly to the side of its head and a bulbous bunny nose that was surprisingly soft to the touch.

"And you shall be called Bunti," I said, patting it on the head.

I took out the cleaner and strained to read the instructions on the bottle. I grabbed Bunti and the cleaner and went into the bathroom. I sprayed the toy as Mahjong and the bottle instructed, rinsed it and then laid the little bunny on a facecloth standing guard over it while it dried. I could see at least four well formed water bubbles on it that I didn't dare touch. Thoughts of the party and the two pencil sketched pictures that Clarissa had shown everyone raced through my mind.

Which one was I?

What was the difference again?

I decided there was only one way to find out.

I had to look.

I locked the bedroom door despite the fact that I was alone in the house and returned to the bathroom to check on Bunti. Two big bubbles still left to dry. I took a deep breath, removed my track pants and my old but comfortable panties.

At first glance I could only see a forest of hair that slightly sprang forward in response to being released from its confines. I stared at the small bushel of hair. It stared back at me. Moments elapsed as neither of us moved.

I pushed at my protruding belly so that I could get a better glance but it flopped back into place forcing me to contort myself more awkwardly. Eager to get a closer look I grabbed a pocket mirror from the side vanity, flipped it open like a police officer's badge, and flashed it at the space between my legs. Just as I looked down, I heard the phone ring.

Manny must have arrived at his hotel.

I ran and grabbed the phone near our bed.

I would really surprise him with my sex talk this time! I lowered my voice and purred into the phone: "Guess what I'm doing? I'm looking at my pussy!"

"You're doing vat?" The shrill voice of my mother slapped my ear. "You got a cat? Ven did you get it? Hoi hoi! Dey are nothing but valking diseases! Dey are rats! Hi hi! I can't believe you got a cat and didn't tell me!"

I dropped the phone and recoiled in horror.

I took a deep breath and picked up the receiver. I could hear my mother screaming from where I was standing at least five feet away.

"Hello mother."

"Vat time are you coming over tomorrow?" she said in the same raised voice. "I am doing many tings tomorrow and your stupid cousin Tarik and his *ghori* wife Catherine are coming for tea. You have to make da samosas. Come at eleben actually."

The spin class was at noon.

"I can't come over tomorrow Ma."

Silence.

The kind of deafening silence inside of which I could hear her thinking what a horrible daughter I was coupled with her personal angst for being cursed with an ingrate like me.

"Ma?" I said gently into the phone followed by a more persistent, "Mother?"

"I don't believe dis! You come at eleben tomorrow Leena! I vill not speak to you again if you do not come."

That threat had some appeal.

"I can't Ma. I have to…" I dropped my sentence. What on earth would be a good enough excuse to get me out of going to her house? She would never understand why it was important to me to go to a spin class. And she certainly wouldn't understand my desire to stay home to masturbate either so I racked my brain to think of something acceptable and believable.

"I can't because I'm going to go to New York with Manny tomorrow for his conference," I lied.

There was another pause. I knew because I hadn't spoken to her for a few days, using tax time as an excuse not to return her calls, that she wouldn't know Manny had already left and that I wasn't going with him.

"Manoo is going to New York? Vy do *you* have to go?" she asked slowly.

"Because I'm ovulating and it's important we're together if we want to have a baby." The lies just kept racking up.

The first three years we were married we used birth control so Manny and I could focus on our careers. When we finally stopped and decided it was time to start a family, we were content to let things happen naturally and even had one false alarm eight months ago.

I waited, holding my breath for her response.

"You had better get on it Leena! Now dis is too long you are vaiting for making baby. I had you right away. First month sexing your father and just like dat, we are having pregnancy. You stupid to vait dis long!"

"I know Ma. We just weren't ready till now."

"Don't be idiot! After I have you doctor say I can't have no more babies. Good I didn't vait na? Vat if it happens to you too? I told you to be sexing Manny from beginning but you don't listen."

"Ma please!"

"Okay. Put a pillow under your bum and make sure you don't eat any winegar," she said simply and without hesitation.

"Okay sure, yeah. Just stop talking about it please."

"Oh and if you are going out don't vear that purple suit. You look like a fat eggplant."

"Yes Ma."

"And don't go too far from da hotel. Dey will cut out your kidney and sell it for drug money hey-na? Don't talk to anyone."

"Yes Ma. I have to go now."

I had to listen to two stories involving muggings and one of stolen identity that happened to *friends* of my mother's that travelled to New York before she would let me off the phone. When she hung up, I stood motionless in my bedroom with only a t-shirt on and the telephone stuck to my ear, the mental image of my mother with a pillow under her bum threatening to imprint itself on my mind for all of eternity.

About fifteen minutes later Manny phoned from the hotel room. Anticipating it was my mother again I answered in a dull, almost sleepy tone of voice. I noted the hotel room number he was staying at on a pad of paper, made some idle chat with him about the plane food and his accommodations finally saying good night to him and then crawling into bed.

No toy.

No adventure.

It was late and I was suddenly very tired.

My desire to play with my toy would have to wait until the sound of my mother's voice had been drained from my ears the next morning.

I woke up excited about my weekend alone. I turned on the television and flipped through the channels. Nothing caught my interest. I turned the television off.

I sat down to my half-finished puzzle, found one piece that fit and then sat and stared at the scattered image for another half an hour.

I decided to make pancakes, maple syrup and French toast, but when I got to the kitchen I opted for yogurt with fresh mango slices, dry toast and half a grapefruit. The image of my belly rolls during the game stopped me from feeding my cravings.

I read the morning paper while I finished my breakfast and then fussed over cleaning the kitchen.

9:30 a.m.

I wandered around the living room looking for something to dust. Finding nothing to clean, I wandered into the garage to tackle sorting out some old boxes that had never been opened since the day we moved in, but felt too lazy to move the rusty old exercise equipment in front of them.

9:45 a.m.

I went down to the basement and rifled through our collection of movies. Nothing caught my interest.

10:00 a.m.

I went upstairs to the bedroom. I saw Bunti on the facecloth. I slowly crept up on the toy as though it might leap to life and hop on top of me.

I picked it up only to be suddenly overcome with fear. I looked for another distraction when I heard my phone register a text message.

It was from Mahjong: "Class is at twelve. TOY-ing with the idea of picking you up at eleven."

I had one hour.

I was suddenly mad at myself for wasting the morning puttering around. I grabbed Bunti and lay down on my bed. As soon as I did, I realized I needed batteries.

No batteries in the bathroom.

No batteries in the spare room.

No batteries in the kitchen.

I finally remembered there were fresh batteries in the television remote control in our master bedroom. I put the batteries in the pack, watching with amazement as the little silver bullet came to life in my hand.

I squealed as the vibration coursed through my entire hand. I turned it off and placed the silver bullet in the tiny hole at the back of the rabbit the way Clarissa did at the party. I turned the toy on watching the bunny's bulbous nose wiggle up and down. It was almost like having a pet animal in my palm. I poked its head and felt the vibrations course through my fingertips.

"Hello Bunti. My name is Leena." It felt like some type of formal introduction was required. His pink head bobbed up and down as if to say, "Happy to meet you." I looked over at the bedroom clock on Manny's side of the bed. I had twenty minutes before I would have to get into my gym clothes.

I lay down on the bed and removed my pajama bottoms and underwear. I placed the loop under the bunny over my fingers so that Bunti was resting like a small bouncy pet on a perch. I inhaled one massive deep breath, closed my eyes and slowly let my hand fall naturally between my legs.

Bunti's vibrating nose landed directly on my right labia. The shock of the sensation made my eyes snap open. I took another deep breath and slowly put the toy back down towards my vulva again. I tried craning my upper body downwards so that I could watch what I was doing but the image of a pink bunny stuck on the end of my fingers looking like it was about to plunge into a hairy black forest made me laugh hysterically. The pressure of the clock ticking started to agitate me.

What if having an orgasm was overrated? What if the entire effort was a waste of time? What if my body exploded?

I sank deeper into the duvet on our bed. Does everyone feel this foolish playing with a vibrator?

I took a deeper breath and placed Bunti back into the wilderness that was my pubic hair deciding that he was a creature of nature after all and would find his own way. A few minutes of the vibration on my labia and a little on the inside lips went from ticklish to something far more pleasant and downright exhilarating.

I instinctively pulled my hand up higher and Bunti bobbed his way up and over my inside labia directly towards the most sensitive part of all: my clitoris. As yet untouched by vibration, my sleeping clitoris instantly reacted to Bunti slamming his head against its sensitive tip. I shivered and my hand flew away in reaction to the sensation.

From deep within and with a growing sense of curiosity, I summoned more courage and placed the toy back on the sensitive spot, trying desperately to settle into the unfamiliar feeling.

It felt so tingly and wild that I had a hard time concentrating on the pleasure itself and instead found myself trying to figure out the mechanics of how it worked.

I looked over at the alarm clock. I had about ten minutes left before Mahjong would be there and it would take me that much time to get into my gym clothes and get my bag ready.

My orgasm would have to wait.

Besides, if it was as earth-shattering as everyone purported it to be, I would probably end up paralyzed and unable to go to the gym to work out.

I turned the toy off ran to the bathroom, cleaned it and left it to dry on the nightstand.

Before I had a chance to get my gym clothes together, I heard a knock at my front door. It started as a gentle tap and progressively sharpened into a loud bang. I scrambled to get my clothes on, grabbing a plastic grocery sac as my gym bag and headed downstairs.

"Well?" Mahjong stared at me like I was about to impart big news.

"Sorry I'm late." I grabbed my house keys and my runners from the front closet.

"What? That's all you've got to say?" Mahjong had tied up her dyed hair in a pony tail and was wearing a bright red top with the words "*Bite me*" written on them. I envied how fit and athletic she looked.

"No orgasm," I said as I closed the door behind me. "I just started to use it before you got here."

"Oh I'm sorry," she said with what seemed like genuine remorse. "I thought you had lots of time."

"I did but I ate breakfast and then cleaned up the house a bit and before you know it, there goes your morning, right?" I tried to sound cavalier about it. Mahjong must have sensed I wanted to drop the subject because she instantly switched the topic to the spin class.

Twenty minutes later we arrived at the gym. I was instantly overwhelmed by the sight of zealous men and women running on treadmills, flying on elliptical machines and climbing on stair machines, the unmistakable smell of sweat in the air. I drew my attention away from the class in progress ahead of us to the gaggle of tiny teenagers idly chatting near the front desk, in tight work out clothes, not a drop of sweat to be found on them.

Mahjong signed my name in the gym's guest book as *Leena Labia*.

The petite perky girl with the word *Staff* written on her shirt looked up at me and giggled. "Foreign names are the coolest."

"I like your name too. It's Staff, right?"

She frowned.

"No, it's Melanie!"

Mahjong led me towards the change rooms. Around the corner from the entrance I saw a large number of very muscular fit men lifting heavy bars in the free weights area. Mahjong pulled my slowly dragging feet into the change room, locked up our bags and then led me back into the main exercise area.

I felt like I had just been dropped on the set of a movie. There were beautiful women with gorgeous bodies and snug tops looking trim and sexy, walking with confidence from one point of the gym to another. I spied only a handful of other women close to my size. The men ranged from above average muscles in tight t-shirts to others who barely exploded in size, looking more like cartoon characters than human beings.

Mahjong led me upstairs where the spin bikes were lined up all facing a long row of mirrors on a back wall and fanning around one central bike that was obviously set aside for the instructor. Suddenly the surreal atmosphere of the gym became frighteningly real with the sight of exercise bikes lined up like soldiers about to go into battle.

I became nervous, shifting back and forth in one spot. I tugged on my oversized t-shirt and baggy track pants feeling like a fraud, horribly out of place. I had hoped I would disappear into the crowd but instead I felt as awkward as a massive black bear would at a children's picnic.

Mahjong stroked my shoulder and smiled at me.

"I'm going to give you my seat cover," she said as she placed a black gel seat on the bike she was setting up for me. "It will help."

"Help what?" I asked with alarm. She either pretended not to hear me or was too caught up in adjusting the seat height and handle bars to answer.

While Mahjong prepared my bike, I looked over the railing of the top ledge and spied down on the group of medium to large men grunting and pulling on the machines in the weights section below. A few women were using the equipment as well. I envied their tight, lean bodies but was more jealous of the look of determination in their eyes than their slender waists.

Amid the small group of men using the free weights, I was spellbound by one in particular. He was tall with long blonde hair tied neatly into a pony tail, precisely sculpted muscles and a long thick neck leading up to a solid square jaw. There was something about his slow precise movements that held my gaze. He looked like he had stepped off the cover of a romance novel, his sword, shield and armor lying somewhere off in the distance.

I imagined how much more stunning his chiseled jaw would look when his hair was let down by the side of his temples. I fixated on the protrusion of the Adam's apple in his neck watching it bob up and down as he eagerly slurped water from a bottle, tiny rivers escaping down the sides moistening his mouth and glistening down to his chest. I felt my own mouth open to drink in the same long stream of liquid when the breath in my throat was suddenly caught mid gulp by a familiar image lumbering past my long-haired vision.

It was Nick.

I only saw the side of his face, the unmistakably sharp angle of his nose and the breadth of his shoulder blades as he casually walked through the weights section towards the front entrance. I couldn't believe how my body instantly tensed at the sight of him. The air around me felt cold and warm sweat began to pool at the base of my spine. I watched as he walked out the front door and out of my range of sight.

Just as quickly as I saw him, he was gone.

"Get on the bike," Mahjong said. "I want to make sure that it's the right height."

I walked like a zombie towards her voice hearing someone in the distance call out my name from the fog around me.

"Leena! Leena!" I heard the bubbles in her voice before her big toothy grin was in front of me.

"Corky," I said under my breath. Could my day get worse?

"*You* work out here?" she said with obvious shock surveying my body in its baggy black covering.

Corky was half of a set of twins born to my mother's first cousin. She was the bubblier half of the pair with a more than generous bust line while her acerbic and far less happy twin had a massive bottom half and a bitter disposition. Corky's giant breasts were squashed into a halter-style white tank top which covered only part of her midsection, showing off the glimmer of a white diamond in her navel just above the band of her lycra black and white leggings. Why did her brown skin look like a tan she just got at the beach and mine made me look like undercooked gingerbread? She made being Indian look exotic, almost ethereal. Meanwhile I could still smell the curry from the previous weekend's dinner at my mother's place emanating from my pants.

"I'm here with Mahjong." I pulled my T-shirt even farther away from my body.

"You're taking the spin class!" she said spying the pink tag in my hand.

"Corky?" Mahjong said as she pulled me toward the bike she had been setting up. "What are you doing here?"

"Oh hi, Mae Mong." Corky ran her hands through the black silk sheet of her hair. "You know, I see you here sometimes, but I don't know if you see me."

"Who could miss you?" Mahjong said sarcastically, her eyes on Corky's chest.

Corky giggled. "I guess that's true! Oh how great you two are taking the class with me! I just love spin don't you? I am so good at it the teacher wants me to become an instructor!" Corky bounced past me and busied herself with the seat adjustment on the bike in front of mine.

"Just ignore her," I heard Mahjong whisper in my ear. "You're gonna love this class. Now get on."

I wanted to tell Mahjong that I had just seen Nick but the words refused to form in my mouth. Did I hallucinate seeing him? What was he doing in my home town?

I put my foot into the first bike peddle. Mahjong fastened the straps down around one runner, then ran over to the other side of the bike and tightened the other buckle so that both my feet were securely in place.

"Make sure you get her feet in those stirrups really tight!" Corky wiggled her tiny bottom at me.

"Mind your own business Porky," Mahjong said over her shoulder. I felt the seat between my legs and instantly shifted my weight. It was uncomfortable and stiff even with the gel seat cover on it. "How's that feel? Is that height okay for you? Move your legs."

I did and with a few more adjustments, Mahjong was satisfied with my positioning leaving me with the instruction to keep my legs moving at all times.

She hopped on her bike, clicked her special shoes into their clips and started to spin her legs rapidly. The instructor came over and smiled at me. When she asked me if it was my first class, Mahjong whispered loudly "It is! She's a virgin."

That was the second time in less than a month I had been referred to that way.

The instructor watched me as I started to move my legs. I felt like everyone was watching me. I swallowed hard trying to absorb what the instructor was saying, her words getting caught between the heavy thuds of my heartbeat in my head. I made particular note of the red bar in front of me that she assured me was my safety stop. I only had to press upon the lever and the machine would halt.

I hadn't been sitting on the bike for five minutes and I could already feel my ass cheeks burning with discomfort.

"This seat is really hard," I whispered to Mahjong.

"It's okay. You'll get used to it."

The class started with a loud bang of music. Everyone else took position on their bikes like a small, well trained army. The combination of loud music overhead with the high energy of the spinners around me served as a good distraction from the fact that I was staring straight at Corky's bouncy ass and that there was something acutely painful between my legs. When the perky instructor started to shout out orders I had the sudden strong urge to bolt for the door but my feet were too tightly strapped into the pedals. With my luck I would fall on my face taking two other spinners with me or worse, run for the door and run into Nick.

The teacher explained that there would be seven working tracks of music and that the goal was to peddle in sync with the rhythm of each song. The first song I recognized from a top 40's radio station and merrily began to spin my legs with as much vigor and excitement as everyone else in the class.

My energy was completely depleted by the second track. I began to pant so heavily that I wondered if there was an emergency kit on the floor in case I passed out and needed resuscitation. Corky shook her bottom back and forth as the song neatly closed on the first twelve minutes of the class. I clutched my chest like my overweight Uncle Banoo before he was taken to emergency.

As the third song started I felt death approach me and a strong desire to pray. A myriad of different memories flooded to my mind as the muscles in my thighs felt like they were being ripped from my bones.

My father studied religious history in university and was most fascinated by Buddhism, Islam and Hinduism. He kept statues of Hindu gods in our home, one of Buddha along with several beautiful scrolls in Arabic mounted on the walls. Despite growing up in a Muslim household, my mother suffered from radical religious confusion. I would often see her whisper mantras in the ear of Ganesh, leave flowers at Buddha's feet and observe Muslim prayer at the same time. She taught me about all three religions and when she began to suspect that Western schooling alone would corrupt me, she sent me to religious school.

The first school she put me in was to learn about Islam.

"Ma, my Muslim friend said that she prays five times a day."

"Good for her," my mother said absently as she fixed a plate of homemade samosas for my snack.

"She also fasts for a whole month. Can you believe that?"

"Ven I vas young girl in India we vould all do da fast. It vould trim us down nicely in time for wedding season."

"I think it's supposed to be so you can observe faithfulness. It's not a diet."

"I know dat!" she said as she prepared the chutney with fresh coriander and lemon juice. "I telling you how I grew up, na?"

"I like the way they think."

"You know, your stoopid great Uncle Hatim did his fast in da hot sun and he fell in love with a willage girl. Oh ho! Idiot love marriage never last!"

"Weren't they married 45 years?"

"Den he got cancer, na? See?"

"I thought he got cancer because he smoked two packs of cigarettes a day."

"Eat your samosa!"

The next day she pulled me out of Islamic study class and signed me up to study with the Buddhist students. They seemed the least bothered by regular peer pressures from high school. They were generally peaceful beings, blissfully smiling all the time. After talking to my new friend Druki about Buddhism, I became very attracted to the concept of nirvana and karma.

"Ma, my friend Druki is a Buddhist. She says we should strive for good energy when we are with other people. She calls it karma."

"Indians invented Karma!" my mother snapped.

"But she says our struggle for peace is here on earth. They don't have a heaven and hell."

"You know vhat? Your stoopid Priya Aunty went to become a boodha and she go to ashram. Now no one will marry her!"

"I thought she was in the ashram teaching yoga."

"Yoga schmoga! She is single girl. na? Now no one will marry her!"

"But I thought she was helping the lepers in the colony and teaching English to the village kids."

"Oh ho! Who vould vant a woman who has touched a leper, na? She will never marry! Her mother have heart attack and die!"

"Wasn't she like ninety-five years old?"

"But doctor say she die of broken heart na? Eat your samosa!"

The next day she moved me to the room with the Hindus.

"Ma my Hindu friend Sunita is getting married and she is only eighteen years old!"

"I like dis girl. She's smart, na?"

"Her parents arranged it and she's going along with it."

"Yah, Hindoos are very clever indeed, na? I too had a Hindoo friend vhen I was your age. Wery vise. Wery vise. You listen to her, na?"

"She doesn't eat meat. I think I might become a vegetarian like her."

"*Pagal!* You have to eat meat!"

"I'm not going to eat any more meat Ma. Please!"

"Okay you eat chicken. Chicken is not meat!"

"Chicken is meat Ma!"

"Eat your samosa!"

I never got to go back to Hindu class again.

With the air escaping my lungs and my thighs feeling like they were bleeding from the inside, I wished I had stayed focused on at least one faith so I could amend for my sins before dying.

By the fourth track I wanted to kill Mahjong. I could make it look like an accident. A kinky sex act gone awry. But that would involve getting off the bike and plotting out revenge. The way my legs were burning I knew there was no way I would ever be able to walk again. With my luck they would fly off my body as soon as I stopped peddling.

I clung to the handlebars of the bike for dear life. I lived in fear of the fifth and hardest track that the instructor kept building up as *the most challenging* of all of them. I sensed it would be the moment my heart would finally stop beating and the world as I knew it would end. This would have been a good time for nuclear war to break out, or for locusts to spring forth from behind the mirrors.

Just when I had lost all hope I would ever see my next birthday, one solitary image floated up at me above the vigorous shaking of Corky's ass and the pounding in my chest. That image was of Nick.

Nick was always so critical of how I looked. The first few months of our relationship I found myself idly nibbling on snack food, mostly chips and chocolate and the weight quickly piled on without me noticing. Nick noticed. He saw every flaw on my body, which spawned comments that were at first easy enough to laugh away but slowly became difficult to ignore.

Several of the comments caught Mahjong's ear and despite her constant reassurances, eventually I began to see myself as Nick did: imperfect, undesirable and lacking sex appeal.

What originally started as a few comments about my body grew to very obvious suggestions about what to wear and what I should be eating. I turned away from food for comfort and sought out his affections more deeply. As the semesters in school passed, the weight slipped off, his compliments increased but my self-esteem had trouble recovering. If he had seen me in the gym, he would see a fat unattractive woman who had let herself go. The dumpier version of the woman he professed to love but refused to commit to.

Memories of Nick fueled me with enough anger that I was able to reach down when instructed to increase the tension on my bike. I pushed past the searing pain in my legs driving the old feelings from my mind until I heard a collective sigh of relief emanate from the other spinners as they settled back onto their seats when the final drum beat played.

I made a hoarse gulping sound as I choked and gasped for air.

As the sixth track commenced I lost all sensation in the lower half of my body. I could see my legs moving but they looked like they were someone else's. The pudgy masses I once called my thighs were so numb from pain they felt like they were made of rubber.

"One more track to go!" the instructor said as she rose on her bike. "And this one's a mountain!"

I wanted her to die.

Slowly and very painfully.

As much as I would have liked to have had a heart attack on the bike to teach Mahjong a lesson for trying to kill me, I did survive the last track in one piece, albeit with only some of my dignity still in tact.

I was so caught up in my full body pain that I didn't enjoy a sense of accomplishment when the class finished. I couldn't wait to get off the bike. I was petrified my legs would collapse under me as soon as I dismounted. I slowly peeled myself off one shoe at a time.

"Woohoo! What a rush!" Mahjong smiled at me through her sweat. "Did you like it?"

"It feels like I just douched with a porcupine!"

"What? Oh the seat. Lee, you'll get used to it!"

"Used to it? *Never again!* I can't feel my ass, and what I can feel hurts like a bitch! I think I broke my vagina!"

Mahjong burst out laughing. "You'll get used to it. I promise. Eventually you don't even notice it."

"You're a liar and you're evil." I said holding my chest to make sure that my heart didn't actually flop out onto the floor. "And oh yeah, by the way, I hate you."

"How did you like the class?" Corky asked me, gently toweling off the dew of sweat glistening on her tanned arms and legs.

"I loved it!" I said refusing to let her see the tears of pain that stung my eyes as I wiggled my toes in my runners to make sure they were still attached to my feet.

"Great! Then I guess we'll see you at another class right?"

"Of course." I smiled feeling pain shoot through my face.

"I guess we'll see you two around. Bye Ching Chong!" she said as she waved her manicured fingernails at me and Mahjong.

"Bye Dorky!" Mahjong said. "I guess I'll wait and see if you really will come back to class with me. For now, let's get you home."

Mahjong gently led me down the stairs to the change room. My legs were shaking, almost vibrating from the inside out. It took all my effort not to collapse into the fetal position on the floor of the women's change room.

Mahjong offered to take me out for a greasy dinner to make up for the calories we had burned but I was afraid I was going to have a heart attack in public and decided I wanted nothing more than to fall into bed and die alone.

"You gonna play with your toy now?" she asked excitedly.

"Are you on drugs? NO! My vagina is still on fire! That is if I *still have* a vagina! I can't feel my lower body at all!"

"Okay sorry!" she said with mock horror. "I was just making conversation."

"Hey speaking of conversation, I think I saw Nick at the gym."

"*Nick?*" Mahjong choked on the long swig of water she had just taken from her bottle. "At the gym? I've never seen him here before Leena. Are you sure?"

"I'm not sure of anything anymore." I felt too tired to continue the conversation and too annoyed that I couldn't even muster up enough energy to breathe without reminding myself of the pain. "I just want to go inside, take a shower, and die."

"Okay, okay," Mahjong said stroking my arm gently. "Go soak in the tub actually. Use that blue bath you bought from the party. It's good for soaking your aching body. You'll feel better in two to three days."

I snapped my head back at her to study her expression but the sudden movement only heightened my overall body ache. I left the subject unaddressed.

I limped into the house and dropped in a heap on the living room sofa. I managed after an hour to draw myself the blue bath with the Dead Sea salt that Mahjong had recommended. Once I settled into the silky bubbles and drew in a deep breath of the refreshing ocean smell, I began to feel my muscles unclench.

Mahjong sent me two text messages while I was in the tub. "*Sorry spin snapped your snootch*" followed by: "*Can't wait for our next class together!*"

How could you love someone and still hate them at the same time?

I lay still in the dark blue liquid of the tub until the sweet enticement of sleep overtook me forcing my prune-like body from its watery bed. I contemplated sleeping on the floor of the bathroom but managed to drag what looked like my legs up and onto the duvet collapsing in a heap of bones and fat. When I finally woke from my nap it was close to 5:00 p.m. My legs were less shaky and only mildly sore, with most of the feeling beginning to return to my limbs. Red hot searing pain had been replaced by an annoying bruise-like ache.

Fixing a snack took a tremendous amount of effort. I expended whatever resources I had left climbing the stairs back up to the bedroom.

I sank down into the duvet on the bed. I didn't have the energy to remove the batteries from Bunti and put them back in the remote so with the television out of commission and the novel I was reading on a nightstand unthinkably far out of my aching body's reach, I lay back and let my thoughts wander.

Was that really Nick that I saw? What had happened to him since I last saw him? Did he have a girlfriend? *Was he married too?* Did he have children? If he had a girlfriend, what was she like? She was probably one of the svelte young tarts I had seen parading around the gym.

My mind replayed the same moment. When I was close to graduation, my Aunt remarked that I had lost weight and that it definitely should help in the matter of my marriage as it increased my appeal as long as I could keep it off long enough to snag a suitor. I knew I couldn't hide in university any longer. My mother was going to start looking for a husband for me as soon as the ink was dry on my degree.

"Nick, I was thinking we should tell my mother about us. You know, tell her we're dating," I said a week before the final exam period.

"Why?" He didn't look up from his textbook.

"Because she will start to look for a husband for me once I've graduated."

"Don't be ridiculous."

"I'm not. I mean it. She will start. She may have already started!"

"You won't get married, Leena. You don't have to do what she says."

"She's my mother. How can I openly disobey her?"

"You're seeing me, aren't you? Isn't that disobeying her?" He put his book down. He looked annoyed.

"Nick that's not how my culture works. I wish you would understand."

"I do. It's your life. You can do whatever you want."

"It's not that simple." I fought the tears that wanted to spring forward.

"Listen, things are good. Don't mess it up now."

I studied him for a moment. I sensed the discussion could turn into a huge fight so I tried to make light of the situation before it got out of control.

"You know," I said shaking my mess of curls, "a sexy, sweet Indian girl with a degree isn't going to stay on the market very long."

"Well now," he said taking me into his arms. "You are sweet and Indian with a degree. But sexy, well I don't know about that."

I looked him square in the eyes.

He wasn't joking.

The man I was sleeping with didn't think I was sexy.

My mind started to reel.

I knew innately that there was something wrong.

"I can't do this anymore, Nick." I got up and started to collect my jacket and shoes.

"What?"

"I can't be with someone who doesn't think I'm sexy."

"Well come on, Lee, you have to be fair. I mean you have a great attitude, you're really kind and I love being with you but baby, sexy just isn't the way I'd describe you. Don't make a bigger deal of this than it has to be."

At the time I was too overcome with the searing pain in my chest to think of a suitable retort. I just needed to be away from him. I needed to be alone with my own thoughts, to straighten things out for myself. My mind was unsettled; my heart felt like it was ripping from the inside out.

I told him we were through and walked out. Admittedly I hoped in the time we were apart Nick would realize how much he loved me and come around to seeing things my way. Instead, he stayed away and I sunk into a deep depression, a dark hole of despair, self loathing and fear.

How did one trip to the gym and a possible sighting of Nick send me right back to where I was ten years ago?

You're not sexy, Leena.

Sexy.

Such a simple word. Such a simple statement and yet loaded with so many different definitions.

What did Nick mean when he said I wasn't *sexy*?

Just what is it to be sexy anyway? I didn't have the D-cup bra size of the girls Nick would point out to me in the malls or the flat stomachs of the women he would openly stare at. Were a big chest and a flat stomach the definition of sexy?

Wasn't there more to it than that?

My brain started to hurt as much as my limbs. Images from my past floated fast and furious around my mind refusing to let me rest. I turned my head towards Bunti.

"Not tonight my little friend," I said to him wistfully.

With the way my luck had been running Bunti would either get lost forever in the forest also known as my pubic hair, or worse, work so fervently to give me an orgasm that he would set off an electrical spark and start a fire between my legs.

Chapter 5

I slept fitfully throughout the night. I dreamt that Nick and I ran into each other at the gym. He looked lean and more tanned than I remembered. I was shorter and fatter than I'd ever been. He kept repeating the same phrase, "Leena, you're not sexy" until his head morphed into a contorted version of a gargoyle.

He chased me through a forest of chocolate-covered pretzel sticks and caramel-covered marshmallows bearing teeth like fangs. Though I wanted to eat them I was too afraid they would come to life and attack me so I kept on running, my legs tight with pain I felt through my sheets. At the end of the forest, I emerged screaming as a building-sized dildo with my mother's face on it approached me. It shook its testicles at me like they were hands and yelled, "Good Indian girls are not fat like you!"

My eyes snapped open. I moaned loudly as I rose from the bed towards the washroom. My legs were so sore that for a moment I thought I had actually run through a forest of evil fattening treats until I remembered the spin class.

I had the whole day ahead of me. No one to answer to, nothing to do that couldn't wait another day and no motivation to do anything more than crawl back into bed. Refusing to let myself get trapped into old habits, I showered right after breakfast, the warm water soothed my aching muscles enough that I wasn't wincing in pain with every step.

As I toweled off in the bathroom I glanced at my reflection in the mirror above the vanity. Something Clarissa had said during her presentation suddenly sprang to my mind again. "Men are born with their genitals on the outside of their bodies. Lucky them! Women, on the other hand, need to go and get a mirror and physically look at themselves and we don't often do that. And if no one has told you before, then I'm telling you, you're beautiful. You're unique."

Unique.

I knew from a very early age in my life that I was different from everyone else but not in the positive, self-affirming way that Clarissa had alluded to in her presentation.

I looked down at the bushel of hair between my legs. Hair anxiety had plagued me from the growth of the very first follicle that ever sprouted on my body at the age of ten.

My mother tried every home cure she had heard of to remove the hair permanently. Everything from turmeric-based powders that left my skin yellow and stubbly to religious prayers chanted in my ear when I was sleeping.

I had a visible moustache until I hit grade school, the envy of most boys my age. Initially, my mother refused to let me wax it off or remove it. She said it was bad luck and that forty more hairs would grow in their place. The day I came home with a black eye from being punched by another girl who called me *monkey boy* my mother acquiesced and showed me how to remove the hair by using a piece of sewing thread pulled between my two thumbs.

I could only keep up with the hair above my lip for so long. By the time I hit puberty there was virtually no inch of my body that was not covered in hair with the exception of my eyeballs and teeth.

In grade nine, our Phys Ed class went off school grounds so we could take part in swim lessons. My mother had agreed to let me shave my legs as long as I only did it before the class. In the change room at the pool, I saw the young girls in my class wearing two piece bathing suits, their light skin luminescent and completely hair free. I had removed all the hair from my shins, calves and thighs leaving the bushy tuft at the top in one piece. My mother was explicit in her instruction: "Shave only da legs. Don't be looking anywhere else! You vill go blind! No one wants a blind bride!"

I hadn't noticed the hair protruding out of my one-piece dark green swimsuit on both sides of my legs until one of the pretty blondes in my class pointed it out to the other girls and started laughing at me. I looked down at what she and her friends were aghast to see, but saw nothing wrong in the winged formation of hair flapping on either side of my suit. Despite my efforts to shove the two balls of fur into the elastic sides to hide them, they simply refused to be tucked away. They emerged like tiny afros on circus clowns peeking their heads out on either side of a canvas tent.

"Eww Leena," Joanie the head cheerleader came over and loudly said to me, "what's going on with your gitch?"

"What?" I asked innocently. "I lost a stitch? Where?"

"It looks like those cleaning pads my mom uses to scrub the pots." The girls laughed and Joanie feigned an empathetic shrug of her shoulders as if there was nothing she could do to stop all the other girls from staring at me.

"No floatation devices for Leena! She has her own!"

I shrank to the back of the change room and cried into the space between two lockers. The gym teacher who was running the class found me sobbing and asked me what was wrong. I wasn't brave enough to utter it out loud so she forced me to join the other girls in the pool where to my horror there was a line up of boys whispering around Joanie and her gaggle of girls who broke into hysterical laughter as soon as I entered the pool area.

The gym teacher caught on to their mockery of me. Maybe it was the blatant finger-pointing or the monkey-mimicking that caused her to pull me out of the class. Either way I was grateful and relieved. From that day on I learned to forge my mother's signature on notes excusing me from swim class.

Jonathan never seemed bothered by the curly black mass on my pubis so I never gave it much thought the entire time we were going out.

With Nick, there was little to no foreplay. He barely spent much time eyeball-to-furball on me. As a result, it never occurred to me that the trees in the forest might need trimming.

I did on a few occasions catch Manny choking on an errant hair that had escaped the mass of its peers and would contemplate it was time for a trim, but by then complacency had set in so deeply that I couldn't find the motivation to do anything about it.

Why did I *need* to look there anyway?

I vaguely recalled Clarissa saying something about knowing what the boat looked like so you could direct the captain to the helm during her presentation. Mahjong doodled a cartoon of sperm at a ship's wheel on her paper and giggled when she showed it to me.

The one quick glance I had been brave enough to take ended too fast for me to really create a strong visual image in my mind.

I locked the bedroom and bathroom door despite the fact that I was alone at home and dropped my towel on the floor taking in my nakedness and the mad disarray of my damp curly hair around my face. I needed a closer look. Somehow the idea of jumping on the vanity and lifting my leg up to see myself felt beyond my flexibility. Perhaps if my mother had let me take ballet when I was a young girl I would be able to do it but according to her, ballet made your toes break and crack and no one wanted a bride without feet.

I found the small pink heart-shaped plastic mirror my *Dadi* gave me when I was in grade school. It was after one particularly memorable Valentine's Day. Our teacher asked us to make our own cards and secretly place them in pouches at the front of the person's desk that we admired most. I worked on my valentines for a whole week, crafting each one by hand and applying the Indian sparkles I removed from my intricate bedspread to them. I was sure they would be the most unique and treasured cards of all and since I didn't want to exclude anyone, I made enough for the whole class.

On Valentine's Day my schoolmates eagerly tore open their pouches and read their cards. I opened mine. It was empty. Later that afternoon I found several of the cards I had made dumped in the trash bin at the front of the class. I cried all the way home. My *Dadi* went out the next day and bought me the plastic heart mirror. "Look in dis Leenoo vhen you vant to see the only Walentine that counts," she said.

She probably wouldn't approve of my use of it to look at my pubic area, but it was all I could find.

I flicked my gaze over to the locked door. My heart started pounding. I spread my legs like I was about to straddle a pony and placed the mirror in between them. My eyes took a moment or two to focus. I almost expected a dramatic "A-ha" moment but at first glance all I could see was hair.

Lots of hair.

Upon closer inspection, I saw two thin brown flaps struggling to press through the massive bush of black curls. I held the mirror in place and pulled the hair to the side so I could get a better look.

It seemed to happen in slow motion.

I reasoned that deep in the forest of blackness, the two outer lips must be my outer labia. After poking them with my finger gingerly at first and then more bravely after a few moments, I moved the two large lips aside to inspect what was struggling to get out from between them. Two brown, wavy at the edges inner flaps of skin released themselves from the thicker hair covered lips that had been hugging them. I tugged at them but couldn't feel much. I spread them back and like the petals of a flower opening, I saw the wonder of the inner skin of my vulva. There before my eyes was the softest looking skin, vibrantly pink in color, a shade so fresh and bright it inspired me.

What a great color for the spare bedroom!

I started to laugh imagining the look on Mr. Chopra's face at our local paint store.

"Mr. Chopra, I want to paint my office the color pink."

"Vat?" he would say bobbing his head, "Okay you pick, I mix."

"None of these colors quite match Mr. Chopra. Have you got something more vibrant and fresh like this?" And then I whip my pants off and flash him my vagina.

Clearly there was too much blood rushing to my head.

Holding the mirror with one hand and trying to explore with the other started to become an issue. I had to strain to keep the outer lips separated so I could continue to study what was inside. I managed to get one of my fingers on the same hand that was holding the flaps back to gently stroke the inner skin, and just as I imagined, it was as soft as it looked with the added bonus of being sensitive to the touch. The sudden tingle of pleasure made me instinctively gaze back up to the locked door.

My heart started to pound again.

I turned my attention back to the little mirror.

I turned my focus up to the top where I saw the bump of a tiny little ball tucked inside the tent of a longer channel of skin. It looked like a little head without a body shielded under a blanket to keep it warm. Images of Clarissa standing in front of the crowd with her bauble ring, her hand mocking a hood, came floating back to my mind.

It all started to make more sense.

It became increasingly more difficult to keep holding all my skin back to look at everything I wanted to see. I pulled the mirror up closer towards me and switched my focus to the top portion. I pulled the hair away from the hood and was amazed to see how well the tiny little button stayed snuggled under its protective blanket. With my thumb I managed to pull the hood back a bit and watched with amazement as the small bauble popped its head out like a turtle from its shell. I immediately retracted the hood and let the bump slip back to its hiding spot.

I poked at it gently with my fingertip and instantly felt a rush of sensation float up from my legs. I caressed it a little more vigorously and noticed with amazement that every stroke seemed to reverberate around its centre from the tip of my toes to the large flesh of my thighs. Unable to hold my skin and the mirror in place any longer I uncurled my naked body back to its upright position and tossed the heart-shaped mirror into one of the drawers in the vanity.

I stood staring at my naked form for a few minutes wondering what other parts of my body were as sensitive as the pearly pink planes I had discovered under folds of skin and hair. I swept my fingers over my breasts, the passage of time showing itself in a discernable droop to what was once a perkier peak, gently stroking the outside skin around to the front watching them react to the sensation and temperature of my fingers against their tender flesh.

My stomach bulged and flopped forward. It was creased in sections that looked like they were holding a place for where my clothes would later be. I traced the skin, crevices and all, rubbing gently and more aggressively in different areas to test sensitivity.

As my hand passed over my hips from the ledge at my belly button where it seamlessly melted into the curve of my sides I felt a sharp ripple of electricity shoot through me. I passed my palm over my hips again to make sure it wasn't a one-time trigger and felt the same pulse of pleasure.

I smiled.

That was a nice surprise.

My thighs, still recovering from the intense workout, responded to a deeper massage. The small virtually hairless patches at the very top where both legs blobbed against each other was by far the most sensitive. My neck was easily stimulated as were the tips of my earlobes much to my delight. My arms and elbows caused little reaction but the feel of my fingertips against my palm created a lovely rush.

Years of indulgence and negligence were obvious at first glance when I stared back at my naked form. I was far from looking like the sinewy wisp I was when I dated Nick. In the two years we were together I had never stopped to appreciate my frame with so much less weight on it. Instead, when I looked in the mirror all I saw were the same imperfections he saw.

What would he think if he saw me now, so many years later, with so many more pounds on my body than when we had been dating? I turned the bathroom lights off, the dim Sunday morning sun the only light streaming in.

I was fat.

I was definitely fat.

Lighting couldn't change that.

My legs, stomach and arms needed work. Images of Nick walking through the gym, his body larger and more muscular than I remembered, floated through my mind again. Familiar feelings of inadequacies I thought I had left far behind suddenly swept over me. I needed to do something to change the way I looked, to change the way I felt when I saw myself in the mirror. I grabbed my bathrobe and picked up my cell phone to text Mahjong.

"*What are you doing today?*" I texted her.

"*Getting a haircut both above and below. Why?*" she texted back.

"*I was thinking of getting a hair cut too,*" I texted her without being explicit about which hair I was referring to.

Maybe I could just take Manny's nose hair trimmer to the bushel of pubic hair between my legs and give myself a tiny trim? What could it hurt? Before I had time to think about the logistics of using such a small trimmer on such a formidable mountain of hair Mahjong was calling my home phone line.

"Lee take my hair appointment with Gregory."

"No, I can't," I said, feeling fear replace momentary bravado.

"I'm serious, take it!" she insisted. "It's in half an hour. I'll come and get you now." I barely had time to dress before she was at my door and pulling me out of my house into her car.

The smell of the salon, the flying scissors and the skinny young girls pushing brooms of hair around the floor sent me into full blown panic.

What the hell was I thinking?

It was too spontaneous, too crazy.

I hadn't had my hair cut professionally in almost four years.

"I'm not ready," I whined as Mahjong forcefully pulled me past the reception desk.

"You've been cutting that shag on your head by yourself for years now. *Enough!*"

I didn't have time to figure out how to back out before I was whisked away by a size two shampoo girl with pink and green highlights in her hair. Before I knew it, I was sitting in the chair of Mahjong's stylist Gregory, a blatantly gay Chinese man, who started to speak in a foreign tongue over my wet hair as it lay limply on my head.

"Tsk, tsk," Gregory kept repeating as he clucked his tongue and shook his head. "Sssso bad dahling. Needs ssso much. Ssso much. Tsk, tsk."

As he combed my wet hair, fighting the tangles down to the split ends, I found myself thinking back to when I was a small child and my *Dadi* would oil and braid my hair for me on the weekends. She applied coconut oil from a glass jar and would sing old Indian songs as she worked it into my hair. I couldn't understand what she was singing, but I loved hearing her soothing voice. She twisted my long hair into two braids and told me to wait at least a few nights before washing the oil out. One Monday, I decided I would wear my hair the way she had braided it to school. By the middle of the afternoon the oil from my hair had soaked into the back of my shirt leaving a large greenish stain on the fabric. A few of the kids noticed it and called me *Greasy Greena Leena* for weeks after that.

Gregory insisted that I needed to cut more than twelve inches of hair from my head in order for it to grow back more healthy. I resisted until Mahjong informed me that I could donate my ponytail to wigmakers for cancer survivors.

"Cut it!" I said taking in a deep breath. "Take what you need."

It was for a good cause; at least that's what I would tell my mother and Manny both of whom would be shocked to see me with so little hair left. When it was all said and done Gregory had brilliantly styled my hair into a shoulder-length mass of layered curls with just the perfect hint of wild abandon.

Did I imagine the other women in the salon looking with envy at my hair? Or the girl sweeping the floor who winked affirmatively at me? Perhaps, but I was so overwhelmed by the smiles at every turn, not the least of which from my own reflection, that I bought every product he instructed me to use to keep the look and vowed to follow through on the process.

"You look fantastic Lee!" Mahjong repeated in the car as I vainly checked my reflection in the passenger side mirror.

"I can't believe what a difference a haircut can make!" I said. "I can't believe I waited this long to get it done. Thanks so much again Mahjong!"

"No trouble at all my friend. My new highlights and cut can wait. I'm kind of used to this colour now anyway. You sore from the spin class?" she asked as she drove down an unfamiliar street.

"I was worse last night." I wasn't sure if she was fishing to see if I had played with my toy or not. The thought of Bunti sitting silently waiting for me on my nightstand made me both sad and nervous. "Where are we going?"

"To my next appointment. It won't take long, if it's okay with you."

"Where is that?"

"I'm getting my wonton waxed. You know I always get my hair cut once every month."

"You mean your *pubic hair?*" I whispered.

"Yes, that's what I mean. It won't take more than ten minutes, I swear. Then we can go for lunch and show off your new hairdo."

I wanted to tell Mahjong that I had just been looking at myself in the mirror before I sent her a text that morning.

What would she think of me?

Knowing her, she probably not only looked at herself on a regular basis but also had an 8" x 10" photo of her vagina on her mantle in her apartment.

"Uh," I said slowly, "speaking of pubic hair, I was just looking at mine when I texted you this morning."

"Good girl!"

"I think I might give it a trim when I get home," I said as matter-of-factly as I could. Mahjong slammed the brakes harder than she had to at the stop sign on the street corner.

"Are you kidding me? Take my appointment with Hannah! I insist!"

"No, I couldn't!" I regretted saying anything. "I've already taken one of your hair appointments today."

"No, really. I don't have enough hair to worry about it. Hannah loves new clients! Oh my God Lee, I'm super excited right now!"

Why did I feel like I was about to throw up?

"I'm scared," I said. "What is she going to do?"

"You'll see." Mahjong had a devilish grin on her face. The leftover red dye in her hair made her look like a satanic gremlin.

"Now I'm really getting nervous!" I squirmed in my seat.

"Oh shit!" Mahjong thumped the steering wheel for emphasis.

"What's wrong?" My voice went an octave higher.

"What? Oh, nothing. I just thought of something." The sheepish look on her face escalated my anxiety.

"*What did you think of?*" Then more calmly, "Is it money? I have money."

"No. No. I'm going to pay. I want to be the first to buy you a Brazilian. It's gonna be great!"

"Wait!" I felt panic cover me like a heavy wet blanket. "*Brazilian?* That means just the sides come off right? That's not the one where it *all* comes off?" Mahjong studied my face as my voice cracked with every other word.

"It means she will take off the hair. She's going to take it all off Lee." She sounded so clinical and matter-of-fact that severe panic took over any rational thought.

"*No way!*" I said wringing my hands in my lap. "No! No! NO!"

"Why not? What difference does it really make once it starts to come off anyway?"

In hindsight, I thought of at least a hundred different retorts to her comment. In that moment, I had none. Her logic seemed too practical and I couldn't form an argument against it.

A large lump began to grow in my throat as we rolled up to a white brick house nestled between two almost identical homes on either side. The only thing that distinguished it from the others was the lineup of rose bushes to the front door. The smell was intoxicating in the late morning air.

Mahjong's esthetician Hannah had been running her beauty shop from the basement of her home for close to ten years. She opened the door and I was surprised to see that she was a very demure woman, all of four feet tall looking more like a doll than a beauty technician. She was so tiny that Mahjong said she had to stand on a small bench to do any kind of massage work or waxing that was required on the table.

Hannah's greatest feature was her large toothy grin and big ocean-coloured eyes. She had a disarming charm about her that put me instantly at ease despite the high level of anxiety I felt. It helped that she was wearing a white lab coat and firmly shook my hand when I first met her at the door.

How bad can it be? She's wearing a lab coat? That's a uniform of sorts right?

"Welcome, welcome!" she said ushering us into her home. "Mahjong so good to see you and right on time. Who is this little lady?"

Little? She *was* a sweet talker.

"This is my friend Leena. If it's okay with you Hannah, she's gonna take my appointment for a Brazilian today. It's her first!"

Hannah giggled out loud and said, "A virgin?" Mahjong tried to conceal the smirk on her lips. "How exciting for me!"

She reached up and hugged me catching me off guard. Her head came up to my chest. Her skinny little arms were surprisingly strong for someone so tiny. "Come downstairs. Quickly! Did you give her an aspirin then?"

"Aspirin?" I said resisting her as she pulled me closer to the basement stairs.

The sheepish expression was on Mahjong's face again. "That's what I thought of in the car. But don't worry! You'll be fine! Hannah is the best!"

"I'm going to kill you Mahjong," I said between clenched teeth. "I don't want to do this! I've changed my mind!"

"Now don't get hysterical darling," Hannah said in her soothing, faint Portuguese accent. "I'll take such good care of you. You will come back. It's not so painful."

I wondered which was causing sweat to pour down my back more: the satanic devil behind me who insisted that it would be over before it started or the wee gremlin with the toothy grin that looked like Rumpelstiltskin on crack.

Mahjong made herself comfortable on the big sofa in front of the big screen TV in Hannah's upstairs living room. She looked as if she owned the house the way she was flipping through the channels and propping her legs up on the coffee table in front of her.

"Is anyone else here?" I asked following Hannah downstairs as the first monster-sized bead of sweat rolled its way down my back.

"No, my husband Jimmy is at work. We won't be disturbed. You just make yourself comfortable darling. Take your skirt off and lay down here."

"I've never done this before," I said like a young virgin about to lose her flower in a badly acted teen movie.

I refrained from telling Hannah I had only really taken a good look at my genitals that morning in a vain attempt to act cool, like it wasn't a really big deal to me that she was about to yank out all the hair from between my legs.

My mind was reeling. I couldn't figure out how I had gone from waking up on a sunny Sunday morning, no different than most, to having the hair on my head styled and all of my pubic hair removed for the first time in my life.

"I'll be gentle," Hannah said like the lead from the same low budget movie.

I removed one shoe.

One shoe down, one more to go, I told myself, but the other shoe refused to come off.

It just stared defiantly at me as though it was saying: "We can still make a quick getaway. *You need me to get out of here!*"

I remained frozen in front of the massage table unable to get myself to take anything else off. The table was situated up against a long pink wall with white stripes that reminded me of a pastry box from a local bakery. The large silver tin of wax simmering on a tiny heater next to the table brought little peace of mind despite its subtle and soothing aroma.

Hannah went to the side of a small hutch situated under a suspended television and picked up surgical gloves to wear. I heard the sound of her snapping a glove on her hand at which point I soulfully looked at my other shoe and whispered, "It's just you and me buddy. We're gonna make a break for it!"

Before I could tell Hannah that I had suddenly remembered that I had left the stove on, the iron plugged in and the water running at home, she turned to me with a concerned expression on her face. It was the first time I didn't see her toothy grin smiling back at me. She had an almost maternal expression.

"What's the matter darling? Is it too cold in here for you?"

Why did she have to be so sweet?

"How's the wildebeest doing?" I heard Mahjong yell from upstairs.

"Come down here!" I shouted back without thinking. I rationalized in a split second that at least if Mahjong was there it wouldn't be as bad. If I had to do this it was going to be equally uncomfortable with a complete stranger so what difference would it make if my best friend was there too?

"What? Are you sure?" Mahjong asked from the top of the stairs.

"Get down here!" I said like my life depended on her presence.

Mahjong raced down the stairs into the small pink room. She looked like she was ready to put out a fire or perform CPR. Her expression changed when she saw me paralyzed by the side of the massage table with only one shoe on.

"Oh good, you got your shoe off. I thought I was going to have to do everything."

Hannah piped in with a throaty giggle. The two of them seemed to be sharing some inside joke I wasn't privy to.

"I think I changed my mind," I said. "I have a lot of hair you know. I'm South Asian!"

"Oh thank God!" Hannah said her big toothy grin emerging again. "If it wasn't for the hairy Indians, I wouldn't have that nest egg of money put away for my grandson's college fund! A few more clients like you and I can buy that winter home in Florida!"

Mahjong and Hannah raised their hands to high-five each other and then doubled over with laughter. I stared down helplessly at my shoe. Even *it* seemed to be laughing at their stupid joke.

"You can leave your panties on," Hannah said as she wiped a tear of laughter from her eye. "Whatever makes you most comfortable darling."

"What do you do?" I asked Mahjong as she took a seat in the chair to the right of the wax pot station. She raised her eyebrow as if to say the answer was obvious. She probably walked into Hannah's house with her pants off before she even crossed the threshold.

I took an exaggerated deep breath and flipped my shoe off and then in one swift movement, riding the crest of that large inhale, took off my oversized granny panties and bundled them up inside my hand.

There was just my skirt left.

It slid off without too much effort. I threw it hastily on the floor with my underwear, trying with great difficulty to leap into position in one fell swoop. Instead of a graceful side hop on to the table it took two tries to get on top of the incline bed causing me to flash everyone in the room in the process.

"Just relax," Hannah said pushing down on the table. I looked over at Mahjong whose expression was calm and soothing, all traces of mockery and laughter gone. Slowly, my heart settled back into a normal pattern.

Hannah took a wooden stick dripping with wax in her hand and gently touched the tip to her exposed wrist above her gloved fingers. She pressed it against the mound of flesh on my pubic bone and slowly scraped it down the edge toward my thighs. The gooey wax was more comforting than I thought it would be. The feeling was so warm and soothing it started to relax me.

I began to settle into the paper covering on the table. The smell of the wax made me think of more tropical climes. It wasn't hard to imagine the paper on the table was a hammock on the beach, the sun beating its lovely warmth down on my tinted skin where the wax was spread.

Hannah started to make idle chatter with Mahjong asking her about her clothing shop and how business was going when the muslin strip of cloth came down to cover the wax.

The cotton felt warm on my skin. I thought I could smell suntan lotion. I waited patiently for my rum to be delivered. I perked my ears up to hear what Mahjong was getting ready to say about her spring line when suddenly my island retreat exploded under volcanic ash and hellfire.

There are no words really to describe what ran through my mind next: hatred, evil, murder. My first instinct, being the primate animal that I am, was to take my fist and ram it down Hannah's smiling face knocking every one of her big teeth to the back of her throat. She held up the wax strip in the air, long lines of my curly black hair suspended from it like released prisoners waving their wiggly arms. I clenched my fists as if to punch her. The only thing that stopped me from doing so was the ear-piercing wail heard throughout the room.

"Aaaah!!! Son of a bitch!" I screamed. "Don't touch me ever again!"

My cry was followed by an equally deafening silence and then after a short pause, the roaring laughter of both Hannah and Mahjong.

"That hurts!" I whined. "I'm bleeding! I know it!"

"Calm down, darling." Hannah wiped a tear from her eye.

As I tried to rise up from the table to run for the door, she pushed me back and with one hand applied more wax to the next small strip beside the first. I'm not sure how that little woman managed to do it, but before I could come to my senses or even get half way into an upright position she was yanking off the second strip and I was begging for mercy again.

"You've got to be fucking kidding me!" I cussed. "I can't take it! I'm bleeding! I have to be!"

"You are not bleeding, darling," Hannah continued. "What doesn't kill you makes you –"

I cut her off and barked: "*Stronger?* You better not say that! Don't feed me that crap! What doesn't kill you makes you lame! I'm lame!"

"Actually," she said holding back a laugh, "I was going to say what doesn't kill you makes me a winter house in The Keys."

Mahjong tried to stifle her own laughter and smacked Hannah on her behind.

I was unaware of anything else. I wished the pain would take me to that sickly sweet dark place where I would pass out from it and wake up in the hospital on the road to recovery, a large bag of morphine already dripping directly into my veins.

"I mean it!" I said. "I'm done! Stop it! For God's sake!"

"You know my other Indian clients aren't nearly as delicate as you," Hannah said with a goading tone. Between the tears of pain swelling in my eyes and the beads of sweat already formed on my forehead, back and feet I had trouble understanding anything that she was saying. "Now go to your happy place."

Happy place?

What was that?

Where was that?

I tried to regain an ounce of composure and flopped back on the table hearing the paper protest and rip under my weight.

My mind was racing.

Happy place, happy place… that *had* to be somewhere in my long lost youth when my father was still alive.

I could vaguely recall being on a swing somewhere and having my Daddy push me high into the air. I remember the exhilarating feeling of the wind rushing against my face, sweeping my long curls all around my head. I believed with each push I might be able to touch the sky. And then mid-swing I remember hearing the high-pitched scream of my mother in the distance telling my father to be careful because I might fall and break my neck. Fear quickly replaced elation.

"I'm sorry we are laughing at you darling. I am just trying to get you to relax, especially now that the worst part is coming." Hannah spread more wax between my legs.

"The mound," Mahjong said knowingly.

"Yes, love, the mound. But really the worst is over."

I heard her say the words but they meant nothing to me as she ripped another strip from the other side between my legs.

Perhaps Hannah was sent by the devil. Or perhaps she *was* the devil. How much would the papers pay, I wondered, to find out that I had discovered the cavern of Satan where you could be tortured and get a pedicure at the same time?

"I want to die." The sound of my own voice annoyed me.

"Listen!" Hannah said sharply. "If you don't think this is wonderful, well, just see for yourself darling. Put a finger here."

She took my hand from its clenched up position on the side of the massage table and tried to pry open my fist. I eased enough to allow one finger loose so that I could gently stroke the tender skin that covered my vulva. I was shocked that the skin was soft and supple, albeit a bit sticky.

Where was all the torn flesh and blood? My skin was almost sinfully inviting, not ripped, mangled and deformed as I had imagined. I withdrew my hand from hers and nodded for her to continue with the same stern expression a prize fighter might give to someone he was *asking* to punch him in the stomach to make him a better boxer.

"Now we do the mound okay?" she said.

I took in a sharp breath and braced myself.

I saw her arm yank forward and the flash of a beige strip covered in black hair go flying through the air.

I think if you can die for one brief second in time that is exactly what happened to me. My heart must have stopped in that instant of scorching pain and before the sound made its way to my throat I was flooded with a series of unrelated images all from my youth.

In an instant I saw the face of the little French boy Pierre who made me a paper rose in grade four and asked me to be his Valentine.

I saw my cousin Vargoo call me out to the parking lot with pockets full of candy.

I saw my *Dadi* smiling in the audience and standing up to clap as I accepted an award for winning my grade six spelling contest. "Dat's my Leenoo!" she was yelling, her sari falling off her shoulders as she vigorously waved her arms in the air.

My happy place suddenly emerged through the muck of other images to a moment caught in time when I knelt at my *Dadi*'s feet on the day of my high school graduation. She put her weathered hands on my face and looked down at me with the most intensely loving eyes I had ever seen. "Leenoo I am so proud of you. I know your father is too."

A small tear escaped my eye. I felt my hands begin to unclench as I breathed into the memory.

"Your samosa is getting stripped!" Mahjong said in a sing song voice. "I get my wanton whacked and you get your samosa stripped!"

She reached into her purse and pulled out a Sudoku puzzle and began to fill in numbers.

"It's not funny. I think I just died a bit."

"You can be one of my regular clients," Hannah said as she mixed the warm wax vigorously and pushed my leg towards the ceiling. "I know so many, maybe some of your friends?"

It suddenly occurred to me that this woman had handled many more lady bits than I cared to imagine. I wondered whose private parts she was handling other than mine and Mahjong's.

"So you have a lot of Indian clients?" I asked in an effort to make conversation and ignore the fact that I felt like a dog about to pee on a hydrant.

"Oh, I do!" Hannah said with delight. "Let's see there is Mrs. Parma and Mrs. Govinda and little Joowania. Poor thing. She is absolutely covered like a bear. There are so many that I have. Do you know them?"

"I don't know every South Asian in this city," I said fighting tears as she yanked another strip away. Hannah merely shrugged her shoulders and smiled as she quietly reached into her pocket and pulled out a small black instrument and then lowered her glasses and gaze towards my throbbing mound.

"What are those?" I said with a shriek, all hope of dignity and decorum thoroughly vanishing out of sight.

"Tweezers, love," she said matter-of-factly as she began to pluck individual hairs out from the root.

With each yank I began to become more and more anxious. By the fourth one I struggled to wade back to the memory of my grandmother but my happy place was now an elusive dream plucked to tiny pieces by a small black tong.

"Uh oh, ingrown," Hannah said as she knelt so close to my vagina I thought her lips might brush against my skin. "Take a deep breath" she instructed as she plunged the tweezers into my soft flesh searing my skin with what felt like a hot poker.

She agitated the same spot, a look of bold determination on her face.

I sought solace skyward.

Dear Allah, I prayed, I promise to give *zakat* to the poor if you make it stop.

Dear Ganpati, I promise to never eat meat again as long as I live if you make the pain go away.

Dear Buddha, I will make my firstborn child study the ways of dharma and cleanse my karma by giving away all my earthly goods if you kill Hannah and shove her tweezers up her nose.

I became aware of Hannah pressing her hands against my hips and telling me to turn over onto my stomach. Perhaps I'm the biggest idiot that ever lived but I thought she was going to give me a massage to ease the sorrow of what she had put me through, so I willingly obliged.

I turned over onto my tummy and lay my head on my hands taking a deep breath. Before I could take a moment to relax I felt Hannah's hands prying my butt cheeks apart, the sizzling feeling of warm wax sliding down a place I had never anticipated it would ever go before that moment.

Much to my surprise, I found the feeling of the warm wax not only soothing and gentle but slightly erotic. I relaxed so noticeably that Hannah gave me a pat on my bottom and said "Good girl" as she placed the muslin between my cheeks. That rip was nothing like the rest. It felt liberating and even a bit enjoyable. The other side was done and in virtually seconds I was hair free from front to back.

"Now would you like me to get rid of this back hair for you too?" Hannah asked as she stirred her pot of wax with her stick.

"Back hair?"

Mahjong looked up from her puzzle and glanced at my backside exposed on the table. She gave me a nod as if to say *get rid of it* so I gave Hannah a reluctant nod to tell her it was okay to remove it. Before long my entire lower body was hair free and for the first time in my memory my bottom was being powdered and patted down like I was an infant again.

"You're done darling," Hannah said sweetly. "You were very brave. Wasn't that bad was it?" She was patronizing me but I didn't feel like getting into words with her about her tone since she had just handled my vagina and I was still lying naked on the table for both of them to see.

"Now when you get a chance, you go home and wash off the rest of the wax with lukewarm water and then maybe add some cream. It will keep it soft okay?"

I sat up on the edge of the massage table and Mahjong very quickly and discreetly handed me my clothes without actually making eye contact. I slid into the skirt directly from where I was sitting on the table. Putting on my underwear was another story.

The moment the fabric hit my tender skin I winced. Before I could even think of removing it, they had adhered to some leftover wax. I thought better of taking them off. I stood up and put on both my shoes. It felt good finally to be dressed and on my way out. I figured it must be mid-afternoon, or several hours since we had arrived as that must be how long it takes for your entire life to flash before your eyes as you writhe in pain and agony.

According to my watch, it was twenty minutes from when we walked in.

"Um, how much do I owe you?" I asked awkwardly.

"I'm paying," Mahjong said rising from her chair with a twenty dollar bill in her hand.

Normally I might have created a fuss about her paying but in light of what I had just been through I thought it was the least she could do for me. Suddenly, I understood why taking an aspirin beforehand would have been a good idea.

"Thank you, Hannah," I said as sweetly as I could, attempting to recover my dignity. "I'm sorry if I acted like a baby."

"Don't worry, darling." Her voice was soothing and maternal. "I have had much worse on that table before. This will last now something like three weeks, so you enjoy it."

I blushed slightly and turned towards the stairs. As I lifted my leg to take the first step I was keenly aware of the coolness of the breeze that floated up from the bottom of my skirt. It tickled, almost teased my throbbing skin with an alluring gentle whisper that squeezed the first smile out of me since I had arrived.

"Wait till you get outside," Mahjong said seeing my face. "Now would be a good time to wear those crotchless panties from the sex party."

The outside air felt warm and wonderful against my skin, climbing in sensual swirls around my newly freed genitals.

"I feel like I lost ten pounds. It's really a freeing feeling. I can't believe it," I said in slow awe. "Am I just in some post-pain euphoria or is this real?"

"It's real." Mahjong smiled broadly. "And it's just the start."

A slow smile curled my lips. I heard a bird sing in the background, the rustle of a tree blowing somewhere behind me, the smell of Hannah's roses wafting up my nose intoxicatingly.

Hannah had said I was *brave*.

I hadn't scaled a mountain, saved a child from a burning house or performed open heart surgery but I had faced down my fears and dammit all, *I did feel brave!* It was ridiculous for me to want to flash my newly bald skin but I wished I could show everyone and anyone who had ever doubted my bravery the results of what I had done.

"Here!" I would flash Joanie from my swim class, "How do you like the look of that freshly waxed vagina?"

And add Glen to the list of people I wanted to eat their words. "Yeah, you think all Indian girls are scared little virgins? What do you think of this bald baddy?" I would wail as I lifted my leg to the sky and flashed him.

And of course I would have to add Nick to the list. "You want sexy? You think I couldn't do anything this wild? Well what do you think of this bare brown baby now?"

"You okay?" Mahjong said as she rifled through the glove compartment in front of me.

"Yes!" I eased myself against the car seat.

"Sorry." She pulled out a bottle of aspirin. "It turns out I had some after all."

"It doesn't matter. I feel good," I said truthfully. "I feel *really* good."

"Oh no, Lee, wait till you actually *feel* it!"

Mahjong's comment gave me pause for thought. Even though she had stayed in the same room with me while I was naked and vulnerable, it somehow didn't seem appropriate for me to reach between my legs in her car and touch my newly supple skin in front of her.

It would have to wait until I got home.

Mahjong and I ate lunch at a nearby restaurant. She mercilessly teased me about screaming like a fool on the table the entire time. I started to get anxious about the leftover wax between my legs. Once I got home, I took a warm shower to remove the small hairs littering my skin from my haircut and the tiny blobs of leftover wax from my genitals. I quietly rejoiced in the feeling of both pleasure and pain from the bar of soap as it glided against the tender skin of my pubic area.

I locked the bathroom door and grabbed the heart-shaped mirror again. Feeling more brave and bold than ever before I propped my leg up on the cover of the toilet seat and placed the mirror squarely between my legs without any hesitation at all. The skin was slightly pinkish in hue, fluffy and plump.

I poked gently at my pubic mound.

I had freckles there?

I noticed a triangle of three small dots on the left that had been hiding beneath the mass of curly black hair. To the right, the still red circle where Hannah had extracted an ingrown hair provided a symmetrical balance. I smiled. I pulled the lips apart and noticed that the fleshy flap of my inner labia looked even more like a tongue sticking out without the presence of hair.

Paint two eyes on the top and two thick eyebrows and you would have my grade seven high school picture.

I found the tiny turtle hiding at the top of my mound. It looked more like a bald man floating at the back of a flesh-tone canoe, no paddle in sight. I gingerly caressed the soft skin and marveled at how sultry it felt, how each stroke sent tiny tingles up and down my spine. This was my reward for climbing the mountain, rescuing the child and saving a life.

There was no stopping the intensely overwhelming feeling of excitement growing under my skin. My freshly cut hair damp from the shower fell in sultry waves around my face. It was such a stark contrast from the mound of messiness atop my head only hours before, that I barely recognized the woman staring back at me in the mirror.

I looked different.

Not just my hair, there was something else.

Something in my expression.

They said I was brave.

I had gone to a sex party.

I had bought a bag of sex toys.

I had taken and survived my first spin class.

I had gotten a haircut that was flattering and flirtatious.

I had my first Brazilian wax and was 100% hair free from the waist down for the first time in my adult memory.

I *was* brave.

Riding the crest of burgeoning self-confidence, I decided there was no time like the present to try out my new toy.

I briefly considered ransacking the secret cupboard where I kept all my liquor hidden from my mother to have a drink and fully calm my nerves but remembered that the only thing left in it was some of Manny's whisky and a bottle of cooking sherry.

I didn't need a drink to relax. The warm shower coupled with my moaning muscles began to take its toll on me. I was feeling lazy, relaxed and fatigued enough to justify slipping into my pajamas without giving another thought to any of the chores I had left to do that weekend.

I lay on the bed, my mind racing back to the night of the party and all the things Clarissa had said. "If you've never had an orgasm before, today is your birthday."

I had lived without having an orgasm for 32 years.

Was I the only woman at the party that night that had never had an orgasm?

I started to think about all the women I knew and wondered if they had ever had one.

Had my mother?

Had my grandmother?

They were from a generation that didn't talk about their sex lives openly. I was from one that did and yet I had never been brave enough until the sex party to admit that I had never had one before. How many other women were in the same situation as me?

"Where is your orgasm, ladies?" Clarissa had asked. I turned to my bedside table where I had left Bunti. His plastic bunny head looked over at me as though he were contemplating life as I had been.

I picked up the toy flicking the switch on the motor. It instantly buzzed to life vigorously. I giggled as I felt the vibrations coursing through my fingers.

"Your orgasm is up here," I remembered Clarissa saying as she pointed to her head.

If your orgasm is in your brain, then how would I ever get past the hurricane of thoughts that plagued me from one minute to the next?

If it wasn't my mother on my mind, the politics of work or the household chores, then it was a news article I had read, a comment Manny had made or a memory from my past that came back to haunt me.

I lay back on the bed in complete exhaustion. The haircut and the waxing had taken their physical and emotional toll on me.

I looked Bunti in his bunny eyes.

There wasn't likely going to be another quiet moment like this again for a while.

I had to find out.

I removed my pajama bottoms and underwear. I hesitantly allowed my hand to go back to my pubic area, the memory of searing pain from being waxed momentarily flooding back to my brain. The skin was so smooth and tender to the touch that I found myself caressing its suppleness with my bare hand reveling in the softness of the flesh.

It wondered what Bunti would feel like against my bare flesh.

I positioned the toy on my finger and slowly slid it down my stomach to the top of my vulva. The mixture of the cool air on my bare and tender skin along with the vibration sent a rush of sensation up my spine.

I instinctually curled my back into it.

I started to relax into the bed, deciding to slowly enjoy each sensation, my focus on every reaction of my body. I moved the bunny's head back and forth over my labia letting it occasionally pause on my clitoris. The sensation was so overwhelming and intense that at first I could only let it linger for a few seconds. With each pass of the toy over my skin I sank deeper and deeper into the warmth of blood that released itself through my body causing my tense and taut muscles to let go and relax.

It felt so soothing that I failed to notice how aroused I had become. I started to moan instinctively, my back arched as I placed the bunny's head directly on my clitoris and reveled in the intensity of the sensation until I met my threshold.

It was a familiar place I had been so many times before.

When faced with pushing past the final barricade, reality overtook my mind and sent my pleasure-soaked impulses crashing amidst the clutter of my brain. Everyday details about laundry, cooking, spreadsheets and personal angst invaded my thoughts refusing to let me surrender to the sensation.

I recalled Clarissa in the midst of the muck pointing her finger at her head and saying, "Your orgasm is up here ladies."

What did she mean?

I suddenly felt defeated.

I was fatigued and exhausted. It had to be the spin class that had caused my entire body to collapse into one throbbing ache.

I let my hand hover over my tender skin, Bunti's vibrating nose dangling over my clitoris. My mind wandered from the bike seat that caused me so much pain to the gym in general. As my grocery list and plans for dinner left my mind they were replaced with the singular image of the tall blonde man with his thick long hair standing by the weights section.

I pictured him in isolation, flexing his biceps until he stops when I walk by.

He smiles.

I lowered Bunti's nose to the side of my clitoris massaging the hood as I pictured my own body sliding up and down the side of the muscular blonde. He looked down at me, his expression smoky and passionate. I saw myself touching and stroking his large muscles, pressing my own flesh against his. My body responded by writhing in unison, swaying my hips towards the vibrations against my skin.

As the sensation spread throughout my body, my muscles released sinking me deeper into the bed.

I imagined the sculpted stranger sliding his hand between my legs, his fingers moving in sync with the bobbing head of the bunny leading directly to the hub of pleasure; my clitoris.

His other hand rested on the peak of my nipple. His large palm opened to cup my breast in his hand. He squeezed gently but forcefully, his pink tongue slick and wet as it descended down the nape of my neck trailing slowly towards my exposed nipple. As his mouth closed and I imagined him gently nibbling, ever so tenderly at the tip of my breast, I suddenly felt overcome by the most intense feeling I had ever felt.

It started with a gentle pull in my legs that spread down to my toes.

I felt the warmth of my blood shooting through my body at breakneck speed, my skin pulsating, almost three dimensionally with heightened sensitivity. There was a rush of tingling everywhere inside my body that I seemed to be aware of in fragments though they happened all at once.

My toes curled down in response to the sudden flame of heat between my legs; my heart was racing, my nipples hard and erect instantly, extremely sensitive to even the light brush of fabric from my pajama top pressing against them.

I climaxed when I felt each separate sensation culminate into a divine peak of pleasure bursting at the crest into a cascade of intense ecstasy awakening every cell in my entire body with heady joy. My whole being shook in response and I felt every muscle, every vein, every bone in my body rise up and scream with pleasure.

I lay back when it ended in a heaving pile of release and euphoria.

Tears sprang to my eyes.

At last I had pushed past all my inhibitions, cleared the space between body and soul and I was amazed, awed and inspired at what lay on the other side.

I was free.

I was finally free.

And I felt alive.

Completely alive.

My body reeled from the intensity of the release. I let myself sob into the pillow next to me until the final wave of blood had rushed through my body.

I curled up into a ball and held my legs, still shaking, into my chest as the last of my tears flowed gently down my face.

When I opened my eyes again, Bunti quietly bobbed on the bed beside me. I watched the battery light go out and wondered if I was hallucinating the wry little smile on his face. I crawled under the covers of the bed and nestled into my pillow.

I had an orgasm.

And damn it was beautiful.

For the first time in my life my soul felt like it was connected to my flesh, my skin felt like it belonged to me and my mind was clearer and more open than it had ever been.

I reached over to the nightstand and picked up my cell phone to send Mahjong a text message: "*I just had an orgasm! I can't believe it. It was amazing!!*"

She instantly wrote me back five words that would make me weep for another hour: "*Welcome to the world baby!*"

Chapter 6

Mondays come and Mondays go but there would never be another one like the one after my first orgasm.

"Morning bagel," I said to the round dough in my hand, "Did you know I had an orgasm last night?"

The cut slice looked as though it was smiling at me.

I smiled back.

"Morning juice. You know I had an orgasm right? Did the bagel tell you?"

I was afraid for a moment that I might wake up and forget what had happened but there was no chance. The smile on my face when

I went to sleep was still carved on my skin when I woke up having never left all night.

I, Leena, had an orgasm.

I wanted to shout it to the world but there was no time.

I would be late for work.

My new haircut made getting ready in the morning especially easy. The reflection of myself in the mirror had definitely changed. Was it more than the hair? Could other people see it in my eyes? Was I imagining it or was my skin glowing too?

I smiled all day at work.

I smiled during a two-hour meeting discussing overtime requirements for all staff and interns.

I smiled while I ate my lunch and dodged questions from co-workers about my especially gleeful state.

I smiled when they noticed my haircut and complimented me on how great it was to see me beaming from ear to ear.

"Clearly the haircut did you a world of good Leena," they said.

You think?

Or do you think it was the incredible orgasm I had with my vibrator last night?

Had Cynthia ever had an orgasm? I wondered as she asked me for the third time that day why I was smiling like a fool?

Had Mary had one?

I was suddenly more aware of all the women around me. I couldn't help but wonder if they had spent their weekend in ecstatic release as I had. If they did, then why didn't they come to work with the same energetic enthusiasm for life as me? How it was possible to have your body reward you with so much splendour and intense sensation and not have that effect you over a conversation about season finales at lunch was beyond me.

Manny would be home later that night. He would notice my haircut but would he notice the difference in me as well? I wondered if he would be upset with me for cutting my hair without discussing it with him. And what would he say when he noticed all the hair missing from my lower body? It had never occurred to me that he might have a negative reaction.

Would he like it?

Would he think I had gone crazy?

Or would he be more upset to find out that throughout our entire marriage I had never had an orgasm?

I decided it might be best to wait and break the news to him after the shock of my haircut had worn off. Bunti had been cleaned and tucked deeply away in the bottom corner of my nightstand dresser.

Mahjong sent me three texts that day.

"Happy Birthday!"

"So glad you got bzz-y last night!" and

"There's no debate when you liberate through that which vibrates!"

Manny came through the baggage area with his work buddy Borgis, still chatting about their conference. Even from a distance I could see how tired Manny was though Borgis looked rested and relaxed.

"Hi Lee." Manny said flatly and then his eyes popped open wider than I had ever seen them before as he added, "You got a haircut! Wow. I didn't know you were going to do that."

"Do you like it?"

"You look sensational!"

I felt tears spring to the back of my eyes and a large lump catch in my throat.

He hadn't looked at me like that since we first met.

"I got it cut on the spur of the moment," I said in an apologetic tone. "I used Mahjong's hair dresser."

It almost sounded like I was blaming her.

"Is there colour in there too?" he asked hesitantly.

I smiled.

"No. I just got a haircut."

And removed all the hair from my pubic area and had an orgasm.

And I didn't do any of the laundry while you were gone.

"Well it looks great. I wish I wasn't so *tired* I would take you out for dinner right now." Manny shot a sinister glance over towards Borgis who was chewing on a candied fruit stick.

"It's okay. I just want to go home."

I slept that night tucked tightly into the cradle of Manny's arms. He continued to shower me with compliments the next day. After a few nights had gone by, Manny caught up on his sleep. I could see the amorous look return to his eyes. I had managed to keep my bald lady bits from his sight but I knew that once we started to have sex, there was no escaping my trip to Brazil. I was a bit afraid of his reaction so I had purposefully avoided any long deep kisses that might lead to something else and managed to dodge any advances he made during the week that might lead us to the bedroom.

I used the excuse that the spin classes I did during the week with Mahjong had tired me out too much. The truth was they had. Although I still found the classes physically tiring, they were becoming easier to get through.

I reveled in the feeling of my cotton underwear and track pants being the only thing between me and the bike seat.

By the weekend I was feeling energized again and anxious to see if my orgasm had just been a fluke or if it was a repeatable phenomenon. After dinner at my mother's place on Saturday night we cuddled at home on one chaise to watch television. We hadn't snuggled in one seat since the first year we were married. After the initial blush of marriage had set in it became very clear which chaise was mine and which was his.

Thirty minutes after we settled in I got agitated and antsy.

"Want to play a game?" Manny asked. I wasn't sure if he was referring to the sex game or not. I couldn't read the expression in his eyes.

"I have other stuff I bought at the sex party we could play with," I said watching his face.

"Oh you do? Like what?"

"I, uh, I have to go see. Meet me upstairs in the bedroom in five?"

"Okay," Manny said pecking me quickly on the cheek.

I ran upstairs ahead of him and locked myself in the spare room fiddling with the contents of the bag from the sex party. I had trouble remembering what one product did and couldn't read the label on another. I pulled out a round canister with the image of a man and woman engaging in what looked like oral sex and decided it was my best choice.

I vaguely recalled Clarissa saying it was the warming liquid and that it got warm when you blew on it.

The key to performing good oral sex on a man is enthusiasm, she had said. For the first time since I could remember, I had no shortage of it.

Manny had placed himself on the edge of the bed. He was wearing his striped black and red boxers, a white tank top and no socks. Was that a nervous expression on his face?

"What's that?" he asked.

"It's something for getting warm. I feel kind of stupid describing it. Shouldn't I just pour it on?"

"Take it easy, Lee," he said. "Come over here." He patted the bed beside him. "Let me see that first." I sat down next to him and handed him the bottle. He opened the container and studied the ingredients and directions like he was studying cooking sauce.

"Manny," I whispered gently, watching him skim over the label on the bottle in his hands. "Are you happy?"

He looked up and surveyed my face. "I'm just reading the label."

"Yeah, I know, what I meant to say was are you happy, specifically, with our sex life?"

"Of course I am," he said instantly. "Why? Aren't you?"

"I am, yes, I am. I just mean, I think things could be better. I feel embarrassed saying it like this. What I mean is I want to be able to talk more freely with you about everything."

"Why? What do you want to talk about?" Manny put the bottle down and sat upright at the edge of the headboard.

I took a deep breath in and tried to let the air will my nerves to the surface.

"Do you wish I was more adventurous?" I realized immediately that it was an unfair question to ask. There was no perfect answer. If he said he wished I was more adventurous, I would have been hurt that he had never said anything before and that he thought our love life was obviously lacking something because of me. If he said he didn't need any more adventure, I would have felt alone in my excitement at trying something new and resentful of the fact that he wasn't willing to experiment with me.

"What do you mean by adventurous?" he asked with obvious caution.

"I mean I think we could be doing more. What I mean is that I could obviously learn more I think. You should have heard this woman, the consultant, go on and on at the party at Isabelle's. She was so informative. She told us all kinds of things and there were pictures too!"

"Pictures?" Manny's eyebrow lifted.

"Yeah, she explained how our bodies worked and even told us some tips on what to do with this hot stuff I bought. It goes on your dick. Penis. Dick." I suddenly couldn't decide what to call it.

"I guess we can try it," Manny said picking up the bottle again. "I've used something like it once before."

"What?" I said in a voice more loud and anxious than I intended. "With who?"

I could see Manny take a few steps back in his head as the gates of caution came slamming down on what he wanted to say. "With Monica," he said slowly. "She bought it at a sex shop I guess."

"You never told me that!" I said petulantly. I could hear my voice and as much as I hated how it sounded, the jealousy, the impatience, the hatred for a woman I had never met, I still couldn't stop.

Monica was one of the four other women that Manny had slept with before he met me. She was the only one of them that I felt even remotely intimidated by.

His first time having sex was when he was nineteen years old and it was with a twenty-four-year-old woman who went to university with him but was several years ahead in her studies. She was his teaching assistant and they had a short but brief affair that ended quickly when Manny realized she was sleeping with a few of her other students at the same time.

His second lover was his first girlfriend, a Vietnamese girl named Loo. They went out for about a year and from everything Manny told me about their relationship it sounded pleasant and comfortable. It broke off because, according to Manny, she was quite insistent upon having children but he felt that they were too young and not ready.

His third lover was Monica.

From the way he described her she was a siren with long black hair, large round breasts and a tight firm ass. She was adventurous and playful but emotionally unbalanced. She would call up Manny in the middle of the night crying hysterically at something he had said four days prior, wanting to break up and then act like nothing happened the next morning. He wouldn't talk that much about her when I asked him questions except to say that she was sometimes a bit too wild and that he found her sexual appetite intimidating. They broke up and got back together three times before Manny finally ended it once and for all.

His next lover was a friend of his from university that he connected with for a brief period but they both agreed there was no spark and Manny wasn't fully over Monica at the time.

Monica.

When I pictured her I envisioned a movie star with long red fingernails and full pouty gloss covered lips. One day I accidentally found a picture of her in Manny's things. I was surprised to see that she looked rather ordinary and almost plain.

The most striking thing about the picture that caused a searing pang of jealousy in my heart was the expression on Manny's face as he sat beside her with a grin as wide as the sea, his arm firmly wrapped around Monica who was half-smiling and almost looked bored. I had plenty of pictures with me and Manny in them but the majority of them were our wedding photos and some shots from our engagement.

In all those snapshots, there wasn't one image of him beaming the way he was in the one with him and Monica.

I never told him that I found the picture.

My fleeting desire to confess the fact that I had never had an orgasm until that week was gone. I was too wrapped up in feelings of inadequacies and lack of sex appeal again. Manny must have sensed my obvious jealousy for Monica because he began to sputter and fidget with the bottle.

"It was just one time. I think she got it for free anyway," he said. I could feel the rational side of my brain struggling to regain control but once the crazy train had left the station, it was very hard for me to call the conductor back. "Want to try this stuff on you?" he asked, hesitation and fear still brimming in his eyes.

"Me? It's not supposed to go on me is it?"

"Why not?" Manny said matter-of-factly.

He started to open the package.

My moment of truth was coming.

Do I feign shock when Manny sees me bald down below and pretend someone stole my pubic hair?

That was ridiculous.

I could blame it on Mahjong. That was always a failsafe.

"Lie down," Manny instructed as he removed the cork top from the bottle and put it down on his nightstand. I couldn't just let him find out for himself.

"There's one other trim I got while you were away."

I removed my pants and underwear. I quickly used my hand to conceal the area.

I kept a close eye on Manny's expression as he watched me slowly, finger by finger reveal the hairless space between my legs.

He swallowed hard. It sounded like he choked on his own saliva.

"Lee! But why? When? Who?"

All that was left was the *where?*

"Where?" he added suddenly.

"It's Mahjong's fault!" I said without the least bit of remorse. "I told her I was going to trim it and the next thing I know she drives me to her esthetician's place and I get a full Brazilian! I only wanted a trim!"

Manny's expression softened. His smile started out small until it grew across his face.

"Let me look," he said with such a low rumble from his throat that it caused the hair on the back of my neck to stand up.

I felt the heat rise under my flesh and knew my brown skin had turned a bright shade of pink as he slowly pried my legs apart and nestled between them to take a closer look.

I fidgeted uneasily.

It wasn't like he hadn't been there a hundred times before. Somehow I felt more exposed. *Literally.* And more vulnerable than I could ever remember feeling with him.

When he looked up at me his expression was unreadable but his smile spoke volumes.

"I think the least we can do is try this stuff," he said taking the bottle into his hands.

Manny tugged at my top and pushed it up under my breasts exposing my belly to the air while pushing me backwards towards the headboard. He dripped a few drops of the liquid on my stomach and then smiled at me before he leaned over and breathed deeply on it.

My body initially reacted to the shock of cold from the liquid he had smeared on my stomach. That shock was quickly replaced by a soothing, warm sensation that started to tingle slightly.

"That's so nice," I moaned.

Manny continued to gently blow on my stomach. The sensation was sensual and enticing. I felt myself relax into the warmth. I could feel myself getting wet between my legs and instinctively parted them without realizing what I had done. Before I could fully allow myself to be seduced by its warmth I suddenly felt Manny's tongue flicking on my skin around my belly button.

I snapped back to reality.

Had I cleaned my belly button in the shower yesterday?

I remembered cleaning my belly button a few days ago.

For sure I did.

But did I do it yesterday?

I couldn't let it go.

Manny picked up the bottle again and dripped some of the hot liquid on his finger tips before nestling his head between my legs.

I raised my head and opened my eyes to see him blowing on his fingers before he rubbed the liquid on my outer labia. I felt him gently rub the gel around the entire mound the sensation of which made my brain spasm into a hundred different electrical impulses.

I felt the warmth of his breath between my legs mixed with the heat of the liquid. I surrendered to the feeling, obeying the insistence of the primal urges that were surfacing under my skin again.

"Do you like it?" he asked as he breathed more deeply and started to press his mouth against my tender skin.

I could only murmur a response.

All I knew was that at once, I was warm and tingly. My body's natural juices reacted instinctively to the intensity of the heat.

I began to experience such a deep need to feel Manny inside me. I lay back and spread my legs farther apart as my back arched and my hips thrust forward.

I felt Manny's tongue on my labia and then felt it darting around near my clitoris. I responded by tilting my pubic area closer towards his face.

He flicked his tongue around my clitoris again. Sensations of fire spread like lightning throughout my entire body right down to my fingertips and toes. I felt the heady rush of every drop of my blood careening towards one area away from my brain.

In the heat of the moment, I didn't even realize that I was clutching our comforter cover so tightly in my hands that I pulled the sheets from their place around the mattress.

As the liquid continued to get warmer and Manny's tongue began to flicker more wildly I was suddenly stopped by one thought: *What the hell is he doing?*

All of a sudden it felt like he had moved from the sweet spot and was nibbling away in a dead zone like a confused woodpecker banging its head against stone. My train of thought took off at light speed.

Did Manny really think Monica was sexier than me?

Would Nick think that Monica was sexier than me?

Did Monica fake orgasms?

Did I rinse my coffee cup on my desk?

There was no way back.

Manny began ferociously licking one side of my labia. I could think of nothing he was doing right, and everything he was doing wrong.

"I'm getting a leg cramp!" I lied at which point Manny darted his head up and asked me if I was okay. "I just need to stretch my legs out a bit. Do you mind?"

He shrugged and began to help me massage out the muscles in my calves. After a few moments his massage turned into a blatant attempt to get back to where he had left off.

My desire to receive had disappeared. It was replaced by my need to test my new secret weapon - *enthusiasm*.

"It's my turn!" I said as I stopped his hands from groping more deeply.

"Don't you want me to keep going?"

"I can't wait to do the same thing to you. It felt so good I want you to feel it to." I felt guilty at first but relieved when I saw him accept my offer.

"Are you sure?"

"Yes!" I said emphatically and pulled myself up on the bed. "I just really want to try it on you… please!"

"Okay, you don't have to beg, Lee. Whatever you want." He propped himself up beside me at the head of the bed. I could see his semi-erect penis pushing at his boxers already.

I let him nestle himself firmly in place debating whether I wanted to tell him to set our decorative throw cushions aside first.

Forget it! I told myself. That's not sexy thinking. Focus Leena. Think sexy thoughts.

I smiled as sweetly as I could at him and picked up the bottle of grape-flavoured liquid.

I settled into the space between Manny's legs feeling the excitement brimming beneath my skin. I removed Manny's boxers from around his hips revealing his half-saluting penis.

With the stopper removed from the bottle, I straddled one of his legs and poured some of the liquid into my hands. How do people get the cork back in without getting liquid all over the bottle?

As the dark purple liquid filled my palm I began to panic about the bed covering and cushions getting stained. A myriad of unsexy images popped into my mind, the most jarring of which was trying to explain to our old Indian dry cleaner what the purple blotches on our bedding were from.

"Oh hi Mr. Chandiwalla, could you get this stain out of my comforter? It's a warming sex liquid I used on Manny that is for oral pleasure, but I accidentally spilled it on the cover."

I could just picture Mr. Chandiwalla falling back and passing out, our stained bed cover still clutched in his wrinkled brown hands.

I placed the bottle upright between the footboard and the mattress. I slid the liquid from one hand to the other between my palms recalling Clarissa saying, "You can put this on the penis to make it hot. You simply need to rub, blow and lick. The liquid does the trick!"

I took the warm liquid from my hands and poured it over his erect penis. I rubbed it between my fingers and smiled as sexily as I could at my husband who was beginning to get lost in thought, eyes closed, with his arms behind his head.

The gooey liquid felt slick in my hands. The more I rubbed it, the warmer it got and the more erect his penis would become. I tried to bend over from where I was straddled on top of Manny to blow air on his penis but I couldn't reach it with my mouth. I would have to shift down further to get my mouth near him which would put me in a highly undesirable position, ass in air and stomach drooping.

I managed to slide down to near the edge of the bed and decided instead to nestle down between Manny's knees where I would have the greatest vantage point of his penis.

Once I was there, I began to rub more aggressively. Manny started to moan and shift a bit. I took a deep breath like I was about to plunge under water and opened my mouth over his penis. I sucked up some of the liquid, instantly enjoying its grapey flavour.

As Manny groaned heavily I felt myself driven forward by my success. I retracted my head and started to blow on his penis with my mouth and rub the liquid more deeply into his flesh.

I couldn't believe how warm he was getting and how hot my hands felt. I reached for the bottle and poured more liquid into my hands. I blew more heavily into my palms. My hands were on fire! I placed them around his shaft again. Manny looked down at me, shifted and let out a deep groan from his throat. I became more enthusiastic about how erect his penis felt in my hands and took a deeper sense of pride than I ever had before accounting it to my passionate efforts. I put another blob of liquid in my hands and vigorously rubbed them together increasing the heat by blowing my hot breath onto my palms and then wrapped my fingers strongly around the length of his penis. Manny shifted under me again.

The heat from my hands, the liquid and his penis seemed to meld into one hot mass. Just as I was about to plunge my head forward to give him more of my mouth, I suddenly felt myself being tossed in the air and off the edge of the bed.

"It's burning!" Manny screamed as he bolted from the bed into the bathroom.

I heard the shower door slam and the quick sound of water running seconds later.

I sat dumbfounded on the floor trying to collect my thoughts.

What the hell happened?

I got up and timidly headed towards the bathroom.

I saw Manny vehemently scrubbing at his penis, his back towards me. He had been in such a rush to get into the shower that he was still wearing his white tank top. I walked back into the bedroom and sat on the edge of the bed. My hands were on fire. The warm liquid had dripped down some of my arm making the length of my forearm tingle with increased heat.

After a few moments Manny emerged from the bathroom, a towel wrapped around his waist, his tank top soaking wet and his hair dampened and disheveled. His expression was so pathetic and drawn that I instantly felt tears swell up in my eyes.

"Did I break it?" I asked chewing vigorously on my bottom lip.

"What?" Manny said snapping out of his expression and heading towards me. "No. Oh no. Lee… it's okay. Honestly. Please don't cry."

It was too late.

I sat on the bed, my hands turned upwards on my lap, weeping quietly. I stared down at my palms as though they were covered in blood like a guilty killer who is suddenly aware of what they have done.

I reflexively lifted my hands to my eyes to wipe my tears when I was met with a sharp shooting pain. The liquid stung the delicate tissue eliciting a larger flow of tears. I raced to the bathroom with the same speed as Manny to wash the liquid off my hands and out of my eyes.

When I looked up at myself in the mirror I was aghast at my own pitiful expression. My eyes were bloodshot and my makeup was running down my face. I looked like a clown caught in a downpour.

Manny sat at the edge of the bed. I noticed that he had removed his wet tank top and laid it out over our side valet. He was barechested with the towel wrapped around his waist and a strange smirk on his face. When he saw me emerge from the bathroom, he instantly raised his hands in the air beckoning me to come and sit next to him.

I started to cry again.

"I'm a loser." I sank into the bed cover next to him.

"You're not a loser. Did you get it all out of your eyes?"

"I think so. Manny, I'm so sorry!"

"For what Lee?" he asked lightly stroking my back.

"For frying your prick like a *pakora*!"

Manny burst out laughing. He began to laugh so heartily that I stopped crying for a moment with temporary shock.

How could he be laughing? Was he crazy?

I had almost melted my husband's penis and he was laughing like he was at a comedy show. When he finally stopped, he looked down at me, a few tears dangling at the sides of his eyes. He squeezed me tightly.

"I swear I'm okay, Lee," he said. "I promise."

We sat quietly for a moment. I felt embarrassed and shy, unsure of what to do next. I found myself instinctively covering his pubic area with my hand as gently as I could.

"I make a mess of everything. And what's worse, it all seems to end up in my eyes!"

"Don't feel bad Lee. I liked some of it."

"Which part?"

"Well speaking of your eyes, I actually really liked the way you were looking at me, when you were doing it." He paused and looked like he wanted to say more but didn't. "I'm okay. I promise."

I wasn't convinced despite how much Manny tried to reassure me. I felt embarrassed and stupid.

"Can I see it?" I asked shyly, gently tugging at his towel.

Manny removed the towel from around his waist. His penis was shriveled up and slightly reddish in hue. I instinctively pet it like a sad little puppy. Manny flinched, obviously still very sore to the touch.

"Let's give him a break for a bit okay?" He put the towel back on his lap.

I loved him so much in that moment for not making me feel worse about what I had done, but mostly for not making the situation more uncomfortable for me.

"Just when I thought I was finally beginning to figure this all out," I said, feeling tears sting the back of my eyes again, "I screw it up."

"What do you mean, figure this out?"

"I mean this whole thing with toys, and sex and playing and being happy."

"I am happy Lee," Manny said. "Aren't you?"

His expression looked like it was on the verge of being hurt or upset. I felt two tears trickle down my face on both sides.

"I'm happy too! I just can't explain it. It's like I feel as though I have been sleeping and now that I'm awake I want to play! I want to do all the things I have been too scared to do. But I'm still making a mess of everything."

"What brought this on?" Manny's expression was unreadable.

"I guess the party I went to really got me thinking about all kinds of stuff."

"Well, it's a good thing that you went I guess."

If only I had gone sooner, I thought wistfully.

I wasted so much time.

I felt defeated.

The party had definitely stirred my desire to be more adventurous and playful but an overall feeling of sexiness seemed to elude me.

Images of Nick telling me he didn't think I was sexy raced through my mind again.

That night I slept deeply and heavily but not restfully. I woke with a feeling of uneasiness like I had had a dream but didn't finish it.

Manny and I spent the next day sorting through old boxes in our basement. We'd made a promise that we were going to get to spring cleaning before autumn turned the leaves and definitely before the snow fell.

It was the perfect distraction for both of us with the rain falling outside and an awkward uneasiness still lingering in the air after the episode the night before.

I rummaged through boxes of old clothing and stacks of papers from university that I had kept. Among the pile of exams and notes I found a stash of old pictures I thought I had long thrown out. With Manny busy organizing the tool section filled with barely used equipment *he had to have* I gathered up the pictures and ran upstairs to have a quick look at them.

The first picture in the pile was of me and Jonathan.

Seeing his smile brought back a flood of memories.

He was always so happy, so easy to please.

We were sitting on the steps of the library, his arm wrapped around me, my face twisting to get out of the winter sunlight. The picture was taken the day after we had had sex for the first time. I vaguely remember Mahjong taking the shot to celebrate my entrance into womanhood but from the expression on my face I hardly looked like I had just had a life-changing moment.

I had been dating Jonathan behind my mother's back for almost the whole first term in university and although we had fooled around a few times, I continued to hold back from the act of sex itself until my first Christmas break home when it became very clear that my life wasn't in my own hands.

Not if my mother had anything to do with it.

On a snowy morning when most people were tearing open presents from Santa, my Aunt Bimli was openly questioning my marital aspirations while having chai with my mother. She made it very clear to both of us that I was getting older by the minute and that no one would want to marry me once I turned 21. The only advantage I would bring to the bargaining table was a university degree and somewhat light-coloured skin.

"Oh ho! Who vill marry her?" she asked my mother tapping her chest for extra drama. "I mean just look at her, na? She's getting fat also."

"Hanh, but she has light skin, na? Don't vorry Bimoo. *Fikir na khur.*"

"But she cannot vait too long, Zarina. She vill be twenty-one vhen she graduates. Too old. Too old."

"Han, but she is getting degree," my mother said as though I wasn't in the room, "Many modern bride has degree now."

"She don't speak Hindi!" My Aunt turned briefly from the subject at hand to complain that her chai was cold and that she was still hungry.

"You vant biscuits?" my mother asked her. "Leena! Go get your Aunty some more biscuits!"

"Na, na!" she said and then shot me a dirty look when I didn't get up to fetch them right away.

I brought out a plate with nine cookies.

She took five.

"Let her finish her studies," my mother said taking the remaining four biscuits. "I get her married. I show her boys den."

"And vat vill you do about her hair?"

I suggested they put out an ad in the paper reading: "Good goat for sale - has some facial hair and degree - needs a good home."

Neither of them was amused.

It became extremely obvious that as soon as I graduated, my mother was going to go into hyperdrive and find me the first mustached brown boy that stepped off the boat.

I felt a surge of panic.

All I could remember thinking was there was no way I was going to give myself to a man I didn't love when I had one who loved and adored me patiently waiting to take the next step with him.

I said so long to my virginal existence in an unceremonious moment on my dorm room floor between Algebra class and Philosophy.

There were no rockets or fireworks like in the movies. I could only remember thinking that I was going to be late for my Philosophy class.

The act of sex itself was anticlimactic after years of build up. Sure it was nice to be touched and held. And it was nice to feel deeply close physically and spiritually with someone you cared about, but the actual act itself let me down. Maybe I had built it up too much, which might account for the sour expression on my face, frozen in time in the palm of my hand.

I flipped the picture over. Jonathan had scrawled on the back, "Love you for all eternity. You will always be my first."

I smiled and clutched the photo to my chest. He was a kind-hearted romantic who I knew, despite his intense love for me, would be an outsider in my culture and even more importantly, would never pass the test of my mother. I slid the picture to the bottom of the pile.

I laughed out loud at the photos that followed of me and Mahjong horsing around on campus and taking silly pictures of each other, and of both of us so drunk that only part of one person's head was fully in the shot.

Two pictures of Mahjong drunk.

One of me drunk.

And one of Mahjong mooning me while we were both drunk.

And my favourite of Mahjong's arms around me after I had thrown up, our feather boas half-shed all over our clothes.

As I put the pictures at the bottom of the pile the next image suddenly sent a chill down my spine.

Nick. Me with Nick.

The picture was slightly tattered at the edges. It was the only one I had kept of him.

The others I burned.

Looking at the picture more than ten years, later I couldn't remember why I had kept it over all the others.

Nick and I were at a restaurant with two of his friends. He had his large muscular arm slung around the chair behind me, his face so still it looked as though it was carved from stone. I was sitting upright, stiff, my body the skinniest I could ever remember it being, my face gaunt and my eyes lifeless.

The first thought that raced back to me as I looked at the picture: *I wish I had eaten the cheesecake in front of me.*

Even in the photograph I could see how on edge I constantly felt with Nick. Because of his formidable size, I felt a certain expectation to be the perfect female complement for a man that prided himself on how he looked.

I didn't eat what I wanted.

I didn't wear what I wanted.

I didn't say what I wanted.

The woman in the picture next to Nick looked like a familiar shadow. I felt an impulse to reach into the photo, shake her by her arms and tell her to run but at the same time I understood why she stayed.

Nick and Jonathan were so different in so many ways. Nick's style of lovemaking was so slow and precise that at one point I wondered if there wasn't something wrong with him. When I would instinctively try to change things up or bring humor and playfulness to our sex life, Nick would retreat emotionally. Sexually he had the endurance one might expect from anyone who dedicated every spare moment of his life to testing his personal physical limits but it wasn't long before I began to realize that longevity in an erection wasn't all that mattered.

I tried in vain attempts to communicate my feelings to Nick but they were either met with resistance or not taken seriously. It got to the point where I began to take everything he said personally; always unsure if there was a double meaning in what he was saying.

A comment about a girl's hair in the lineup for the bank machine would make me think he thought her hair was nicer than mine.

A comment about a server's blue eyes made me think he preferred them over my dark brown ones.

It got so bad that even a comment about a cloud in the sky made me think he was trying to tell me I was fat.

How could I be so different with different people?

I felt like I had changed so much from the innocent but slightly jaded girl in the picture with Jonathan. I hardly recognized her anymore.

But the gaunt and exhausted version of me in the picture with Nick felt like she was still inside me hiding under years of complacency and pounds of fat.

Why had my love life been such a mess all these years? I figured once I had sex, everything else would just fall into place.

With Jonathan, I was so caught up in the spiral of negative thoughts that haunted me thinking that my mother would find out about us that I never truly enjoyed the time we spent together as a couple.

With Nick, I thought I had found true love. He claimed to love my culture. He wanted to go out for Indian food all the time. He even had a history of dating only South Asian women.

We had broken up not long after the picture had been taken and my delusions of thinking I had found someone who could surpass my mother's expectations and would transcend the barrier of cultures between us came crashing down when our relationship ended.

All my dreams had been shattered and I was at the mercy of my mother's matchmaking skills, bitter and angry that I wasn't going to have my fairytale romance like all the non-South Asian girls I knew.

After university and a year of living at home with my mother I agreed to several arranged set-ups of boys that my mother deemed worthy and willing, all of whom either disgusted me or insulted my intelligence.

There were the ones with thick accents and head-bobbing, fresh-off-the-boat attitudes that I could barely finish one conversation with.

"So you are having degree?" one of them asked me as he slurped his tea from the cup I had given him.

"Yes, she does," my mother answered eagerly.

"Vat you planning to do?"

"She doesn't do anyting okay?" my mother interjected again.

"Actually I am applying to some administrative positions and hoping to get something soon."

"Hanh, I tink it okay for woman to work. I *let* you work."

"Gee, thanks," I said sarcastically, avoiding my mother's gaze.

"Hanh, I good. Not working of course when babies born. I vant six."

"You want six what?" I asked barely swallowing my own tea.

"Six babies of course." Crumbs of biscuit fell from his thick black moustache.

"Are you planning on having some of them yourself? Because I'm not having six children."

Complete silence.

My mother made me promise to keep my mouth shut when the next one rolled off the docks.

"You vent to university?" the next candidate asked.

"Yes, she did," my mother answered for me. I began to think it wouldn't be long before she just started handing out my marriage resume at the door when they came in.

"These *ghoras* they be doing da heroine in der na?" he whispered. "Did you do da heroine?"

"I prefer to call it smack," I answered with a smile.

My mother refrained from more set-ups for another six months so I could *straighten out my attitude.*

There were the ones that were born abroad like me which I reasoned were more sound choices based on at least the basic understanding that we shared the same cultural confusion.

One of them named Rahul was a running favourite for the first two meetings. He behaved like an angelic prince in front of my mother, but on our first outing together alone he drove me to a secluded beach where his true nature came out.

"So you can give me a blow job now," he said flatly as I started to head for the ice cream stand I thought we were going to.

"I beg your pardon?"

"I'll take that blow job now."

"Blow job?" I asked studying him to see if he was joking. "You're kidding right?"

"No. All the girls do it. Don't worry Leena, it won't count."

"*Count?* What are you talking about?"

"I mean if you don't have actual sex with someone who is brown then you're still a virgin. If you have sex with someone who's not brown then *namaste* to your virginity. And a blow job is that grey zone so it's not really sex. It's okay to do that. You get it?"

"Rahul, you're serious aren't you?"

He nodded and began to fidget with his belt buckle.

"I'm not giving you a blow job. I can't believe you would ask."

"You don't want to be single forever do you Leena? You better learn to play the game."

"Take me home, Rahul," I snapped. "I'm sure your mother can explain the rules of the game to me."

"Don't tell my Ma, Leena," he said sounding panicked. "I'll buy you ice cream okay?"

I didn't tell his mother despite wanting very badly to expose his blatant hypocrisy. To end the issue with my mother as to why I would reject such a wonderful candidate, I told her that he had said he had no plans to let his future mother-in-law live with us when she was older. That put an end to Rahul and brought the next suitor Dinesh to our door.

Dinesh was tall, muscular, suave and sophisticated. A real Bollywood hero that made me believe for one brief moment that all my dreams might still come true.

He was equal in size to Nick but where my former lover had no charm whatsoever, this oversized brown version had ample to spare. I was smitten the second his large frame filled our door.

I almost drooled chai out of the side of my mouth as I watched him texting on his Blackberry throughout most of the evening.

How did someone with such large and lovely hands work such a small device effortlessly? More importantly, how would those same beefy fingers feel against the delicate softness of my skin?

I felt myself getting warm. His hands were like the giant paws of a manicured bear. Before long I was fixated on them, thinking of nothing other than what they would feel like on my body and in my mouth.

My mother could take care of all the details of our wedding; I was mentally having sex with him before the tea had gotten cold.

"Leena has a degree!" my mother said proudly to Dinesh in the middle of my reverie. Dinesh's mother sat next to him and informed us that her son had graduated from Harvard and had taken a position in a prestigious law firm.

"You are doing da upper lewel job, na, Dinoojaan?" she cooed to her son.

I pictured his fingers in my mouth as he deftly continued to type.

"Un-hunh," he said without looking up from his Blackberry.

"He is driwing the porcha car," his mother continued to brag.

"Porsche," Dinesh corrected as I fixated even more on his large hands.

I imagined how his hand would look like a visual piece of art complementing his perfect body wrapped around what had to be the world's largest and loveliest penis.

"Leena also got a job," my mother said impatiently. "Tell them about it Leena."

I only heard some of what my mother had said. I was too lost in the fantasy I had created in my brain and my obsession with his oversized hands that instead of saying what I wanted to say I blurted out: "Job? Yes, I give lovely hand jobs."

"What did you say?" Dinesh asked looking up sharply.

My skin was red hot.

What had I said?

I only knew that from the expression of horror on both mothers' faces something had been lost in translation.

"Who vant more chai?" my mother asked pulling me roughly into the kitchen. "Vat you said in dere? Hand job, na? Vat is that? Like dis?" she asked as she motioned up and down with her hand on an invisible penis. I nodded unable to get the image out of my brain and stop the vomit from pushing itself to the surface of my throat.

"Please don't do that, mother," I begged her.

"Take dis plate of samosas out dere and shut your mouth, na?"

I obeyed but for the rest of the evening any lascivious thoughts of Dinesh were erased by the mental image of my mother signaling how to do a hand job to me in the kitchen. Even when he smiled at me upon my return, I was too embarrassed to make eye contact with him. I was scared that if I looked at him I might blurt out something even more inappropriate and from the look on his mother's face I could tell there was no turning back. Needless to say, a proposal never came from Dinesh's side of the family.

The set-ups continued and with every failed attempt to find a mate I sank farther into despair. I packed on all the weight I had lost and then some, stuffing cake, cookies and pie in my mouth whenever I felt the urge to pick up the phone and call Nick.

Months and months had passed and I still found myself blocking my number, calling his phone and hanging up just to hear his deep voice. I heard from mutual friends that he had become a project manager at a company called Traincom, but my efforts to find a contact number for him were in vain.

I momentarily covered the dark expression in my eyes in the photo of Nick and me and then lovingly stroked the image before seeing the last snapshot in the bundle that triggered another massive flood of memories.

Though the picture was of my father, I would always associate it with Manny and our wedding day.

I remembered some of the details of my courtship with Manny with alarming clarity but most are a general unromantic blur. Mahjong had been taking night school for small business owners when she met Isabelle, who was newlywed and taking the course to improve her husband Peter's company. They instantly became friends. Isabelle invited Mahjong to her thirtieth birthday party and told her to bring anyone she wanted. She brought me.

I was twenty-six, fat, single and unwilling to go out and meet a happily married woman celebrating a milestone birthday I was dreading myself but Mahjong threatened me as only she could so I gave in. My first thought when I saw Manny at her party was: *Even for a brown guy, that's a big nose. How does he find sunglasses to fit that thing?*

Manny spent most of the night talking to his buddies near the pool. He only said "Hi" to me once during the evening. I openly stared at his nose and said nothing in return. His smile was a disarming distraction from the tent perched above his lips.

He left early and I vaguely recalled thinking that since the only other brown person at the party was gone, I could safely drink my face off without fear that he would tell a cousin who knows a cousin who knows a mother who will tell my mother that I was drunk at a party. Everything after that thought is a blur since the only other important introduction I had that night was to a bottle of something called *tequila*. In my drunken haze I remember he returned to the party because he forgot to give Isabelle her birthday gift at which point I reintroduced myself to him spelling my name with three 'e's and a 'j'.

When Manny and I ended up meeting again it was almost two months later and completely due to chance. I was at an Indian grocery store, one of dozens that my mother had dragged me to that weekend in her quest for one ingredient to complete a new curry she wanted to create.

Manny was picking up some samosas. My mother was busy gossiping with the shopkeeper off in the corner while I was scrolling through the Hindi movies in the back trying to see if I could figure out which Western flick they were copies of.

"Don't I know you?" he said tapping my shoulder with his finger.

"That's original," I said sarcastically.

I turned to see his face and the sight of his nose instantly brought me back to that hot summer night. My eyes widened when I realized he might blurt something out about my drunken state to my mother and I would have to endure endless lectures about what a heathen I was and how hell would have a special place for hussies like me.

"I met you at Isabelle's party, didn't I?"

"Yes, I think I remember." I regretted uttering the words as soon as they were out of my mouth.

"*Think?* I'm surprised you can remember *any* of that night."

I would have been taken aback by his rudeness if it were not for his smile.

I was overcome by how dramatically his whole face altered, softened by the warmth in his easy grin and the crystal twinkle in his almost black eyes. I didn't have time to react because my mother sniffed the scent of a single boy, and came rushing to my side, waving ecstatically.

"Hoi hoi! Aren't you Shaila's boy?" she said extending her hand to his. He didn't have a chance to answer because her eagle eyes had picked up on the stainless steel ring on his pinky finger. "An engineer!" She beamed like she had just won the lottery.

"Yes Aunty." Manny smiled. "I am Shaila's son. How are you?"

My mother didn't answer right away. I could tell the wheels in her head were spinning at a thousand revolutions per minute.

"I am taking it you have met my daughter Leena? She has degree from university. She is accountant. She is working out at gym now. She is twenty-one years old."

I had gone through this routine before. There was no point in correcting my mother and embarrassing her publicly.

I worked *for* accountants but wasn't one myself. I had never stepped foot in a gym in my life and I was twenty-six, not twenty-one years old, but pointing out the inaccuracies of her tale only served to increase my anxieties at home. It seemed the older I got, the more she embellished until the only thing that was close to the truth was that the fact that I had a degree.

"You forgot to mention I can drive and brush my own teeth," I said sarcastically under my breath. My mother ignored me but Manny smiled and winked at me.

"I work out at the gym too," he said.

Poor fool. He had no idea what he was getting into.

"You do?! Na, na, of course you do," my mother gushed, "You be so handsome and so fit aren't you? Your mudder must be being so proud. You were living in England, na? Just moved back, na? Oh, but you did not get marriad yet, na, Manoj?"

I took a deep breath and tried to count to ten. I got to two.

"I prefer to be called Manny," he said to my mother.

"Like Almonzo from 'Little House on the Prairie'?"

"Exactly. I just haven't found my Laura yet."

I knew the reference would be lost on my mother.

"Who is Laura? You should only date *Desi*, na?" My mother shot me the *I'm going to smack the crap out of you later* look to get me to stop interrupting and cuddled up closer to my future husband.

"Uh, Ma, we should go," I said before my mother could invite him to our house for dinner, offer him a car to marry me and possibly slide him some cash on the side.

"Actually Aunty, your daughter and I have met before," Manny said smiling at me.

I was suddenly paralyzed with fear. My secret was about to be exposed.

Your daughter is a lush. She behaves like a dirty Western drunk girl behind your back.

"I was taken by her beauty then and she looks even lovelier now," he said. "I wish we had more time to talk that night but unfortunately I had to leave early to catch a plane."

My mother was actually speechless.

She must have been making silent vows in her head because no other words came out of her mouth. In her wildest dreams she could never imagine me married and out the door - *TO AN ENGINEER* no less.

It was the jackpot of all jackpots with the payoff not in dollars but in bragging rights to her other sisters and the elderly Aunty down the street who berated my mother every time she passed by about the fact that I wasn't married.

I smiled politely, tried hard to read the glint in Manny's eyes and fearing any outbursts on my part or my mother's, pleasantly bid him adieu and rushed my wobbling parent out the door. Once we were home, my mother raced to the phone, made four calls and by the same time the next day Manny was calling me to go out for dinner with both families' blessings.

We mutually agreed to take it slow despite the ever watchful eyes of our respective families who thought that when we were out on dates, we were merely waiting for a sufficient time to pass before announcing our engagement. Truth be told, Manny and I were finding interesting places to fool around without getting caught.

It took me a while to completely warm up to him, but his sincerity and his kindness won me over. Manny's greatest appeal laid in the one character trait he had that no other suitor before him ever possessed. He made me laugh.

When things my mother would say or do caused me anxiety, Manny was reassuring and patient, ready with a joke to make light of the situation or able to make me smile and take things less seriously.

On the eve of my twenty-seventh birthday, without any great romantic gestures, proposals or fanfare, we agreed to tell our families that we had made a choice we could live with.

Manny and I had already had sex several months before our wedding in a hotel room he rented because we were both still living at home with a parent.

The most shocking thing about having sex with him was the contrast of his darker skin against mine. I had only been with Jonathan and Nick whose skin tone was a crisp blank backdrop for my mocha-tinted flesh.

Our wedding was the traditional flash of brilliant colors, buckets of gold jewelry and literally hundreds of people I had never met before who were friends of my mother and late father or people that *had* to be invited for the sake of decorum.

I found myself sinking into sorrow before our wedding as I had little to do with the actual planning of the event. My mother planned Muslim, Hindu and village traditional ceremonies together. She had made the arrangements herself. All I had to do was show up. She did a special prayer asking for blessings in our marriage including one for my father specifically, which made me cry so hard that I had puffy red eyes the day of the wedding itself.

A non-denominational officiate conducted the ceremony. As I sat on the altar, listening to her speak about love and commitment, Manny leaned in and whispered to me to look under the trim holding down my headpiece. I discreetly fiddled with the edge until my fingers snagged against a small tear in the side from which I pulled out a picture of my father.

Manny bent down and whispered, "He's here with me, too." He showed me the same picture stitched into the flap of the vest of his *kurta pajama*.

I never found out how he managed to do it, but I knew at that very moment there was no other man for me.

It eradicated any doubts I may have had and only served to deepen my love for him.

So many years later, the picture still bore tiny holes at the edges where it had been sewn into my suit.

I wiped the tears away from my eyes as I stared back at the image of my father smiling back at me.

Finally, I flattened out the sides and placed it on the top of the pictures stashing them all away in an old philosophy text book I knew Manny would never open.

After a few more hours of sorting boxes in the basement, we decided it was time to break for a snack. I warmed up the handmade samosas my mother had sent us home with putting three on his plate and one on mine.

The afternoon sun had faded but was still streaming in the last of the day's light. I studied Manny's face as he sat across from me at the kitchen table. He prepared the three samosas on his plate filling each one with equal amounts of tamarind and coriander chutney. He was so meticulous when he ate his food.

I studied his hands as he began to tear up small pieces to eat. Somehow I had never really noticed how well manicured he kept them, how masculine but long his fingers were. They were the same fingers I had felt on my skin, in my hair and inside me for the last five years.

I squirmed in my chair and watched him lift small bite-sized pieces to his mouth; the same mouth that kisses me tenderly when I am sick, passionately when aroused and eagerly when between my legs. And yet in all these years those same fingers and mouth so adept at stuffing samosas into his hungry belly, were somehow awkward and fumbling when it came to pleasing me. Were those fingers and mouth actually capable of satisfying me or were they best-suited to pedestrian pleasures like eating and waving hello?

I couldn't stop staring at his hands.

As Manny opened his mouth to stuff a piece of samosa into it I caught a glimpse of his pink tongue glistening with saliva as it descended on the food. The sight of it triggered back the image of the ponytailed man in my fantasy that had brought me to orgasm. I averted my gaze to the food in my hand.

"Aren't you going to eat?" Manny said his mouth still full of samosa.

"Sure, sure," I answered absently.

Manny licked chutney off his lips and the sight of it made my mind race to the previous night.

I couldn't get sex off my brain.

As I watched him slurp the tamarind sauce from his fingers, I was suddenly struck by how awkwardly he maneuvered his own tongue.

Was he bad at oral sex or was it me?

I had enjoyed the sensation with Jonathan and even thought I felt myself come close to orgasm with him once. Nick was proficient enough at intercourse but oral sex always felt like it was something he did begrudgingly on me. I assumed if I got more proficient at oral sex on him he would make more of an effort, but I never got past the fact that I could tell his heart wasn't in it and as a result I never enjoyed it with him.

Manny always seemed to make a valiant effort. His heart was in it, no doubt, but his technique lacked precision. I felt like I knew what it would take to make it better, but I never told him because I was nervous that if I insisted he perform better he would ask for the same in return and I knew my own skills were sorely lacking.

I looked down at the samosa on my plate. Triangle shaped, just like the bald patch between my legs.

I traced the outline of the pastry with my fingers. That kind of stroking would probably feel good around the outer edge of my labia, I thought.

I fiddled with it studying its shape and texture.

"Did you ever really *look* at a samosa before?" I said to Manny, wondering if I was the only one who could see the similarity.

"These are good. You made them with your mother right? They aren't the store-bought ones." Manny stuffed the remainder of one of his samosas into his mouth, coriander chutney dripping from his lips.

"Uh, yeah I made them. But what I'm saying is *look* at it. Look at its shape. It's a triangle. It's a triangle shape."

"Yes," Manny said in a mocking tone, "and the table is a round shape. And the door is a rectangle."

I ignored his tone and broke the samosas in my hand, removing its potato and pea filling onto the plate in front of me leaving only the shell of the hollow triangle exposed.

I stared intently at it.

The top of the triangle rose up like the crest of my vagina where my clitoris was situated and the soft folds of the pastry trailed down gently like the flaps of my labia. I cleared the plate of the contents and cradled the shell in my hand as Manny absently watched in silence. I picked up one of the larger peas and placed it at the top of the triangle, the hood of the samosa gently cradling it in position.

"This is me." I showed him the carved out samosa. I could see he was unable to follow my logic. "This is like the shape of my vagina." I stared at him waiting for some recognition in his eyes.

Manny smirked and mindlessly grabbed more chutney.

How could he not see it?

I was so proud of myself for turning a samosa into a vagina but somehow Manny didn't seem to share my enthusiasm. I wasn't expecting him to keep it under glass on display it in his office like a piece of art I had sculpted with my own two hands, but a little recognition for the similarity would have been nice.

"Are you going to eat that?" He stuffed his mouth with the second last piece on his plate.

"Can't you see it?" I tucked the sides down more so that they resembled labia and pressed the bottom of the triangle up a bit so that the hollowed hole was more obvious. I held up the pastry to my mouth and when he still didn't respond I tried to prompt him by sticking my tongue out and mimicking a licking motion. He watched my tongue dart in and out. I instantly had his full attention. Something Clarissa said at the party came back to me as I watched his expression intently: *Men are very visual.*

"Oh yeah, sure, I see it now." Manny smiled broadly. "Especially when you stick your tongue out like that."

"Do you really, or are you mocking me?"

"No, I really see it, Lee." He leaned forward, shoving his plate away. Rejecting his last piece of food? He must be serious. "Do that again."

"No. I feel like a fool."

"Come on. Show me how it's done."

There was something playful but mocking about his tone. I realized I actually had a chance to tell him exactly what I thought I would like.

I just had to find the nerve.

I looked at the hollowed out pastry in my hand. I had already made a fool of myself by likening a samosa to my vagina so how much worse was I going to make it if I started to mimic oral sex on it?

I watched the Adam's apple in Manny's throat go up and down, his smile suspended, almost fixed in a quiet state of disbelief. I couldn't remember the last time I had his attention so fully.

What the heck? My dignity was already long gone.

I had nothing to lose.

I lifted the empty samosa up to my mouth and blew on it gently to remove the excess flaky pastry from the sides. From Manny's expression, he thought I had already begun to make love to it so I began to blow around the outside edge again, feeling the heat from my mouth emanating out.

"It should be gentle at first," I said blowing warm air on the rim and at the little green pea peaking out at the top.

I wasn't sure if he could even hear me. My voice was barely above a whisper.

"Nothing too shocking at first."

The floor vibrated from Manny's leg shaking under the table.

"It's nice to have small little licks here on the side," I said as I flicked my tongue over the edge of the pastry. "That always feels nice. And then maybe the tongue comes up here slowly," I said as I mimicked the words and gently opened my mouth to where the little green pea was waiting at the top of the triangle.

I looked over at Manny's expression, the sun almost completely gone; his face hidden in shadows. I couldn't read him fully but from what I could see of his face, I knew that he was engrossed, his smile replaced by the gape of his open mouth.

I turned back to the samosa in my hand, the light glistening off my saliva. I noticed the pea was about to slide out of place, so I put my finger inside the hollow and pushed gently up towards it rolling it into position at the crest. I lifted my finger to my mouth and moistened it, rubbing the wet tip against the pea so that is sealed itself firmly in place. I played with the little green ball twirling and rotating it gently under my dewy finger until it glistened like a jeweled emerald.

No longer aware of Manny's presence, I continued to finger the pea in place attempting to secure it at the top. I intermittently darted my tongue around the top edge of the pastry to moisten it hoping it would adhere the green sphere to the top of the triangle. I started to lick more vigorously, the saliva in my mouth increasing with each stroke, the pea securing itself neatly in place.

I opened my mouth wide to allow my tongue to protrude forward and darted it steadily in and out of the centre of the triangle in an effort to keep the hollow open. I could taste the remnants of flour and butter at the edges triggering a different type of reaction from my taste buds.

I was hungry.

I sucked at the little green pea tasting its salty residue, gently nibbling at the crispy hood atop it. A low moan escaped my throat as the pea wobbled at the crest. It started to sink towards the back of the triangle. I groaned fearful I would lose it and not get to enjoy at least some of my snack. My tongue flicked wildly at it trying to cajole it back to the front. Several seconds later it was back where I had placed it ready to be devoured.

I lifted my head up and surveyed the moist pastry in my hand.

The pea was practically glowing at the top of the samosa, the sides of the pastry were limp and damp from my saliva.

I looked over at Manny. His eyes were glassy, his mouth wide open, both of his legs were shaking heavily.

I sat back in my chair placing the glistening pastry on the plate in front of me. I wanted to eat it until it dawned on me that I had just performed cunnilingus on a samosa.

I suddenly wasn't sure if I should consume it or buy it a drink.

Embarrassment coursed through my veins.

How was I ever going to look at another samosa again? What was I thinking?

Did Manny wonder if I had finally snapped after years of repression into some kind of twisted snack molester?

I was too afraid to look up from my plate displaying the carnage of peas, pastry and saliva.

I saw Manny rise from his chair out of the corner of my eye. In a heartbeat, he was by my side reaching down to grab me by the wrist and pull me from my seat, his eyes so dark in the light they looked black.

"Right now," he growled under his breath, his words almost inaudible. His intention was very clear from his expression.

He drew me passionately to his chest and kissed me, a bit too forcefully at first and then with more controlled vigour. I wasn't able to process anything fast enough, my thoughts beginning to cloud over in the steam from the obvious desire I could feel firmly pressed against my hip.

"Here?" I said between breaths.

I realized what I was suggesting was sex in the kitchen, something we had not done since our first month in the new house, and even then on a carefully laid out blanket Manny had put down when the cupboards were still in disarray and we were waiting for the contractor to show up.

"Right here." His voice sounded even deeper as it reverberated in my ear. I started to sink into the intensity of it.

I felt him lift me onto the top of the table. In a moment of sheer indulgence and stupidity I threw the plates of food, tablecloth and chutney to the floor clearing the surface behind me. I heard the dishes break as they hit the ground and felt a splash of chutney against my ankle and foot. Before I could let my practical sensibilities take over, I felt my pants and underwear deftly being removed and Manny's fingers rushing between my legs along with a swirl of cool air.

The sudden touch of coolness with warmth left me shuddering and in shock. I felt him pushing my legs up to my chest and forcing my back down onto the table. My last coherent thought left when I felt the hot air of his breath against the slick baldness of my tender skin.

I involuntarily moaned with pleasure.

He licked the sides of my labia with slow and precise control.

My legs started to shake.

I felt his finger tip, warm and wet against my clitoris rubbing slowly and precisely, his tongue moistening it with small and rapid licks.

My bones felt like they were melting into the table.

When his tongue darted inside me I lost all trace of thought and succumbed to the intense pleasure of the feeling of his mouth so intimately seducing my skin.

I arched more instinctively towards him clenching fistfuls of his hair in my hands, feeling the repercussion of his heavy moans as they reverberated through my tender skin and deep inside me. A pulsation of feeling shot through my entire body as I felt myself crest towards that familiar place I had been to so many times before, my breathing more shallow, my mouth dry and opened wide.

Just as I felt myself rise to the sensation, Manny's tongue vigorously flicked up and down directly on my throbbing clitoris bringing with it a tidal wave of blood and warmth until I climaxed and felt every vessel in my body explode in hot ecstasy.

The magnificence of the moment brought me not only to orgasm but to tears as I relaxed against the table weeping; my heart as swollen with love for him as my genitals were with blood, pleasure and rapture.

I felt the tears gently cascade down the side of my face into my ears.

I raised my head to see Manny's expression, a mixture of passion and concern.

What little light was left in the room glistened against the moisture on his mouth. Impulsively I pulled his lips to mine kissing and tasting the union of his tongue with the salty sweetness of my own juices as they mixed in my mouth. We kissed ardently until I gasped out loud feeling the pressure of Manny's penis delving deeply inside me. I felt my inner muscles instinctively pulsate around his hardness and struggled to keep the tight sensation as he continued to thrust in and out.

I leaned my head back, pushed my hips forward and felt Manny's fingers gently rub the top of my clitoris. Then, without any warning, a deep wave of pleasure overcame me, the crest of ecstasy larger and more intense than the one only a moment before.

I felt the tears flow from my eyes again as I felt the warmth of Manny's own emission gushing inside me, his breath as shallow and jagged as my own.

He cradled me in his arms, my legs wrapped tightly around his body as we held each other on the table for what felt like hours until the brisk reality of spilled chutney and broken glass beckoned both of us back to reality.

Chapter 7

It's funny how time flies. A month had passed and I was already beginning to see a change in the mirror. Three regular spin sessions a week with Mahjong and the weight I had indulgently put on during the last ten years of my life was slowly starting to melt away.

My clothes were starting to sag around the hips, my blouses for work were too big and even my shoes didn't feel as tight as they used to. When I showed up at Mahjong's work to meet her for dinner, she commented on how loose my clothes were and insisted we forego the movie we had planned for a night of shopping instead.

"You've lost weight, Leena," she said beaming. "I can see it in your clothes!"

"I haven't lost enough yet, Mahjong," I said defensively. "I don't want to spend money on clothes now."

"Don't be ridiculous! All that sex you're having will make the rest of the weight just peel right off." I blushed. "You are having lots of sex aren't you?"

"I'm not answering that!"

It was true though.

Manny and I were having the best sex of our entire marriage. It was no longer something we scheduled to fit in to our weekend errands or a duty performed out of guilt or obligation.

It felt more fun. More inspired.

We grabbed a bite to eat in the food court and I followed Mahjong from shop to shop trying on whatever items she picked out for me, vetoing the ones with too deep a neckline or too snug a fit. In one of the stores, I came out of the change room in a pair of jeans that were so low my underwear rose up above the belt line looking like an extra flap of fabric accentuating my belly.

"What are you wearing under those jeans?" Mahjong asked as I stumbled back into the change room and tried to peel the pants off like an extra layer of skin.

"These jeans are the wrong size! I told you they were too tight."

"No, I mean were those your panties, Lee? What the hell have you got on under there?"

"Underwear. What else?" I heaved a long sigh when my legs were finally free.

"We have to go to the lingerie store. NOW!"

I looked at myself in the dressing room mirror.

My stomach had shrunk considerably but it was still lumpy in places, curvy in others. My breasts shrunk from the weight loss, were sagging slightly under the old fabric of my bra which was dulled and yellowed from frequent washes and time. I pulled up the straps of the bra and watched my breasts bounce up, looking perky and firm for an illusory moment.

I moaned inwardly.

I never enjoyed lingerie shopping. It made me feel uncomfortable and unsure of myself from the very first bra I ever tried on.

When my mother first noticed that it was time for me to wear a bra, I was excited because I thought my experience lingerie shopping was going to be as lovely as when my closest friend at the time, Carol, had bought hers with her mother.

They turned the whole experience into a special day, going for tea, shopping for shoes and buying lingerie like grown-up ladies. Carol was so proud of herself that she showed her fancy white cotton bra to all the girls in the washroom and regaled us with stories of how her mother called her a *little lady* and that they would be shopping for makeup and other special *big girl* items in no time.

I ran home and excitedly told my mother that we should go for tea and buy my first bra since that was what Carol and her friends had done. My mother winced, shook her hands at the sky and gave me $20, telling me to buy whatever Carol had bought. I was too embarrassed to ask Carol outright for any advice and avoided making the purchase clutching my $20 until the edges were frayed, the centre was torn and it was a wrinkled mess.

After a very painful gym class I realized I had no choice but to go shopping. I knew my mother wouldn't go with me so I asked my grandmother.

"We vill get you da best training bra dere is," my *Dadi* said as we trolled the discount bins in the local mall.

She managed to find a white cotton bra with a Velcro clasp in front that she told me to try on in the fitting room. I was uncomfortable and horrified when she lifted her weathered old hands to my breasts and squeezed them tightly to see if they would come out of the brazier. "Nothing like a bra dat doesn't keep dem locked in place. It can be wery embarrassing for you my darling Leenoo."

Having my elderly grandmother feel me up in the change room of the discount store wasn't all that wonderful either.

"I think this one will do," I said wanting to get the experience over with as soon as possible.

"Just like all de other girls now, na?" my *Dadi* said with a smile, her front teeth missing, her old skin rising up in lines around her mouth.

"Carol's had a small pink flower on it but this one will do." We paid for the bra. Instead of going out for tea, my *Dadi* took me to her house and made me chai and fresh samosas. While I cleaned up the kitchen she emerged from her bedroom with my bra in hand out of its box and dangling from her arthritic fingers.

"What is that?" I asked spying something on the front flap of Velcro.

"Just like all de other girls," she said with a smile lifting the bra up for me to see. She had crocheted a tiny pink and white flower to the front of the fabric and stitched it in place over the closure.

I was immensely proud of my new lingerie until one of the girls in the locker room spread the rumor that my family was so poor I couldn't afford a real bra like everyone else so I had to make one myself. My patchwork bra became a greater source of mockery as within weeks, all of the other girls had upgraded their cotton bras for lacey ones with wire.

I was too embarrassed to ask my *Dadi* to go shopping with me again so I turned changing my clothes in the locker room into an art, managing to hide from everyone and emerge fully clothed when it was time to take the field for class.

I didn't give my lingerie another thought until I started dating Jonathan.

I rationalized that it was my first real relationship and worthy of an investment in some sort of sexy undergarment that might come close to what I had seen other girls in the dorm wearing.

I found what I thought was the sexiest pair of lace panties I had ever seen for less than a quarter of what I paid for my first bra. They were a full panty of black lace with a red bow at the front. I wore them to class one day anticipating with excitement the look on Jonathan's face when he saw me in them.

As I sat in class, the lace dug into my skin and began to irritate the tender flesh between my legs and on my thighs. I started to subtly scratch at it at first and then itch it more aggressively until the professor noticed me vigorously rubbing myself between my legs and evicted me from the class for the rest of the lecture.

"Get your rocks off in your dorm room like everyone else," one of the girls sitting next to me commented snidely.

"Pervert," another shot at me as I fled from the room.

"Call me!" one of the boys from my row shouted.

I was too mortified to ever go back to that class again and instead of returning to it I borrowed notes from someone and settled for a C- rather than face further humiliation. My mother was very upset about the grade but I let her nag me about it endlessly rather than fess up and tell her the real reason I didn't do well in the class.

Nick made several comments to me that I needed to update my lingerie when we were together but never gave me any guidance as to what he liked. One day I bought a pink lace baby doll to surprise him but he laughed when I wore it and told me it made me look like swollen cotton candy.

I cried for two days.

Manny never made any comments about what I wore. Somewhere along the way, I stopped caring. The only thing that became important was function and simplicity.

Mahjong took me to a high-end lingerie store in the mall and showed me the wide variety of panties I could wear. Most of them looked uncomfortable and others looked like they would make me scratch myself in public again.

What was the point of sexy lingerie if your body protruded in directions it wasn't supposed to when you had it on? Looking at myself in the harsh lighting of the change room only increased my anxiety.

"These bras are too racy," I whined to Mahjong as she slammed the door shut on me in the change room.

"Just put one on Lee. Trust me. See how it *feels*, then decide."

I begrudgingly put the first one on.

Not only did it fit well, it looked good and it felt good.

It felt *really* good.

Nothing was bulging, nothing was squeezed in and the satin cups actually felt so soft that I was barely aware of the fabric against my breasts.

"Your underwear says something about you," Clarissa had said at the presentation.

I looked down at my tattered bra on the floor of the change room.

Mine looked like it was saying: "Put me out of my misery" or "She's quit on herself".

I picked out six new bras and promised to toss my old ones out. I was afraid that if I didn't Mahjong would check under my blouse to make sure I did. She had set aside the matching French cut panties for me and told me to pick out five G-strings as a gift from her.

I had no intention of buying them.

As I fiddled with one particularly stringy pair, a manicured brown hand crossed mine to pick up a white lacey thong.

"Leena?" I heard the delicate soft voice of my cousin Tinoo.

"Hi Tinoo," I said feeling the rush of blood floating to my face. I threw the G-string in my hand back towards the table. "How are you?"

"Engaged!" she said with delight and shoved her large three-carat ring towards my eye.

"Yeah, I heard. Good for you."

She was wearing a tight black vest, her tiny but perky chest pointing straight at me, her skin a soft brown hue. Her long straight hair cascaded like a soft black sheet from her head down past her shoulders. She was the epitome of youth, beauty and style.

I felt like vomiting.

"Where are your sidekicks?" I asked referring to my cousin Pinky and her friend Dimple who were never far from her side.

"I don't like to do my lingerie shopping with them around, you see?" she whispered. "They get a bit, uh, jealous. Are you going to buy that G-string?"

I followed her eyes to where the G-string I had tossed landed. It managed to snare itself to the protruding flap of my belt like a holster.

"I, uh, I don't know,"

"*You* wear thongs?"

It wasn't the sentence itself that bothered me.

It was the look in her eyes.

Like how could *you* Leena wear something sexy? Something risqué and so bold?

"As a matter of fact, I've just run out of all my thongs and I'm buying new ones," I said as though G-strings expired in the fridge like groceries.

"Oh, I didn't mean anything -" she said. I grabbed a pile of G-strings and headed towards the cash register. "You look like you've lost weight!" she shouted as I walked away.

Three stores, four new skirts and five new blouses later, there was practically smoke coming off my credit card.

I was emotionally and financially spent.

I awoke the next morning brimming with excitement. I had so many new clothes to wear I didn't know which ones to pick.

I decided on a pair of simple black pants paired with a white top adorned with large red and orange flowers and lacey sleeves. The perfect spring ensemble!

Okay, that's what I'm going to wear on the *outside* I said to myself… what about underneath?

I ran downstairs and grabbed the bunch of thongs that I had left to hang dry in a crevice under the stairs so that Manny wouldn't see them. He rarely did the laundry but on the off chance that he decided he wanted to do something nice for me, I decided to keep them hidden until I was ready to show them off.

I rifled through them and decided on the orange and black polka-dotted thong, one of many I would have thought twice about buying if I had not felt so enraged by Tinoo's comment.

I put the panties into the pocket of my robe and ran upstairs. Manny was running through his morning routine like clockwork. Showered and dressed, he would sit and read the headlines first, open sports page next, read the comics last and then fix two bagels, one crispy for me and one under-toasted for him. In that same twenty minutes I would have showered, dressed and joined him for our morning coffee before we would both head out the door to our respective cars and work.

I got out of the shower, slipped my new bra on and then fumbled with the G-string.

How the hell do they go on?

I turned it right.

I turned it left.

I hung it upside down and tried desperately to figure out which hole to stick my leg through.

Each opening looked equally as large as the last.

I may as well have strung it around my head because I didn't have the foggiest idea how it was supposed to fit.

I took a deep breath and grabbed the thickest part figuring it must go in the back, sliding one leg in the adjacent hole and then the other leg down the other side. I instantly cringed at the feel of the fabric crawling deep between my ass cheeks and my labia. I tugged on it and tried in vain to get it to settle into a comfortable position but no matter what I did, it felt unnatural and odd.

Mahjong had warned me that it wasn't going to feel *right* the first time I wore them. But was it supposed to be so invasive and uncomfortable?

Was this the reason supermodels always had such stern expressions on their faces?

I shifted a few more times until it felt moderately more comfortable.

Manny was right on schedule, putting his snack in a bag and two bagels in the toaster; one for him and one for me.

I put on my new black pants and white top. I threw on a pair of big gold earrings I usually wore to Indian functions as a last minute addition.

I had my hair styling down to a five minute routine growing more fond of my brilliant hair cut and bouncy curls with each passing day.

I took an extra few minutes to put on some mascara and lipstick and when I looked up at my reflection in the mirror even I was surprised by the results. I fussed with my pant seams trying to pull them away from the fabric of the thong and raced downstairs.

"You're - " Manny said and then paused as he saw me enter the kitchen. "You're late," he added sternly.

"Sorry," I said, more than a bit hurt that he didn't comment on my new outfit.

Was he angry at me that I had spent money on new clothes without telling him?

Did he not like the way I had done my hair and makeup?

Did he think the clothes were too tight and that I looked fat in them?

I wanted to ask him why he was in such a sour mood but I couldn't concentrate on anything but fabric riding up between my legs.

"Fuck! My bagel is burned!" he said angrily. "I'll have to get something at work now."

He grabbed his lunch bag and was out the door just as the words, "You didn't kiss me goodbye," left my mouth. I knew it bothered him when I dawdled in the morning, but I had hoped the extra effort I made would make up for it.

I grabbed my lunch and headed to work. Within an hour I was beginning to look like a backup singer in a Michael Jackson video constantly pulling on my crotch and wiggling my ass.

I sent a text to Mahjong reading, *Mahjong this thong is weird! I am so uncomfortable!*

A few minutes later she wrote me back. *"Call me Mah-thong. Ha ha! Sounds like that thong is on wrong. Call me."*

I went into the ladies room and made sure it was empty. I quickly dialed Mahjong's number at work.

"What do I do?" I whispered in complete panic. "This thing hurts me! It can't be right!"

"Did you put the tag in the back?" Mahjong said stifling laughter.

"There was no fucking tag! I'm not a complete loser. I looked. Now what do I do?"

"Take it off," she said matter-of-factly.

"What? I don't have any other underwear here!"

"So?"

I paused.

I hadn't even considered the possibility of not wearing any underwear. I took off the thong and tried to describe it to Mahjong on the phone. I heard someone come into the ladies room so I couldn't answer her as she gave me directions on how to put them on properly.

"Okay, I see," I said into the phone. "Yes I will be there for dinner." I waited until the lady who had come in left, and then hissed into the phone, "This is humiliating!"

"Don't take it so seriously," Mahjong said in a soothing voice. "I can't even count the number of times I've put my underwear on wrong. Mind you it's usually after a drunken night in a bar or because of a quick getaway from some guy who looked super ugly once the sun came up, ya know?"

"You're not helping me." I listened to see if there was anyone else in the ladies room. "Now tell me what to do."

She instructed me to place the thicker part of the fabric in the front insisting that there must be a small bow or rose at one of the joints to indicate where the back was. After closer inspection, I found the little bow she was referring to at the narrower portion of the G-string. I reluctantly slid the thong on wincing in advance at the thought of the chaffing to come but was pleasantly surprised to be met with a strange feeling of comfort.

"Oh that's not half bad," I said into my cell phone. "It feels so much better."

"Yeah, you had it on backwards," Mahjong said matter-of-factly. "No more swan thongs from now on okay?" She laughed at her own joke and hung up on me.

I wiggled my waist around and admired the way the fabric hugged my hips and thighs. From what I could see, it actually fit really well once it was on, and even looked a bit flirty and fun!

I slid my pants back on but then reasoned that while I was in the washroom I might as well pee. I sat down, slid the thong past my hips and began to relieve myself.

Something seemed odd.

After a few moments I found myself wondering why there was no sound accompanying the urine trickling out of me. Was this one of those *silent* pees you pray for but don't get when you know the person right next to you in the stall? I didn't give it much more thought until I began to stand up and felt something drip against my leg.

I had peed through my thong!

It was never fully off!

It must have been stuck in my butt crack, the thicker fabric still squarely in place.

When was the last time I urinated on myself? I thought in horror. When I was two?

My mind rushed in a thousand different directions.

How was I going to work with a urine-soaked G-string?!

What was I supposed to do now?!

I had no time to think or call Mahjong back to ask her what to do as I heard the sound of two women enter the washroom. I sat back on the toilet and tried hard not to cry.

I peed on my thong.

My thong was soaked with pee.

No matter how I put it, I was mortified. Instead of feeling like a sexy desirable woman, I had reverted back to the awkward embarrassments of a toddler.

There was only one thing I could do.

I removed the thong, cleaned myself up and put my pants on without any underwear on. The thong was damp and surprisingly only wet at the gusset so it wasn't difficult to bundle it up in paper as I was leaving the cubicle.

I waited until both ladies entered their own stalls before I left mine. The moment I stood up to leave, I immediately felt the brush of my slacks against my bare skin. To my surprise and delight, the gathered seam of my pants nestled itself between my labia lips sending tiny erotic spasms throughout my body.

When one of the accountants came by and asked for a photocopy I rose up from my desk, felt the tab of the seam in my pants press against my clitoris and giggled drool straight out of my teeth.

He took the paper and walked away, staring at me with a dazed expression as he left.

When a junior intern came in after lunch she asked me if I could help her bring in the boxes of cutlery and paper plates for our upcoming work party. We took the stairs down to the lunch room, the seam of my pants gliding devilishly in and between my inner labia.

"Are you okay, Leena?" she asked as she handed me a bag of paper napkins and plates.

I responded with a giddy laugh. I climbed the stairs, the rise and fall of my legs causing gentle nibbles of pleasure against my throbbing clitoris. I intermittently let out gasps and moans with each step up.

"I'll - gasp - take these - ahhh - to the - dear God! - conference room!"

I thought I might have an orgasm at the top of the stairwell but managed to keep myself in check.

Later that day, I made an appointment with Hannah to get myself waxed again. My hair had grown back and was starting to annoy me. I craved the smoothness of the skin after waxing and selfishly wanted to prove to myself that I wouldn't be as big a baby the second time around. She fit me in on my lunch the next day and though the waxing itself was still painful, I had taken aspirin beforehand, which helped.

I hadn't seen Manny almost every night that week because his hockey practices ran late. He seemed easily agitated when I did talk to him and since he could sometimes get into bad moods for a spell, I decided it was best not to irritate him further by parading around too much in my new clothes and lingerie in case we got into a fight about money.

By the weekend he was in a better mood but by then I had a few days of letting my imagination wander and was beginning to feel crabby by Saturday morning.

If he was so bothered by me spending money, why didn't he just say so? Did he think he was the sole bread winner in our house?

Did it bother him that I was starting to feel better, look better and take more pride in myself?

Was he only happy when I was fat and miserable?

Did he figure out that I had never had an orgasm with him until recently?

Was he angry with me for not telling him?

My mood was decidedly down after eating my morning bagel. I looked over at Manny mindlessly chewing an orange slice and writing out our grocery list.

I wasn't in the right mood to grocery shop with Manny, following him around on his regimented and established breakdown of the supermarket. As I watched him reach for the flyers and coupons knowing he was about to map out his strategy according to what was on sale, I excused myself and rummaged in the crevice in the basement where I hung my underwear out of sight. "Having a bad day? Wear these crotchless panties to the grocery store and I guarantee you that you will feel better when you get home." I could still see Clarissa in my mind's eye wearing the bright white panties over her black pants.

I wore a medium length skirt made of thin Indian cotton with a white t-shirt and slid my black parachute panties on underneath, careful to keep the bow at the back as instructed. My freshly waxed skin fluffed itself into position neatly between the two outside strings.

I couldn't help but take a quick peek before I headed downstairs.

From where I was standing, it looked like I was staring at a sideways smiling face with the tongue slightly sticking out. I smiled to myself and dropped the fabric of my skirt down, a pleasant and refreshing breeze tickled me as it wafted up around my legs.

My bad mood had already begun to dissipate.

"I can't wait to go grocery shopping with you!" I said to Manny as I grabbed my purse and cell phone.

Manny smiled for the first time that week.

"Really? Okay, let's go."

In the car I sent Mahjong a text message, *"I'm wearing my crotchless panties while I run my errands today!"*

She wrote me back, *"I'll look for the ho in the grocery sto'!"*

The normally mundane drive was made more interesting with every bump, pot hole and curve in the road. I had to keep turning my gaze away from Manny as he drove to avoid letting him see the grin on my face.

Opening the car door to the warm summer breeze brought my skirt up to my knees and a huge smile to my face.

Was it the fact that I *felt* like I had underwear on but at the same time I felt exposed?

Was it because I could feel the back of the panties ever so gently rising up and tickling me between my cheeks?

I was only sure of one thing. Clarissa was right. It was the best $17.95 I had ever spent in my life and we hadn't even gotten out of the parking lot yet.

The grocery store was its usual bustle filled with weekend shoppers, children and the elderly. The moment we entered the main foyer a small child ran up to me and tugged on my skirt. It set off a white hot panic and instant twitch between my legs as the little girl's mother ran to pick up her daughter and apologized profusely.

"Are you okay?" Manny asked in response to the obvious fear frozen on my face.

"I thought she was going to lift up my skirt."

"I thought that was my job." Manny's expression was dark without the slightest hint of playfulness in it. The look in his eyes and the tone of his voice shocked me almost as much as the threat of the child outing my scanty underwear.

Why was he angry again?

"Let's get started on the list," he said sounding a little less agitated.

He headed off towards the oranges as he always did, every Saturday without fail.

I took a few steps hesitantly at first and then in longer more open strides towards the vegetable section.

The crisp air conditioned coolness felt invigorating against the warmth of my legs. Every step I took forward forced long breaths of air under my skirt, up towards my exposed genitals. I could feel a moist dew between my legs, a mixture of both sweat and excitement.

My senses went into hyperdrive.

I noticed no one in particular and everyone at once.

Were they looking at me?

Did they know?

I smiled at an old lady bent over the watermelon bin.

"Can I help you pick one?" I asked, a huge smile already on my face anticipating what it would feel like to bend myself forward into the crate with the large melons in it.

"Aren't you kind?" she cooed. "Yes, please dear."

I reached into the crate flopping my tummy over the edge and sticking my ass into the air, the folds of my skirt gently wafting down towards the crease in the back of my panties.

I giggled.

I tried to lift one of the larger melons towards me and felt myself lose my footing slightly. My legs started to shake, liquid sweat beading up between my thighs.

I reached down for a smaller watermelon and raised myself from the crate producing it for the old lady to inspect. She thumped it with her wrinkled knuckles and shook her head. I put it back in the bin feeling myself lift up higher into the crate, my ass teetering at the edge.

Could she see up my skirt?

I started to panic.

I pulled another watermelon out of the crate. She thumped and rejected it again.

By the fourth choice, I was giddy with excitement and panic mixed together.

"It's so good to meet a nice young lady like yourself," the old lady gushed.

I'm actually a pervert ma'am, I said to myself as I slowly walked towards the veggie section.

I picked up a tomato in my hand, plump and red. I slowly stroked its thin skin feeling its firmness against the softness of my hand.

It felt familiar. It felt ready to burst under the slightest pressure.

What did it remind me of?

I closed my eyes and continued to stroke the orb gently squeezing it at the top of its fleshy mass bringing mental images of my own breast tissue to mind. I picked up a firmer, less red one, the leafy green stem attached to it nipped my finger tip and I was suddenly reminded of the eighth grade.

I had become lax about hiding when I changed in the locker room. One morning in gym class, I removed my top and bra when one of the girls getting dressed next to me plunged her face towards my nipple area as I was reaching for my towel.

"Ewww!" she said. "Is that hair on your titties?"

I looked down to where her eyelashes were almost brushing my areole.

I covered myself quickly.

"Ewww!" she continued. "Leena has hair on her titties!"

I cried for a week.

Manny placed a large bag of navel oranges into the cart he wheeled towards me.

He stared at me in silence for a moment.

"Do we need tomatoes?" he said with a puzzled tone, snapping me out of my reverie. "You didn't write it on the list."

He seemed bothered again.

"Have you ever really felt a tomato?"

"Do you want them or not? I'm heading over to the pineapples. They're on sale."

I gingerly placed the tomato back to the stack.

"Meet you there," I said as he walked away with the cart.

I stopped in front of the large bin of green English cucumbers at the end of the aisle.

Was it just me or did everyone see that they looked like large green dildos wrapped in cellophane condoms?

I plucked a long cucumber from the bunch in the bin and began to stroke the length of it with my hands.

It was so firm, so much denser than the tomato. I caressed the length of it in my hands as a long forgotten memory came rushing back to me.

It was my first trip away from home. My mother had deemed it worthwhile because it was organized by the *Desi* community.

I was sixteen years old and joining several of my cousins and a few kids from school for a weekend multicultural camp and workshop. We were supposed to be discussing how culture made an impact on us as developing sons and daughters of immigrants. Instead, most of the kids spent their time sneaking alcohol into their water canteens and cavorting in the bushes at night when our trusting chaperones were long asleep.

I hid in my dingy bed in the tiny log cabin I was sharing with my cousin when she was called out by the other kids to join them by the lake. She pleaded with me to come but I decided against going. Moments after she left, sitting alone in the smelly cabin, I decided I did want to join them after all and raced into the dark hoping to find her.

I ran into Amrish Gupta half way to the lake. He emerged from behind a tree clutching his pants.

"Lee!" he said, waving his arms in the air. "Come over here! I want to show you something."

I could barely make him out in the dark, his tanned skin blending seamlessly into the night.

"I'm looking for the others at the lake," I said cautiously heading towards him.

"I have something for you," he said as I drew nearer.

He reached out for my hand and placed it in his.

He slowly led my hand down to the crease of his jeans where he placed my fingers and gently squeezed them.

I wasn't sure what I was feeling at first.

"It's okay," he said, "I put a cucumber in my pants."

He laughed nervously and I felt the large bulge move under the weight of my hand.

I screamed and ran back to my cottage barricading the door with two chairs and a desk.

I moved my hands up and down the length of the cucumber smiling at the thought that Amrish was now married with two children and living in Canada successfully running a pizza franchise.

I wondered if he ever thought about that dark night near the lake.

"Do we need cucumbers? Oh yes, we do," Manny said grabbing the one from my hand, placing it in the basket and carefully crossing the item off his list.

"Not that one," I said with a smile and handed him a different one. I didn't want to look into the fridge at the length of the green vegetable and think of Amrish all week.

"Whatever. Okay I'm going to go and get some coriander for the chutney. You're making me samosas with your mother tomorrow right?"

I nodded.

Even the thought of spending an afternoon stuffing and sealing samosas with my mother didn't upset me.

I silently wondered if I should wear my crotchless panties to her house as well.

I might never take them off.

"I want to make eggplant," I said as Manny picked up a bunch of green coriander and raised it to his nose gently sucking a leaf in and out of his large nostrils.

"Okay you get it," he said absently.

I walked briskly towards the beans, carrots and seasonal vegetables, feeling the breeze between my legs as I spun on my heels around the edge of the bins.

I slowly dragged my hands over the eggplants feeling their tight skin against my finger tips. I picked up a large dark purple one and thumped its bulbous end with my thumb listening to the hollow echo underneath. I cradled its chubby end in my hands and held it up to my gaze.

"You look like a fat eggplant in dat suit," I could hear my mother saying to me as I walked into her house on our way to a wedding function earlier in the winter.

It was the only suit I owned that still fit me and that I felt good in.

She criticized the length of the top of my suit and the style of the pants telling me that everyone would be mocking me if I showed up in it.

I didn't care.

I heard her and a few of the ladies she was sitting with say eggplant in Hindi several times behind my back at the ceremony. They weren't serving it at dinner so I knew they were talking about me.

"Leena?" I heard the accented voice of my Aunt over my shoulder.

"Jumma Aunty," I said bowing my head respectfully to her and putting down the eggplant to kiss her hand.

"No need yaar for formalities. Vat you doing here?"

"Grocery shopping," I said trying to fight back the urge to be sarcastic.

"Vere is Manny? You pregnant yet?"

"Which question do you want me to answer first?" I asked, biting my tongue inside my head.

"You must be getting pregnant now, na? It's really getting on late, yaar. Come now okay? Don't eat this eggplant to get pregnant okay? You eat *bhindi*. It works, na? I eat *bhindi* every day for one month and yeah, got me pregnant. I get you some."

"No!" I said to her as she hurried away to pick up some fresh okra for me.

"Here's the coriander," Manny said placing a large bundle of the green herb into our basket. I could smell its fragrant perfume waft up gently towards my nose, triggering a memory of the first time Jenny came over to my house for dinner just before announcing her engagement to Johnny.

We had been preparing a salad together waiting for Manny and Johnny to join us after their hockey practice.

"I just love exotic spices," Jenny said watching me, her eyes wide with excitement. I smiled and chopped up some coriander to put in the salad. "How traditional! Are you going to put corry-ender in the salad, Leena?"

"Uh, yes," I said slowly. "Why? Is that a problem?"

"No, no! It's just so exotic! I never do that. But I do love the corry-ender. I eat moosala ch-eye too."

"I don't put coriander in my tea," I said with a wry smile.

"I know!" She had a gentle and sweet laugh that I suspected must have been the first thing Johnny fell in love with about her. "I'm just saying how excited I am about the traditional food we're going to have. I guess you're making *dosas* and butter chicken for dinner?"

"I was going to serve a casserole actually."

"Corry-ender casserole?"

"No. Just vegetables and pasta. I'm only putting coriander in the salad."

"So what's a casserole? Is that like a casserole I would make?"

Dinner that night was a torturous affair for me. My cheese and vegetable casserole failed to impress, and feeling the need to make the night more suitably exotic for Jenny, I pulled out our wedding pictures for them to see despite Manny's rolling eyes and hand gestures.

Jenny gushed over the vibrant colors and foreign fabrics as I showed her photos of the different ceremonies and tried to explain their significance to her. Johnny lost interest as soon as the album came out, exiting the room with Manny to watch a hockey game in the basement while Jenny and I made small talk over the pictures.

Jumma Aunty plopped a large bag of okra into my basket and pinched my cheek followed by a smarting slap against my face. "You try dis now. It will work for the baby, na? Okay bye Manny. Good to see you darling. You're such a good boy."

"I'm craving my veggie casserole," I said to Manny as Jumma Aunty plodded off towards the cash registers. "I want to put the fake meat in it though."

I spied the refrigerated salad section nearby and walked legs further apart than necessary towards the packaged foods and gourmet cheeses.

The cooler, as though it knew I was wearing crotchless panties, greeted me with a crisp breeze emanating from the wire grates at its base. I instinctively spread my legs a bit wider and pushed my hips backwards to angle the breeze straight up my skirt.

I bent myself into the cooler to survey the array of tofu-based products unable to focus on anything directly except for the coolness coming from the vents.

I absently picked up products and put them back imagining how sultry and seductive I must look to anyone walking by.

I felt so good, so sexy.

I thought I must look just like a runway model posing over the cooler in an ad for veggie meat.

I caught a glimpse of myself in the side glass of the cabinet.

I looked like I had rickets.

"Did you hurt yourself on the chair this morning?" Manny asked as he picked up the same package I had put down twice already.

"No."

"Why are you standing like that then? Does your back hurt?"

"I want to buy these tofu sausages," I said matter-of-factly, my smile more playful and mischievous than my words.

Manny rolled his eyes and put the package into our cart, added the item to his list and then crossed it off.

"I need more cold stuff. The cold stuff is good. I'm going to the freezer section," I muttered to myself.

"Not yet, Lee!" Manny said in a snapping tone. "I have to get this other stuff first. We'll get there in time. That's last on the list."

I didn't think I could wait.

Walking away from the cooler I felt myself long for the refreshing feeling as soon as it was gone.

I watched Manny meticulously mark things off his list from noodles to tea bags growing more and more anxious with every item he put in the cart. I commandeered control of the buggy so that I could walk with my legs slightly apart leaning against the top rail feeling the swish of air all around me.

"Are you sure you didn't hurt your back?" Manny said as we rounded the bread section where the freezers were finally in sight.

"Not at all. We need french fries!" I said in a voice louder than I intended.

"Jeez Lee, if you want to get all this stuff why didn't you tell me about it on Wednesday when we wrote the list? I think I have a coupon for some. Hold on."

Manny fished in the pocket of his summer coat to take out the weekly flyer. He nodded and smiled as he ripped out a 50¢ coupon for wedge fries placing it gingerly in his wallet between the others he had already collected.

I resisted the urge to run full tilt through the aisle towards the frozen food section. Seeing no one around several of the cooler doors I broke free from Manny who was squeezing buns for sandwiches and headed straight to the glass cabinets all in a row.

I pulled the door open so forcefully that the cold air from the compressor behind the frozen goods made a hissing sound and blasted a snap of frosty air that wafted over me like an icy wave.

I felt my nipples instantly pop erect, the impulse to squeeze my legs together immediate and overwhelming. Instead I pulled my skirt up a bit to let the frozen air find its way up my legs toward my bald and goosepimply body.

Why hadn't I bought these panties in every color?

"Not those fries," Manny said as he threw some bread into our cart. "I have a coupon for the wedge ones. Those are in the other door I think."

"I'll get them!" I said whisking past him to pull on the next door and feel the rush of air again.

"Why are you standing like that Lee? What the hell is wrong with you today?"

I heard his words floating like clouds around my head. I could vaguely see his concern from the corner of my eye but my grip on the door was tight and unyielding, my desire to crawl right into the cooler becoming dangerously high. Manny grabbed a carton of ice cream from the section next to where I was standing, the cold breeze doubling in intensity with both doors open.

"Lee? Lee! Are you listening to me Lee?"

"Ahhh," I murmured. "Frozen food section. They should call it sextion. Like sex you know? Spell it with an "x". Ahhhh…"

Manny backed up and stared at me with an expression I had never seen before and could only assume would be the kind he might sport prior to admitting me to a mental institution.

Fearful he would completely lose patience with me, I decided to let him in on my secret.

"I'm wearing crotchless panties," I said to him in a voice above a whisper.

His eyes widened as he absently dropped the tub of ice cream into our cart. I assumed he didn't understand the concept, after all it was foreign to me up until a few months ago, so I emphasized in a slightly louder voice: "There is no crotch to them."

Manny's expression was as frozen as the bag of peas I was dying to straddle.

"My girlie bits are hanging loose! You get it? *I have no crotch in my panties!*"

"We are doing alterations now *beta*," I heard a familiar voice behind me say. I turned to see Mr. Chandiwalla standing next to me with his large white grin against his dark brown skin. "You can be bringing your pants to the cleaners now. I put the crotch back in dem for you okay *beta*? We are doing alterations now. Do tell your mother also so she knows."

I stood with a smile as frozen as Manny's and nodded to the old Indian dry cleaner, muttering a polite thank you and good day. He trundled off with his cart, the smell of curry mixed with chemical cleaner wafting behind him.

"You could have told me he was there!" I snapped at Manny.

"Are you *really* wearing crotchless panties?" he said in a voice just above a whisper, his expression slowly changing from shock to something more playful and bright.

I nodded and smiled, afraid to declare anything else out loud since, with my luck, my grade two school teacher or a nun might walk by next.

Manny's eyes widened even further.

"Do you really think it's a good idea to get me so aroused in the grocery store?" he asked in a hushed tone.

"What are you going to do? Throw me down on the lettuce and fuck the croutons out of me?" I said with a smile. "Oh, that reminds me, we need to buy stuff for a salad. You know what that means? Back to the refrigerated cooler!"

I closed the frozen food door and quickly strode to the vegetable section with Manny in hot pursuit. For the first time in years and some hundred grocery lists later, Manny left his well planned attack of the grocery store aside to blindly follow me as I twirled my skirt around, giggling with each burst of fresh air.

Standing in the checkout line, Manny stroked my arm, face and back like he did when we were first married, leaning in to randomly kiss me on the shoulder or forehead. He got flustered when he paid, completely forgetting his coupons until I mentioned them before the final tally.

Sylvie, the barely nineteen-year-old cashier, rolled her eyes at what she must have thought were repulsive older people canoodling in the checkout line.

I took the opportunity to whisper in Manny's ear as he fumbled for the coupons. "By the way, did I mention that I had another Brazilian wax done? I'm as bald as your Uncle Vindoo down below."

For a brief moment I was afraid that Manny might have a stroke in the grocery store. His eyes widened so far that I could see the whites all around them.

He suddenly became hyper focused, throwing our groceries into our enviro-sacs with abandon and barking at the checker to go faster. I picked up a few bags and barely caught up to Manny as he tore through the parking lot, dodging small children and a man with a walker pushing past everyone impatiently to get to our car. By the time I reached him he had already loaded the trunk and was recklessly throwing our cart into the receptacle area.

"What's the rush?" I asked as I slowly slid into the car.

"I feel like taking you to the back parking lot and having sex with you there," Manny said slightly out of breath. "I'm not kidding Lee. I'm so turned on right now."

I impulsively guided his hand up my thigh feeling the warmth of his fingers against my cool skin until it met the heated centre between my legs. He flashed me the same smile I fell in love with so many years ago, his eyes wide with excitement.

"Manny we haven't *parked* since we were first going out."

"Are you kidding me?" he said as his fingers wandered over the flesh of my exposed skin. "God, that feels so good."

I stopped Manny's hand before he could delve any deeper as Mr. Chandiwalla walked past our car and absently smiled at us while mimicking the motion of weaving with his free hand.

I thought I would be more mortified than I was.

Nothing could stop how good I was feeling.

Not even the look I knew I would get from my mother when Mr. Chandiwalla told her to make sure to tell me to bring in my crotchless pants for repair.

It was the most spontaneous, young and alive I could remember feeling in a long time.

Manny shoved the car into drive whirling around the backstreets towards our house. I felt the edge of my panties crawling towards my inner labia. I reached under my skirt to make what I hoped was a subtle adjustment. Manny must have thought I was touching myself because he slammed the car to within an inch of the one in front of us.

My stomach lurched from the jolt.

His jaw clenched and unclenched as we sped around the residential area dodging cyclists and a dog walker until squealing the car's wheels he maneuvered us into our driveway.

He was in the house before I could get my seatbelt off. I held my stomach feeling queasy and uneasy on my feet.

I entered the doorway slowly, unsure of where he had gone or why he hadn't taken the bags out of the trunk.

As I came in Manny grabbed me and lifted me towards the front staircase. I could feel the pressure of his fully erect penis against my inner thigh.

He kissed me passionately, without precision but so intensely full of hunger that I found myself reeling between shock and arousal.

I arched against the steps marveling at how the angle of how I was sitting forced my legs into a more open position. Manny who never wanted shoes cluttered in the foyer and was meticulous about the cleanliness of our entrance way was making love to me at the foot of our front stairs.

I took in a long, deep breath of air, reveling in the moment until I finally succumbed to the heat radiating from his skin and the pressing need of his body with mine. We made love passionately, fusing into one seamless entity, like the ice cream melting in the trunk.

The next few days were blissfully wonderful. Manny was in a good mood, I was in a *great* mood and life was sweet.

One night in the middle of the week I attempted to seduce Manny into having sex with me, but my gestures and comments still felt awkward.

I tried oral sex on him without the warming lotion and though I oozed enthusiasm and he seemed very grateful, my technique was still lacking. I was too embarrassed to ask Mahjong for tips fearing she would whip a banana out of her purse and perform fellatio on it in the middle of lunch. I sent her a text hoping to ease myself into the conversation before she picked me up for our next spin class.

"*I need help improving oral sex on Manny,*" I wrote.

"*I was PORN to help you,*" she wrote back.

I started to sweat the moment I read it.

What did she mean by that?

Mahjong didn't bring up the text the entire time she drove me to the gym or during the class. Finally, once we were in the change room she shoved two movies into my hand insisting it was going to be the best three hours of my life.

"*Porn?*" I whispered to her. "Are you kidding? This is offensive. I can't watch this. It's degrading to women!"

"What the fuck are you talking about?" Mahjong said shoving the videos in my purse. "These were *made* by women. I have the whole series."

"What? Women made them?"

"Yes!" she said. "I often thought about going into that business myself but I love buying clothes and shoes so a boutique suited me better. I might still try my hand at it one day. I have this great idea for a movie set in the future but with vampires and some robots. I know it sounds weird but it all works in the end. The robots are vibrators you see! Anyway it's temporarily called *"Buzzy and the Blood Suckers"*. I work on the script in my spare time."

I had no comeback and was too nervous about delving deeper into her twisted psyche so I took the movies, covered them with a towel and my shoes and headed out the door.

Mahjong whizzed through the security gates at the front door of the gym.

I followed two people behind her promptly setting off the alarm.

"Do you have videos in your bag?" the taut young man behind the counter asked me nicely. I felt new sweat spring to life on my body.

"I, uh," I sputtered. "Mahjong!"

But it was too late.

She was already heading out the door and out of ear shot.

The gym rented current movies to members free for the weekend and if you didn't check them out at the front desk the alarm would go off. There must have been some kind of electronic tape still on the movies Mahjong gave me.

How did she get them in without a peep and I set off the alarm?

"You can just give me the movies and I will swipe them here. They likely didn't get demagnetized," he said extending a well formed muscular arm towards me.

"I didn't rent movies," I said feebly. "I don't have *any* movies on me." Just as I uttered the words Mahjong returned and asked what was taking so long.

She looked from the guy at the desk, to me frozen in the middle of the security gates, and said, "Oh did your movies set off the alarm?"

The young man's expression turned from kind to harsh within seconds.

"I thought you said you didn't have any videos," he said accusingly.

"I don't!" I considered bolting for the door, taking my chances with the police and suffering through the look on my mother's face when she came to bail me out of jail.

"They are my videos," Mahjong said brightly. "I bought them at the mall and they must have forgotten to take the strip off."

"I'm going to need to see them." The young man crossed his arms making his frame even more imposing.

"Sure," Mahjong said in a sweet tone, pulling the videos out of my purse and knocking my shoes to the floor.

She handed them to him.

He looked down at the covers, looked at me and then looked back at Mahjong.

They exchanged a smile that made me very uncomfortable.

Two days later they went out on a date.

I held on to the movies for a few days waiting for the best possible time to watch them alone.

The opportunity presented itself when Manny went on a course the next weekend. As luck would have it, my mother had gone out of town with her sisters so I had no responsibility or fear of being caught.

The timing couldn't have been more perfect!

I ran to the laundry room where I had hidden the two movies behind the dryer and decided to watch them on the big screen downstairs instead of the tinier television in the bedroom.

I popped the first one in. "*Dirty Danger, the Midnight Bone Ranger.*"

The cover had a busty blonde bent over, ass in air, standing beside a wooden fence on a ranch. I couldn't remember the last Western movie I liked but I figured it wouldn't make much of a difference in this case.

I made myself comfortable, remote in hand, while the initial warnings of sexually explicit and dangerous behaviors flashed on the screen.

I fast forwarded the opening sequences as names like Tarty Bazooms and Hugo Bigboner whizzed by.

The first scene opened on a lush field of grass scaling up to a large red ranch, with apple trees and mountains in the distance. A scantily clad brunette with a round nametag reading *Sugar* on her tiny top mumbled to herself that she was lost on the range and was going to have to get someone to help her find her way back to the highway.

She wandered around the field for no apparent reason flashing her pink G-string to the camera as she walked towards a red brick house. Her breasts were easily four times bigger than mine, her ass was round and tight and her fingernails were long, obviously acrylic and manicured with tiny diamonds in each nail.

What the hell was she doing in the countryside?

Sugar came up to the front door, unbuttoning the top two buttons over her heaving cleavage before ringing the bell.

The door opened.

An oversized, very pumped up and tanned man in overalls with a toothpick in his mouth came out of the house.

"I'm the Bone Ranger" he said in a horrible attempt to speak with a Southern accent.

"I'm Sugar," Sugar cooed back to him. "I'm lost."

"Is what you're looking for in my pants?" the Bone Ranger asked.

I stopped the movie and rewound it just to be sure I hadn't hallucinated how ridiculous the dialogue was.

Another two rewinds more and I was convinced that this movie wasn't going to provide me with anything of value I could use in my own sex life. Without further introduction, Sugar was on her knees and the overalls were down around the Bone Ranger's ankles as she promptly started to spit and suck on his oversized penis.

I picked up the phone.

"Mahjong! Bone Ranger doesn't even *know* this girl! What the hell is going on?"

"Ah," Mahjong said easily. "You're watching the movie. Yeah, just suspend your disbelief and keep going. You can learn a lot from Sugar's technique."

"She spit on him!" I said in disgust. "And that thing in his pants is massive!"

"It's not that big," Mahjong said calmly. "And spit's okay. Keep watching."

I hung up the phone and continued to watch as Sugar swallowed the entire length of Bone's penis in her mouth. She sounded at one point like she was going to gag on it but came up for air and flashed him a devilish look with her eyes which caused the large Ranger to groan.

Sugar slobbered at great lengths on the Ranger's great length for a few more minutes until she was lifted onto a porch swing nearby so that she could be ravaged by the cowboy.

As soon as he had removed her panties I was intrigued.

She was as hairless as I was and didn't look anything like me.

I silently wondered to myself if I had ever seen another woman that close up before.

I hadn't.

I was fascinated.

The big cowboy had some good tricks up his sleeve that made Sugar writhe about on the wooden swing. She's going to get a splinter in her ass, I thought. That won't be pleasant. How will they write that into the script?

Before long the Ranger had slipped his large circumcised penis into Sugar with the camera so close I feared it might get covered in liquids flying out of either one of them.

I wasn't aroused.

I was nervous for her on the swing and wondered why I didn't find the storyline tantalizing despite the fact that Sugar wouldn't stop talking and kept on repeating, "Fuck me harder cowboy! Fuck my wet pussy!"

"Mahjong, I don't think I like porn," I said calling her again.

"Give it a chance Lee," she said calmly. "Fast forward that one to the third scene."

"You know the scenes by heart?"

"Just do it. And relax would you?"

I hung up again and fast forwarded over Bone Ranger's explosive finish on Sugar's busty chest and through another scene in which another similarly clad cowboy got busy with a blonde who was sitting in a car that I assumed belonged to Sugar.

The third scene started in a softly lit dinner hall with candles burning on the edges of a long sideboard with two very provocatively dressed women sipping wine and chatting.

There was a blonde with large, natural breasts and a brunette with an average-sized chest not much bigger than mine. They were both engaging in easy, natural conversation as soft music played in the background. I had no idea how the range house could be transformed into such an elegant dinner hall or who these two women were but I assumed it was because I hadn't followed the storyline through its prescribed scenes.

The brunette softly touched the blonde on the arm and the pair started to deeply kiss each other and stroke each other's bodies.

To my surprise, I was getting aroused.

I watched intently as the two of them slowly undressed each other, gently caressing arms, necks and the soft curves of each other's breasts. I sat upright and keenly watched as they began to lick each other's nipples. The music died down slightly so that I could hear them moaning and asking to be touched in their provocative sweet voices.

Soon the two of them were undressed and writhing atop the large dining table. I was so riveted by everything they did that it never occurred to me until they were done that I had just watched, for the first time in my life, a same-sex couple making love. I reached between my legs and found myself completely aroused.

"I'm gay," I said flatly to Mahjong stopping the video to call her again.

"You're not gay," she said calmly.

"I only got aroused when I saw those two women going at it. Doesn't that mean I'm gay?" I said in a high pitched tone unable to bring my voice down.

"No," Mahjong said reassuringly. "I think it's hot to watch two women go at it."

"You do?"

"Of course," she said easily. "It's natural."

There was a long pause.

"Uh, have you ever been with a woman?" I asked slowly and tentatively.

"We should probably talk about this in person," Mahjong said in a very business-like voice.

"Is there a woman over there now?"

"Fuck off!" Mahjong snapped. "I'm trying to do my taxes."

"Oh! Really? I'm so sorry!" I added quickly. "I didn't know that! And I keep interrupting you. I'm really sorry! If you want I can ask someone in the office to take a look at them for you."

"Maybe. Let me see how much I get through on my own. Now I recommend that you lie back and try to enjoy the movies instead of dissecting them with your brain."

I did my best to take her advice and watched the next scene unfold with Sugar and two cowboys. I watched Sugar's technique for performing oral sex intently. She did things that I never even thought to do. The main move she repeated was the eye contact she made with the person receiving oral sex. It seemed to elicit the most positive feedback from the man. I suppressed the urge to take notes or to call Mahjong to ask her more questions.

Everything the women said in the movie, though the acting was wooden at best, sounded natural once the act of sex started.

"Slap my ass!" or "Fuck me harder with that big fat cock of yours!" and "Fuck my pussy! Make me cum!" all sounded fine within the context of the movie.

When I tried to utter the same words aloud to the open air in the room I felt like a fool.

None of it felt natural.

"You make me so very wet. I would like your big dick inside me," I said to the rubber tree plant in our basement.

I watched as its leaves seemed to wilt.

Even the plant wasn't impressed.

The last scene of the movie saw Bone Ranger with the small-breasted brunette from the dinner hall engaging in intercourse when he suddenly pulled out a rubber toy from behind the bale of hay she was lying against and began to lubricate it with his mouth.

I recognized its shape from something I saw at Isabelle's party.

I tried to get past my obvious disbelief that an anal toy would be lying around in a barn, and that if it was it would be clean enough to use on someone, and intently watched as he gently thrust it back and forth inside the anus of the brunette. She squirmed with delight and then Bone Ranger discarded the toy and slowly inserted himself inside her rectum.

After a short period of time, he was thrusting with as much enthusiasm as he had when he was in her vagina and I was glued to the scene not to mention the cushion of my chaise seat.

I picked up the phone.

"But I don't understand it! That area has stuff in it!"

"The first five or six inches are empty," Mahjong said calmly.

"But what if she has to go for a number two?"

"Number two? How old are you?"

"I don't get it. I mean she really looked like she liked it."

"Some people do. It feels different in the back door than it does in the front. It's tighter, and you're more sensitive by a mile. If you don't believe me, next time you're in the shower just stick your thumb in there and see for yourself. "

There was another awkward pause on the phone.

I think she was waiting for me to ask her if *she* liked it. I couldn't bring myself to say the words. I heard her calculator ticking in the background. "Did they use lubricant in that one?"

"No."

"You have to use lubricant for any back door loving."

"I guess the barn was all out."

I hung up the phone and decided there was enough time for me to try "*Slut, Slut, Guys on a Truck*".

The video opened with two women in the backseat of a pickup and again as before, I was riveted and completely aroused. I fast forwarded through the video to a scene with an extremely well endowed man. A woman performed elegant and artful oral sex on him until he ejaculated on her neck and chest. The scene caused me to suddenly flash back to university when I was first dating Jonathan, and Mahjong gave me a picture-book she had made called 'Fun with Cum'.

She had drawn cartoon images of women with splashes of glue in different places on their bodies. Some were in their hair, on an arm, on a foot or the chest. The ones for the stomach were broken down in categories including the happy face series and the fireworks extravaganza.

The book frightened me.

When Mahjong bought glitter glue in the craft shop down the street to update her picture-book, I realized she would always be in a league all her own.

The next scene took place inside the mechanic's shop. I was especially intrigued by the dialogue of one couple.

Woman: I just don't know anything about cars.

Man: Well baby, you came to the right place.

Woman: How much will it cost?

Man: What have you got? (Man begins to pull on her tank top)

Woman: Gee, I think I only have five dollars.

Man: It's more than five dollars.

Woman: It is? How can I pay? I just can't pay.

Man: Well you owe me for the service. I think we can do a trade though.

Woman: What kind of trade? (She says as her tank top comes off and her breasts bounce out).

Man: Let's say you suck my dick first to pay for the tires I put on your truck.

Woman: Oh, I guess I could. (She begins to unbutton his pants).

Man: But just know you're going to have to pay for the lube job too.

Woman: How about I give *you* a lube job.

The idea of role-playing triggered something powerful in me.

I wondered if Manny would play along to dialogue like the one in the movie.

Was I even capable of uttering any of it with a straight face?

I imagined greeting him at the door when he brought home a pizza and acting like he was the delivery boy and I was the girl who couldn't pay.

Would he just tell me to get out of the way because the pizza was getting cold or would he play along?

Maybe I could ask him to fix the light bulb in our garage that he hadn't replaced in almost six months of nagging and then tell him I couldn't pay for his electrical services.

Would he tell me to quit badgering him or follow my lead and insist that I give him something else in return for his services?

The possibilities seemed endless, and what's more, I might finally get him to do some things around the house!

The movie continued with another scene which saw a young redheaded woman driving a truck and picking up a robust young hitchhiker. She told him he would have to pay for gas and he said he had no money so she lay down a blanket in the flatbed of the truck and said he could repay her with oral sex.

Clearly there was a theme throughout the movie.

To my surprise, the hitchhiker allowed the redhead to insert an anal toy, conveniently stored in the glove compartment of the truck, into *his* ass while she performed oral sex on him. He moaned with unabashed delight until he came to his explosive conclusion in her mouth.

This scene required rewinding several times as there was no part of my marriage to Manny that made me think there was any way he was going to let me stick anything in his bottom even if I promised him he would look as ecstatic as the man in the movie.

"Manny, can I shove this plug in your ass?" I could see myself asking while watching the smoke rise from his heels as he ran straight to our lawyer to serve me with divorce papers.

I sent a text to Mahjong instead of calling her again.

"I didn't know you could blow a guy with something in his ass!"

"Lookout Manny's fanny!" she texted back.

After two and a half hours of watching videos I felt like I had just had a crash course in sex.

They were certainly unlike any video I ever saw in health class.

I shut the television off and placed the movies back in their cases hiding them at the back of our extensive collection alongside the handful of Bollywood flicks my mother had loaned me in hopes I would enjoy them and have something to talk to her about.

I practiced a few lines of dirty talk to a mirror, laughed hysterically and then fell into a heap on the bed. Feeling the moist wetness between my legs, I seized the opportunity to ignite my bunny buddy and within moments had fully climaxed with little to no trouble at all. Images of the women in the hall, the hitchhiker and the Bone Ranger floated endlessly through my mind as a massive orgasm overtook me with a series of smaller ones that quickly followed.

I couldn't stop thinking about the scenes from the pornographic movie and what Mahjong had said. I took a shower later that night and found myself soaping between my cheeks for an extra long time. I lathered the soap and gently slipped my finger inside my rectum out of curiosity.

I was surprised at first by how soft the skin was and how instinctively the membrane closed around my finger like a padded hug. I withdrew it quickly and closed the shower curtain tightly despite the fact that I was alone in the house and then did it again. I plunged farther in until the heavy pounding of my heart forced me to stop. I was amazed at how even without my finger inside me I could still feel its shadow moments later.

My fascination with that area really shouldn't have surprised me since my earliest memories centreed on cleaning myself there as far back to when I was a little child.

My mother trained me to use water at home instead of toilet paper.

I was five years old in kindergarten when I was faced for the first time with the challenge of how to get water out of the sink to clean myself after using the facilities. I had never seen toilet paper before that. I didn't know what to do so I would either try to hold my bladder for the entire class or I would end up relieving myself by accident to the teacher's horror.

Mrs. Fitzpatrick told my mother I was *special* and a *slow learner* because I couldn't seem to master the art of using the washroom by myself. She also noted that whenever I did manage to go, I would always leave the floor covered in water causing the children in my wake to slip and fall when they went in.

In response my mother sent me to school with a small vase and told the teacher to give it to me whenever I needed to go to the bathroom. The other children became jealous of the porcelain vase. They called me Jug Head and wouldn't speak to me. I came home crying every day until my mother broke down and bought toilet paper mumbling something about how it was a conspiracy brought on by the *ghora* culture to suppress Indians everywhere.

Fully refreshed from my shower I lay down on my bed contemplating what to do next.

A few minutes later I received a text from Mahjong reading, *"Want me to give you more movies now?"*

"Yes! Yes! Yes!" I wrote back.

"Looks like that sex talk is really cumming along…"

Chapter 8

I picked up Manny at the airport wearing one of my new blouses, a new skirt and bright red lipstick I had bought with Mahjong that weekend. His initial reaction when he saw me seemed to go from happiness to confusion to anger. I spotted Borgis behind him who, as usual, looked well rested, waving his meaty hands at me and leaving in the opposite direction.

"Have a nice flight?" I asked Manny cheerfully.

"Why is your skin glowing?" Manny said between clenched teeth.

"I'm wearing makeup!" I said proudly.

He said nothing in return. His gaze got darker and darker as we drove home. I fidgeted restlessly becoming more and more agitated by the fact that each time I tried to wear something new, he refused to compliment me or acknowledge my efforts.

We didn't say another word to each other until we got home. Manny was taking his clothes out of his suitcase when I heard a loud yelp. I ran upstairs.

"What the fuck is this?" he asked dangling Bunti from his finger.

I forgot to put him away!

"My, uh, my vibrator," I said trying to sound casual.

"I don't even know who you are anymore," he said angrily, flicking Bunti back onto the nightstand.

"What do you mean?"

"I mean what the fuck is going on? You never wanted to go to the gym with me and now all of a sudden you're going to the gym!"

I was confused.

I could see how angry he was but I couldn't follow his logic.

"What does my vibrator have to do with going to the gym?"

"I can't believe you, Lee. I was begging you to go to the gym with me for years and you came, what, maybe six times all year? Then every time I say I'm going to cancel your membership, you tell me that you swear you will go. Now all of a sudden you're going to the gym all the time. You're doing a spin class three times a week. Three times!"

I still couldn't see the connection. I could only see his disbelief.

"So what are you saying Manny? That you thought all this time I *needed* to go to the gym?"

I knew what I was doing was wrong.

I was trying to deflect his anger by twisting his words. I started to feel myself panic because I couldn't figure out why he was so enraged.

"You said we were going to try and have a baby. You wanted to start a family."

"I still do. We agreed we would just let it happen naturally."

"Is that the real reason you're having sex with me? Or is there some other reason?"

"How else are you supposed to make a baby? Did they invent some other way I don't know about?"

He looked me up and down, his eyes growing more dark and distant.

"And the new clothes Lee. Did you think I wouldn't notice?"

"As a matter of fact, I was beginning to wonder if you ever would!"

"Of course I noticed. The new tops, the new skirts. Not to mention the thongs. Let's not forget those!"

Why did itemizing my wardrobe make him so angry?

"If this is about money-" I started.

"And the haircuts. The waxing!"

"I thought you liked my haircut!"

I felt tears springing to my eyes.

I didn't want to start crying especially when I wasn't sure what we were fighting about.

All the changes I had made over the last few months had not gone unnoticed. For some reason they were a source of angst and resentment for him instead.

I felt anger start to boil inside me.

"You just want me to stay fat and unattractive for the rest of my life! *Stay home and eat samosas, Leena. Get so fat no one will ever mistake you for a sexy goddess, Leena,*" I said seething sarcasm. "You don't care that I'm finally taking care of myself now. You're such a jackass, Manny!"

"*Who is he?*" Manny asked all of a sudden. His expression was the darkest I had ever seen it.

"Who are you talking about?"

"Who is responsible for the change?"

"You mean Bunti?"

"His name is *Bunti*?" Manny said, his voice squeaking.

"Yes! And I love him! I don't care who knows!"

Manny flopped down on the bed, his shoulders drooped.

"How could you do this to us?" he said, his voice so low I barely heard him.

"*To us? Do this to us?* I did this for *me* Manny! I was tired of feeling numb all the time. I was tired of going through the motions. I feel free for the first time in my life! If you can't understand that, it's your problem, not mine!"

Though my blood was boiling, saying the words out loud seemed to lift a massive pressure off me.

I felt the air around me clear.

"I hope he makes you happy," Manny said in a dejected voice.

I thought I saw a tear cresting at the corner of his eye but I was too enflamed to care.

"He makes me very happy!" I said, "And I'm not giving him up for you or anyone else! I'm tired of living my life for everyone but me!"

I grabbed my coat from the closet and stormed out of the house.

I found myself driving down the highway with no destination in mind, the warm summer night's air doing little to cool me off. By the time I realized where I had been driving to, I was at the doorstep of my grandmother's home.

I knocked on the front door of my Uncle's house where my *Dadi* stayed, tears beginning to stream down my face. My Uncle Vim answered the door and in one fell swoop scooped my sobbing form into the entrance.

"Vhat has happened? Has he beaten you?" Uncle Vim asked in his thick Indian accent.

"No! No!" I said quickly wiping away my tears.

"Is he drunk? Has he lost all his money doing the gambling?" he said in a frenzy. "Suman get down here!"

"I'm okay, Vim Uncle. Really. I just wanted to make a surprise visit to *Dadi*. Is she here?"

Of course she was there. Where else would a ninety-something woman be on a Monday night?

Vim's wife Suman rushed down the stairs of their house and instantly started to pace around in circles.

"What has happened? Oh *Baghvan*! What has happened? Tell me!"

Her voice was like a shrill drill in my brain.

"Is *Dadi* here?" I asked again.

"What is it, Lee?" Auntie Suman asked in an overly concerned voice. "Is he beating you?"

Why did everyone assume the problem was with Manny? What if I was having some kind of emotional crisis of my own or maybe I lost my job or got hurt?

"No. Look, I'm sorry I'm crying. I must be tired. I just want to see my *dadi* if it's okay," I said wiping the last of my tears away and putting on a brave face. The two of them surveyed me like twin police officers.

"I'll get her," Uncle Vim said.

He motioned for me to take a seat in the living room. I knew better than to go and sit on their formal plastic covered sofas which were reserved for visitors and arranged marriage proposals for any of Uncle Vim's five girls. I sat on the old chesterfield they refused to throw out because it still had plenty of life in it. It was over twenty years old and if one of the coils didn't catch you by the bum and secure you down for life, the softer cushions would suck you into a deep abyss that was impossible to get up from gracefully.

I took my chances and picked the middle cushion.

I sank right to the bottom.

"Want something to eat? You are losing weight, na?"

"I haven't lost any weight," I said defensively.

"Is it because you are having the problems? Is he drinking too much? You know your Uncle Vim he does drink too much too," she said sitting on the coffee table in front of me.

"He does?" I asked in surprise.

My Uncle Vim had worked hard his whole life to get out of my father's shadow. Though my father had died young, he had a well established career that was the envy of his simpler brother.

My father was a professor and author of two books. Uncle Vim could barely read and had held blue collar jobs all his life. My father left my mother with savings and insurance money. His pension also more than adequately covered our needs. Uncle Vim had trouble keeping a job. I always respected him for being a dutiful and kind man. When my *Dadi* became weaker and was unable to live on her own, Uncle Vim took her into his already overstuffed home, though my father's sister who had never married could have easily looked after her.

Uncle Vim showed up at the doorway with my frail grandmother on his arm. She had wrapped a long paisley printed shawl over her white Indian cotton nightgown. Her long gray hair was slightly askew as though he may have just woken her up.

She patted his hand gently and took the two steps down to the living room from the hallway. Once she was on the main floor she let go of him. He asked her if she wanted a pillow and she gently told him not to fuss and go back to doing whatever he was doing before. Uncle Vim kissed her gently on the forehead and smiled at me. He still had a look of concern in his eyes though it was slightly muted. Suman Aunty had sat herself down on the coffee table and seemed blissfully ignorant of the fact that I might want some time alone with my grandmother. Uncle Vim shouted at her to leave us alone which she reluctantly did as soon as my grandmother sat herself down in an old wooden chair by the sofa.

I immediately propelled myself from the sofa to kiss her. I knelt at her feet holding her legs and placed my head in her lap.

"How is my beautiful Leena?" she said in her old frail voice. I felt the tears welling up in my eyes again.

"I'm sorry I woke you," I said between sniffles.

"Vhat is wrong my child?" she said patting my hair gently.

"I don't know *Dadi*. I'm so stupid!"

She slapped me on the head sharply. "Don't ever call yourself stupid! Now tell me vhat is going on?"

"I don't know," I said between half sobs. "Manny and I had a fight!" I was sure to keep my voice low as I knew if Suman Aunty wasn't at the door trying to listen in on my conversation, one of my snoopy cousins would be.

"Oh my darling Leenoo, all couples have fights."

How could I explain to her that he wasn't supportive of my personal growth? That he didn't seem to appreciate the efforts I was making? That he was jealous of my vibrator?

It would all come out sounding trite to a woman who had lived through five births, two miscarriages and countless deaths of loved ones in India.

"*Dadi*," I said wiping the tears from my face, "I'm so confused. Just when I think I've got things figured out I make a mess of everything and I don't know what I'm doing anymore."

"Dis is normal in life *jaan*. You vill figure it out my darling." She handed me her cotton handkerchief smelling like a familiar mixture of sandalwood and balm.

"*Dadi*, why am I married?" I asked suddenly.

I had no idea where the question came from. It shocked me as much as it seemed to surprise her. My grandmother patted me gently on the head.

"I was married to your *Dada* for some forty years," she said gently.

"I don't remember him much."

He had died when I was still a small child.

"I know," she said warmly. "It's okay. He loved you wery much. I still remember vat he said ven you were first born. Dat one has a gift, he said and he was right."

"He did?"

"Yes he did. And do you know what I said?"

I shook my head.

"I said she does have a gift. It's the gift of love."

The look in my grandmother's cataract-riddled irises made me well up again. It was the same unconditionally loving expression she had given me so many times before in my life. She was always there for me when I needed support. At my high school prom I wore a pink and blue Punjabi suit instead of the puffy strapless gowns that all the other girls were wearing. Dateless but still determined to go I did my best to mix with the other students. I even worked up the nerve to ask one of the boys from the audio visual club to dance. He said since I was already dressed in my pajamas we should just skip the formality of dancing and go straight to bed. I was mortified. I cried for hours that night soaking my *Dadi*'s sari with tears.

When I was seventeen and wanted to leave home to go to university, my *Dadi* was the one who spent night upon night fighting with my mother to let me go. She insisted the experience would be good for me and she relentlessly badgered my mother until she finally gave in. The day I left for university she took my face in her hands and looked deeply into my eyes. "No matter vat you do in university, I am already proud of you," she said.

At my wedding, near the close of the ceremonies, my mother and some of the Aunties started to pressure me to get pregnant. Just before I got into the car my *Dadi* took me aside and placed a sweet candy in my mouth.

"Are you going to tell me to get pregnant too *Dadi*?"

"No, my darling Leenoo. I only vant one thing for you. I vant you to be happy. Be true to yourself."

The expression of love she had in her eyes had never changed. No matter what I went through, her support was unfailing.

"I love you so much *Dadijaan*," I said and fought back fresh tears.

"My beautiful Leenoo, why are you crying now? I hate to see these tears in your eyes but I know it is part of every marriage. It vasn't always so smooth for me and your *Dada* either you know. Ve had some wery hard years. Vhen ve first married he spent a lot of time at work. Long, long hours alone with his secretary. I didn't like it, na, but vhat did I know? I was a stupid young bride. You just have to trust. Times are different now, hey-na? Ah I was so happy to live long enough to see you get married and to a good soul. Good prowider. Good potential. And vhat a smile!"

My mind started to race. Was she suggesting that my grandfather had cheated on her? I couldn't read the expression in her tired old eyes.

A memory flooded towards me. It was one of my earliest that I could recall. I was playing with a pot and spoon on the floor when the woman who had been visiting my grandmother at our house suddenly began screaming and shaking her arms. My grandmother reached down, took the spoon from my hand and started to bat at the woman's hips and thighs with it. I don't remember what they said, I just remember my *Dadi* passing me the spoon back after the woman had left the house and muttering "We got rid of that *chaloo* didn't we?" I asked my *Dadi* what a *chaloo* was a few days later and she told me it meant secretary.

The image of my husband slumped over on our bed came back to me and it all seemed to connect instantly.

Did he *actually* think I was having an affair?

Is that what he was talking about?

The words he said came floating back to me in the tangle of memories from the last few weeks and the rash change in his behaviour.

Could *he* be that insecure?

I wanted to ask my *Dadi* if my grandfather had ever cheated on her but something in her eyes made me stop.

"I shouldn't keep you from your sleep," I said softly lifting her hand up to my mouth to kiss it. Her fingers had become so gnarled over the years that they now resembled lumpy masses of joint swells leaning in one direction, a cruel replacement of the strong and powerful hands that had once held future generations and cooked a lifetime of meals.

"You are losing veight, my darling Leenoo," my *Dadi* said as she lifted herself slowly from the chair. "Not so much you don't give me a great grandchild to play with, na?"

"I started working out at a gym with my friend Mahjong."

"Good for you. And vhat colour is that child's hair now?" she asked sweetly.

"It's kind of orange," I said and smiled.

My *Dadi* rolled her old eyes around and held her head for a moment. I eased her back up the stairs to her room and lay her down on her bed.

She nestled into the mattress with a long and heavy sigh. I kissed her forehead feeling tears swell up in my eyes again. Memories of her stroking my head when my knees were scraped as a child, of her surprising me with a box of chocolate when I brought home perfect marks in school and of her rocking me in her arms when I sobbed for hours on end after my father had died, came rushing back to me as I breathed in her scent.

"I'm sorry I'm such a baby," I whispered in her ear.

"I love you my darling Leenoo." She smiled. "When I look at you I can see so much of your father. You look just like him you know? Ah, I miss him so."

"I miss him too. I love you *Dadijaan*," I said kissing her on the forehead.

"How I miss him so." She closed her eyes.

I settled back into my car and started to drive home trying to make sense of my fight with Manny. By the time I rounded the corner, I still had no idea how things got so out of control.

How could he misunderstand me so much? Was it his fault for not paying attention to me all these years? Couldn't he see that our mediocre existence was killing us both?

Why wouldn't he celebrate a more exuberant approach to life? Was he afraid of change?

If he was I could hardly blame him. I was only just beginning to understand that I could demand more from life.

Demand more from me.

I climbed the stairs to the bedroom and found Manny slumped in the same position I left him in.

"I'm an idiot," he said without looking up.

"I went to my grandmother's place." I couldn't think of anything else to say.

"I thought you were having an affair, Leena." He looked up at me, his eyes caked with what looked like dried tears at the side.

"Why would you ever think that?"

"Because I'm an idiot." He managed a half-smile. "Didn't you catch that part?"

"I'm not having an affair. Unless you count the one I'm having with myself."

"I know. Bunti, right?" he asked lifting the toy up from the nightstand. "It's just that you've been changing so much and I didn't know what would happen next. I thought you might not want to be around me anymore."

For the first time since I had known him, I saw Manny from a different vantage point.

I had always thought he was more self-confident than me. That he was so laid back, nothing truly fazed him or shook up his self-esteem. I had thought for years that he wished I was more sexy and adventurous like Monica but it suddenly dawned on me as I saw him slouched on the bed, Bunti idly hanging from his fingers, that he was as intimidated and unsure as I was.

"You're my husband," I said taking a seat next to him on the bed, "and I want to be with you."

"I love you, Leena." He held me close to him. "I'm sorry."

I wanted to freeze the moment in time.

We fell asleep in each other's arms until the phone rang suddenly at 1:00 a.m. My grandmother intending to call my mother dialed incorrectly and apologized profusely for waking me up.

I tossed and turned in bed restlessly. By 3:00 a.m. I realized there was no way I was going to get to sleep again. I reasoned that a warm bath might help me feel dozy. I took a quick but steamy shower hoping not to wake Manny. The hot water did the trick. I was feeling worn out and relaxed when I slipped back between the sheets. Manny was awake with a curious look in his eyes.

He started kissing me slowly at first and then more ardently.

"My sexy wife," he moaned between kisses.

Images of the pornographic movies I had watched floated in and out of my semi-sleepy state of mind and my brain raced to the memory of the shower I had taken after I watched them all.

"Want to fuck me in the ass?" I whispered in his ear, slightly unsure I had actually said the words aloud.

"What did you say?"

"Uh," I said. "I thought maybe we could try it. You know some 'back door loving' as Mahjong calls it."

"Seriously? You want to try that?"

I smiled and nodded. "Let's give it a go. But you have to go slow."

"Of course!" Manny said. "I will!"

I reached over into my nightstand to take out the bottle of lubricant I had hidden in it. I slid my pants and underwear off as Manny ripped at his boxers and the sheets around us.

"I say you can fuck me in the ass and suddenly you don't waste any time!" I said with a smile.

"Say that again," Manny said turning on his side.

"Say what?" I said as I removed my pajama top.

"That first part."

I blushed when I realized what he was referring to.

"Fuck me in the ass?" I asked in a voice above a whisper. "That part?"

"Yeah. Say it again."

I hadn't even realized I had said it.

In the dark light of the room, his eyes and mine still barely adjusting to being awake, I felt natural and relaxed. More free.

I leaned in closer to him and pressed my naked body against his. "I want you to fuck me in the ass," I said with the same slow drawl I had heard in the Bone Ranger movie.

We kissed each other's morning breath into one general amalgamation of flavor and smell. My body was still warm from the hot shower, giving me a languished, relaxed feeling beneath my skin which heightened every sensation. Manny flipped me onto my back and to my surprise and delight began to tease me with his tongue on my backside just under my cheeks. I squealed with joy as his tongue snaked back and forth until it slipped farther down below.

For a moment my mind stopped functioning.

I quickly found myself searching for the clinical term I was sure I had heard for what he was doing.

What did Clarissa call it? Lingus something. Anal something? What was the grade I got in Psychology 101 class?

Just as my mind began to trail into a spiral of bizarrely connected thoughts, all traces of cognizance left me when I felt his tongue begin to move in rapid circles around the rosebud of my rectum.

I was suddenly drowning in deep waves of pleasure that coursed from the arches of my feet to the nape of my neck. I moaned so loudly that the sounds coming from my throat fueled my arousal.

"God that feels soooo good," I moaned. "Yes, right there. Don't stop." With every command I moaned Manny obeyed until I started to sound exactly like Sugar. I climaxed in a flurry of spoken words mixed with moans and screams.

Sugar would have been proud.

I melted against the sheets. The sound of Manny fussing in the side drawer of the nightstand shook my head back to reality.

"What are you doing?" I asked with choppy breathing.

"I need something," he said gently. "There's nothing but candles. I guess it will have to do."

I sat up and watched him take a condom from the side drawer of his nightstand and open the package.

"That must be expired," I said as he unraveled its slippery shadow.

"It's not for that. It's for this," he said as he lowered the condom over a tapered golden candle he had yanked from the side dresser.

I forgot they were there. I had left them in the nightstand before our third anniversary intending to create a romantic mood for us but we ended up fighting over who was supposed to make the dinner reservations and never ending up having sex that night.

Manny finished wrapping the candle up tightly in the condom and then gently pushed me onto my back.

"It's not optimum but I think it will do," he said.

"You have to hold onto the end or the lamp will go straight into my ass!" I said with alarm.

"What lamp?"

I couldn't remember why I associated anal sex with possibly getting lamps stuck in my ass but I did recall Clarissa sternly warning us about needing to hold on to the base or it meant a trip to the hospital.

"I won't let go. I promise," Manny said. From the way he was looking at me it seemed like he was referring to more than the toy.

I decided not to get into a discussion as to what inspired him to wrap up the candle or of how he knew using it would help relax the area. I lay back and the next thing I felt was the cold and silky texture of the lubricant being applied to my rectum.

The shock of temperature was at once wickedly arousing as well as unnerving.

I took several deep breaths as I felt something push against me and realized it was the head of the tapered end of the candle. I felt a myriad of different sensations.

I wanted to scream, cry, laugh and moan all at once. I arched my back and closed my eyes heightening the sensation and intensifying the feeling.

"That feels funny," I said suppressing a giggle of nervousness.

"Let me know if it's too much," Manny said gently and then pushed the candle deeper inside. As it was being pressed into me, a feeling of fullness started to sweep over me leaving me aching for a sensation I could relate to. Everything up to that point was foreign and difficult to process in my brain.

Manny asked me how I felt.

"Weird but don't stop."

He told me that he was going to withdraw the candle but I didn't expect the sensation of it coming out to be as remarkably overwhelming as the feeling of it going in.

"Tell me if it's too much," Manny said as he readied himself to enter me anally. The feeling of the head of his penis felt simply like external pressure until the head pushed through and I felt a searing awareness rise in that area again.

"Oh!" I said catching my breath and closing my eyes tightly shut. "Go slow!"

"Take deep breaths and try to relax," Manny said like a doctor inserting a speculum.

Wrong hole.

He wasn't a doctor.

And I wasn't relaxed.

The feeling of fullness started to numb my mind and just as I was thinking of stopping, Manny started to gently massage my clitoris, his thumb still covered in lubricant.

I became even more overwhelmed by the different sensations and before I knew it I was being swept up in a tidal wave of feelings.

I felt the urge to cry.

I felt the urge to laugh out loud.

I wanted to vomit for a brief second and then I started to moan deeply.

Manny applied more lubricant to his penis. The shock of the cold liquid against my skin snapped me back to the reality of the sensation with its icy coolness. I took a few deep breaths to relax and as I slowly became more comfortable, the sensations became more pleasurable, even exciting.

"You okay, Lee?" Manny said as he gently started to slide back and forth.

"It feels so, so, weird having you fuck me in the ass," I said forcing my eyes open.

I saw Manny kneeling just over me, his eyes dark and full of passion. As soon as I made eye contact with him I started to relax even more. He began to moan and breathe heavily. I reached up and dug my fingers into his biceps pulling him closer to me. As I moved with his thrusts, his breathing became more erratic and before I could fully begin to immerse myself in the sensation, he had exploded inside me with a large grunt and a deep draw of air.

"I'm so sorry," he said quickly. "I wanted to last longer for you. It was just too much." He tried to catch his breath as I adjusted to the heightened awareness of him pulling himself out of me.

"Don't apologize," I said as he fell on top of me and began to kiss me gently on my head. "That was, uh, different."

"Did you like it?" he asked with hesitation.

"I'm not sure." I turned and smiled at him. "I still feel weird. It's odd. I can't describe it."

"That was the most erotic thing I have ever done," Manny said lying flat on his back. "I've always wondered what it would feel like."

For a moment I was smug with satisfaction. Like I had broken down a barrier between us and I was the braver of the two for having taken the initiative to do it.

I felt almost drunk with power but it was extremely short-lived.

"Am I leaking?" I asked putting my hand between my legs.

"Oh, sorry. I came inside you. You probably have to go get rid of that," Manny said sheepishly.

"Hunh?" I asked and followed his eyes towards the bathroom door. "Oh."

I kept my hand between my legs and hobbled towards the bathroom shutting the door behind me.

I sat down on the toilet and heard a decidedly unpleasant sound as I lowered myself and realized that the mess of lubricant and ejaculate had to be forced out of me. *This* was definitely *not* one of the scenes I saw in either of the two pornographic movies I had watched. The series of sounds coming out of my ass were far from sexy or romantic.

I cleaned myself up and jumped into the shower again to make doubly sure that I was completely pristine. Manny joined me in the shower and soaped my back and neck for me. I was surprised to see that he was semi-aroused again when I turned to face him.

"I should always tell you how much I love you, Lee. I'm so lucky to be your husband." His words touched me so deeply that I felt tears sting my eyes. "And you are my sexy wife," he added, his eyes still dark with passion.

His words hung in the air like the mist from the shower.

My sexy wife.

I felt the words revolve in my brain.

I felt good.

I felt loved, no doubt.

I felt brave.

But sexy?

We toweled off and lay in bed naked for an hour falling into a deep sleep in each other's arms. I dreamt that I was weightless floating above a cocoon that had been cast aside with the peeled layers on the ground each sporting an image of me from my youth, from high school, from university. I reached down to pick up the fragments when a loud ringing snapped me awake.

"Hello?"

"Leena!" my mother said. Her tone of voice sounded like a mixture of fatigue, sadness and emergency. It instantly forced me awake.

"What is it Ma? I know you want us to come over today, but we just got out of bed. I will come over after work okay?"

"Come over *now*." The tone in her voice forced me to bolt upright and look at the alarm clock on Manny's side of the bed.

"No way! It's 6:00 a.m."

"Come now. Your *Dadi* has expired."

Your *Dadi* has expired.

They were simple words in theory but complicated in reality.

Expired. Like a loaf of bread or a carton of milk.

She was dead?

Yesterday she was fine. Didn't I just speak with her? My brain was scrambling to remember the last thing she said to me.

"*Dadi* has died?" Heavy blankets of pressure bore down on me. "Are you sure? What happened?"

"Come over, Leena." The sharpness in my mother's tone had gone.

"I'm coming over now."

I hung up the phone and shook Manny awake.

"My *Dadi* has died!" The pressure in my chest grew.

"What? When?" he asked, wiping sleep from his eyes.

"I don't know all the details. We have to go to my mother's now."

We readied ourselves in fifteen minutes and were at my mother's place by 7:30 a.m. There were already at least twenty-five people inside the house made up of family, distant relatives and friends.

"Ma?" I called out like a small child, stepping over multiple pairs of shoes in the foyer. How had so many members of my family gotten there before us?

It took me almost ten minutes to find her in the growing throng of people bustling themselves with moving furniture, grabbing food from the cellar and making phone calls.

"Ma!" I said when I finally found her. She looked as though she had aged dramatically since the last time I saw her. "How did all these people get here so fast?"

"I have been on da phone since tree in da morning. God, na, I am feeling so tired. Help your Aunty get da rice."

"Three? You called me at 6:00 Ma!" I said sounding more petulant than I wanted to.

"Leena I called you later. I didn't vant to vake you too early. Go get da rice."

I felt the heat rise under my skin as I walked to the cellar to get the bin of rice. I saw my Uncle Vim sitting quietly on a brown cushion on the floor in the hallway.

"I loved her so much," Uncle Vim said as he looked up at me, tears streaming down his face.

"What happened?" I asked him, settling down on the floor next to him.

"She was fine when I went to check on her before bed. She said she had a phone call to make so I brought her the phone. That was it. Around three in the morning I got up to get some water and I noticed the phone wasn't on the cradle. I thought I would just creep into her room and put it back. But there was this look on her face. I had never seen it before Leena." I felt the pressure tighten around my heart. "She looked so peaceful."

Two long tears streamed down his face into his mouth. He sighed heavily. I watched his large black eyebrows rise up and down as his face contorted in sorrow.

"She must have called my mother," I said absently.

"No," Uncle Vim said wiping his face with the sleeve of his white *kurta pajama*. "No. Your mother said she didn't call last night."

"But she called me!" I said and as I heard the words come out of my mouth, I put the connection together at the exact moment he did.

"She called *you* last night?"

"It was around one in the morning actually. She said she meant to call Ma."

He paused and took in a sharp breath. "Leena *beta*, you were the last one to speak to her before she died."

I felt the fingers of familiar pain squeeze around my heart again restricting my breath, but no tears.

Why wasn't I crying?

I heard my mother yell for me from the kitchen for the rice. I left my uncle and ran down to the cellar to get it out of the metal tin my mother stored it in. When I got back to the kitchen, it seemed like the number of people in the house had already doubled.

I was the last person to talk to my *Dadi*?

What was the last thing she said?

Was it "I love you"?

Why did she call *me*?

Did she mean to call my mother because she was worried about me? The pain around my chest shifted down to the growing knot in my stomach.

Oh my God! The last person to talk to my *Dadi* was me and then she died.

And what was I doing? I was having anal sex with my husband.

I felt like throwing up.

"Leena!" one of my aunts called out. "Leenooo!" Only my *Dadi* had ever called me that. I instinctively looked for her.

"Have you seen Manny?" I said to the older lady who was calling my name and stuffing a mourning sweet in my mouth.

"No darling. Your *Dadi* is in a better place. Eat. Eat." I pushed her hands away from my face and squirmed past the people in the hall all trying to put food in my mouth or touch my head.

"Manny? Manny?" I called out.

"I'm here," I heard Mahjong's voice over the general chaos. "Lee!"

I saw Mahjong, without any makeup on, looking weary, her concern for me deeply etched on her face. I felt the sting of tears pricking the back of my eyes but they still refused to flow.

"Mahjong, thank you for coming!" I said wrapping my arms around her.

"Where else would I be?"

She hugged me so tightly I thought she might squeeze the tears from my eyeballs, but still nothing. The weight of guilt that was sitting on my chest clouded my mind from anything else.

"I have to tell you something," I whispered to her. "Come outside with me."

Mahjong and I found a quiet corner in the backyard of my mother's house free from mourners and outside the earshot of everyone else.

"I don't know how to say this. It's so embarrassing and stupid at the same time."

"What is it?" she asked clasping my hands in hers.

"My *Dadi* called me last night at one in the morning. I was the last person she talked to before she died." Mahjong's expression of sorrow would normally have set me to crying, but I had to get the rest out of me before I lost my nerve. "And the thing is, I talked to her, she told me she loved me and then Manny woke up." I could see the look on her face move from concern to confusion.

"Why are you telling me this? What are you trying to say?"

"I'm trying to tell you," I said in a low whisper not even the birds around us could hear, "that after he woke up we had sex. Not just regular sex... *aaanal* sex." I paused and studied her expression.

She looked concerned, shocked, proud and upset all at once.

"Let me get this straight," Mahjong said pulling me towards a raggedy lawn chair near the fence. "You did it – you did it – in the –"

"Ass!" I said taking a seat in the chair. "I can't believe you are torturing me like this."

"What? No Lee, I don't mean to torture you. I can't even believe it myself. That I can't bring myself to say it, I mean. I just can't believe you did it. That's all. I mean in the – uh- ass as you say."

"Mahjong," I said feeling the tears begin to sting the back of my eyes again, "I was the *last* person to talk to my *Dadi* and what was I doing when she was floating up to heaven? I was being sodomized by a candle with a condom on it and taking it in the ass from my husband! Oh my God, I'm so ashamed of myself!"

I covered my burning eyes with my hands unable to look her in the face.

"Hold on a sec, what's this about a candle?"

"It was to get me to relax I guess."

She paused. "Creative. Creative. I didn't think Manny had it in him. I don't see why you are so upset though."

"What if she *saw* me?" I whispered. "What if my *Dadi* saw me doing that while she was floating up to meet her maker?"

"Oh," Mahjong said, solemnly crouching down at my feet. "I see what's going on. All that aside, can you tell me how it was? The anal sex part? Did you like it?"

I should have been shocked she would ask me about it at such a sorrowful time but a part of me had been longing to tell her since it happened and I wanted to share every detail, gory and magnificent with her.

"I'm not sure. I mean I think I did. It was really different. I mean *really* different. I didn't expect my head to explode with so many thoughts and my body to feel so, so full. I felt so overwhelmed." Once I started, I couldn't stop. "Oh and there was one part I really, really liked. At one point he had the candle in me and he was licking me at the same time and oh then there was that feeling when he was just licking around the bud before he put the candle in. What's that called again?"

"Analingus."

"Amazing-lingus is what they should call it. I thought I was going to leave my skin!"

"So all in all it sounds like it was a good experience. Nothing too traumatizing."

"That is until I found out that while I was doing that my *Dadi* was watching me from above."

"Sorry, Lee." Mahjong took my hands in hers. "I'm sorry that your *Dadi* is gone. I really liked her and I know you loved her, but I just can't believe that people in their afterlife have nothing better to do than spy on us when we're having sex. I just don't think she would do that."

I couldn't believe that I had gone from barely ever talking about sex with anyone to discussing anal sex at my grandmother's funeral with Mahjong.

"I guess you're right. Now every time I think of that first time for me it is always going to be associated with how my grandmother was floating above me and taking notes."

"You think she'd take notes?" Mahjong said with a gentle smile. "I always knew there was a reason I liked that woman."

"She's dead," I said in a low voice. "I don't think it's sunk in. Somehow I can't stop thinking about what we did this morning that's why I think this feels so surreal. But the reality is she's dead. Mahjong my *Dadi* is dead."

She said nothing.

She wrapped her arms tightly around my shoulders.

"It can't be real. I just saw her yesterday. I spoke to her on the phone this morning."

From the edge of the fence where we stood, I heard the low hum of chanting starting to emanate from the house. Mahjong and I went back inside. I saw uncles I hadn't seen in years, cousins that had grown since the last time I saw them and strangers with their faces drawn and sullen.

"Wow," Mahjong said as we made our way to the kitchen. "Your grandmother sure knew a lot of people."

"Leena!" I heard my mother call my name over the crowd.

"Here Ma," I said as loudly as I could.

"We are starting now! Go sit by your *Dadi*."

"*What?* Where is she? She's *here*?"

"In your father's room. Go!"

My Uncle Vim gently explained that he had made arrangements with the funeral home per my grandmother's request to have her body moved to my mother's house for the prayer ceremony before she was to be buried.

Mahjong squeezed my hand as we made it through the growing crowd of people into the room my mother dedicated solely to my father. It contained an oversized picture of him hanging on the wall with a sandalwood wreath around it. Incense burned below. Statues of Buddha, Ganesh and an Arabic scroll were draped in fresh flowers on the mantle.

It was the room I would go to whenever I felt like my life was falling apart and I needed guidance. I often had long conversations with my father as I burned incense for him and gently wept my sorrows into the lavish Persian carpet he had bought for my mother as a wedding present.

The room was stuffed with visitors gathering into the corners respectfully clearing the space around the body of my grandmother laid out in the centre of the room under the picture of my father. Her tiny frame was neatly wrapped in white muslin. She had white cotton stuffed into her nostrils and ears. Her wrinkled old face lay motionless, unstressed; almost ageless. Her expression radiated a solid beam of peacefulness from where she was resting like a beacon of white light slicing the room down the centre.

I felt the burning sensation behind my eyes again.

Instinctually, I went to her side and stroked one of her gray hairs from her forehead and placed a small kiss on her cheek. I could smell the sandalwood from the cotton and the faint mixture of her familiar scent intertwined in the fabric of the muslin. Before I could absorb any more, my mother walked in, her head covered, praying in a language I didn't understand. The room fell silent, everyone listening with reverence, their heads hung so low I couldn't see the whites of anyone's eyes.

My mother placed a wreath of flowers on the chest of my grandmother and prayed aloud, her voice more beautiful than anything I had ever heard before. I watched her as though I were removed from my body, entranced by a mystical being that was unfamiliar to me and far too alluring to ignore.

As she finished her prayer she lay her head down by my *Dadi*'s feet and began to sob deeply, her head and chest heaving. A few of my aunties knelt down and wrapped their arms around her their own tears flowing onto her head, the thin white fabric of her Punjabi suit catching each one of their tears and imprinting a small grey shadow on her.

A few people gathered around me, hugging and kissing me while whispering their blessings into my ear. I was passed seamlessly from one member of the family to another until the procession of condolences took me from my father's room back into the kitchen. The smell of the curry bubbling on the stove and the fresh smell of *roti* being rolled out on the counter bypassed the pain in my chest waking my sleeping stomach out of its stupor.

Moments passed into an hour.

I searched every room.

"I'm right here," I heard Manny say from a distance.

It wasn't him I was looking for.

"I'm here too," I heard Mahjong speak over my shoulder.

It wasn't her I was looking for either.

"Where is my mother?" My voice cracked slightly.

Someone informed me that she was still in my father's room. I started to make my way back toward her. As I passed one woman I had never met before, I felt her hand clamp down on my wrist. She was an elderly woman of Hispanic descent, her face a mess of lines, her eyes bright green.

"I knew your grandmother so well." She pulled me towards her. "I met her at the mission where she volunteered."

My grandmother was never one to brag about what she did for the community. I only knew that she volunteered three days a week, sometimes at a women's shelter, sometimes at a local mission and on the odd occasion at the local hospital.

I nodded and smiled politely at the woman.

"I would be dead if it weren't for her." The lady's green eyes swelled with large blue tears. "She saved my life."

"How?"

"She was there when no one else was there. She came every night to check on me when I was in such a bad state. She was so dedicated. She listened when no one else would. She made me want to get up and fight. I didn't want to but she believed in me. She told me a woman can do anything. She saved my life. God bless her. God bless -" Her voice trailed off, caught in the mist of her tears.

I hugged her tightly and moved toward my father's room again.

"You have my condolences," another elderly lady said as she extended her arms to me. "Your grandmother was a saint. She saved my life. She made me believe in myself."

"Did you know her from the mission?" I said as the woman tightly wrapped her arms around me.

"No, I knew her from the shelter. I was assaulted by my husband and living there when I met her. I was so lost. I felt so alone. She gave me hope. She taught me to stand on my feet. She was such a good woman. She was a fighter and she told me all about how she came to this country so young and how her husband was so controlling. How she learned to stand on her own two feet. She's a real inspiration."

"He was controlling? Is that what she said?" I remembered the look in my grandmother's eyes the previous night, the look I couldn't read.

No one really talked about my grandfather except in vague references to the past. My grandmother had never remarried after he died and lived on her own despite the grumblings of my mother and her other children until only a few years ago when she was no longer able to take the stairs of her house and began to need more medical care. She acquiesced and moved in with my uncle.

"I'm sorry dear. I don't mean to upset you. It's something she brought up in the speeches she gave when she came to lecture at the shelter."

"She lectured?"

Why did it suddenly seem that my grandmother had an entirely secret life I knew nothing about?

"Yes she often came and gave us inspirational talks about her struggle to acclimatize and to regain her life when she was living on her own. She was a real hero to me. I will miss her." Like the other lady who had sung my grandmother's praises, tears choked her up and prevented her from continuing to speak.

I passed my uncle on the way to my father's room.

"Vim Uncle, can I talk to you?"

"What is it? Are you okay *beta*?" I pulled him out of the general mass of people into the only quiet corner I could find near the end of the front hall.

"I am hearing all these things about *Dadi* that I never knew. Did she lecture at a women's shelter? And did she volunteer her time at a mission and give them inspirational speeches?"

"Your *Dadi* was a remarkable woman," my Uncle said solemnly. "She didn't like to boast about what she did. She was wery humble."

"Why wouldn't she tell me?"

"Vhat vould it make a difference?"

"She was like a hero to these women! I should know about that!"

"But wasn't she a hero to you too, na?" my Uncle said gently. "She didn't need to tell you vat she was doing, she just did it."

I felt the burning at the back of my eyes again and the tightening around my chest.

My grandmother *was* my hero.

She had loved me so intensely.

And still I only saw her as the old lady who showered me with kisses and kindness, never looking past her role as grandmother to see the bigger picture of her as a woman and a member of her community. I was suddenly overcome with a feeling of longing.

I began to wander the house aimlessly accepting condolences and hugs from random strangers and the odd prayer whispered into my ear from relatives, my limbs numb, my chest one tight unrelenting knot. My eyes felt like sandpapered empty shells in my head, hollow and dry, begging for tears that refused to fall.

Manny found me and handed me a plate of food I absently picked at. Mahjong held a tissue in one hand, ready at the first sign of a breakdown, her other hand always gently stroking my back.

Before I knew it, another ceremony had begun and there were more prayers followed by a loud chant that echoed throughout the house. My grandmother's body was gingerly carried into the main foyer where two very sober looking men from a nearby funeral home came in and bundled her into a red bag while we all waited in other rooms. I watched as their large black van drove off slowly into the late evening air.

With the absence of my grandmother's body in the house, guests slowly began to leave until only immediate family and a handful of close friends remained.

Mahjong had never left my side the entire evening, prodding me to eat something or to drink water. Despite her pleas I barely ate or drank anything. By the evening I was feeling parched, tired and hungry my body barely able to stand erect. My mind had been racing all night and with the lack of sustenance to keep it going even my thoughts were drawing to a halt.

My grandmother was dead.

She was a hero to countless women I had never met before that night, an inspiration and an advocate for change. She had consistently loved me without judgment for as long as I could remember, her love a form of comfort and the only thing I could solidly rely on for support. And now she was gone and with it that source of love.

I knew all too well the long agony of mourning the death of a loved one. Of how the journey towards acceptance came with years of tears and sorrow until the longing becomes something manageable but still unsavoury.

I walked slowly through the house, my shadow Mahjong soberly marching behind me gently stroking my hair. Manny had fallen asleep on the sofa in the basement almost three hours earlier. I reasoned it was time to wake him and get home to prepare for the upcoming service and help make the necessary phone calls.

"I'm going to go home now," I said to Mahjong who immediately nodded and offered to wake Manny for me. While she ran to get him, I gathered my purse and shoes taking one last moment to peer into the empty room that once held my *Dadi*'s body, my father ominously smiling at me from the wall.

I heard a quiet whimper like the sound of a small child coming from just behind the entrance. I moved the door to find my mother curled into a small ball, my grandmother's long white scarf wrapped in her hands, her face stained with tears.

She looked up at me and held the scarf to her nose taking in a long deep breath.

"Oh Leena, she was like *my* Ma. My Mama has died."

I had only seen that look of sorrow and complete devastation on my mother's face once before.

I felt my chest tighten, the tears that refused to flow all day beginning to well once again.

"I'm sorry Ma," I said gently. "I'm so sorry."

"How vill we do dis now?"

I knew she was referring to life in general. To something abstract for which I had no answer and even if I did, it is doubtful I would have been able to make her feel any better. Hunched over in the corner, she looked as small and fragile as a young child.

The only thing I could think to say was, "We have each other Momma," knowing that it wasn't enough and that she would likely find it poor solace at best.

Her chest lifted high as she heaved and I heard her tears catch in her throat on the way down her cheeks.

"I always have my beautiful, Leena," she said in a soft whisper. "All dese years I would be dead without you."

Her soulful words sliced through whatever barrier was still keeping my tears at bay. The first one of thousands to come that night slid down my face.

"Come to me, my Leena."

My mother opened her arms to me.

I fell into her embrace and cried harder than I could ever remember crying before.

Chapter 9

With the feeling of profound loss, sometimes a bright dawn awakens within directing you forward through the darkness.

My grandmother's death left me with the deep resonating need to fulfill a destiny I knew she was bold enough to envision for me even when I was too afraid to do so myself.

She had made a difference, had generated change by sharing her personal battles and story of survival in order to inspire hope in others. My life in comparison seemed lacking of enough strife to adequately move anyone. Sure I had a series of small triumphs over the past few months but I doubted they were enough to be considered inspiring. Was having my first orgasm really something any other woman would care about?

"Isabelle just ran out of all her stuff from the sex party. You could be next!" Mahjong wrote in a text message to me.

That's when it dawned on me. I should host a party of my own. Wouldn't that be the best to way to create positive change since the sex party at Isabelle's was the impetus for my own growth? I talked myself out of the initial rush of reasons why I *shouldn't* host the party and then called Clarissa before I changed my mind.

"Leena, you are very lucky," Clarissa said. "I am booking into November right now but my hostess for next Saturday the twelfth said she has to change the date because the bride isn't available. I was just about to call some former hostesses to see if one of them wanted to move the date."

"The 12th?" I said in shock. "That's next week!"

"Then you better start inviting everyone you know right now," she said with a laugh.

"Okay, I will invite everyone I know."

That would be four people in total and one was Manny.

I booked it, gave her directions to my home and began to plot out the guest list.

"Mahjong, I'm having a sex party and you're coming to it," I said to the only guest I was sure would come.

"Yeah, sure you are Lee, and I'm organizing a church bake sale this weekend. Get serious."

"I am serious!" I said empathically into the phone from work. "I'm having a sex party dammit!"

"Okay, okay! Who else is coming?"

"I only have you on the list so far."

"Great party."

"Actually my cousin Tinoo is getting married, remember? Maybe I should ask her if she wants me to make it a bachelorette party. What do you think?"

"A Bollywood Bachelorette? Sure why not! Just tell them they can't bargain for the toys. And no bartering chickens for vibrators."

"We only do that for brides. You really think I should do it? I mean Tinoo is cool but what about the others? What will people say? What if my mother finds out?"

"Why do you care? You have to stop thinking like that, Lee."

I hung up with her and made four different lists of people I could invite.

That night I had a vivid dream that my mother, my cousins and my aunts were all being chased by cyberskin dildos with legs. Fire was falling from the sky and I saw Ganpati and Buddha shake their round heads at me and sigh. I narrowed the list down to only the brown people I trusted not to squeal to my mother and the few Western friends I had kept in touch with but rarely saw.

I had managed to keep the whole thing a secret from my mother until two days prior when she heard I was having a party and wanted to know why she wasn't invited.

"Ma, it's a party for cooking food. You know like pasta and stuff like that."

"Dat is not food! Hoi hoi! Vhere is the chilli? So bland! Yuck. Don't buy anything, hey-na?"

"Trust me I won't. I think I already have everything I need."

With the guests on their way and the impending hell I knew I would be in after the party, the only thing I had left to stress about was the menu. Did I serve Indian food or Western food? Curry was too messy to dish out during the presentation and cucumber sandwiches and scones felt too pretentious and not my style. I reasoned deep frying was the way to go so I prepared *pakoras, bhajias,* jalapeño poppers and mozzarella sticks. I made chocolate chip cookies, and a full batch of brownies. I had nothing I could lay out provocatively on the table like Isabelle had done at her party, so at the last minute I made *gulab gamuns* from scratch and stuck a note under the bowl calling them Brown Ball Surprise. The final menu item was a full plate of homemade samosas.

I figured if the evening tanked, I could always perform cunnilingus on one to get things going.

The afternoon before the party I decided the house was as clean as it was going to get but something still didn't feel right. Mahjong's phrase "Bollywood bachelorette" kept running through my mind over and over again.

In a flash of inspiration I covered the cushions on the sofa with the fabric my mother had given me from India for my wedding. I dug up my wedding head scarf; a long rectangular red silk piece heavily embroidered with gold thread, beading and small diamond sequins and tacked it up on the wall above the dining room table.

Manny came down from his afternoon nap just as I was draping a bright blue and gold sari across the blinds of our bay window. "What the fuck?" he gasped. "You're going to fall, Leena!"

"Are you upset?" I asked him as I tacked the last edge of the sari to the wall.

"It looks a bit like a bazaar in here with all the fabric. You're going to take it down after the party right?"

I didn't answer. I might have haphazardly thrown the fabric up, but somehow the bright colors and detailed embroidery made me feel more at home in my home than I had the entire time we had been living there. I silently wondered why I had never thought of decorating with them before.

"When are you leaving for Tushar's party?" I asked him as I chopped coriander to throw into a mixed salad.

"Can't wait to get rid of me for your girlie party, eh?" Manny snuggled up behind me in the kitchen.

"Be serious, Manny!" I said smacking his hands away. "I still have to finish this salad and make the chutneys."

"You don't want my Manny *masala*? I make it special for you!"

Laughing turned to kissing and kissing turned to loving. Before I could finish the salad, we were squeezing in a quickie in the kitchen. Manny was still scrambling to get his clothes on when I heard the first insistent doorbell ring.

"Let me the fuck in!" I heard Mahjong scream. "I want to buy a great big dildo!"

I ran to the door and ushered her in quickly.

"I have neighbours you know!" I pulled her into the house almost knocking two large bottles of red and white wine from her hands.

"I have to tell you about last night, Lee. We had sex!" she blurted as she threw off her shoes and ran towards the samosas in the kitchen. "And, Lee, it was like no sex I ever had before."

"Who did you have sex with?" I asked almost afraid of her answer.

"Steven of course!" she said impatiently.

I had recently asked a junior accountant in our office if he could help Mahjong get her business taxes in order. Steven was thin and wiry with large round glasses and nothing like the type of man she usually dated, so it never occurred to me that she would find him attractive. I knew that they had had a few business dinners together so when I found out that in the midst of muddling through her finances they started calling and texting each other every day I teased her that they were dating.

She vehemently denied it.

"I thought you said you weren't dating him?"

"I wasn't! God, last night was amazing!" She was glowing.

"Amazing how? Like kinky?"

"No! Like *amazing*." Her smile spread across her whole face. "I don't know how to describe it. It was the connection. We laughed the whole time."

I was speechless. I couldn't remember ever seeing Mahjong so happy before.

"What's his nickname?"

"Uh, no nickname, this time. It just doesn't feel right somehow. He even got me a gift. He made me matching towels with our initials on them." She stared at me as though she was waiting for it to register. I stared blankly back at her. "The towels have an S and an M on them. Get it?"

I smiled.

"God look at the time! I have to change!"

I ran upstairs, Mahjong trailed behind me stuffing a samosa in her mouth. In the midst of throwing my clothes around, Mahjong picked up a black T-shirt with a golden monkey in the centre of it.

"What about this?"

"Don't be ridiculous. I bought that because it's my Chinese sign. It's a silly T-shirt."

"If you're not going to be a silly monkey tonight, when are you?"

I took the T-shirt from her, remembering when I bought it.

My nicknames in grade school went from monkeyface to monkeybum. When I saw the T-shirt, I remembered wondering why the monkey looked so happy. Didn't he get teased about being hairy? Wouldn't that hurt his feelings too? But the golden monkey danced merrily on the T-shirt, not bothered in the least. I envied his happiness. I bought the T-shirt hoping to feel as carefree as he looked.

I slipped on the shirt with a pair of black Capri pants.

"Spin is paying off." Mahjong smiled. "Good for you, Lee!"

The doorbell rang sending me running downstairs with no time to change or rethink my outfit.

"Hi Monkey!" Tushar said. "I came to pick up Manny."

"Where's Tinoo?" I feared my guest of honour wasn't going to show.

"She's coming with Pinky and Dimple. They were still doing their make up when I left." He rolled his eyes. "*Ustaad!*"

I wanted to ask him what they were wearing. Was it traditional or Western? What if they all showed up in Punjabi suits?

"Let's get our drink on groomy!" Manny said as he slammed his chest into Tushar's.

Just over Tushar's large frame I saw my first guest approach: Svetlana, the wife of Manny's coworker Borgis.

She was strikingly tall, slim and had slightly mannish features. I didn't directly invite her. When Manny went to work boasting that his wife was hosting a vibrator party in his house, Borgis begged him to let Svetlana attend. I had no choice but to extend an invitation. She towered even over Tushar, her long red hair loosely blowing around her face, her statuesque frame imposing and intimidating.

"Uh, hello," I said craning my neck up to meet her gaze.

"I am Svetlana," she said in a thick Russian accent. "I am being Borgis wife."

"I'm so glad you made it! Come in please. Meet my friend who is here already."

I turned to see Mahjong in my living room rearranging a wooden elephant and turtle so that they were humping each other doggy style.

"Hi," Mahjong said extending her hand to Svetlana. "My, you'd need a step ladder to kiss this woman. How tall are you?"

"I am being six foot three inches. I am wearing flat shoes though," she added in a more sheepish tone.

Svetlana was immaculately dressed in white linen trousers with a royal blue blouse. She stood in sharp contrast to Mahjong who had dressed in orange overalls with a green checkered blouse and matching green and orange *bindis* at the side of both her eyes. There were several neon orange stripes of hair running through Mahjong's tresses only slightly dulled in comparison to the aquamarine eyeliner she was wearing.

I felt like I was standing next to two circus performers.

I could fill out the trio as the bearded lady.

"We're off!" Manny said from the doorway.

Tushar didn't want a traditional bachelor party. He simply wished to watch the World Cup of Soccer and have a few drinks. Unbeknownst to Tushar, Manny and a few of the groom's cousins were planning to take their bachelor out to a local bar dressed in a sari and make him *bungra* dance all night for money.

No sooner did they leave when the doorbell rang again.

It was the guest of honour Tinoo flanked by her two sidekicks, Pinky and Dimple.

Pinky was Tinoo's best friend and also my first cousin. She was the epitome of Western style from her designer clothes, bags to her expensive shoes.

Pinky was decidedly wilder than Tinoo. Her parents were often seen in the temple praying for her to mend her shameful lifestyle and find God.

Dimple was equally as stunning as the other two but came from a poorer family. She carried imitation bags and wore knock-off shoes, not that I could ever tell the difference. No invitation went to Tinoo or Pinky that didn't automatically include Dimple. Not even the impending wedding could break up the trio girls who called themselves The Three *Muska*-teers.

I was actually shocked when I heard that Tinoo was marrying Tushar.

Tinoo was young, gorgeous, with long straight black hair, expressive hazel eyes and light mocha coloured skin. She had been paraded in front of a long line of suitors all of whom vigourously sought after her hand. Tushar, an arrogant man fifteen years her senior, was best known for his sharp business sense. He was the last person I thought Tinoo would ever consider for marriage.

She said that past the hairy, sullen exterior was a prince she had fallen in love with.

Manny said it was more likely his wallet.

I ushered the three brown beauties into my home. They entered in a cloud of sickly sweet perfume. I offered them drinks and introduced them to Svetlana who was thumb-wrestling with Mahjong just as the doorbell rang again.

Isabelle had warned me that she was going to bring her friend Harriett to the party. I had met Harriett at a dinner party that Isabelle and her husband Peter threw for Manny and me after we were married.

Harriett was a slender woman with mousy brown hair, one massive eyebrow and a large black mole on her chin. I don't remember what she said that night but I did remember what she wore: a shapeless black frock with a huge white cross at the neck. Isabelle said she was Born Again and struggling with her own ethics having come from a life of stripping for money in her youth.

To look at her, I would never have guessed that anyone would pay two dollars to see her take off anything. Harriett would have been at Jenny's bachelorette party but it was the same weekend as Christ Camp.

Standing meekly by Isabelle's side, Harriett's long overcoat and stooped posture were a strong contrast to the pink and black leather vest her friend was wearing.

"I brought you pasta salad," Isabelle said cheerfully.

"Nice to see you again," Harriett said in a quiet voice. She took me by surprise reaching out to hug me.

"That's a super shirt," Isabelle said. "Why does it say *Monkey*?"

"It's my Chinese sign," I said as I peeled Harriett off me.

"I'm born in the year of the Rooster," Harriett said shyly. "We're not that far apart."

"I know plenty of cocks too!" Mahjong said from behind me.

"It is the year of the *Rooster*." Harriett shifted uncomfortably. "Forgive her, sweet baby Jesus."

I looked at Mahjong and desperately pleaded with my eyes for her not to respond.

"Well do come in!" I motioned to take Harriett's overcoat.

"Oh no!" She clutched her coat to her chest. "Not yet. I'll keep it on if you don't mind."

Tinoo made herself at home on the sofa proudly displaying the henna designs on both her hands and feet to Svetlana and Isabelle. Harriett motioned the sign of the cross when she saw the wooden elephant humping the little turtle on the coffee table.

The next guests to arrive were Corky and her twin sister Aquila.

Aquila was painfully thin, tall and dark-skinned with an ass so bulbous that Manny said a cup of coffee could rest on top of it without being disturbed. I had never known such opposite twins. Aquila was dour and sarcastic. Corky was beautiful and prized.

Aquila wore black jeans and a long-sleeved black shirt. Corky's sizable chest was barely contained in a figure hugging white V-neck shirt with sequined hearts on the sleeve.

"I heard this was a sex party!" Corky said as she handed me a container full of fresh *jalebi*. "I hope you don't mind but I invited Jumma Aunty. She heard about the party and wanted to come."

I felt my heart sink to my feet and my stomach turn. The last time I had seen her was in the grocery store when I was wearing my crotchless panties.

"Dahling!" Jumma Aunty said in her thick Indian accent. "But why we don't see each other so much more? We should be going to pahty ever night! Tank you for inviting me!"

I bit my tongue and shot Corky a dirty look.

"Come in," I said motioning to the three of them.

Over the rising voices in the house, I heard Corky tell her sister, "I can't wait to tell you about this guy Nick at Traincom."

It was like the words floated up over what everyone else was saying and hung in the air like a hand mid-slap in front of my face.

Was Corky dating Nick?

My Nick?

How many Nicks could there be at Traincom?

Of course, he would be dating her. She was the epitome of everything I wasn't: chesty, self-confident, *sexy*. The image of Nick smiling smugly locked in a Kama-sutra-type embrace with Corky's big breasts bouncing about kept rolling around in my mind.

It was a moment before I realized the doorbell was ringing.

"I'm so glad you called me!" Mary said as she plunged forward and wrapped her tiny arms around me.

Mary was the current girlfriend of Dinesh. She was a young petite blonde who was disarmingly charming and the only girl so far that Dinesh had brought home to his parents. He recently did the unthinkable and introduced her to his family as his *beloved*. It caused many tears, one fake heart attack and a threatened suicide, but Dinesh stood his ground.

"That's a lovely blouse you have on." She wore an Indian embroidered top with faded jeans. "You look nice."

"Thanks Leena! I just love anything from India with this kind of stitching."

I found myself imaging how her entire torso must disappear under Dinesh's massive paws.

Nalini bounded in shortly after Mary, carrying her oversized pregnant belly in her hands and heaving up the four stairs to the front door.

I couldn't remember a time when Nalini wasn't pregnant. She was my second cousin and the mother of three very annoying and precocious children, the worst of whom was her youngest Pindoo. He constantly broke things, tore clothes and smacked people with a wooden spoon.

I decided to invite her expecting she would turn me down. She had barely hung up the phone when she called back five minutes later to tell me she had made arrangements for a babysitter.

She wore a light pink Punjabi suit, her hair was disheveled and her shoes didn't match but she smiled valiantly as she handed me a bag of Indian sweets she had bought from a local restaurant. I put them in the kitchen next to my brownies.

"Brownies?" Corky said with a devilish smile. "Is this your ode to *Desis*?"

Could she really be dating Nick?

Why on earth was it bothering me so much?

Was it because a part of me didn't want to admit that he was probably happier with a bubble-headed, big-breasted idiot like Corky than he ever could be with me? Would he settle down and marry her though he never had the courage to commit before?

"They're just brownies," I said sharply. "They're tasty."

"Like *Indian* women!" Corky said her gaze squarely on Mary.

I felt the tension in the room rise with the pressure in my brain and the feeling that my world was spinning out of control.

The doorbell rang.

I sprinted from the room and almost knocked over a potted plant in the foyer.

The last guest to arrive was my old high school friend Kathy. She had an affinity for Indian culture I never understood.

Kathy had always marched to her own drummer, or in her case, her own *dohl* drum. She would wear bangles to school, *bindis* on her head and tie-dyed embroidered T-shirts, often to the ridicule of others around her. She ignored them despite their harsh words and taunts. I could never understand why she seemed to revel in a culture I railed against. Her obsession with all things Indian confused and scared me. I stayed away from her until one day, while I was sitting by myself in the cafeteria eating lunch out of the stainless steel container my mother made me take to school, I felt something graze the top of my head and fall into the curry in front of me. I looked down and saw the edge of a half eaten bun floating in my lunch, my white top covered in turmeric-coloured blotches from the sauce that had sprayed up.

"Leena stinks of curry!" I heard someone scream from across the room. "Now she looks like it too!"

"That's what you know ignoramus! I'm the one eating curry!" Kathy screamed back taking the bun out of my lunch and throwing it wildly across the room. She grabbed me by the hand and quickly pulled me out of the cafeteria. When I started crying because I knew my mother would be furious with me for getting curry on my shirt, Kathy took her poncho off and offered it to me in exchange.

"I kind of like those splotches anyway," she said. "Just tell your mother there was a shirt swap at school or something. She'll believe you."

Standing in my doorway so many years later, Kathy still stayed true to her fashion sense. I did everything in my power not to openly shield my eyes from the bright glare of the vivid fuscia Punjabi suit she was wearing. It had a mass of circles with metallic mirrors in the centre amidst a backdrop of tie-dyed orange squares.

"Kathy!"

She plunged forward into my arms.

"Leena! Thank you so much for inviting me! Thank you! I am so excited! Here this is for you," she said handing me a small golden box with red ribbon. I opened it to find several misshapen squares resembling Indian sweets. "It's barf-ee! I made it myself! I make so many of the mee-ties myself. You're gonna love it! I can give you the recipe. Oh what am I saying? You probably already know how to make it already! Ha ha!"

I added it to the pile of store-bought Indian sweets I wasn't going to eat, felt my stomach turn on itself and prayed for strength to get through the night.

"Everyone, this is my friend from high school, Kathy," I said to no one in particular.

"My Indian name is Urmilla!" Kathy said. "Urmilla Jasbarsingh!"

Everyone in the room fell completely silent.

The doorbell rang.

"Clarissa! Thank God!" I said as I saw her friendly and familiar face. She had small beads of sweat forming on her forehead. "Let me help you with those!" I took two duffel bags off her shoulders and carried them upstairs to the bedroom.

"Sorry I'm a bit late." She dropped the other three bags she had on her shoulders. "I hit traffic."

"It's okay. I figured everyone would show up after you so I told them the wrong time and now everyone is here."

I helped Clarissa settle into our bedroom where she would take the sales orders and then guided her downstairs to the dining room table where she could set up and do her presentation. As she began to unload her large bag of toys, games and products from her display bag, I paid especially close attention to Kathy and Jumma Aunty's reactions as they were the only two I was worried might run screaming from the room.

Jumma Aunty had a look between constipation and excitement on her face. Kathy just looked constipated.

"That's my sex Momma!" Mahjong said pointing to Clarissa. "Go big or go home!"

"Nice to see you again!" Clarissa laid out the last of the contents from her bag on the table. "That is a beautiful piece of fabric," she said motioning with her eyes towards the gold embroidered piece on the wall.

"It was my wedding head scarf," I said proudly.

"It's stunning. What a beautiful bride you must have made." Her bright green eyes twinkled as sharply as I had remembered them from so many months ago.

I felt the urge to leap into her arms exclaiming my eternal gratitude to her. Instead I stood paralyzed in one spot unable to speak or move.

"Get the drinks going," Mahjong said twice to me. "Did you hear me Lee? Get these bitches drunk and let's get this thing started."

After Mahjong kicked me in the shins, I did a general round of inquiries as to what beverages everyone wanted and then busied myself making conversation and preparing the long list of requests.

While I was making the drinks, I was bombarded by a flurry of comments about my weight loss. My Western guests applauded me for taking off the weight and asked me how I did it. My Indian guests asked me if I was sick and told me to go see a doctor.

The group settled in to their seats as the last of the drinks was handed out. Tinoo sat on the large sofa with Pinky and Dimple flanking her on both sides. Jumma Aunty sat on the floor between the coffee table and sofa despite my insistence for her to take a seat on a chair. Nalini squeezed her pregnant form into an easy chair with Isabelle and Harriett on the floor in front of her. Corky and Aquila created the book-ends for Kathy's seat on the smaller sofa while Svetlana, Mary and Mahjong took seats on the floor directly in front of the display table.

The only one left to sit was me.

"You look so good," Clarissa said warmly as I handed her a bottle of water. "You've lost weight since I last saw you."

"I have," I said shielding my eyes from her.

"Good for you!" she said enthusiastically squeezing my arm.

"I need to work on my biceps," I said sheepishly as she withdrew her hand. "Is there anything else you need before you get started?"

"No. Are you going to keep the discount or should we give it to the bride?"

I hadn't thought about it. I had assumed since I was the one who was going to have to deal with the repercussions of having the party, it was only logical that I get some kind of monetary compensation for being excommunicated from the Indian community at large and shunned from whatever was left of my mother's affections.

"Uh, we can give it to the bride. That's her, the pretty one on the sofa."

"Which pretty one?" Clarissa said in a slightly sarcastic tone.

"Tinoo hold up your arm!" Tinoo held up one exquisitely delicate arm showcasing her extensive mehndi design at the same time. "Maybe I should have put a penis on her head or something so that she would stick out."

"I have one in my bag if you like."

"You do?"

"Yes," she said and reached into a side pocket of her display bag and pulled out a flesh-tone penis attached to a plastic headband with small pink and white feathers dangling on the sides.

Everyone was quiet.

I looked over at Tinoo whose face betrayed not even the slightest sign of fascination, fear or anticipation. "Is that for me to wear?" the delicate little bride-to-be asked.

"If you'd like," Clarissa said as she took giant steps over Mary and Mahjong to approach the bride.

"It doesn't go with my outfit but I think it would be fun." Tinoo started to giggle, setting off the two beauties to her right and left.

Clarissa put the penis crown on her head. Even the tacky row of phalluses flopping from side to side with pink and white feathers took on an elegance atop the thick matte of black hair on Tinoo's head.

"Are you be taking MasterCard?" Svetlana asked abruptly.

"Yes dear," Clarissa said with her back still to the crowd. "But I'll get to all that soon."

"Are you guys sure you don't want anything else to drink?" I asked a little too loudly.

Anxious drops of sweat began to bead up on my lower back.

"I'm ready." Clarissa reached under the golden fabric of her large woven basket and pulled out a small cellophane bag of pencils. She slowly walked around the room and handed each person a small paper menu folded in half along with one pencil the top of which was adorned with a small pink penis.

The first person to receive the pencil and paper was Mary who squealed with joy and then poked herself in the nose with the tip of it.

Pinky joked that the pencil was her favourite color.

Dimple took hers and started to lick the top of it vigorously much to the delight of Tinoo who outstretched both her hands eagerly as Clarissa came by. Once her pencil was in hand, she mimicked Dimple until the two of them started dueling and blowing air kisses at each other.

I couldn't believe my eyes.

I held my breath as Jumma Aunty was next to get a pencil.

The older Indian lady bobbed her head like a heroine from a Bollywood flick and gently tapped her chin with the pencil while singing a Hindi song I couldn't understand. The Indian girls on the sofa laughed hysterically. Nalini began to laugh so hard that I thought her pregnant belly might burst open like a piñata stuffed with babies and candy corn.

Even Corky and Aquila joined in the laughter.

Harriett used her pencil to make the sign of the cross while she bowed her head into her lap.

Kathy's face was frozen in a lifeless smile that seemed born of fear as it must have finally dawned on her that it wasn't going to be the Bollywood bachelorette she was expecting.

Svetlana reached her immensely long arms up in the air and grabbed her pencil holding it up over her head. "It look like my Borgis! I be needing something bigger than this!" she said, switching the focus of laughter to her.

I surveyed the room for a comfortable place to sit and still be able to serve my guests.

"So who gets the discount?" Clarissa whispered to me.

"I do," I said without hesitation. "I want it."

"Okay love, sit down then. Make yourself comfortable. You know how I love to talk."

I parked myself next to Mahjong squeezing between Svetlana's long legs and the coffee table adorned with drinks and small plates of food.

"Good evening ladies. My name is Clarissa. Who here has been to an *Outside the Box* party before?"

She surveyed the room as I did. Isabelle, Mahjong and Mary's hands all shot up. "Good! The rest of you are virgins!"

"Especially the bride!" Pinky said. "She has never seen a *dunda* in her life!" The girls around her howled with laughter.

"What's a *dunda*?" Clarissa asked me.

"I guess you could say it's the Indian word for a penis," I said.

"I can work with that. Yes, so the bride is a virgin! Excellent! I've only broken up one wedding in all the years I've been doing this so worry not."

"You have?" Harriett asked from the back of the room.

"Yes," Clarissa said redirecting her attention to Harriett. "But they were never well suited to each other. I think you have to be on the same page physically, psychologically and spiritually to be able to go the distance with your partner these days."

Harriett lowered her head and picked up her pencil scribbling something in the corner of her menu.

"I have seen a penis," Tinoo said in a loud voice and then took a long swig of her cooler. "Or forty!"

I almost choked on the samosa I had just stuffed in my mouth.

Through the tears forming in my eyes from the reflexive shock of gagging, I could see Mahjong smugly smiling back at me.

"She wrote the Kama Sutra!" Pinky said and then clinked bottles with the bride-to-be.

It felt like I had left my body and was starring in a movie with unfamiliar people and a plot line I couldn't follow. It may as well have been a bad Bollywood remake. The only thing missing were the subtitles.

"This is going to be a long night," Clarissa smiled at me. "So listen ladies, this is how it works. My hostess Leena will be getting the discount tonight of 10% of whatever I make before tax in product. So the more you spend, the more she gets free!"

"Lucky Manny!" Isabelle said from the back. "I know Peter was happy!"

"I can give you the discount Tinoo," I said over the gaggle of mixed voices in the room.

Mahjong shot me a dirty look I ignored.

"No Lee," Tinoo said. "I want you to have it! You deserve it! Tushar can afford whatever I want. He gave me his credit card and said break the bank or don't come home tonight!"

The young Indian girls broke out in a chorus of laughter and began to wave their penis pencils in the air as though they were at an outdoor concert. I couldn't picture her uni-browed fiancée telling her to break anything unless it was to break out the wax strips.

"Well then," Clarissa said bringing their attention back to her, "I guess it's a done deal. Or should I say *DUNDA*?"

The women laughed at such a high octave I pictured my neighbors calling the police.

"I assure you that your sales are private as they will be done in the upstairs bedroom. You will get your bag of goodies tonight when you leave."

"I can't wait to see the love shack upstairs," Dimple said as I became deeply wistful of my boring grey bedspread and white walls in the bedroom.

"What are you drinking?" Mahjong asked me as I reached for her bottle of water.

"My stomach hurts," I whispered back to her. "I've been nauseous all week planning this party. I just know my mother is going to find out."

"Forget about it," Mahjong said watching me rub my belly. "You just relax. Try and enjoy this night Lee. You are doing a wonderful thing here."

It didn't feel like I was doing anything but screwing up my future in the community and possibly bringing shame to my *Dadi's* reputation and my mother's.

My stomach twisted on itself.

Clarissa began to instruct everyone on how to take notes giving a brief background of the company and its history. Mahjong took my paper out of my hand and wrote down "I'm buying you the King" on it and a smiley face.

"Now that we all understand this," Clarissa said, "let's quickly run though a true and false questionnaire I came up with to educate ourselves about our bodies. I can't stress enough how important it is that you know your body better than anyone else."

I sat back against the cushions I had gathered to prop me up and leaned the rest of my body against Mahjong.

Clarissa began her questionnaire asking whether couples masturbate less after marriage. "That's when they start!" Isabelle said and was quickly hushed by Harriett.

She then asked whether women become indifferent to intercourse if they frequently use a vibrator. Mahjong shot her arm up and Clarissa motioned for her to speak.

"I just want to say, the King is by far the best sex I had until I did it with my boyfriend for the first time yesterday."

That was the first time I heard Mahjong use the term *boyfriend* in a very long time and not *fuck buddy* or *sex server* or my personal favourite *fuck jockey*.

"That must be some boyfriend to come even close to the King," Clarissa said.

"He is," Mahjong said smiling directly at no one but me.

My emotions had been so erratic over the last few weeks that I felt my eyes instantly well up and fought the deep urge to openly wail my internal joy for Mahjong.

"What's this King?" Pinky asked.

"Well, you might as well make a note of it now." Clarissa directed the group to the number of the product she was referring to.

"I think we should call him *Raja* all night," Tinoo said. "It is our word for King."

"Then *Raja* it is," Clarissa said. "Let him be known as The Thunda *Dunda*!"

I couldn't hear my own laughter over the loud screams and yelping from the other ladies who were saluting Clarissa and alternately bobbing their heads side to side as they clapped with joy.

"Thunda Dunda!" the ladies on the sofa took turns exclaiming.

"Okay, so that's established," Clarissa said as the noise finally died down. "Let's move on. True or false, approximately 50% of women have never had an orgasm?"

"True!" I heard someone say.

"Good for you, Leena," Clarissa commented on my sudden outburst.

Throughout the night I had felt like I was floating outside my body, experiencing the evening from an altered state of mind. When I heard the question asked, only one thought emerged above all the clutter in my mind: *This was my moment*. I could own up to my own shortcomings and come clean about my struggles or keep it to myself for all time.

A sudden stark quietness filled the room when I said out loud, "I never had an orgasm until I met you!"

I caught my breath loudly. As I exhaled, I heard loud laughter and cheering. It took me a moment to realize what they were laughing at.

"Oh! That didn't come out right!" I said quickly. "I meant I never had an orgasm until you sold me Bunti."

"Bunti?" Clarissa said, raising an auburn eyebrow.

"The little bunny, you know the toy with the bullet inside. I never had an orgasm until I played with that toy." Suddenly there were no filters left in my brain. It was a tidal wave and free for all. "It was my first orgasm ever. I had never had one before in my whole life! I swear I floated up off the bed! My whole life has changed!"

Mahjong smiled and squeezed my knee.

"Oh no, we don't do," I heard the thick Indian accent of Jumma Aunty from behind me. "We don't do dis".

Here it comes, I thought.

"I don't do! My husband he do and so I don't have to. Right?"

"Do what?" Clarissa asked.

"Doing dis masta-bating. It's not for me to do. He do."

Tinoo shifted uneasily in her seat. I tried to dig a hole in the carpet with my plastic fork to escape.

"I'm a big advocate of masturbation," Clarissa said slowly. "So I believe like I said just now, that you need to know your body better than anyone else."

"To touch yourself is simply not divine," Harriett said and then stuffed the top of her penis pencil in her mouth and looked away.

"It feels pretty divine to me," Mahjong said in a voice louder than anyone else's.

"How do you do dis? Dis mastoorbating ting? It's what, na? A *dunda*? What you do?" Jumma Aunty continued with unabashed confusion on her face.

"Listen," Clarissa said, "Why don't we just carry on here and see if some of your questions get answered along the way, otherwise I can answer them in the sales room for you.

"Okay, let's try another question," Clarissa prodded. "True or false, things can get lost in the vagina?"

"I tink dat's what happened to Mr. Parma. I don't buy dis extended wacation in India ting," Jumma Aunty said, bobbing her head side to side.

I dug my plastic fork deeper into the carpet.

"That's false," Clarissa said and took a deep breath. "Nothing gets lost in the vagina. So let's say you're going out on a night on the town and you don't have a purse to match your shoes. Well you can put your keys in your vagina no problem!" Harriett dropped her paper on the floor and Kathy crossed her legs tightly over each other, hugging them close to her chest. "Just kidding! Don't do that! I was just trying to lighten things up."

Was Clarissa nervous?

She seemed less confident than the last time I saw her do her presentation.

"Now how about the anus? Does anything get lost in there?"

Can anxiety make you deaf?

Suddenly there wasn't a sound to be heard in the room except the gentle ticking of a wall clock in the kitchen.

"True," Clarissa answered when no one responded. "The rectum is empty at the bottom. There is a natural vacuum after which it will take anything you put in there straight up. So if you do put anything in there it has to have a loop on it or something you can hold on to that maybe flares out at the bottom, like the lamp, but not the lamp."

"You are putting the *dunda* in your bum?" Jumma Aunty asked through the deafening silence.

I knew for the first time what it must feel like to have one major artery in your heart clamp shut.

"Only if you want to," Clarissa said and gently smiled. She definitely looked tired, even a bit impatient. "Okay, so does everyone get that? And nothing goes in the back door and then straight into the front door because that is a urinary tract infection."

"Who be at the doors?" Svetlana said to no one in particular.

"Now here's an important question," Clarissa said, "True or false, the clitoris retracts under the hood just before the point of orgasm?"

There was a great deal of confusion. Several women asked for the question to be repeated. Clarissa obliged as I sat back to watch their reactions remembering how I felt during her presentation the first time around.

"It's true," Clarissa said and then held up her hand with the large stone ring on it that she had used at Isabelle's party. "For the rest of the night we are going to pretend that this ring is my clitoris."

"It looks like Tinoo's clitoris!" Dimple said and then held up her hand to high five Pinky.

"I want a clitoris that big!" Pinky said and slapped Dimple's hand.

"Okay, we're pretending now," Clarissa spoke like she was talking to a group of kindergarten students. "Let's pretend that this ring is my clitoris and that I'm getting some loving. At the point of orgasm, the clitoris is so engorged that it will retract up under the hood at which point you cannot get at it. She then needs to be gently coaxed back out for you to have your orgasm."

"What if you don't have a clitoris?" Aquila asked loudly from the back of the room.

"Excuse me?" Clarissa asked.

"Some women have had their genitals mutilated by religious tradition and dogmatic, misogynistic bastards who believe in oppressing women and controlling them so that they can't experience pleasure."

"Okay, yes," Clarissa said slowly. "That is a serious issue. Sadly it's still practiced in some places today."

Clarissa began to fidget with her big clitoris ring. I noticed a glint of sweat beading on her forehead.

"What?" Tinoo asked choking back her drink. "People do that? Who?"

"We shouldn't go into it here," Clarissa said in a calm even tone. "It's a serious issue and I think it's something we should all be educated about so we can put an end to it. I can go over details of things that can be done if this is an issue with you in the sales room."

From the awkward silence and small whispers in the room, I doubted that Clarissa could salvage the atmosphere previously created.

"It has happened to me," Jumma Aunty said flatly, slapping her hands for more emphasis. "I didn't do dis to my girls. I couldn't do. No, I pay price for it but I didn't do."

The plastic fork I had been trying to carve my way underground with suddenly snapped under the pressure of my hand as I turned to see Jumma Aunty's expression.

I saw sorrow in her eyes.

It had never occurred to me until that moment when I saw the face of my mother and grandmother woven into the weathered lines of my Aunt's face that the same horror might have befallen them.

In a flash, my mind sought out a haggard memory of women screaming at my mother when I was eight years old about a ceremony I couldn't understand. I only remember her shouting at them with tears in her eyes and ushering the women out of the house. I was angry because I knew the ceremony was for me and I was bitter that she was denying me what I thought was a happy occasion.

The reason that night stuck out so vividly in my mind was because I remember half waking to see my mother, her eyes full of tears, lovingly stroking my head as I slept, whispering in my hair, "Never to you my darling. Never to you."

Had my mother lovingly spared me from this horror the same way Jumma's girls were saved?

A lump formed in my throat and my stomach stirred uneasily.

Caught up in the various trains of thought running through my mind, I hardly noticed how low morale had become in the room.

"Tonight is a celebration of us," Mahjong said waving her pink penis pencil in the air. "Let's deal with the heavy stuff later!"

Clarissa mouthed the words "thank you" to Mahjong and carried on. "So ladies, where is your orgasm? This is the most important thing I can teach you tonight."

Everyone was still very silent and morose.

"In your bum?" Jumma Aunty asked. The ladies around her shook with laughter.

"Up here," Clarissa said pointing to her head. "Up here. If you're not concentrating up here, conducting your fantasy up here, living in your erotic state of mind up here, then forget it. You aren't going to have an orgasm and it is likely the reason you have never had one before. And by the way, if you haven't had an orgasm, today's your birthday because you're going to!"

"She's right! And what a happy birthday it was!" I said to the clapping and cheering of the women around me. Jumma Aunty reached down and over Svetlana to tussle my hair and pat me on the back.

"Happy Birthday," Svetlana whispered in my ear.

"Yay Leena!" someone from the back of the room shouted.

"Let's carry on then shall we?" Clarissa said. "The next thing is about foreplay. Statistics show that you need at least thirty minutes for your body to become ready for intercourse or to play with a toy."

"My husband Borgis not be doing the licking and sucking for that long," Svetlana said. "He pass out."

"No," Clarissa said gently. "That's not exactly what I meant. It has to start up here in your mind. Fantasy is a natural part of the sex act. You may watch a Johnny Depp movie and that's it! You're done! You want to have sex and you're picturing you and Johnny in his pirate costume going at it on the kitchen table while your partner is getting busy with you. Think of the fun!"

"Oh for me it's Shahrukh," Tinoo said with a sigh.

The two beauty queens and Jumma Aunty all sighed in unison.

"I'm a big fan of Salman Khan," Kathy said eagerly. "I just love his movies! I watch them all!"

"Nice suit by the way," Dimple said as the trio of beauties began to giggle in unison.

"Thanks!" Kathy said, oblivious to their dig, "It reminded me of a suit I saw in '*Koosh, Koosh, Hoota Hay*'. I love it!"

"We love to use costumes!" Mary squealed and started to shake her arms wildly in the air. "Dinesh and I are way big into it. The other day he wore a construction worker hat he got from a friend and we had a totally wild time!"

"Everyone pressures you to get married but no one asks you if you're happy," Nalini said over everyone else in the room, absently stroking her swollen belly.

"I agree," Aquila said. "No one cares if you're happy. They just want you to get married, have a baby, or four," she said looking down at Nalini's tummy. "And lastly all they care about is how big your house is and how much gold you have."

"It's not that bad," Tinoo said lightly.

"This coming from the princess who is marrying into more money than she can spend," Aquila said.

"And that is also for me," Svetlana interjected suddenly, her loud, deep voice bellowing over the general commotion in the room. "I not so much with the gold, but no one is asking, is Borgis doing his oral duty? Does Borgis do the fingering? Does Borgis tickling you? I likes these things. Does he be doing it? Only when we are first to be married. Now, not so much. And who can sleep with that noise in the ears? He is snoring so bad, I put pillow on his head."

I looked down at my broken plastic fork and decided to tunnel my way through the floor with the head of my penis pencil instead. As I snapped its pretty pink head off I looked up at Clarissa who was rapidly twirling her large glittering clitoris ring on her hand.

"There is an unspoken understanding in our community that we go the distance. We are set up based on what works, social stature, class, money, education," Tinoo said ignoring Svetlana's outburst and directing her conversation to Aquila.

"Please!" Aquila said sharply. "That's completely antiquated thinking. People are mixing it up now and doing just fine with it. Look at little whitey down there and her costume-freaky boyfriend. They're fine."

"We played with a police costume once too," Mary said and smiled at Mahjong.

"And so what if Juzer is a goof in public? No one has ever treated me better!" Corky suddenly screamed out loud. She burst out crying and buried her hands in her face.

There was not a sound to be heard.

Corky and *Juzer*?

Did she not say Nick's name when she came into the house?

"You're dating *Juzer*?" Tinoo gasped in unison with Pinky and Dimple.

"Juzer the loser?" Pinky continued.

"Juzer the goof who thinks he's *black*?" Dimple said and started to laugh.

Juzer was often seen wearing saggy blue jeans, long silver or gold chains around his neck, pimp-style hats and dollar-sign rings on his fingers.

He was thirty-four years old, lived at home with his parents and spent all of his money from working at local night clubs on an array of flashy clothing, cars and women. His parents had four daughters and one son. As their only son, he took liberties with his parent's affection for him, dropping out of medical school to pursue a more profitable future as a DJ and night club owner in the seedier part of town.

Corky on more than several occasions at various wedding functions joined in the myriad of others poking fun at Juzer's clothing or style of walk and talk. The idea that one of the prettiest of the young women still *available* and on the market dating a cartoon character like Juzer was absolutely unthinkable to me.

"Stop it!" I heard someone sharply admonish the girls when their laughter had risen to a squeal like pitch. I was surprised to see Aquila rise to her feet, both hands on her hips, fire flying from her eyes. "Can't you see how happy he makes her?"

Everyone turned at the same time to study Corky who was heaving so hard that her breasts were rising and falling like balloons bobbing in the choppy waters of a tsunami tidal wave. "I'm happy," she said between cries, "I'm *haaaappy*."

I surveyed the room.

Aquila was standing protectively over her sister who was curled into a heap of tears on the floor.

Nalini was wiping away tears of her own, a tissue box teetering on her swollen belly.

Isabelle was trying not to look at Harriett who had taken out a rosary and was praying on her knees. The trio of Indian beauties on the sofa fumbled with their pink pencils, heads hung down to the floor.

Kathy was admiring a hand-painted plate on my coffee table as she stuffed a samosa in her mouth while Jumma Aunty tore errant strays of fabric from her bright orange suit when she wasn't looking.

Mary sat anxiously in front of Clarissa trying to peek into her basket of costumes and lingerie as Svetlana typed a text message to Borgis. The word *fingering* in capital letters was all I could see.

Mahjong rolled her eyes at me and Clarissa looked at a loss.

My party had gone from bad to disaster and the consultant hadn't even begun to show anyone any products yet.

I stood up and joined Aquila on her feet.

"That's it!" I said in a loud sharp voice. "This is supposed to be a fun time, with sex products, information and a wonderful woman who has come out here to give us the benefit of her time and knowledge and I am now on my last nerve! I am sick to my stomach you hear? I mean it! Shut up, take notes and buy some stuff so you can at least have a good sex life if you can't have a good life!"

I felt Mahjong stroke the back of my calf.

"You're right, Leena!" Harriett said and rose to her feet. "We have to follow our hearts and live!"

In one swift motion she removed her large overcoat and shapeless clothes revealing a shiny gold one-piece dance leotard sequined with blue and black stones resembling a Vegas costume for a showgirl in a chorus line.

Everyone gasped in unison as Clarissa's hands went up to her forehead. "Okay! This party officially takes the cake."

"There's cake?" Jumma Aunty asked excitedly.

All eyes were directed towards me.

I couldn't tell if they wanted dessert or my blood.

"No one is getting any cake if you don't all shut the hell up and start paying attention! I've lived in this fear for too long and I'm not putting up with it anymore. We all have our hang ups and our problems but we have to get past them. If my *Dadi* hadn't decided to move past her own sorrow she wouldn't have been able to help the women she did. And my mother might be a piece of work but she loves me and she did her best raising me on her own. You three princesses over there owe Kathy an apology. She knows more about Indian culture than we do! At least she has a strong sense of self and she sticks to it! Kathy, I mean Urmilla, I envy you for that."

Kathy bowed her head and smiled.

"And Corky, if you're in love with Juzer, then it's nobody's business but your own. For God's sake, we all just want to be happy so what should it matter who the object of our affection is? As long as you aren't hurting anyone, who cares?" Corky raised her head enough to smile at me and then turned her face into her sister's arms. "Svetlana, if your husband isn't giving you what you need, then you have to find a way to tell him what you want. And please buy some nose strips for that man! His snoring keeps Manny awake all night and he comes home to me super grouchy and cranky."

"Nose strips?" Sveltana whispered to Mary. "What be this?"

"And Mary, I think it's wonderful that you and Dinesh found each other and that you two obviously are really well suited. Everyone in the community should just get past the fact that you are white and thank their lucky stars that you two are making each other happy."

"Leena!" Mary said with delight. "Thank you!"

"And you Harriett," I said my ceaseless tirade coming to a close, "If you want to dance then dance. No one understands religious confusion better than me. I don't know much but I do know that my Gods always practice forgiveness and the first person you have to forgive is yourself." Harriett reached down for her trench coat and quietly wrapped it around her glittering suit. "Jumma Aunty I simply can't think about you having sex with anyone. But I admire you for coming here and for being so candid with everyone."

I surveyed the ladies in the room and then turned my attention to Clarissa whose expression looked tired and beaten.

"And lastly Clarissa, to you I want to say thanks. You inspired me to make a huge change in my life. After your presentation I really started to take stock and take ownership. I owe the greatest debt of thanks to you for inspiring me to face my fears and really live." I felt tears well in my eyes in a rush of emotion careening to the surface after years of oppression. "Thank you," I heard the words get caught in my throat as I reached out to hug her and feel her arms wrap around me in return.

"Group hug!" Mary screamed as her tiny arms clung to my sides and she flung herself onto me and Clarissa. Mahjong got up to pull Mary off of me but was pressed deeper into our huddle by Svetlana's large frame as she came crushing down on the small group wrapping herself around us and crying tears onto my head.

Corky and Aquila both squeezed themselves into the group followed by the three beauties that had picked up Kathy from her place on the floor to sweep her into the large hugging mass. As I felt the air around me close in and my breathing become shallower I heard a voice in the back of the room shout, "Fat pregnant lady over here needs a hug too!"

Several of the women separated and formed another small huddle at the back of the room hugging and embracing each other.

Eventually I shifted out of position until everyone managed to go back to their seats quietly awaiting my next words. I looked around the room filled with adoring eyes as tears welled up inside me again.

"I'm sorry, there isn't any cake!" I said as Mahjong pulled me down to the floor next to her.

"Can we get back to the sex now?" Mahjong asked to no one in particular.

"What a good idea," Clarissa said as she straightened her blouse and adjusted the big pink ring on her finger. "How about we skip the questions for now and go straight to the products? In particular the costumes because I have a feeling there is someone here who really wants me to start there."

Mary beamed with joy clapping her tiny hands and squealing.

Clarissa pulled out a few exquisite pieces of lingerie noting numbers and prices as she quickly sped through her collection.

"Okay that concludes the lingerie in the basket now I want to show you the *costumes!*"

"Yippee!" Mary said. "I've already spent a hundred dollars!"

"This one," Clarissa said pulling out a school girl outfit, "you might wear and say, "*I haven't studied for this class but I really want to pass*". And guess what? You pass every time!"

Clarissa seemed back in her groove. I felt my shoulders come down from my ears. She then pulled out a costume with a badge, plastic nightstick, handcuffs and hat which she held up and said, "You put this on and say "*You're under arrest for violating the anal code. Now bend over, I need to frisk you!*"" Mary screamed with delight and for the first time in what seemed like forever, things felt light again.

"You give it to him up the bumhole?" Mahjong whispered to Mary.

"He totally loves it!"

Mahjong looked over at me with an expression I rarely saw in her eyes; a mixture of intrigue, respect and surprise.

Clarissa then held up a white and red nurse's outfit. "You wear this and say, "*It's time for your medication. Would you like it orally?*""

Everyone laughed. Mary scribbled down the number, Svetlana reached out to touch the fabric and Mahjong checked it off her list.

"The doctor is in," someone shouted from the back.

"And of course, last but not least in the lingerie is the crotchless panties." Clarissa began to loop her legs through the open holes to demonstrate how they worked.

My smile was a mile wide.

"If we do buy all da colours, you give me discount. *Egdum* good price, na?" Jumma Aunty said.

There was some gentle ribbing and laughter throughout the presentation of bath products and lotions. Corky seemed to have snapped out of her sour mood and was beginning to make a few self-deprecating but funny comments about her breast size that had me and everyone else laughing alongside her.

"How about we take a very small five-minute break before the toys?" Clarissa asked to the rousing agreement of everyone in the room.

The ladies rose from their seats heading for the bathroom or the island of food in the kitchen. I hurried to offer drink refills and shoved food at my guests so that I wouldn't be tempted by too many leftovers. Tinoo came up to Kathy who was making a plate of *pakoras* with chutney for herself.

"I don't think we've met," Tinoo said extending her delicate little paw.

"I'm Kathy but my Indian name is Urmilla Jasbarsingh," she said easily and turned to shake Tinoo's hand.

Tinoo's expression was blank.

"Yes, that's what you said when you came in. I heard you. I just wanted to say I'm sorry if we got off on the wrong foot. You know with the comments about your suit. I'm under too much stress with this wedding." Her tone was so haggard and tired that I didn't recognize it as Tinoo's. "I didn't mean anything by it."

"It's okay," Kathy said easily. "I love your henna! I was going to have it done myself for tonight but the tube exploded on my kitchen table and I couldn't do it."

"This is bridal henna," Tinoo said slowly. "It's not usually this elaborate."

"Oh I know," Kathy said, "I saw it like that in the movie *Kabbie-Kooshie-Kabbie-Gam*."

Tinoo didn't bother to correct her pronunciation. "Are you married?"

"No, I'm still single. Just waiting for my Shahrukh to come along and sweep me away!" Kathy said with a dreamy expression in her eyes.

"I see. I think if it wasn't for Tushar, I would be single too."

"Really? Why?"

"I just couldn't find anyone who understood me, you know? I mean my parents set me up with all these rich boys with lots of potential and lots of arrogance."

"So your fiancé is a poor man?" Kathy asked innocently.

I heard Pinky choke on her beverage.

"No! Oh no! He is very well to do. On his own of course, not just from the family. No, it wasn't about money but I do like it. I won't lie. I want to live in a luxury I have grown accustomed to. Is there anything wrong with that?"

Kathy couldn't answer with a piece of *barfi* stuffed in her mouth.

"He just lets me be me," Tinoo continued though Kathy seemed to lose interest in the conversation once she had spied a full plate of *bhajias* with tamarind chutney. "And Leena, you will appreciate this, he is the only man I have ever been with that can give me an orgasm while I'm having sex."

I dropped the serving spoon in my hand.

"Sorry?" I said spewing spittle in her direction.

"Yeah, he is so amazing in bed and I was the last person who would think that. When we went on our first date you know without his parents there and mine, we went to this small dump of a restaurant. I totally wasn't impressed but then he tells me he brought me there so he could be freer with me and no one would see. And then you know what he did? He put his tongue in my ear and whispered there was so much more to come. I was so disgusted and excited at the same time."

"Tongue in the ear is old school," Mahjong said as she fixed drinks for Pinky and Dimple who seemed bored with a story they had likely heard several times before.

"No, I know. It was *what* he whispered in my ear that made me wild. Come here and I'll tell you."

Tinoo leaned in, her headband of penises lightly brushing Mahjong's hair and whispered something into her ear. Whatever she said made Mahjong's eyes stretch round and curled the lower half of her mouth into a wry smile.

Miraculously over the din of the ladies, I managed to hear a beep from my cell phone indicating a text message.

I picked it up and saw that it was from Manny. It read, "*This party sucks. Drunk Desis making dumb jokes. I hope your party is better. I love you. Buy whatever you want.*" I smiled and put the phone away.

I had put out another tray of cookies along with the small pastries in the box that Svetlana had brought when I felt a hand on my shoulder. "Sorry I've been such a downer tonight," Corky said traces of her mascara darkening the light skin under her eyes.

"It's okay," I said soothingly. "Everyone has a bad day. I just snapped at everyone back there and I'm still feeling bad about it."

"You shouldn't," she said with her voice lowered. "You're doing a *brave* thing here, Leena."

"Brave? What do you mean by that?"

"Brave because people in the community just won't understand. They don't get it. I'm tired of always trying to put on a face for them you know? I'm such a naturally upbeat person. I'm always on but lately I just can't get over these blues. I have everything going for me. I'm young, beautiful, hot, desired but something is just off you know? I guess you don't."

I took a deep breath and tried for all of twenty seconds to put myself in Corky's shoes.

"How is your job going? Are you still working at the coffee shop?"

"No," Corky said. "I got fired because this woman who used to come in and always tell me she wants a double, double with skim milk caught me putting cream in it instead and she got me canned. Stupid bitch."

"I see. Well I'm sure something will come up."

"Oh, I got a job offer. Didn't I tell you?"

"Where?"

"It's this place called Traincom. Have you heard of it?"

An image of Nick instantly jumped to mind and I dropped the plastic bowl in my hand watching the two grapes that were still left in it roll and hide under the sink counter.

"How did you get a job there?" I asked as calmly as possible.

"It's a really interesting story actually. I was at the gym a few weeks ago and I totally saw you there in the spin class. I meant to tell you."

"Yeah, I've become addicted to spin," I said, my stomach starting to turn on itself again.

"Anyway," Corky said playing with strands of her long hair, "so I'm at the gym standing behind the counter when this big guy, he's like 220 lbs, hook for a nose and not that good-looking really but super full of himself, comes over to me and says he wants a towel. I didn't want to tell him I didn't work there and that Marcus at the gym lets me stand back there and steal towels for myself sometimes so I give him one and he tells me he's the project manager at this company and that they are looking to hire someone for their customer service department. The truth is I caught the sod staring at my tits the whole time like they were a sandbox he wanted to jump head first in, but I played along, you know?" I nodded hoping the story would end soon. "And so he gives me his card. Nick Frontenac."

There it was.

I *had heard* her say his name. I didn't hallucinate it after all.

"The interview was all set and I was supposed to go there at 2:00 p.m. but I showed up a bit early hoping to steal some magazines from the lobby when the secretary goes into his office and starts screaming at the top of her lungs. Apparently she caught him beating off to some porn on his computer at work and she walked right in on him! Can you believe it?"

She had painted the image so clearly in my mind that I could almost see the shocked expression on his face. The image made the edges of my mouth curl up.

"He was jerking off right there in the office!" Corky reiterated her eyes aglow with delight. "The company was so embarrassed by the incident that they gave me the job and said not to mention it to anyone ever. That guy Nick got fired anyway because the secretary was the cousin of the CEO and apparently she was really traumatized by the whole thing. Poor old bird."

I sat down on a nearby chair and tried to fully absorb what Corky had said. Should the opinion of a man who was disgraced at work for masturbating to porn on his computer really matter to me?

What was I thinking? How could I have put so much stock in what *his* definition of sexy was and not my own? Why did I let Nick and everyone else I had ever been with determine what I thought was right for me? And it wasn't just Nick's ideals I struggled to fit into. For so many years I let everyone else carve out their expectations of me and then forced myself to fit them even when it didn't feel right.

"Are you okay Leena?" Corky said stroking my back. "Don't worry about me. It's okay. I got the job out of it but that poor slob is the talk of the water cooler every day now."

"You okay, Lee?" Mahjong asked noticing me sitting on the kitchen chair.

"I'm fine."

"Let's get people back to the room," Mahjong bellowed over the conversations in the kitchen. "Hey you horny bitches! Get your sexed-up asses back to the living room!"

Once everyone was settled in their places, Clarissa walked around the room as she did at Isabelle's party putting a shiny bullet toy in the hands of all the guests so they could feel its vibration.

I watched each guest's reaction with fascination.

Mary eagerly lifted her tiny hands and put them both around the toy giggling like a small girl. Svetlana, in the middle of sending another text to her husband, stopped typing, closed her eyes and wrapped her long fingers around the vibrating bullet.

Clarissa yanked it out of her hand and walked towards the long trio of girls on the sofa. They each took turns quietly holding the toy and snickering with delight.

Jumma Aunty looked startled and screamed, "Hoi hoi!" as the bullet danced merrily in her palm.

Harriett, her gold lamé suit flashing from underneath her long overcoat, shed years off her expression when she smiled like a teenager at the sensation in her hand.

Isabelle, Nalini, Corky and Aquila all politely extended their hands to the consultant for a sample of the sensation and the last one to feel its powerful vibration was me.

I quietly closed my eyes and felt the energy from the toy race through my limbs invigorating my body from the tips of my fingers to the ends of my toes.

Clarissa espoused the benefits of a vibrator in a woman's life, causing Jumma Auntie's hand to shoot straight up into the air.

"How do I do dis den?" she asked. "I bring it and my husband will say he can do. We don't need to do. Then what do I do?"

"That woman can only conjugate one verb: *to do*," Mahjong whispered in my ear causing me to burst out laughing.

"If you want to introduce a toy to your partner, you simply *show* your partner how *you* use the toy and I guarantee they will pounce on it too and try to use it on you. Masturbating for your partner can be a tremendous turn on. It helps you to think outside the box." Clarissa smiled at her own joke. "I am a firm believer that every woman has the power to enhance her sexuality literally in the palm of her hand. Which moves us on to another toy." She then pulled out a familiar friend; Bunti.

Clarissa finished displaying the toys on the table and then began her extensive presentation of the King to everyone. Mahjong's legs were paddling back and forth on the floor in front of her with unbridled excitement. "I have to tell you about the other night with Steven in more detail!" she said excitedly into my ear. "He is the most in-tune man I have ever met! And he's a fucking accountant!"

As Clarissa finally wound down her presentation of the King, I felt tired, emotionally and physically. I thought it must be close to midnight.

My watch read 9:00 p.m.

The Indian girls on the sofa, Jumma Aunty, Nalini, Corky, Aquila and Kathy all started to chant unabashedly: "*RAJA! RAJA!*"

"Okay, are there any questions?" Clarissa asked.

I braced myself for any last minute outbreaks.

"Well then, this has been a most interesting night. I want to thank you ladies for your attention and honesty and above all things I want to thank Leena for having me over." As the last words left her lips, everyone in the room began to clap, whistle and cheer.

The sound was overwhelming.

I felt tears sting my eyes again.

Clarissa began to load her display bag up with her products as I became acutely aware that the ladies were suddenly my responsibility to entertain. I stood up and asked if anyone wanted anything to eat or drink. Mary rushed over towards me as Corky did to ask if she could be first in the sales room.

"I want to go first!" Corky whined.

"I think Mary called it," I said as diplomatically as I could.

"I want to go next then!" Corky said.

"And I will do next," Jumma Aunty said, making notes on the paper in her lap.

"I'm fourth!" Pinky said.

"I'm pregnant!" Nalini declared pointing to her bursting stomach.

"I'm the fucking bride!" Tinoo objected. "I want to go first!"

I settled the arguments in the room by drawing numbers from a stainless steel bowl.

Clarissa packed up her bag and whispered that I should come in last after the final guest had made their order. She disappeared upstairs with her display bag on her back, her briefcase and basket of lingerie in either hand. Mahjong drew the first number, but gave it to Mary. I watched the tiny blonde run upstairs practically screaming with delight, busily dialing her cell phone as she headed towards my bedroom.

"I am buying the King and that little bunny thing for sure," Kathy said, loading a plate of food for herself in the kitchen.

"I thought you were single," Pinky said taking a small morsel of *barfi*.

"Happily single," Kathy corrected. "My other vibrator broke. I want those two to replace it."

I choked on the mozzarella stick I was eating.

The entire night I felt badly because I thought that Kathy was uncomfortable with sex toys.

"I want the rubber lassie sleeve," Tinoo said. "It's an inside joke with Tushar. He calls his ejaculate *lassi* like the yogurt drink you know? I think he'll really get a kick out of it! Oh sorry, Jumma Aunty. I hope that doesn't gross you out!"

I doubted I would ever look Tinoo's hairy groom in the eyes again.

"My husband is having such small *dunda*," Jumma Aunty said wistfully, silencing the room with her heavy sigh. "I hawe roll of quarter is bigger. But ah, well, what to do?"

"Get Hank," Mahjong said when no one in the room addressed her statement. "Next to your hubby, he will seem like a horse!"

"I had relations with a horse once and it was quite unpleasant," Harriett interjected.

Suddenly, it became so quiet in the room I thought I could hear my neighbor's conversations.

"You mean that as a metaphor right?" Isabelle said slowly.

Harriett studied the room before answering. "Uh, yes. A metaphor. It's a metaphor."

"I was with this one guy," Dimple said, "who was so easy to talk to, so wonderful to be around, so handsome and smart but he had the dick of a little bird. I couldn't feel the stupid thing. I never knew if it was in. I mean it! I mean I would ask him if he was still in and he would get upset and then go flaccid but it's not like I could tell that either you know?"

"What happened to him?" Isabelle asked.

"I dumped him," Dimple said sadly. "I really miss him. The guy I mean. Not the dick."

Were these women really divulging their secrets so easily? I would never have guessed they could be so frank and open out of fear that everyone in the community would start gossiping, but none of them seemed the least bit fazed.

Just as I asked if anyone wanted more to eat, Mary rejoined the party carting two very large bags in her hands shouting, "Next!"

"Did you leave anything for us?" Tinoo asked.

"I know Clarissa said what we bought is our own business but I asked her if it was okay to show you what I got and she said I could if I wanted to!" Mary knelt down in the centre of the room and began to spill the contents of the two large black bags. "I bought these three costumes, two of these panties. Oh I'm so excited! And I bought this feather thing. I love being tickled! And I bought the King of course and I bought the bunny that Leena recommended. I bought this set of handcuffs too."

"Handcuffs?" Isabelle said with a laugh. "Don't they come with the police officer outfit?"

"I need an extra pair," Mary said in a shy tiny voice. "And I bought this big canister with all the licky stuff in it and some of the lubricant. Smell it! It smells awesome!"

As Mary showed off her purchases to the ladies in the room, I took a moment to stand back and quietly observe everyone. I saw smiling faces, expressive hand gestures and heard bursts of giggles and laughter from every corner of the room.

"How much did you spend?" Isabelle asked as Mary reloaded her large bags.

"In total? $580. Spend your $58 wisely, Leena!" Mary smiled and then sprang up and ran across the room to give me a big hug.

"Are you serious?" I whispered in her ear. "You didn't have to do that!"

"Dinesh wanted me to. He gave me his credit card and he told me to spend as much as I wanted and I even called him and asked him about some of it and he said go for it!"

"Is this a butt plug?" Pinky asked as she pulled out a pink toy with a flared bottom resembling a tiny lava lamp.

"Oh yeah! We love that!" Mary said and then gleefully ran back to her bags on the floor. Her youthful energy and enthusiasm, her loving and sincere expression made her impossible to hate. I could see why Dinesh was so attracted to her.

Harriett came down from the upstairs bedroom with two large bags of her own. At some point after Mary had come downstairs, she quietly left to make her purchases.

"Two bags too?" Tinoo asked. "There won't be anything left!" Several ladies laughed and studied Harriett in the doorway of the living room.

"You can keep your stuff in the bag," Mary said lightly. "I was just so eager to show everyone what I bought!"

"I will keep it in the bag if you don't mind."

"Of course!" I insisted. "You don't have to show anyone. No one does. Do you want something to drink?"

"I don't want to drink," Harriett said slowly. "I want to dance."

"Yay!" Mary exclaimed. "Put on some music, Leena!"

Did they want Bollywood or Western?

I rushed over to the CD player in the living room and searched through the small collection of music in the case underneath it. Nothing seemed suitable.

"I'll get something out of my car," Mahjong said. She was gone and back before I had time to figure out how to turn the machine on.

I pressed play and was immediately assaulted by the sound of someone wailing and screaming. "Try this one," Mahjong said handing me another disc. I put it in as the room filled with the soft but sensual sounds of belly dance music.

"You belly dance?" Isabelle asked Mahjong instantly rising as the music became louder.

"I took it for a while a long time ago. I haven't done it in ages."

"I always belly dance," Nalini said stroking her large tummy. She asked for help getting out of her seat so she could be the next buyer ready to go upstairs.

As the first track began to reverberate throughout the living room, the Indian girls all stood up and started to dance instinctively shaking their hips and holding up their arms in the air. Every time Tinoo moved her head, the row of penises atop her hair would flop into her face causing screams of laughter from her inebriated sidekicks. The first track stopped. The next track was a sensual top forty song with a heavy club beat. Seconds into it, a snapping sound was heard drawing everyone's attention to Harriett who had ripped off her long overcoat exposing her flashy gold outfit again.

She began sliding against the door frame as though it were a pole in the centre of a stage. Corky and Aquila started clapping and encouraging her.

Harriett writhed against the frame and then walked towards a chair and began to undulate rhythmically over the seat. With deliberation and skill, she arched her back over an imaginary person seated before her, slowly and playfully wiggling her shoulders so that the soft gold fabric began to slide down her body inch by inch.

I was completely mesmerized watching her dance, until fear kicked in as the top of her outfit pooled at the curve of her hips exposing her milky white skin in contrast to the dark leopard print of her bra.

Was she going to get naked in front of everyone?

I imagined the headlines in the Indian press reading: "Leena's sex party turns into naked orgy. Mother dies of shame."

"Mahjong, *do* something!" I said pleading with her and shaking her arms, trying to snap her out of her fixated stare at Harriett.

"How the fuck is she doing that?" she asked her almond eyes wide with awe.

"She's going to get naked right here in the living room!"

"We didn't learn this in belly dance class," Mahjong said, her attention unwavering.

"Harriett!" I shouted.

She didn't hear me over the screaming women who were clapping and encouraging her to dance.

"Harriett!" I yelled.

She was lost in her own world. As the next song, with a heavier drum beat began, Harriett began to shake herself out of the bottom of the outfit until she stood in her matching leopard bra and panty. The panty had sequins laid out in the shape of an arrow pointing downwards.

I was reminded of my own ghastly attempt to do a strip tease for Manny. I sat down reluctantly deciding that if she wanted to dance and get naked in front of all my guests, there was nothing I could do to stop her. In fact I may as well sit back and take some notes as the woman obviously had a long history of dance and was, after all, at one point, a professional.

By the end of the third song Harriett was panting heavily.

"Can you teach me to dance like that?" Tinoo asked her eyes wide with excitement.

"I gave up this type of dance when I found enlightenment," Harriett said between choppy breaths.

"Enlighten us!" Dimple said. "Teach us!"

Before I could offer Harriett a polite means to get out of the requests, she grabbed one of the dining room chairs and forcefully placed it in the centre of the room.

"Who wants to go first?" she asked. Eleven hands went into the air.

Harriett grabbed a CD from her purse and handed it to Mahjong to play. As the music filled the room, she gave individual instruction on the fine art of lap dance to each woman.

She told Tinoo to use her hands to make broad gestures because she had lovely long fingers that could be used for dramatic effect. When Tinoo took her turn at the chair she used Harriett's advice captivating everyone around her.

She told Dimple to use her long black hair in the art of seduction. Dimple's first attempts made it appear as though she was trying to swat flies with her hair until Harriett came up behind her, gently placed her hands on her neck and rhythmically swayed with her until she moved with the grace of a silken blanket gently wafting in the wind.

Kathy took to the dance naturally after watching years of Bollywood movies. To streamline her sex appeal, Harriett told her to only move her hips when she danced and place her hands by her sides. The isolation was instantly effective. She snaked up and down with ease over the chair, the light in the room occasionally reflecting on the mirrors in her suit like tiny diamonds in an orange sky.

Jumma Aunty's attempt was more comical and awkward but her hearty laughter and exuberant enthusiasm made her appear ten years younger.

Mahjong pulled me to the centre of the room after almost everyone had their chance to dance by the chair.

I began to gyrate, to swivel around the seat like I had seen all the other women do.

"Ah, Leena," Harriett said. "Most beautiful Leena. You should dance with your heart."

That was my advice?

Everyone else got specific tips on using their, hair, hips, hands or lips but I got an organ you couldn't even see!

"I'm not sure what you mean." I was annoyed by what I believed was the crappiest piece of advice she had given all night.

"Close your eyes," Harriett instructed.

I did as she said mostly because it prevented me from having to see everyone else staring at me.

"Who is in the chair, Leena? Who do you see? Picture them in your mind. Now listen to the music and follow your heart."

The music hummed a sensual low drum beat with the sound of a woman softly singing in the background.

"Listen to your heart," Harriett said gently. And then she whispered directly into my ear, "Listen with your soul."

The words sent a shiver down my spine.

I closed my eyes, took a deep breath and tried to understand what she meant.

When I looked back up at her she offered no more advice, she merely guided my eyes back to the empty chair in front of me and lightly nodded her head.

I looked down at the vacant seat, feeling my heart begin to beat more intensely, knowing that everyone's eyes were on me.

A sea of images floated towards me.

I pictured Jonathan in the chair, his smile relaxed, his expression loving. My heart warmed at the thought of him but the love felt childlike and innocent. My body instinctually stiffened at the memory.

An image of Nick came to mind, his sharp features, angular jaw and brooding disposition filled the chair in front of me. He was no longer the ideal of physical perfection. His body seemed more like the muscular carcass of a man with no moral substance and low self-esteem. My body recoiled at the thought of him. I felt my heart clamp shut and my body respond in kind.

I lowered my gaze and tried to picture Manny in the chair. I could see his big nose and goofy smile. My heart opened and my limbs began to relax but a part of me still felt like it was holding back.

Manny's image began to dissolve, replaced by the vision of my mother sitting cross-armed in the chair.

Her glance was stern, her expression angry. My heart instantly reacted by pounding harder in my chest. I began to feel my spine lift up from inside, the heat from my body turning into a fire in my belly.

Memories of my mother holding me while I cried after being bullied at school emerged like a slide show in front of me. I saw her cradling me at night and whispering, "Never to you my Leena." And I saw memories of me embracing her while she wailed out the pain of sorrow for her dead husband. Each image softened her expression until she began to slowly dissolve, her arms unfolding; her eyes open and bright.

My heart opened, melting me from inside, until it was not her face I was looking at but my own.

I saw my curly hair, my dark brown eyes and the soft turn of a smile on my face.

I began to feel myself move.

As the vision before me became as clear as the reflection in a mirror, I could see with precision every line on my face, every curve of my body.

I began to feel myself sway.

I circled the chair and then glided down onto the seat. I felt the energy rise inside me as though the image of myself was pushing me forward.

My eyes were closed, my focus unshakable. I could see myself, so much younger as a child, covering my dark skin and wishing I was more like the other kids around me. I felt my childhood pain resurface, the frustration of wanting to fit in overcoming my entire being. I floated up to the image, caressed my small head and instead of feeling isolation, I felt appreciation.

I then saw myself hiding as a teenager in the bathroom stalls during gym class ashamed of my figure and of my hairy body. I heard the taunts again, the teasing. I felt the tangle of insecurities and inadequacies creating tension inside me. I absorbed every feeling, embracing my young image, exactly as it was, until I felt acceptance instead of resistance. The pain slowly released.

The image transformed from teenager to woman. I saw my body and all its curves, its bumps and its raw femininity. My mocha skin, my curly hair, my imperfections were all compiled into one canvas before my mind's eyes and I saw the image not as the sum of its parts but as a whole.

I began to see it from the inside, not the outside.

And what I saw were the various acts of love I had received over my lifetime, and the gifts of love I had returned, which built the foundation of the person I had become. The myriad of moments that it took me to get to where I was each glittered like jewels that seamlessly came together to form the image before me. As that image became stronger, more powerful, more confident, I floated up into a languid dance that felt more like it was emanating from my soul than from my body. I had no idea what the singer was moaning about but imagined instead the words I had long to hear being sung in her lyrical voice.

I am beautiful.

I am sexy.

I am unique.

The music stopped.

I collapsed in a heap onto the seat of the chair. I heard clapping and whistling like a distant train in the background.

Nalini broke the silence by asking to see me at the door.

I opened my eyes, tears crystallizing the corners and bowed my head to the broad smiles and cheers from the women as I excused myself to the foyer where she waited.

"I had a really good time," Nalini said in a low whisper. I could hardly hear her over the loud drum beat of the next song and the jumping sounds of the women in the living room.

"Did you?" I asked tentatively. "I'm so glad. But you hardly said much all night."

"I'm so fat and pregnant. What was I to say?"

"Don't call yourself fat!" I said harshly. "You're beautiful!"

"Oh Leena, you are beautiful! I never saw anyone dance the way you just did now!" Nalini said pressing her belly against me as she leaned forward to give me a hug. "It means so much to me that you invited me. I am so glad that you had this party. I learned so much."

"Thank you. I'm glad too."

Without thinking I looked down at the small bag in Nalini's hand.

"I could only buy the bath for making the babies sleep," Nalini said sheepishly. "Nishit would kill me if I bought anything else. He just doesn't like this kind of thing. I'm so sorry."

"Don't apologize!" I said. "I don't care. I just wanted you to have a good time."

"Oh I did!" She leaned forward and hugged me even tighter.

"Give my best to Nishit and the kids will you?" I said out of habit.

"I will. Your braveness really inspired me. Thank you so much again, Leena."

I closed the door after watching her get into her station wagon, the weight of her body sinking the car down.

When I re-entered the living room the CD had been changed to a top forty collection Mahjong had compiled. The Indian trio were dancing Bollywood style and singing the lyrics out loud. Kathy jumped in the middle with them never missing a beat.

"Who's next?" I asked. "Who is number four?"

Jumma Aunty heard me over the music and held up her ticket like I had just screamed Bingo and she was the winner. She tore upstairs and wasn't seen for another half hour.

Slowly over the course of the night, each lady went up to the bedroom to make an order. Tinoo went up and came down with two large bags exclaiming that their honeymoon was going to be the raunchiest Paris had ever seen. She gathered up her two bookend friends who had already made their purchases and readied herself to leave. She must have given the crown of penises back to Clarissa upstairs because when she returned to the party, her hair slightly askew, there was no headband in sight.

"Leena honey," she said to me quietly in the corner of the foyer as the other girls strapped on their shoes, "it means the world to me that you threw this party. Thank you so much!"

"Are you sure this is the kind of party you wanted to have?"

"Oh yes! It is the best of all the functions I have had so far!" she said her face a veil of love.

"Woofuckinghoo!" Dimple said in the background, unsteady on her feet, trying to balance her large bag with one hand.

"Well I'm glad you had a good time," I said and opened the front door.

"I can't believe the time! It's midnight and I'm getting married soon!" Tinoo said leaping forward to hug me and kiss me on the cheek. "God bless you, Leena!" she whispered in my ear. "I can't wait to see you at the wedding!"

The girls piled into a cab. The noise level in the house dropped as the few guests still lingering quietly watched television on the small screen in the living room.

As the other guests discussed the show they were watching, Corky and Aquila quietly conspired over what purchases they would make when it was their turn to go upstairs.

Isabelle grabbed her large black bag remarking that there were several things she had regretted not buying at her own party that she decided to purchase at mine. Harriett picked up her black overcoat and the two of them walked towards the front door.

"I hope I didn't do anything upsetting," Harriett said quietly to me as she made her goodbyes in the foyer.

"Not at all!"

"I have seen some lovely dancers in my time, Leena," Harriett said softly to me, "but I have never seen anyone dance from their soul like you did tonight."

"You should teach people how to dance for a living," Kathy said joining us in the foyer. "I'm really serious about that offer I made you before. Call me."

Harriett smiled shyly, her complexion still dewy from sweat.

"I will call you," she said. "I will. And Leena – God bless you." She kissed me on the mouth so quickly and gently that I hardly had time to react. I waved goodbye as I watched Harriett load Isabelle's drunken body into her car.

Kathy moved closer to hug me and thank me for the evening.

"I didn't know for sure it was going to be a party like this," she said, clutching her big bag like the others before her, "but I have to say Leena, it was absolutely amazing!" I thanked her for the *barfi* and promised to call her the next time I was going to a Bollywood movie.

I began to tidy up with Mahjong and Mary's help.

At some point Mary had changed into her nurse's costume. She smiled when Mahjong said she should have bought the French maid's outfit instead as she watched the tiny blonde pick up cups and plates that had made their way throughout the entire first floor of my home.

The doorbell rang and before I could get to the front door Mary ran and opened it. I heard a high pitched squeal of delight and came around front to see Dinesh broadly smiling, scooping up his petite bundle of medical help into his big arms.

He looked dashing in his casual shirt and pants as his large frame filled the doorway and his even larger infectious smile shone out against the night.

"Hey Leena or should I say Monkey?" he said over the shoulder of the tiny woman clinging to his torso. "Looks like you had a good party, hey?"

"We did!" I said as he slowly lowered Mary to the floor in front of him and studied his tiny nurse with hungry eyes. I felt like I was intruding on their lovemaking as I watched him slowly lick his lips and slide his hands around Mary's tiny waist.

"It comes with a hat," she whispered playfully.

"Let's go!" Dinesh said quickly. "Where's your stuff?"

Mary gathered her two large bags together. I got the feeling Dinesh was in for a medical checkup as soon as he got back to his car.

Mary gave her bags to Dinesh, who smiled broadly at me again. She turned and lifted her tiny arms towards me and ran into my arms hugging me tightly. I could feel the rubbery fabric of her outfit pressing against my hands and arms.

"I had such a good time!" she said with a heavy breath into my ear. "Bless you, Leena!" The two of them smiled and said their goodbyes to everyone rushing off to Dinesh's sports car parked partially on the grass of my front lawn.

I closed the door and sighed. Fatigue was setting in.

Corky and Aquila had slipped upstairs together as soon as it was their turn returning a short time later carrying three large bags between them. It was the first time I had ever noticed anything similar about them. They both had the same smile.

"We had such a good time," Aquila said easily. "It's so late. We're going to go. Unless you need more help with the dishes?"

"No." I ushered them towards the front door. "It's all under control but thank you."

"No!" Aquila said very sternly. "No, Leena. Thank *you*." She turned and hugged me. As she pulled away she planted a deep kiss on my right cheek. "God Bless you Leena," she said as she pulled away.

"Yes," Corky said in her bubbly tone. "Yes! Thank you and bless your sweet heart!" Before I knew it, Corky had her large breasts pressed up against me almost knocking the air from my lungs.

"I'm glad you two had a good time," I said. "I guess I'll see you at the wedding."

"I almost forgot about that!" Corky said and then in a less high-pitched tone, "Juzer and I are going to announce our engagement that night. Please don't tell anyone until then."

"You're engaged? I can't believe it!"

"Yes, we are," Corky said jumping slightly in one spot, sending her bosoms into motion.

"Where is the ring?" I asked instinctively.

"Oh," Corky said blushing slightly and then turning away. I looked over at Aquila who was suddenly sporting a huge grin on her face.

"Tell her," Aquila said to her sister.

"I don't have a ring exactly," Corky said slowly. Then in a low less irritatingly high tone of voice, "We got matching tattoos instead."

"Are you kidding me? *Where? What?*"

"Well I can't show you where," Corky said as her skin began to lighten. "But I have his name and he has mine and we both got piercings down *there* that match."

"You're pierced there?" I asked again looking down unabashedly between Corky's legs. No wonder she seemed to enjoy the spin class more than anyone else!

I wanted more details but Jumma Aunty had joined us in the foyer carrying her large bag and demanding Aquila drive her two blocks down the road to her house since she hadn't had anything to drink all night.

"I bought da Thunda *Dunda*! My very own Raja for real," she said as she stuffed her swollen feet into her sandals.

"Um, thanks for coming," I said and hugged each of them individually.

"*Beta*," Jumma Aunty said, her round cheeks lifting up to her eyes, "your Pappa would be proud to see what a beauty you have become."

Her compliment surprised and elated me. I instantly felt tears sting my eyes.

I closed the door and turned to see what I expected to be the house in disarray. Instead it was more pristinely clean than when my guests first arrived. Mahjong told me to start the dishwasher while she ran upstairs to make her order.

As I filled the small tray with liquid I was suddenly startled by two hands on either side of my hips pulling me back towards them.

"Manny!" I said as I turned and saw my husband, his eyes glazed from too much beer, his clothes reeking of the same. "When did you come in?"

"Me so horny," he said dry humping my Capri pants.

"You're so drunk!" I pushed him away from me.

"It was the only way to survive the night!" Manny slurred and wobbled back against the island in the kitchen. "Those pricks are a bunch of dead-beats. We just drank and watched cricket all night. For once, I'm not the designated driver and this is the lame ass night I get!"

I gently guided him to the living room and placed him on the long sofa. Back in its natural state, it was hard to imagine only hours before that my living room resembled the dance floor of a bawdy strip club.

I turned and headed back to the kitchen. I was startled again to hear a tiny peep coming from somewhere in the room. I looked around in the dim light and then screamed in fright at the sudden image of Svetlana standing with her looming height in front of me.

"Oh my God!" I said catching my breath. "I didn't see you. Where did you come from?"

"I was being here in the corner of kitchen. On cell phone. Sorry to be scaring of you. I was on phone with Borgis. I be talking long time. No battery left," she said shoving her red phone towards me to show me the flashing battery light.

"Do you want to use my phone?" I willed my heart to calm down.

"No." Her brilliant white teeth gleamed in the low light. "I talk to him so good now. We really talk since what I am hearing here. I go make my order now."

"Wait!" I said trying to catch up in four steps to one of her long legged strides. "Mahjong is up there now."

"No, I'm not," Mahjong said in a sing song voice. "I'm done. Go up Rooskie. See if she has anything left."

"I be going!" Svetlana said taking the stairs three at a time.

"Is that your husband passed out on the sofa?" Mahjong said as she put down her bag on the floor.

"That would explain why he didn't come running when I screamed just now."

"Why did you scream?" Mahjong asked.

"I didn't know Svetlana was still here. I didn't see her in the kitchen."

"Yeah," Mahjong said soberly. "She was on the phone with her husband for about an hour and a half. I think they had some big talk. I couldn't make it out. It was in Russian. But I think the gist of it was start fingering me like you used to or it's over. That's a universal language you know."

We both smiled.

Mahjong got out her lipstick and started to put it on Manny's lips as he laid snoring and drooling on the sofa.

"Don't do that!" I whispered.

"Why? Is it turning you on?" Mahjong applied eye shadow to his closed lids.

"I am be going now," Svetlana said as she filled the frame of the doorway. "I am telling you what lady says. Now it is your turn. I had very, very good time Leena," she said and flashed me her brilliant white smile again. "I am thanking you so much for this night. It has been changing me. I am learning so much."

"I'm so glad." I feared what a hug from such large woman would feel like. To my surprise, it was warm and deep. I felt moved almost feeling her heartbeat against mine when we embraced.

I closed the door behind Svetlana as Mahjong carried on applying blush to Manny's face.

I went upstairs to the bedroom where I saw the carnage of empty bags scattered on the floor. Clarissa looked up and smiled at me.

"Sit down here." She motioned to the flattened spot on the comforter where everyone had obviously sat all night.

"You look so tired," I said carefully. "Can I get you anything? Water? Coffee?"

Clarissa shook her head and extended her hand.

"What?" I asked in confusion.

"Shake my hand," she said with a smile.

I reached over and shook her hand as I sat down on the edge of the bed. "Why?" I asked.

"Because you darling, are my highest party to date. Are you ready for your discount?"

"I'm your highest party to date?" I asked, clapping my hands over the monkey on my chest. "Are you kidding me? At one point I thought you were going to charge *me* for coming over!"

"I'll do a party for you any time, honey!" she said with a smile. "Are you ready for the number?"

I braced myself on the edge of the bed and smiled hesitantly. "Okay tell me."

"Your party tonight, Leena, capped out at $4,159.00. You get 10% of that in product so you have $415.90 to spend. What would you like?"

I slipped off the bed onto the floor before I could answer.

It took almost thirty minutes for me to use my discount. Once I had completed my purchases, Clarissa threw nine extra free gifts at me ranging from a make-your-own porn movie kit to kinky scratch cards.

"There's so much stuff!" I said as I gathered the last of her bags.

"You have the time of your life, sweetie," she said. She turned to hug me. "This was an incredible night for me too."

"It was amazing, wasn't it?"

I finally felt like I had my life in order.

For the very first time, I felt like I was in complete control.

I helped her with the last of her things, watched her drive down the empty streets in the early morning hours and then closed the door quietly behind me.

Mahjong had curled up on her cell phone and was talking to Steven, her grin so large and lascivious I felt as though I was intruding on her private time with him. I headed upstairs to lie down when a strange and dubious thought crossed my mind. I rummaged through the bathroom cabinets hoping I hadn't thrown out the extra kit.

As I waited for the line to emerge, I surveyed the surface of my bed resembling the landscape of a sex toy explosion and mindlessly stroked my tummy.

I felt like I was starting a whole new chapter in my life.

My wonderful life.

I wasn't even worried about what my mother would do when she found out about the party.

I felt giddy with excitement.

Elated with anticipation.

What will tomorrow hold?

Where do I begin?

The double pink lines on the stick left me with no doubt.

I raced downstairs bypassing my passed out husband to where Mahjong was still giggling into her cell.

"Get off the phone." I handed her the pregnancy test. "Everything's about to change."

Loving Acknowledgments

I would not be the person I am today without the love and support I have received from my family and friends. It is a blessing to have so many people in my life to thank for their constant support of me and this project. Sadly, there isn't enough room for me to thank all of them here. I am especially filled with a great deal of love for those that have been there for me from the start of this journey.

I'd like to thank my buddy Maxx (Jackie Taylor) for taking me to my first sex party and for encouraging me throughout the process of my novel. Maxx, you are my love because you were "Sex and Samosas" first critic and champion. I lovingly dedicate chapter 8 to you buddy.

I owe a huge debt of thanks to my coaches. Jennifer Carruthers you are my love for showing me support, talking me through the bad times and celebrating Consultant of the Month with me. Sharon Nixon a.k.a. "Coach" you are my love because you got me through countless breakdowns. I could feel your love for me and how it never wavered from day one to end of blog.

I want to thank my spin teachers and most especially Sophie at Queen Street. Some of the hardest rejections I ever got came on Thursdays and despite my overwhelming sorrow, your energy always managed to pull me through from our first class with just you and me to the countless that followed.

Thank you to Sylvester Stallone. You are my love for looking right at the camera and telling me not give up.

I am indebted to my countless hostesses and clients who wrote me letters about how I inspired them and who in turn inspired me. You are all my loves for welcoming me into your homes and for showing me kindness but mostly for affirming my life's passion.

My sincere and warm thanks go to Karen Opas of Partner Publishing as all roads led back to you and in your kindness and your incredible generosity of spirit you gave me support out of sincerity alone. You are my love for the wealth of knowledge you have but above all for introducing me to Donald.

Donald Lanouette (Partner Publishing) you are my love for absolutely being the most brilliant graphic designer I could ask for. You not only got what I was saying with regard to the cover but your professional and timely responses have made the process of self publishing worry free. I simply can't express what that means to me and how very grateful I am for your dedication and commitment to excellence.

And a great big thank you to André Scott for being a sweet love and taking professional pictures for the book and the website! You are my love for being so candid, so kind and so passionate about your work.

I want to thank the many people who helped me in the editing process of the behemoth novel that this once was into the crafted (and I'm sure wrought with mistakes still) story that it is today.

First and foremost of all of them I thank "Paul." You are my love not only because you were my first-and-last-editor but because you have been my support system ever since the orange-floatie days and beyond. You have endured fourteen years of rants, tears and heartbreaks (I'm referring to mine here, not yours) and somehow you have managed to help me keep sight of where I could go even when you weren't sure of where you were going yourself.

Jen Roundell you are my love for having faith in this story and for making me dig even deeper. And for being the first person to really reflect love for Leena.

Alex Binkley you are my love for your edited version of this novel but more than that for crossing your arms over you chest and telling me I had to pursue this no matter what. In that moment I redefined my definition of success.

And to my Pen and Paper group most especially, June, Alex, Ken, Katherine, Roberta, William, George and the Moo: you are all my loves for laughing at things I didn't think were funny. I would be lost without you all.

I can't think of a better compliment to my love Zoe Yuan than to see in print an incredible character born out of my imagination that became my personal reality. I envisioned Mahjong before you showed up and you have been as solidly unwavering in support to me as she is to Leena. You are my love for putting faith not only in a project you had never seen but for literally putting it in my hand and for not letting me let go. You fill my heart in ways only someone cosmically connected to me can.

There are no words for the love I have for my family. Anyone who knows me knows what they mean to me.

Reidbhai you are my love for being unfailingly supportive at every turn not just of my journey to get published but with my life as well. Thank you for calling me Authorbhen even when I wasn't sure I was worthy.

And my baby sister Shonnie, you are my love because there is no other person on earth that I can say has been through the same hell we have endured and can still laugh at it. You are the only one in my life that I have a secret language of jokes with and you are ever more precious to me for it. Thank you for telling me that fateful night to go "whack off". Who knew how it would change our lives? I love you with all my heart, but especially with the pieces you have helped me put back together. I love you for that 3am drive back to Ottawa, for the long talks and all the laughs and for believing in love. Above all, for believing in me. You will forever be the best sister any soul could ask for. You are the Greatest Sister of All Time. I am blessed because you love me.

The ultimate thanks and love go to my mother. There simply are no words that can completely convey what I feel for you; how I look up to you, wake up every day striving to be the best I can be and praying you will be proud. Thank you for being nothing like Leena's mother, for being brave enough to let me carve my own path and for supporting me even when you don't agree. You taught me not to fear and with your heart at my side I never do. I am always secure that I can get through whatever life throws at me, because you are with me. Thank you for not only giving me life, but for making the life I have a quality one that I treasure. You are and always will be the love of my life.

My sweet Daddy, you're at the top of the world and looking down on this creation. I hope you are proud. I miss you infinitely and every day.

And lastly to my darling Leena; you are beautiful, you are unique and you are free now. Be happy.

Glossary of Terms

Atta – flour used to make dough

Baghvan – God

Barfi – Indian sweet/dessert

Besharam – shameful, heathens, naughty folk – you get the idea

Beta – dear one (usually in reference to younger children)

Bhajias – fried appetizer made with gram flour and a vegetable - yummy

Bhindi – okra (won't really make you pregnant but when properly cooked, very tasty)

Bindi – small decorative sticker usually placed on the temple between eyebrows

Bungra – genre of Punjabi music/dance

Chaloo – cheap and easy tramp, hussy – you get the idea

Chappati – flat bread not unlike a tortilla

Chuddy – underwear/panties

Cinnai – type of Indian flute

Dada – Paternal grandfather

Dadi – Paternal grandmother

Dadijaan – Paternal grandmother along with term of endearment to mean "dear grandmother"

Dahl – lentil dish, thick like a stew (usually vegetarian)

Desi – term for South Asians

Dhoti – cloth worn around the hips and between the legs (usually by men)

Dohl – type of Indian drum

Dosa – South Indian savoury stuffed crepe

Dunda – slang term for penis

Ghatia – deep fried gram flour snack – fattening but delicious

Ghora – white person (specifically male)

Ghori – white person (specifically female)

Gulab Jamun – Indian sweet shaped into balls and deep fried until they are dark brown, served in sugar syrup

Jaan – dear/darling

Kurta pajama – men's two-piece outfit (can be casual or formal) made up of a long shirt and loose pants with drawstring

Lassi – yogurt drink served sweet or salty

Lengha – women's two-piece outfit usually consisting of a short top with flowing skirt (this changes with the current fashion trends)

Masala – spices

Muska – soft, as in buttery soft or sensual to the touch

Namaste – greetings (hello and goodbye)

Pakora – fried appetizer made with gram flour and a vegetable – yummy

Pagal – crazy

Raja – King

Ustaad – wise one/learned person

Zakat – alms (charitable donation made by Muslims)

ABOUT THE AUTHOR

JASMINE AZIZ

I am a coconut, brown on the outside, white on the inside.

I have struggled with two cultures and my place in them for over 40 years. My South Asian side wrestles with the cultural stigma of being single while my Western side rails against misogynist trappings and an ever expanding definition of what modern day commitment means.

I am a fighter.

I am a dedicated daughter.

I am a retired vibrator seller.

I believe that every woman should know her own body better than anyone else and that she should have an unshakable sense of self before endeavouring to pursue a relationship with anyone else.

I am a Buddhist, a Muslim and a Hindu. I have learned that faith will pull you through anything life throw's at you.

I am addicted to spin, love chocolate and therefore must continue to spin.

And I am a writer.

To follow my adventures please visit
www.jasmineaziz.com